"Love Regency? How about a swoon-worthy hero and a plot that twists and turns yet ties up in a neat bow at the end? Then get thee to a bookstore! *The Lost Lieutenant* is all that and more, from the battlefield of Salamanca to the gowns and suits at Almack's. This is my favorite Erica Vetsch title to date and earns a place on my keeper shelf."

MICHELLE GRIEP, Christy Award–winning author of the Once Upon a Dickens Christmas series

"An enchanting tale, *The Lost Lieutenant* was quick to capture my heart and engage my hopes. A wounded hero meeting a heroine on the run is always a perfect recipe for romance; throw in a spy for good measure, and you've got a winner from Erica Vetsch! This is a Regency novel that will have fans begging for more."

JAIME JO WRIGHT, Christy Award winner of *The House on Foster Hill*

"A riveting Regency read, with captivating characters, that will tug at your heartstrings."

CAROLYN MILLER, best-selling author of the Regency Brides series

"Erica Vetsch brings such a fresh, true voice to Regency romance. She catches all that's best about the genre while weaving together a fast-paced, intriguing story full of characters I cared about so much. I can't wait for book two!"

MARY CONNEALY, author of the best-selling High Sierra Sweethearts and Wild at Heart series

"Original, engaging, and oh so romantic, *The Lost Lieutenant* is a delightful tale sure to satisfy Regency fans and inspirational readers alike. Evan, a battle-scarred war hero, earns his place alongside the leading men of Austen and Heyer, and Diana is a heroine you'll relate to and root for as she falls in love with her unintended earl. Rich historical details, authentic faith elements, and a dash of intrigue combine in this winning first installment of the Serendipity & Secrets series, certain to gain a permanent place on your shelf . . . and in your heart."

AMANDA BARRATT, author of *My Dearest Dietrich*

"Two brilliantly developed characters forge a future together at the intersection of love and war in this compelling and immersive historical romance. Well matched in spirit, courage, and intelligence, together they graft a world through secrets, espionage, and unexpected acts of chivalry. My romantic's heart will continue to skip a beat every time I think of them. With Vetsch's deeply compassionate look at the mental scars of war, readers of Carla Kelly, Mary Balogh, and Julie Klassen will find their next favorite read in *The Lost Lieutenant*. I fully intend to revisit this world time and again for years to come."

RACHEL McMILLAN, author of *The London Restoration*

"With this stunning novel, Vetsch has seamlessly created a story and characters firmly set in Regency England. From the court of Queen Charlotte to the renovated English manor known as White Haven, we're taken on a breathless journey of intrigue, romance, and historical depth. This is a must-read for those who love Sarah Ladd and Mimi Matthews."

GABRIELLE MEYER, author of *A Mother's Secret*

The LOST
LIEUTENANT

SERENDIPITY & SECRETS

The Lost Lieutenant
The Gentleman Spy
The Indebted Earl

SERENDIPITY & SECRETS

The LOST LIEUTENANT

ERICA VETSCH

KREGEL
PUBLICATIONS

Published in association with the Books & Such Literary Management, 52 Mission Circle, Suite 122, PMB 170, Santa Rosa, CA 95409-5370, www.booksandsuch.com.

ISBN 978-0-8254-4617-7, print
ISBN 978-0-8254-7600-6, epub

Printed in the United States of America
20 21 22 23 24 25 26 27 28 29 / 5 4 3 2 1

To Peter, as always
Love, Erica

CHAPTER 1

Seaton Estate
Berkshire, England
January 4, 1813

"You'll do as you're told if you know what's good for you. I won't be humiliated again."

Diana Seaton gripped the back of the chair she stood behind, grateful to have the piece of furniture between her and her father. Red suffused his face, and his eyes glittered. He paced the oriental rug in front of the fireplace in the drawing room of Seaton Manor.

She gathered her courage. "But wouldn't it be better if I remained here this Season? I could look after Cian—"

"Do *not* mention that name here. Not his and not his trollop of a mother's." The Duke of Seaton halted his pacing and jabbed his beringed finger toward Diana. Her pleas wadded into a lump in her throat, and fierce tears pricked her eyes.

Her half sister, Catherine, hadn't been a trollop. She'd been an innocent, a naïve debutante taken advantage of by a true rake and scoundrel—a mistake that, had word gotten out, would've cost her reputation, and in the end had cost her life. But Diana knew better than to protest aloud to her father.

"It's bad enough to have her spawn here in the house. At least she had the decency to die and rid us of her shameful presence. I wish both of them had." He stalked to the drinks cabinet and poured himself a whiskey, though it was barely ten in the morning. This would be a bad day, if he was starting his drinking so early.

Diana only wished he didn't mean it when he said he was glad his daughter had died in childbirth, but she had too much evidence to the contrary to deny it. The Duke of Seaton was at once a womanizer and woman hater. He had not loved any of his three now-deceased wives, marrying them for either their fortune or the power the alliance would bring him. Each had borne him a child, and he hadn't loved any of them either. He was not capable of love. Only power. Control. And cruelty.

"You'll go to London with your brother and me, you'll be presented at court, and you'll marry the man I choose for you. Beyond that, keep your mouth shut and mind every rule. There had better not be so much as a hint of scandal attached to your name, or you'll regret it. Your sister cost me far more than she was worth, outfitting her and bringing her out last Season. She barely lasted until Easter before she was compromised. I had almost brokered a marriage. The bids were set to come in, and she ruined it. If you do the same, you'll regret the day you were born." The skin tightened along his jaw as he glared.

Brokered a marriage. Sold into bondage would be more accurate, and such a fate awaited her too. She would be his pawn, and she had no say in the matter.

The lump in her throat grew. How could she keep her promise to her sister to care for Cian as her own if she were in London, married off to a stranger, when the baby was here in Berkshire under the dominance of her father? Her thoughts scrambled as she tried to subdue the panic in her chest. She had to ask.

"What will happen to the child?"

"He'll stay in the nursery here until I decide what to do with him. I should've sent him to the orphanage the day he was born." It was a threat he had uttered for months before the baby's birth as a means to keep Catherine in hiding, and one he'd breathed often in the three weeks since Cian's arrival in order to quell any rebellion on Diana's part.

The worst was knowing he'd do it, either in a fit of rage or as a calculated move to bring someone under submission to his will.

"And will we stay in London the entire Season?" She infused her voice with innocent inquiry.

"Of course. It takes time to arrange a marriage and a proper society wedding. After you are presented at court, I'll start the negotiations. Once I find a suitable husband, your sponsor will take care of the wedding details." He waved his hand, as if what happened to her after the wedding were of little consequence.

Diana must be careful here. If he thought she was manipulating him . . . a shudder went through her. "Are you worried about news spreading in your absence that there's a baby at Seaton Manor, if you're not here to quell the gossip?"

He had gone so far as to forbid having a midwife or *accoucheur* in attendance at the birth for fear of word getting out, and when complications had set in, neither Diana, who was completely inexperienced, nor Mrs. Hudsworth, the housekeeper, had been able to prevent Catherine's death.

"Perhaps bringing the child to London, where you could have more control over who might learn of his existence . . ." She hated herself for even uttering these words, but it was all she could think of to sway him. "If you turn him over to the orphanage here, everyone in the village is likely to know where he came from. But in London, there are many orphanages, and you would be assured of anonymity."

Her father's gaze narrowed over the cut-glass tumbler, and she held her breath. Beyond the heavily curtained windows over his shoulder, snow fell in fat flakes, two weeks too late to give them a white Christmas. Traveling to London would be arduous, even if the snow melted soon. The roads would be a muddy morass.

She should be excited about a trip to the capitol, a place she'd never been, though her entire life had been spent in preparation for the event. She should be eager to wear the elaborate gown created for her appearance before Queen Charlotte at court, about attending the social events, about meeting new people. She should be anticipating an escape from Seaton Manor—where the mullions and muntins in the windows might as well have been prison bars—and the dominance of her father. And for most of her life, she had expected this Season to be her emancipation.

But now all she wanted was to stay. To stay hidden in the Berkshire countryside with a newborn boy she loved as her own and had promised to protect.

"Hmph. You could be right. Tossing him into a London orphanage would be easier if we want to keep it a secret." Father set the glass down hard on the rosewood table. "Very well. Tell the nurse to get ready to travel. We leave in the morning."

Waiting until he strode out, slamming the door in his wake, Diana rounded the chair and sagged onto the brocade cushion. She felt like a rag doll with all the sawdust leaking out. Elation that Cian would be coming along warred with fear that she had only hastened his being placed in an institution, and clamminess swept over her skin. *Lord, help me find a way to keep him safe, to keep my promise to Catherine.*

It was a prayer constantly in her heart and on her lips, but did praying do any good? Was God listening? Did He care about an illegitimate child that nobody but her seemed to love? Diana had never been certain that God cared about her prayers or that she was of enough significance to arouse His interest. When Diana had been small, her nurse had prayed aloud, but only that Diana would be a good girl and not tax her nurse's patience. The rector at the girls' school Diana had attended had read all his prayers from a book, as if he were bored. Only the assistant matron in her dormitory had taught them that God wanted a personal relationship with them through His Son, Jesus. That it was right and proper to read Scripture and pray from the heart. How Diana wished she had Miss Bonham to talk to now. Diana prayed, but she sometimes wondered if her words reached any farther than the chandelier, since nothing she had prayed for seemed to have changed her circumstances. Before she could summon the strength to rise and head to the nursery, the drawing room door opened again. Her heart leapt to her throat. Had her father returned? Had he changed his mind about taking Cian with them? She straightened and folded her hands in her lap, lowering her chin to present the properly demure daughter her father required.

But it was only Percival who sauntered into the room, giving his gold-topped cane a twirl. She hated that cane. He pretended to need it whenever he wanted to elicit sympathy, but his ankle was well healed by now. Her half brother might like to act as if he had suffered a "great war injury," and that somehow it made him a romantic figure, but Diana knew the truth. There was nothing romantic about her brother beyond his good looks, and even those were tainted by the character she knew lay behind the facade.

Was there such a thing as an honorable man in all of England? A man without a cruel streak, an uncontrolled temper, a need to dominate every woman in his life?

Not in Diana's experience, admittedly limited as that might be. All men were alike—forceful, controlling, and unpredictable of temperament.

"Fetch me a drink." Percival dropped to the sofa, swinging his legs up and propping his dirty boots on a satin pillow, clearly not caring about the servant who would be tasked with removing the stains he caused. "I'm worn out."

She straightened, ready to flee if he started toward her, fed up with his sneering demands. "No one broke your legs on the way downstairs. Get your own drink."

"Aren't you feeling saucy this morning?" He tapped his cane on the rug. "If I weren't so tired, I'd give you a smack to remind you of your manners. Has the trip to London got you all in a lather? I might be too, if I were silly enough to think that getting married would solve any of my problems. Father's already got a list of prospects. All old, fat, and in need of an heir. I don't envy you."

Saying nothing was often the best defense when Percival baited her, so with an effort, Diana bit her tongue.

Percival dropped the cane to the carpet, raising his chin and staring at the plaster filigree work on the ceiling. "You don't think he's going to give *you* that inheritance money, do you? The minute you marry, it won't belong to you. It will go to your husband . . . and only as much as Father has to shell out to get somebody to take you off his hands. The rest he will pocket. It's been his plan all along." Percival pinched the bridge of his nose, as if bored with dealing with such an inferior intellect. "It's galled him right along that he couldn't get his hands on your trust, but if you think he's going to turn over thousands of pounds sterling without a fight, you don't know our dear father."

Frustration boiled under Diana's breastbone. Her hands fisted on her thighs. Her grandmother had left that money to Diana to be inherited upon her marriage. The old woman had done it to spite the Duke of Seaton, revenge for the way he had treated her daughter, his third wife and Diana's mother.

"Still, having a debutante sister will fit nicely into my plans for the Season. It's a good excuse to show up at parties you're invited to, and I'm sure there will be a few swains willing to do whatever I want them to in order to secure a formal introduction. Your looks are passable, and you are a duke's daughter, which should be enough to have them swarming around. I shall have to see how I can leverage things to my advantage." He rubbed his fingertips against his thumb and grinned. "Sheep to the slaughter. I hope you last longer than Catherine did in town. I missed out on several opportunities to fleece the young bucks at the tables when she scuttled home. Whoever ruined her better hope neither Father nor I catch up to him, since he cost us so much money." He stacked his fists and twisted them in a neck-wrenching pantomime.

Before she said something she might regret—or that would earn her the aforementioned slap—she stood. There was plenty to do in preparation for tomorrow's leave-taking. She'd waste no more time on Percival or his hateful words. The notion of him making suitors pay for an introduction to her, of having him show up at every social function she attended, and of luring unsuspecting prey into gambling with him in order to get on his good side made her want to break something, preferably over his head. She slipped out of the drawing room and through the hall to the staircase.

Upstairs, the servants went about their packing duties quietly and quickly, trunks and boxes open and spilling their contents, maids hurrying to Mrs. Hudsworth's directions, and everyone tense. The servants at Seaton Manor were always tense, it seemed. Like Diana herself. What would it be like to live in a peaceful, happy home, where people were kind and treated one another with respect? Did such a household even exist?

From the sounds of her father's plans to marry her to the highest bidder, she would never know.

"I don't see how you're going to make sense of all this by tomorrow. Have the lists I made helped?" Diana touched the gowns lying across her bed, letting her fingers trail over ostrich feathers, tulle, satin, and silk.

Several of the dresses were leftovers of her sister's, never worn after she'd fled London last spring.

But the rest had been sewn for Diana's debut by a seamstress imported from the city for the purpose. Diana had enjoyed the process of collaboration with the *modiste*, selecting fabrics and trims, adding her own special touches. Though Diana had been sequestered at a girls' school for the past several years, she had always had a flair for design, and she took pleasure in the tiny sense of freedom making her own dress choices had afforded. She'd been popular amongst the girls at school for her taste and creativity. Then her father had summoned her home. Ostensibly to be with Catherine in her confinement, but Diana surmised it was more that her father feared he was losing control of his daughters and wanted her where he could watch her.

"Don't you worry, dear. We'll get it all sorted. And your lists have been most helpful. No, not that trunk. That's for the court dress." Mrs. Hudsworth shook her head. "Do you want any of your books and art supplies packed?"

Diana didn't hesitate. "I want everything. If things go according to Father's plan, I won't be returning to Seaton Manor. I don't want to leave anything behind."

Not that she had much beyond the clothes she would need for her debut—and she could argue that those did not really belong to her. Her father had been reluctant to spend money on daughters, even for necessities. Leisure items were rare indeed. Diana had her schoolbooks and a few sketchpads and pencils, but little else to call her own. Even her mother's jewelry, which should have passed to her, had been confiscated by her father.

Mrs. Hudsworth's lips trembled, but she took a deep breath. "I'll miss you, lass."

Diana squeezed the older woman's fingers, something her father would be shocked to see. One didn't treat servants with familiarity. She left the packing in the capable hands of the housekeeper and climbed the stairs to the nursery.

A fire blazed behind a protective screen, and the nurse her father had reluctantly hired sat before it, her toe slowly rocking the cradle on the floor. The girl couldn't be more than fifteen, but she had the necessary skills to care for the baby, being the eldest of nine, the daughter of one of the crofters on the Seaton property. Father had refused to hire a wet nurse, but thankfully, Cian seemed to be thriving on thinned cow's milk.

"Beth, you and the baby will be accompanying us to London, so I need you to pack Cian's things and have them ready to go before first light tomorrow." Diana bent to the cradle and lifted the warm sleeping bundle. She inhaled the newborn scent that still clung to him, closing her eyes for a moment, her heart torn with love and worry.

The girl's eyes grew round, and a flush suffused her pale cheeks. "London, miss?"

"Yes. His Grace has relented, and he wants the baby where he can keep an eye on him. But the same rules apply. The less you're seen, the better. Keep Cian as quiet as possible, because if His Grace feels like he's being inconvenienced, he might ship our darling to the nearest orphanage."

Diana's arms tightened around the baby, fear wriggling its chilly way up her spine. She had to do whatever it took to protect Cian.

"Tiens! Attrape bandit!"

Evan Eldridge bolted upright in his bed, his arm sweeping wide to fend off the advancing enemy, only to make contact with the bedside table and send a porcelain pitcher flying across the floor. The blankets wound around his legs, trapping him, and he kicked free, pain piercing his thigh like a bayonet. He lashed out again at the French soldier, shouting, "Get back!"

Sweat prickling his chest, his ribs pumped like bellows. Blinking, swallowing, he shook his head, trying to clear the panic and cobwebs. An orderly rushed down the ward, scowling. "What's going on here? This is a hospital, not a melee." He didn't wait for an answer, bending to pick up shards of pottery and mopping up spilled water.

No French soldier, no cannon fire, no smoke or broken, bleeding bodies. He wasn't on the battlefield of Salamanca. He wasn't fighting for his life.

He was in the hospital. Still.

"Sorry, bad dream," he muttered. It was as good an explanation as any, and partially true, though he didn't remember falling asleep. His heart hammered against his breastbone, and he forced himself to take slow breaths, willing the panic to recede. The dream had seemed so real, he could almost smell the burning gunpowder and hear the shriek of the cannonballs as they whistled through the air.

A bad dream that seemed to repeat every time he relaxed his guard and fell asleep.

Evan dragged his hands down his face. He couldn't admit what was really bothering him. He couldn't talk about the cold sweats, the panic, the nightmares, the memory loss, the flashes of anger, the sense of impending disaster that he carried constantly. If he breathed a word, he'd find himself on a one-way trip to Bedlam. He had hopes of getting out of St. Bartholomew's soon. If he landed in Bethlehem Hospital for the Insane, where others with his malady had been taken, he'd never get out.

He held his hands out flat, palms down. Tremors shook his fingers, and he had no power to stop them. Every sudden noise had him jumping out of his skin. Pulling a handkerchief from his dressing gown pocket, he wiped his temples. One would think, after enduring the sweltering heat of Spain, he'd be suffering from the cold of January in England, but the ward resembled a furnace today, though no one else seemed bothered. The soldier in the cot next to him lay under several blankets, and one of the orderlies stumped by, a coal hod banging against his leg as he went to feed the fire.

Evan rolled his neck, trying to ease the knots that had taken up permanent residence between his shoulder blades. Perhaps, if he could only get a decent night's sleep, this internal jangling might cease, but at the moment he felt like a box of musket balls that had been dropped from a height. Bouncing, rolling, scattering.

The French had a term for it. *Vent du boulet.* The wind of the bullet. A term for a soldier who heard bullets even when he wasn't under fire, someone who was losing his grip on reality. Evan had seen such men, vacant expressions, quaking muscles, jerking movements, unable to eat or sleep or cope with the world around them.

Evan feared that was happening to him. If he couldn't bring himself under control, he'd be thought unfit to rejoin his regiment, unfit for command—or worse, insane and in need of incarceration.

A familiar squeak drew his attention. The cart with the protesting wheel. Why didn't someone fix that? Every meal, the same thing, *squeak, squawk, squeak, squawk,* hailing the arrival of pathetic food grown cold in its journey from the basement kitchens to the ward.

"Morning." The porter removed the cover on the kettle and ladled out a bowl of pasty-looking slop.

"Gruel again?" Stuffing the handkerchief back into his pocket, Evan accepted the thick porcelain bowl and heavy spoon. What he wouldn't give for a slice of bacon or a piece of toast with butter.

"Doctor's orders." With a shrug, the porter moved on, *squeak, squawk, squeak, squawk.*

Evan lifted a spoonful of porridge to his lips, but at the monotonous taste of bland nothing, he let the utensil drop. It was ridiculous, him even still being in the hospital. His leg wound had nearly healed. He should be convalescing at his father's parsonage in Oxfordshire, where his mother could fuss over him, or at the company barracks, preparing to rejoin the Ninety-Fifth on the Peninsula. Six months since the battle and being shipped back to England was long enough to linger in a sick bed. In fact, compared to the others on the ward, those with amputations, blindness, burns, bullet wounds, Evan felt like a fraud. A few headaches and a nearly healed shrapnel wound in his left thigh were nothing.

Setting aside the bowl, he levered himself upright, tightened the belt on the dressing gown—a luxury his father had brought to him when Evan arrived at the London hospital—and began his slow, determined walk to the far end of the ward and back. The sooner he regained the strength in his leg, the sooner he could get back to his men.

"On the march again, sir?"

He stopped at the bed of Freddie Cuff, an infantryman with a cheeky grin. Freddie always had a quick word for everyone on the ward even though he had lost his right leg. The young man struggled to pull himself up in the bed, and Evan hurried to adjust pillows.

"How're you feeling?"

"Like I'll be joining you on your walks soon. Maybe we can have a race." Freddie's eyes twinkled. "Doc said he's going to fit me with a wooden leg as soon as this thing heals up enough." Waving at his abbreviated limb, he sighed. "Not much use for an infantryman with one leg though. Soon's I'm healthy enough, they'll discharge me. Then what am I going to do? I can't go home to my folks. They barely have enough to live on themselves. That's why I joined the army in the first place. No job, no training, no money." It was a question he posed daily, it seemed.

With a twinge of guilt, Evan patted Freddie's shoulder. "Something will come up. You just work on getting better so we can have that race." Freddie's condition, one shared by many veterans, made Evan more grateful than ever to have survived his wounds relatively unscathed and that he would be back in uniform soon. He, too, had joined the military because it was one of the few options open to him, and he'd found a home with his fellow soldier brothers, one to which he was anxious to return. Not to mention, there was still work to be done on the Continent that wouldn't be finished until old Boney was dead or behind bars.

After six laps of the ward, up from yesterday's five, Evan's legs trembled, especially the left. The fresh scar burned and ached where a battlefield doctor had dug out shrapnel and splinters, and later had reopened it to drain infection.

Evan didn't remember receiving the wound. He didn't remember anything about that day. And yet something drifted at the edge of recall, something important. Something urgent. Or was it just his addled brain playing tricks on him? He couldn't trust anything his mind conjured up at the moment.

He sank onto his cot and swung his weak limb up with the help of his hand. Breathing heavily, he shook his head. If his mates could see him now, weak as a half-drowned kitten, they'd laugh and tease the life out of him. Where had all his strength gone? The strength that had enabled him to march, ride, or climb, whatever the terrain and situation called for, carrying a heavy pack of supplies and ammunition?

Evan was the best sharpshooter in a regiment of sharpshooters—or at least he had been. Again he held up his hands, noting the tremors. How could he shoot straight if he couldn't even hold his hands still? What if he never regained his ability? *God, You wouldn't do that to me, would You?* Evan had only ever had one real talent, a talent revealed when his father scraped together the money to purchase Evan's commission six years ago. A talent for shooting far and straight and hitting what he aimed at. If he lost that, what use was he?

He eased back and closed his eyes, trying to lock up his anxiety and shove it into a dark corner. Right now the men of his regiment were in winter quarters, preparing for the next campaigning season, and he should be with them, leading, strategizing, gathering intelligence for the encounters to come. Instead he was stuck in a dreary London hospital, fighting boredom and doubt in equal measure.

"Morning, sir."

Evan cracked his eye open and beheld a familiar face.

"Sergeant Shand." He wanted to leap from his bed and shake the man's hand, thanking him for alleviating the mind-numbing monotony of his days, but his sergeant hated any display of emotion. "Good to see you."

"Not sergeant anymore, sir." Shand patted his breast pocket, where papers crinkled. "Got my discharge today."

Evan mulled the idea of a military life without David Shand in it. The gray-haired, weathered sergeant had been with him since his first days in the army, keeping him on track, showing him how to lead, making up for all his novice shortcomings. And along the way, becoming a friend.

"Your discharge? Already? What are you going to do now?" Evan scooted up in his bed, his leg and his head protesting. The room spun, but then his equilibrium caught up and things steadied. He couldn't wait for that side effect to subside completely. The doctor had warned him he had been severely concussed and it would take time to get over the symptoms. Six months should have been long enough, shouldn't it? It was just a knock to the head, after all.

"Look for work, I suppose." Unlike many of his fellow soldiers, Shand's discharge hadn't come through being wounded, but because of age. "I've got a bit laid by, but that won't stretch too far." He scrubbed his chin, a gesture that meant Shand was thinking hard. "Don't know what else I'm qualified to do, but surely there's something. You wouldn't have any ideas, would you, sir?"

Weight settled in Evan's chest. He had no ideas for Shand, seeing that unless or until Evan could pass the physical himself and rejoin his regiment, he was in the same situation. England must be full of out-of-work former soldiers, with more coming all the time. What would happen to them all?

"I'll give it some thought. What will you do in the meantime?"

"Stay with my brother across the river until I can find a place. Bit crowded though. There are four daughters still living at home." Shand shook his head. "Sure is different from what I'm used to, sir. Females are a talkative lot, aren't they? They laugh most of the time, but it's the crying that's the worst. They can cry over the slightest thing, even things that make them happy." Again he shook his head. "I don't believe I will ever understand them."

Evan chuckled. "I think better men than us have tried since Adam himself." He didn't envy Shand. Encounters with women had been scarce on the Peninsula—Evan had shied away from the camp followers and laundresses of questionable reputation. He'd seen too many of his fellow soldiers choose that path, to their sorrow. Being a sharpshooter called for clarity of mind and focus, and women were a distraction that Evan couldn't afford.

"How much longer will you be here, sir?"

Sighing, Evan shook his head—gently, so as not to start up the swirling again. "I'm going to break out if the doctor doesn't let me go soon."

"Would you like me to hold the ladder, sir? It's only three stories to the ground." Shand grinned and motioned to the window beside Evan's bed.

"The idea has merit, Sergeant. I'll let you know. The sawbones should be doing rounds soon. If he gives me the 'not just yet' litany again, you and I will need to hatch a plan."

"We're good at those, sir. Many's the time we've concocted a scheme to foil the enemy." Shand grinned. "It would be like old times, sir."

"Now that you're out of the army, you don't have to call me sir. You could call me Evan."

Shand's eyebrows rose. "I don't think so, sir. Some habits shouldn't be broken."

"Well, get used to civilian life for a while, and see how you feel about it then." Evan smoothed the cotton sheet over his legs. Would he have to get used to being a civilian himself soon?

Evan shook his hand as he took his leave. "Thanks for visiting. Keep in touch, and let me know how you're doing."

"I will, sir. And you let me know if you need me to help you escape. I'll come running."

Before the sergeant made it to the ward door, there was a stir in the hall, followed by many footsteps. Evan's doctor all but sprinted into the room and straight toward Evan's bed. "Lieutenant, you've got visitors." His face was pale, and his side-whiskers bristled. "Sit up, comb your hair, and look presentable."

"What is it?" Evan, used to taking orders as well as issuing them, reached for the comb on his bedside table and dragged it through his hair as the doctor twitched the covers and tucked them in tight.

"The Home Secretary, Henry Addington, Viscount Sidmouth, just showed up downstairs asking for you."

The comb clattered to the floor. "What? Me? Why?"

"I've no idea, but . . ." hissed the doctor, "he's here." With form that would thrill a drill sergeant, the doctor snapped to attention and stared at the door.

A ripple went through the ward as heads turned. Using his foot, the doctor nudged the comb out of sight under the bed.

Five men entered, four clearly underlings surrounding the principal personage. One carried a rolled paper, the others appeared to be . . . guards? What danger did the Home Secretary expect to find lurking in a hospital ward?

They stopped at the foot of Evan's bed, and embarrassment swept over him. Clad in a nightshirt and dressing gown, hair half-combed, propped up in bed, he made a sorry sight next to their court dress, fancy waistcoats, and buckled shoes. He reached for the edge of the blankets in order to stand, but the Home Secretary stopped him.

"Don't rise, my good man." He looked around, and one of the guards supplied him with a chair from somewhere in the ward. Perching on the edge of the seat, he adjusted the tails on his coat, shot his lace cuffs, and touched the intricately tied neckcloth at his throat.

"It's an honor to meet you"—Evan cast about his mind for how one addressed a Home Secretary and fell back on the military safe zone of—"sir."

"The honor is mine. It isn't every day I get to meet a hero like yourself, Lieutenant."

Evan flushed. People had been bandying that word about since he'd arrived here at St. Bart's, and he didn't think he'd ever be comfortable with it. Especially since he couldn't remember what he'd done to earn the accolade.

"It was nothing." He waved the compliment away, aware that everyone in the ward was listening.

"Saving the Prince Regent's godson from certain death is more than 'nothing.' If the story reported in the papers is anywhere near accurate, you will go down in the annals of British history as one of the bravest men in His Majesty's army."

Evan couldn't deny the account in the paper, since he could remember nothing of that day, but the way he'd been portrayed made him out to be so noble and self-sacrificing. According to the article, he'd rushed onto the battlefield, cut a horse away from its dead teammate, and leapt aboard the horse to drag an artillery wagon behind British lines, rescuing one Percival Seaton, the Prince Regent's godson, who had been hunkered down in the wagon, in the process.

His hands fisted on the sheets, and the familiar prickle of sweat broke out on his skin. Images of battle seared through his head—the concussive explosions of cannon, the whistle of musket balls, the clash and rattle of sabers, the screams of men and horses. In flashes he saw himself skidding down a slope, rifle in hand, racing over open terrain. The horse, rearing, plunging, white showing around his eyes. A few slashes of his sword cut the dead horse's harness loose, and Evan swung aboard the remaining animal, still hitched to the wagon, and kicked him in the ribs, praying his comrades would give him enough cover fire for him to reach safety. Was his memory returning, or was he merely reconstructing what he had read in the paper?

The doctor laid his hand on Evan's shoulder, and he realized he was panting and swallowing hard. He forced himself to take a slow breath through his nose and exhale through his mouth, repeating this several times, smothering his panic lest the doctor become aware.

"My dear man, I've come with an invitation." The Home Secretary held out his hand, and one of his attendants placed the rolled paper in it. Slowly, he opened the page. "The Prince Regent wishes to convey his gratitude in a ceremony at court one week hence. He requests your presence at that time." The viscount let the paper roll up again. "I trust you will be fit and able to attend?"

The doctor nodded. "He will be there. He's making a splendid recovery."

Which was news to Evan, since the doctor had been elusive about the subject every time Evan asked.

"Very good. I am looking forward to the occasion, and I know His Highness is as well." Putting his hands on his knees, the Home Secretary levered himself up. With a nod, he laid the paper on Evan's bedside table. "Good day."

Evan sagged against his pillows, and the doctor dropped into the chair the viscount had used, his eyes on the departing figures.

A meeting with the Prince Regent. Old Prinny, the butt of many a joke in the Ninety-Fifth Rifles, scorned as a hedonist, dilettante, and philanderer. Evan's regiment mates would never let him hear the end of it.

Still, he'd lived through worse. It would be a few minutes of his life, a bow, a few words, and then Evan could focus on getting fit once more and back to his men and his mission of stopping Napoleon from taking over Europe. All while hiding his lack of memory and the attacks of sheer panic that struck far too often.

He couldn't let anything distract him from getting back to his regiment.

CHAPTER 2

DIANA COULD HARDLY breathe against the pressure of the stomacher laced against her middle. Or was her breathlessness because, in a few moments, she would be presented to the Queen? Every deportment lesson her schoolmistresses had drilled into her tumbled over in her mind, and she couldn't concentrate on anything for long. Her hands trembled as she smoothed the silver-shot white satin draped over her panniers.

It was a costume that had been in fashion in her grandmother's time, but the elderly Queen Charlotte's requirements for court dress were firm. One wore the style she deemed proper, or one did not appear in her presence.

Four other debutantes waited in the anteroom, each grappling with her own state of nervous panic, if they were anything like her. Diana turned her head carefully so as not to dislodge the ostrich feathers in her hair. Round eyes, tense lips, and fluttering hands met her gaze.

Gowns in pastels and whites, proper colors for a debutante, and no jewelry. Elaborate hairstyles and many, many ostrich feathers. They must look like some exotic strange birds indeed.

Mentally, Diana rehearsed her curtsy, wishing she could work some moisture into her mouth.

A liveried footman opened the ornate doors into the drawing room at St. James's Palace and stood back. Father had hired someone, a Lady Cathcart, to sponsor Diana. Before a few moments ago, Diana had never met the woman, but all debutantes must have a female sponsor—one who had herself been presented at court before. The sponsor was supposed to be able to vouch for the girl's character and chaperone her through various social events.

Lady Cathcart had looked Diana over, peering through her lorgnette, sniffed, and said, "I suppose you'll do."

Which made them quits, because that was how Diana felt about Lady Cathcart.

One of the footmen beckoned to them.

"Come." Lady Cathcart raised her hem and headed for the doorway, turning sideways slightly to fit her wide skirts through the opening. Diana followed in her wake, her heart pounding so loudly, she could barely hear her own shallow breaths.

Gawping probably wouldn't endear her to the Queen, so Diana forced herself to keep her eyes forward, fixed on the stair-rod-straight back of her sponsor. Members of the peerage lined the perimeter of the room, and Diana kept her chin parallel to the floor, taking careful steps on the thick carpet that led to the small dais where the Queen waited.

Don't speak until spoken to. Curtsy without falling on your face. Keep your voice steady. Never turn your back on the Queen. Oh, my mercy, is that the Prince Regent with her?

She almost stopped. The Prince Regent at a presentation of debutantes? Was that normal? Her schoolmistresses hadn't mentioned his possible presence. What was the proper protocol? Did she acknowledge him first? Or the Queen?

"Lady Diana, daughter of the Duke of Seaton, presented by Lady Cathcart." Her name echoed in the silent room as the Lord Chamberlain announced her. Lady Cathcart curtsied and stepped to the side, and Diana faced her Queen.

Queen Charlotte, resplendent in ice blue, her white wig piled high and her throat draped with jewels, looked down at Diana. The Prince Regent fussed with his lace cuff, his considerable girth encased in a brocaded silk waistcoat and his calves bulging in white stockings. Diamonds winked from the buckles of his red-heeled shoes. He sighed, looking out over the room with disinterest.

With knees made of water, she dropped into a low curtsy, bowing her head, but not so far as to tip her headdress onto her nose. Because she didn't know who had precedence, she directed the gesture somewhere between the royal pair.

"You look lovely, my dear. Please step forward." The Queen had a pleasant voice, husky and precise with the thickened vowels of her Germanic heritage.

Diana kept hold of her skirt, lifting the hem and moving to the base of the two steps.

The prince gave a small flick of his hand. "This is one of my goddaughters." His voice reeked of *ennui*, but he remembered that much about her, at least, though he'd never laid eyes on her, to her knowledge.

"One of many. Too many, if you ask me," the Queen said with a touch of asperity. She brought her attention back to Diana. "I believe I met your sister last Season? And did she find a suitable match?"

Heat prickled across Diana's skin. What should she say? If she breathed a word of the scandal, her future in the *ton* was finished. Not to mention that her father had forbidden her to even whisper her sister's name, much less her illegitimate child and her death. But she couldn't lie to the Queen, could she?

A small stir behind her had the Queen looking up. Diana daren't look over her shoulder, but whoever had caused the distraction had her gratitude, for the Prince Regent rose laboriously from his ornate chair, a smile splitting his face. The pleasant expression made him look almost handsome in a florid way—at any rate, better than he looked when he was bored.

"Ah, there he is." The prince motioned to several of the courtiers, who seemed to have nothing more to do than wait to fulfill his wishes. The group of men stirred and separated, as if to some prearranged task.

The Queen nodded to Diana. "Perhaps we will have a moment to speak again later."

Lady Cathcart gave a small jerk of her head to Diana and bobbed a quick curtsy. Diana followed her lead, dipping her knees and bowing her head again. "Thank you, Your Majesty." Now the tricky part—backing away from the Queen gracefully without tripping on her train. In a maneuver she'd practiced at least twenty times, Diana took an infinitesimal step to her right and began to retreat. Lady Cathcart did the same, and halfway down the aisle of onlookers, she took Diana's elbow and drew her to the side to stand amongst the peers.

Diana took a deep breath, or at least she tried to, but the boned panel of the stomacher thwarted her. She had survived her presentation without any major *faux pas* and without having to speak of Catherine. A sigh rose as far as her throat before she stifled it. Already her feet pinched in her satin shoes, and she had possibly hours to go before she could sit. One did not sit in the presence of the Queen unless invited to do so, after all.

"You did fine." Lady Cathcart spoke behind the edge of her folded fan. "And the Queen spoke to you, so you have that in your favor. Now, just stand there and look decorative."

Across the room, her eyes met her father's. He wore a shrewd, calculating look, and he nodded once at her, sharp and short, which she took to mean do as Lady Cathcart had said. Stand still and look decorative. Beside him stood a portly man, balding, with his hair brushed forward on the sides and red cheeks that denoted either great excitement or a fondness for drink, she couldn't decide which. The duke bent and whispered in his ear, motioning with his chin in Diana's direction, and the man's gaze sharpened on her, sweeping her from feathers to feet. Was this the man to whom her father intended to marry her off? Her stomach flipped. Surely not. The man had to be thrice her age. But if not him, then who?

A bitter wave swept through Diana. She had no power, no say, no rights in her father's eyes. She was under his command, and he loved to remind her of that fact. Without being overt, without turning her head, she looked from one male face to the next in the room. Chances were excellent that her future husband stood amongst those watching. Having been isolated at a less-than-fashionable all-girls' school for most of her life, she didn't know a single face in the crowd other than her father and brother. Was there anyone whom she could trust? Anyone who might see her for herself and not as a means to an end?

Percival stood near their father, sneering, standing with his weight on one leg, his obnoxious cane in his hand. Beside him, another young man leaned in to whisper, though he stared at Diana the entire time, leering, actually. She tore her gaze away, flushing uncomfortably. Insolent man. Who was he?

The Prince Regent beckoned toward the doorway, and a man in a green military uniform came forward. His triple row of buttons winked in the light, silvery rather than brass, and Diana thought she might well be able to see her reflection in his tall black Hessians. He looked pale and thin, as if he hadn't been well, but his bearing was erect, his black square-cut shako under his arm. The slight clanking of his sword echoed with each step.

Something in his face drew her. Dark hair, worn longer than current fashion dictated, the indication of a dark full beard if he weren't clean-shaven, a straight nose, and heavily lashed eyes. But drawn skin, a tense-ness about his mouth, and a hint of panic—or was it just wariness?—in the way that he held his head. Was he, too, nearly overwhelmed by the occasion?

When he reached the foot of the dais, he bowed low from the waist.

A movement across the way caught her attention. Percival had stopped slouching, his gimlet eyes trained on the soldier's back. Perhaps they were acquainted? Percival had gotten the opportunity to join a delegation of members of Parliament to Spain six months ago as an aide. Father had ordered him to go because it was advantageous to Father at the time to have his son as part of the envoy, and somehow Percival had wound up embroiled in the Battle of Salamanca and had come home slightly wounded, looking for accolades and sympathy in equal measure. What-ever he had done there, her father had been furious, but neither had shared anything about the experience with Diana.

"Lieutenant Eldridge." The prince spoke only to the soldier, but his voice carried to every corner of the room. "I trust you've recovered from your injuries?"

Ah, so he *had* been ill.

"Yes, Your Highness. Thank you."

Diana wished she could see the soldier's face again. He wasn't a titled gentleman, for the prince had addressed him by his rank. Lieutenant. An officer, but barely.

"I am pleased to hear it. I imagine you're wondering why you are here? Your actions on the battlefield deserve a reward. Some would say your deeds deserve a knighthood."

A murmur went through the crowd.

The prince narrowed his eyes, scanning the room. "I, however, think such bravery on the battlefield, and doing such a service for your regent, deserves more. Kneel, young man."

A collective intake of air happened amongst the onlookers.

"Oh my," Lady Cathcart whispered. "He wouldn't. Not again."

Diana wanted so badly to ask what was happening, but she bit her lip, not wanting to be reprimanded or to miss anything.

The soldier knelt, slowly, as if it pained him, tucking his sword out of the way, his hat clamped against his side.

The Prince Regent accepted a sword resplendent with a jeweled hilt from a courtier and stepped down to place the blade on the kneeling officer's shoulder.

"For bravery in the face of the enemy, and for saving the life of my godson, Percival Seaton . . ."

Diana's eyes shot to her brother. This soldier had saved his life? What had happened to her brother in Spain, and why hadn't anyone mentioned it before?

Evan knelt at the foot of the dais, wishing he were anywhere else. His thigh throbbed at the pressure of being on one knee. Every eye in the room seemed to be on him. What was he doing here? He never thought he might long to be back in the hospital, but that feeling teased the corner of his mind. The prince took a ceremonial sword and rested the steel against Evan's shoulder. Was it really heavy, or was that his imagination? He'd never expected anything like this . . . whatever *this* was.

"For bravery in the face of the enemy, and for saving the life of my godson, Percival Seaton . . ."

Something Evan couldn't even remember doing.

"I confer upon you the title of Earl of Whitelock, Viscount Slaugham, with the lands and holdings entailed to that title."

Evan wasn't sure if it was everyone else in the room who gasped or himself. What?

The sword lightly bounced on his left shoulder, then his right, then his left again. "Rise, Earl of Whitelock."

This was a farce, right? Somewhere, there was a hidden joke, right? Him?

An earl?

Hoisting himself upright, trying not to favor his wounded leg, his mind galloped like a horse loose on the battlefield. A flash went through his mind, a shudder in his soul. Why had that image—a horse loose on a battlefield—rocked him? A cold snake of anxiety coiled up around Evan's torso, and his hand gripped his sword handle.

There must be some mistake. He wasn't an earl. He was a soldier. He was Evan Eldridge, not Whitelock or Slaugham or whoever else—

"Well done, my good man. Never let it be said that the Prince Regent does not reward those who serve him faithfully."

A buzz went through the room as Evan bowed again. What did he do now? There was some rule about not turning your back on royalty, right?

He took a few steps backward, careful not to stumble. A hand reached out and touched his arm, and he glanced at a man of about his age, dressed in knee breeches and satin coat.

"This way." The man drew him to the side to merge with the crowd.

Evan followed him, grateful for the direction, wishing they could've gone all the way to the door and out onto the street. People continued to stare, and many whispered to one another with shocked expressions, frowns, disdain. No one could be more astonished than he. What had just happened here? Evan wanted to escape the speculation, the bewilderment, and . . . the guilt. Guilt that rose up to smother even the shock.

He'd been rewarded for an act of bravery he couldn't even remember, saving the life of someone he didn't know. Rewarded with an earldom? A title and . . . lands?

What did any of this mean to his future? His mates in the regiment weren't going to believe this. When he returned to the Peninsula, he'd never hear the end of it.

The man beside him leaned in. "Ninety-Fifth Rifles, correct?"

Evan stared straight ahead as a young woman in a wide-hooped pale-pink gown floated down the aisle in front of him. He felt out of place in his military dress, but he'd rather that than the antiquated costumes of the rest of the assembly. He felt as if he'd stepped into a fifty-year-old painting. "That's right."

"I recognize the uniform. Marcus Haverly, late of the Fifty-Second Oxfordshire Light Division."

Some of the tightness went out of Evan's shoulders. A fellow military man, someone to whom he could relate in this alien world.

"We can talk more once the presentations are over. Stick with me when things break up."

Evan nodded, wanting to turn and shake the man's hand. He felt as if he'd been thrown a rope to pull himself up the cliff he'd been pushed over.

Three more young girls were announced, curtsied before the Queen, and were shepherded into the ranks along the walls. The audience stirred when Her Majesty rose, took the arm of the Prince Regent, and was escorted through a doorway. Those nearest to her bowed and curtsied, and she nodded right and left. Once she was out of the room, everyone seemed to relax a fraction. Voices rose, and Evan found himself the focus of much scrutiny.

Marcus steered him back toward the wall. "Best to only have to defend one front." He smiled as he said it. "Did you have any inkling? Were you given any indication in the invitation?"

"Not so much as a warning shot across the bow." And what it all meant was still a mystery. Perhaps once he got out of this crowd, which pressed in on all sides, cutting off his escape routes, he could start to make some sense of what had happened. Until then, the growing noise of the people around him sent fluttery, anxious feathers across his chest and tightened his throat. He hated crowds at the best of times.

"Well, congratulations, I guess." Marcus shrugged, his shoulders sliding under the dull bronze of his embroidered coat. "What are your plans?"

"Plans?" Evan's mind blanked at the notion. "Beyond passing my physical and getting back to my regiment?"

A quick bark of laughter from Marcus had heads turning. "Put that notion away for good. You're a peer now. A war hero. You're going to be the talk of the Season. And here's the Home Secretary. By the way"—Marcus lowered his voice even further—"you now outrank him."

Evan shot Marcus a look. What did he mean Evan couldn't return to his regiment? What else was he to do? They needed him, and he needed them. And he had unfinished business on the Peninsula, something he'd left undone. He could feel it, even if he couldn't remember it. All this fuss and frippery with the nabobs was temporary, right?

Marcus turned to Viscount Sidmouth. "Good afternoon. Quite a 'Drawing Room' session today, wasn't it? Five debutantes and a new earl."

"Indeed." The Home Secretary looked as if he'd just tasted puddle water as he turned to Evan. "I had no idea when I met you in the hospital so recently that the Prince Regent would be conferring such an honor." Pure vinegar couldn't have puckered his mouth more. "I've been sent to discuss the properties and responsibilities that come with the Whitelock title." He opened a sheepskin-wrapped bundle of papers sewn down the side with legal tape.

The Home Secretary scanned the front page, flipped to the second, and said, "There is a townhouse here in London that is currently being rented. You will have to decide if you wish to evict the current tenants or let them finish out the Season in the property. And there is an estate and manor house in Sussex south of Crawley. The earldom has been vacant for twenty years or so, and the manor has been closed up for that time. I understand there was a caretaker. The previous earl's executor wasn't up to the job, it seems, and things have gone untended for too long."

Land? A manor? A townhouse? What was he supposed to do with an estate? He felt as if shackles were closing about his wrists and ankles.

Sidmouth cleared his throat. "There's also the matter of funds. The last Earl of Whitelock was not known for his circumspection when it came to personal finances. He left behind a meager bank account that has accrued some interest, and of course there is the income from the town-house rents." He handed the papers to Evan, his finger on a number at the bottom of the page. His lips were pinched, and his brows drawn together, as if he felt the task of educating the newest peer of the realm beneath him. He clearly didn't approve of the Prince Regent's generosity. At the moment, he looked at Evan as if he were a stray mongrel sneaking into the pedigree kennel.

Which was just how Evan felt.

Letting his gaze land on the page where the viscount pointed, Evan tried not to show his surprise at the amount. Who called a bank account of over five thousand pounds meager? He would never amass that amount as a soldier if he stayed in the army for the next fifty years.

"Those documents will allow you to take possession of the properties and accounts. Have them with you when you go to the bank and when you receive the townhouse and manor keys from the law firm of Coles, Franks, and Moody on Orchard Street, near St. James's Park."

The Home Secretary bowed to Evan, nodded to Marcus, and turned on his heel, clearly glad to be finished with his assignment.

"Poor Sidmouth. I don't envy him his job, keeping the Prince Regent happy. He's caught between Parliament and the prince." Marcus grinned. "Ah, now it begins. Brace yourself."

"For what?" Evan swiveled his head, looking for danger but seeing only overdressed noblemen and women.

With a chuckle, Marcus turned Evan toward an advancing party. "You're about to join an exhilarating hunt, and it's up to you to determine if you're the hound or the hare. You have just become a very eligible bachelor, my new friend."

Evan held up his hand. "No, not me."

"Yes, you. The introductions to debutantes and their eager mamas will now commence. Or eager papas, as the case may be." Marcus straightened. "Here's one now."

"Good afternoon, Lieutenant. Or should I say Lord Whitelock now?" A tall, thin man with a square jaw and deep-set dark eyes covered the last few feet between them. His iron-gray hair rose thick and full from his powerful brow.

"May I present the Duke of Seaton? Your Grace, the Earl of White-lock."

Marcus made the introductions, and though his words were deferential, something in his tone put Evan on his guard.

"I came to express my gratitude. It was my son, Percival"—he indicated the young man at his shoulder—"whom you saved in Spain." Nudging his son, he looked away, as if his duty had been fulfilled.

Percival held out his hand, leaning on his cane. "Obliged." He pulled out of the brief handshake, his eyes languid. Candlelight from the mirrored sconces glinted off his golden hair. "Glad to see you suffered no lasting harm."

Other than the fact that I can't remember anything about you, about that day, about the battle? Evan searched the man's face for any sign of familiarity but found none.

"And you as well, I hope?" Evan indicated the cane, sizing up the young man. He would last about three minutes in the Ninety-Fifth. Fancy fop with a weak chin, a weaker handshake, and a lazy demeanor. How had he wound up in the middle of a pitched battle?

"Oh, you know. Making progress. At least the ladies find it dashing." He cast a rather leering eye toward a pair of the debutantes who whispered and fluttered their lashes at him from a few yards away. One debutante stood nearer, the one who had been standing before the Queen when Evan had entered the chamber, though she paid no attention to the young viscount, keeping her eyes lowered. The duke stirred, as if just remembering she was there.

He cleared his throat. "My daughter, Diana."

Her chin came up, and Evan blinked. Light-brown eyes with a fringe of dark-brown lashes. Not limpid, doe eyes, but intelligent and perhaps . . . wary eyes? Her chin was small and pointed, and her lips the palest rose. Her waist was cinched tight, her bodice showing the barest hint of bosom, her slender neck unadorned, the hollows of her collarbones somehow making her look vulnerable. Glossy brown curls framed her face and clustered on the back of her head. He was instantly aware of her in a way that took him off guard.

A beauty to be sure, the kind of beauty his fellow soldiers had rhapsodized about on long homesick evenings around the campfire.

A flush rode her cheeks, and she dropped a small curtsy. "Lord Whitelock."

Lord Whitelock. Evan felt like an impostor. At any moment, someone would elbow him and say it was all a prank, right?

How should he address her? Totally out of his element, he wondered what she would do if he snapped a salute and clicked his bootheels together.

Marcus took command before he did anything so silly. "Lady Diana, congratulations on your presentation. You look lovely. Don't you agree, Whitelock?"

"Yes." Had he really just croaked out the word like an awkward school-boy? Evan cleared his throat. "Yes." He took the fingertips she presented, gave a small bow, and said, "Lady Diana." Her fingers felt petite and delicate in his, and he found himself wishing she wasn't wearing gloves so he could feel her skin.

His arm jostled, and her hand slipped from his. A man of about his height forced his way forward, putting himself partially between Evan and the young lady. "I say, Perce, I believe introductions are in order." He ignored Evan and Marcus, focusing his attention on the girl.

Percival Seaton shrugged. "My sister, Diana, Fitz. I told you she was in town."

"Fitz" reached for Diana's hand, not waiting for her to offer it, and held it between his own, bowing over it and pressing his lips to the back of her glove. "Delighted, my dear."

Her brows came together, and she had to tug twice before he relinquished her fingers. Evan had the urge to haul the fellow backward and put himself in front of Lady Diana.

"Since Percival here is too lazy to do it, I guess I'll have to introduce myself. Viscount Fitzroy, at your service." His lip curled in a sneer.

Diana's hand went to her throat, her brown eyes wide enough that Evan felt he could fall right into them. She took a step back and bumped into her father, who was speaking with a pair of men.

"Don't be clumsy, girl," he growled, his face a thundercloud.

She moved quickly away from him, and as Fitzroy reached to clasp her arm, she slid away from him too.

"My lord." She placed her hand on Evan's elbow. "I would love you to meet my sponsor. She's over this way."

Evan threw a quick look at Marcus, whose eyebrows had risen. He nodded, and Evan took this to mean he had little choice but to go with her.

When they were out of earshot of her family, she lessened the pressure on his arm. "Thank you. I apologize for taking you away from your friends. That really was most bold of me, but . . ."

"Don't trouble yourself. They aren't my friends. At least, I didn't know any of them before today." He could feel each of her fingers through her glove and the sleeve of his woolen uniform. An only child, going straight into the army at seventeen, he'd had few dealings with women, and none at all with a woman of her station.

She smelled like flowers.

He realized he was staring and tried to think of something smart to say. "Though, I suspect that Marcus might become a friend." He glanced back to where Haverly stood in front of a tall set of draped windows. Marcus grinned at him with raised eyebrows, no doubt amused at how quickly an unmarried lady had cut him from the pack.

Eligible bachelor? Him? "You wanted me to meet your sponsor?"

"Oh, I do beg your pardon. I said that just to get away from the viscount." She blinked and looked down at her hand on his sleeve, withdrawing it and stepping back to lace her fingers together, her fan dangling from its loop at her wrist. "I'm afraid I don't care for the man."

Evan frowned. "But, I thought you'd only just met."

She shrugged, her shoulders delicate, her eyes not meeting his. "Yes, that's right. But sometimes you just know about people." With a small curtsy, she left him standing there staring after her.

Was this an example of "women's intuition" he'd heard of? If so, what was her first impression of him?

Not that it mattered. He had too much on his plate to have his head turned by a woman, no matter how pretty.

CHAPTER 3

"IF I'M NOW a man of leisure and am not supposed to work, why do I need so many clothes?" Evan held still, lest he impale himself on any of the dozens of pins holding the fabric that would become a new suit coat in place.

"Because"—Marcus slouched in a chair in the tailor's shop—"there are expectations."

"Whose expectations? A group of people I've never met, who last week wouldn't have been caught out even speaking to me? What about *my* expectations?" He winced as the white-haired little tailor jabbed him in the ribs to get him to do a quarter turn. Trying not to squirm as the man marked down his side with a piece of chalk, Evan sighed. "Actually, I take that back about being a man of leisure. I've worked harder this last week than I did as a raw recruit. Lawyers, bankers, tailors, boot makers, hatmakers, haberdashers. What's next?"

"A trip to Tattersall's to look over some horseflesh, even if you don't buy anything today. We can't have you afoot everywhere. You need a coach and pair, and a saddle horse."

At this rate, Evan would burn through his bank account in a fortnight. He'd have to put a stop to the spending.

"I also need my own place to live. After meeting the renters of my townhouse"—it still felt so odd to say that—"I couldn't exactly turn out the baron and his three daughters mid-Season. Until their lease has run its course, I'm homeless. I can't keep imposing upon you." Marcus had insisted that Evan stay with him until he "found his feet," as Marcus put it. If this week was any indication, finding his feet might take the rest of his life.

Being Marcus's houseguest had proven an education in itself. Marcus lived in an opulent brick townhouse on Cavendish Square. Not his alone, he admitted. It was the city headquarters for the Duke of Haverly, Marcus's father, but Marcus had the run of the place at the moment.

"The old boy rarely comes to town these days, and my elder brother, the marquess and heir, is busy on the estate in Oxfordshire. My mother isn't expected for a few more days, so I'm knocking about in the great town pile by myself. There's plenty of room, and you'll be good company. Be a friend and stay."

Put that way, Evan could hardly refuse. Marcus made it sound like Evan would be doing him a favor. But the boot was really on the other foot. Marcus had taken seriously the task of getting Evan outfitted and educated to look and act the part of the gentleman he'd so suddenly become. Evan had to wonder at Haverly's generosity and interest. Did he have an ulterior motive, or was he just bored and looking for a diversion? Thus far, he'd been generous and friendly, but Evan was still fighting panic attacks and nightmares, not to mention being thrown into the deep end of the aristocratic pool, and he didn't know whom to trust.

"Deliver everything to my place, Pierre, and send the bill to Coles, Franks, and Moody. They'll take care of paying for everything." A situation Marcus had set up for Evan last week, and which Evan still thought strange. Lawyers to handle his bills? He'd always managed his funds, meager as they had been, himself. He didn't like the idea of letting others take care of his accounts. Yet Marcus assured him that all gentlemen had secretaries, lawyers, and stewards to see to their affairs.

Marcus stood as the elderly Belgian tailor tugged the jacket off Evan's shoulders, and Evan reached for his uniform coat. With no proper civilian clothing—at least none that Marcus would allow him to be seen in—he'd continued to wear the green tunic and trousers of his regiment. At least he was comfortable in those, feeling like himself in that respect.

"Make one of everything first, then the duplicates," Marcus instructed the tailor. "Complete the evening wear at once though. We need to get him outfitted properly before tomorrow night."

Evan paused in slipping the pewter buttons through their holes. "What happens tomorrow night?"

Marcus smiled. "The first bash at Almack's. I got you a voucher, of a sort."

"A voucher? To Almack's?" Even a recent commoner such as Evan had heard of the famous social institution.

"Of course. One can't just show up uninvited. You have to be approved by one of the Patronesses. Unless you're the Prince Regent, of course. Though I don't know that I've ever seen him there. Almack's is the most exclusive entertainment in the city. The social dragons who run the place keep a watchful eye on everyone who enters. Debutantes' Seasons can be made or broken by a single evening at Almack's."

Marcus picked up his many-caped cloak and swirled it over his shoulders with a panache Evan envied. Once his new cloak arrived, he'd have to practice that maneuver.

"I spoke with the Prince Regent yesterday," Marcus continued, "and he wrote you a personal pass. We'll see what the Patronesses have to say about it when we get there."

A smile played about Marcus's mouth, and Evan frowned. Who were the Patronesses, and why did they wield such power?

"What am I expected to do there?" *And how am I supposed to do it without making a fool of myself?*

"You mean beyond be an eligible bachelor and dance with the ladies?" Marcus slipped on his calfskin gloves.

"Dance?" Panic skittered through Evan. He buttoned his tunic. "I have a wounded leg." The leg was coming along fine, had improved over the last week of activity in fact, but it would make a handy excuse not to make a cake of himself on a dance floor.

"Nonsense. Your leg is nearly healed. You said so yourself, so no malingering. There is a new dance that is scandalizing and thrilling London society at the moment. It's the waltz, out of Vienna, and it allows you to get very close to your dancing partner. I find it quite exhilarating, and you've got all of tomorrow to master the steps. Good thing it's fairly simple."

Evan's head ached. Dance with ladies of the *ton*? Surely there was some way out of this. Though . . . the memory of Lady Diana Seaton's face surged into his mind, something that had happened all too frequently since their brief encounter last week. Dancing with her might not be too bad. Officers had hosted occasional dances, and he'd partaken, but he was sure the reels and country dances he knew would bear little resemblance to a high-society affair at a place like Almack's.

Marcus pushed open the door and stepped into the brisk air. The tailor's shop had no front window, no sign over the street. Customers were by referral only. Evan never would've located the place without Marcus, much less been allowed through the door.

"Don't people do anything else at Almack's besides dance?" Evan dodged pedestrians to keep up with Marcus's long strides.

"Certainly. There are card rooms, and lots of business transactions get done, but the most important thing is shopping the Marriage Mart. Now that you're a nobleman, you're expected to marry well and produce an heir and a spare as soon as possible to consolidate the title firmly into your family." Marcus stopped at the corner where his carriage waited. The Haverly Family crest adorned the door, and the coachman sat high above a pair of dappled grays with glossy rumps and braided manes. "Tattersall's," he instructed the driver.

Evan had no desire to marry. His circumstances were too new, too foreign. Not to mention the fact that he far too often woke in the middle of the night drenched in sweat and reliving a battle he couldn't remember. Wouldn't that just endear him to a wife? She'd have him committed to an asylum before the ink was dry on the marriage license. He needed to keep all of that private until he sorted it out. Daily life amongst the aristocracy was proving challenge enough. Pursuing a wife would only add to his problems. Reasoning that the best way to defend himself against Marcus's suggestions was to go on the offensive, he said, "What about you? You're an eligible bachelor. Aren't you searching for the perfect mate?"

Marcus grinned. "Ah, that's where I have the advantage over you. I'm a mere second son. As such, I have the connections ladies like but not the title or fortune that makes them so eager. I can afford to take my time, look around. No pressure since I have an elder brother who is already married. That's why I went into the military for a time. I am the spare and thus not as valuable as the heir, in my parents' estimation. Anyway, I find life as a bachelor quite interesting." He looked out the carriage window.

Evan watched him, sensing the hurt beneath the light tone. What kind of culture had he been thrust into where any child not an eldest male was surplus to requirements?

The carriage finally rolled to a stop near Hyde Park Corner, and they disembarked. Marcus waved to several men he knew as they entered a high-ceilinged building. "Tattersall's. Biggest blood-stock auctioneer firm in England. Perhaps the world. The best of the best falls under the gavel here."

Evan found the auction fascinating. As a true horse lover, he enjoyed seeing the animals, and the witty and occasionally barbed interactions of the auctioneer with the bidders had him laughing and wincing by turns.

Coach horses, racehorses, saddle horses, broodmares, weanlings, stallions, the variety was amazing. But he wasn't ready to bid, Marcus's wishes notwithstanding. He'd never bought a horse of his own before, though he'd learned to ride as a boy, and he wanted to take the time to make the right choice.

"Let's go round the barns and get a better look at what's coming up. Maybe you'll find something there that catches your eye." Marcus led him away from the ring. Several onlookers slapped Marcus on the back, greeting him with smiles and handshakes.

"Is there anyone you don't know?" Evan asked as they left the building through the rear, emerging into the shed rows. Grooms walked horses for prospective buyers, who felt equine legs, peered into equine mouths, and looked into equine eyes.

"London society really isn't all that large when it comes right down to it. Maybe three hundred families? Anything catch your fancy?" Marcus studied a bay with white socks as it strode by.

"Plenty, but probably all out of my price range." Evan sidestepped a red-faced large man.

"You, boy, make sure you keep him moving in the ring. Let everyone get a good look," the man shouted as he hurried down the cobblestones.

Marcus grimaced. "Crack McGibbons. Be careful buying one of his horses. He knows every trick in the book to get them looking fine for the auction, but the minute you get one home, its faults all show up." He kept his voice low, and Evan nodded.

"*Caveat emptor.*"

"Indeed. Where did you learn Latin?"

"My father's a minister, and he was the local schoolmaster as well. Latin, Greek, logic, and rhetoric were my meat and bread as a youngster. Speaking of my father, I need to send him a letter. He won't believe what's happened." Evan pulled a face, knowing he should've written sooner.

"Will he be pleased?" Something down at the end of the row caught Marcus's attention, and they started that way.

"Hard to say. He's never been one who cared much about social classes. Everyone is the same in God's eyes, so they're the same in Reverend Eldridge's too. What my mother will make of it, I have no idea." They reached the far end of the barn row, and Evan stopped. Before him, in a round pen, a dozen horses stood, heads down, eyes dull. "What's this?"

Marcus gripped the top rail with both hands. "Army horses. Well, former army horses. When the military is done with them, some wind up here."

Evan went still. The looks in their eyes reminded him of his fellow patients in the hospital. Used up and cast aside by the army, futures uncertain. Behind him a door slammed, and he jumped, every muscle tense. And he wasn't alone. One of the horses, a chestnut, jerked his head up, white showing around his eyes as he crowded against the fence.

I understand, boy.

"What will happen to them?" He feared he already knew the answer.

"Cabbies buy them cheap. Farmers too. Those that don't sell wind up at the knacker's yard." Marcus followed the progress of a leggy colt toward the sales ring. "Most stay on the Continent, but those that do return are sold in an effort by the army to recoup some of their investment money."

Not much of a reward for faithful service, for all the danger they had lived through, the lives they had saved by being brave, strong, fleet, and loyal.

Surely someone should do something? But what?

"I say, if it isn't the new earl." Viscount Fitzroy sauntered up, Percival Seaton in his wake. "What are you doing back here with these nags? Or is that all you can afford? I heard your title didn't come with much money. I suppose you'll have to find some well-heeled debutante eager to be a countess in order to fill the coffers, eh?" He looked Evan over from his head to his boots. "Still wearing the uniform, I see."

Percival turned his cane in his hands, his face pink with cold. He nodded to Evan. "Eldridge."

"It's Whitelock now," Marcus reminded him. "We've seen all we need to here for the time being. We were just heading over to Gentleman Jack's. Perhaps you'd care to join us?"

Evan quelled a questioning look. From what he had ascertained, Marcus had little time for Fitzroy or Percival Seaton. Now he wanted their company? And who was Gentleman Jack?

"Not today, my good man. We've got an appointment, don't we, Seaton?" Fitzroy grinned. "Thought we might check out what's going on over in King's Place to see the new merchandise. Maybe you'd like to skip Jack's and come with us? You can work off some steam either way." He elbowed Marcus, whose mouth tightened.

"No, thank you."

Evan looked from Fitzroy to Marcus, unsure of what was passing between them, but sensing it wasn't friendly, invitations aside.

"Your loss, old boy." Fitzroy walked away but turned back after a few steps. "Just a friendly warning, Eldr—I mean Whitelock. Don't get any silly ideas about the Seaton girl. I noticed the attention you were paying her last week at her presentation. I'm considering a move in that direction myself, and it would be bad manners for you to upset those plans."

Percival snorted. "Nothing to worry about there. My father would never consider someone like *him* for Diana. He'd as soon marry her off to one of these spavined horses. Though that's about all she deserves. She's cost him a packet with her come-out and all. He'll be looking to recoup his losses when he brokers a match for her. You'll have to move fast, Fitz.

He's lining up a couple of his cronies into a bit of a bidding war, last I heard."

Fitzroy winked, a lurid grin on his face. "Not to worry. I wasn't planning on *marrying* her. They're welcome to her . . . after I've had a bit of fun." He nudged Marcus in an old-boys gesture.

Evan stepped forward, anger surging through him at the slander against the woman he had been unable to put out of his mind for a week. If this was an example of the way so-called gentlemen spoke about ladies, he would rather stay a commoner. Either way, Percival and Fitzroy needed someone to teach them a lesson.

Marcus put a staying hand on Evan's arm before he could plant the young jackanapes each a facer.

"This is the gratitude you have for the man who saved your life? Curious." The even, condescending tone in Marcus's voice made Percival flinch. "Not to mention speaking about one's sister in such a fashion."

"She's just a woman. And I didn't ask him to save my life. I would've gotten out of it myself if given the chance." Percival swelled his chest.

Evan held his breath. Was he going to say what had happened at Salamanca? Shed some light on the missing memories? Before Percival could speak, Fitzroy punched him in the shoulder.

"You're dotty. Let's go. We're wasting time here." Fitzroy gave a nasty laugh and tugged Percival away. "We can talk *to* some women rather than just talking about them, which is much to be preferred. There's a new girl, Pippa, that is said to be smashing, and I want to see for myself." They sauntered through the crowd, looking back once and laughing.

Evan slowly unclenched his fists. "Too bad you stopped me. A good thrashing might improve both of them."

"You're going to have to give up your Philistine ways now that you're a gentleman. You can't resort to brawling in public, however much satisfaction it might give you. Next time, perhaps he'll take us up on the invitation to Gentleman Jack's Boxing Establishment, and you can fight with him in the accepted way. If you do accost him, however, and manage to draw claret, preferably from his aristocratic nose, I'll buy you dinner." Marcus pushed away from the fence. "In fact, I'll buy you dinner anyway, at my club."

"I'm never going to keep track of all the places you're taking me. You have a club? And what's in King's Place anyway?"

A man they passed overheard, barked out a laugh, and nudged his companion, who laughed too. Marcus tugged Evan's sleeve. "Come on. And keep your voice down. King's Place is where the highest-priced doxies live, looking for gentlemen callers and hopefully a rich patron who wants a mistress. The most exclusive brothels in the city are on that street, just off Pall Mall."

Evan said nothing, staring ahead, trying to quell the blush he knew crept up his cheeks.

"Yes. Well." Marcus headed toward his carriage. "The one I feel sorry for is Diana Seaton. A brother like Percival, and a rake like Fitzroy after her? Not to mention her father. Someone should marry her and take her away from all of that." He raised his eyebrow and looked at Evan from the corner of his eye.

"I'm no knight in shining armor. Maybe you should marry her yourself." Though that notion didn't sit well with him either. Rescuing damsels in need wasn't in his purview. Look where rescuing a viscount had gotten him.

This gentleman's lark was no picnic.

Diana followed her father and brother up the stairs, her muscles tense and her heart thudding. Neither had offered their arm as her escort, but she didn't mind. Physical contact with either of them made her skin crawl, and she was nervous enough.

Almack's.

The building certainly didn't look the part of London's most exclusive ballroom, being plain brick and otherwise unadorned. Light spilled from the tall arched windows on the upper floor, and she clutched her cloak at her throat, unsure if the chill was from anticipation or the cold evening.

At the door, she showed her voucher, obtained through one of her father's many contacts and delivered that morning, and was admitted. She breathed a little sigh at having gotten that far.

"Meet us right here, and don't take forever. There are a couple of gentlemen who want to look you over. My negotiations are at a delicate stage, so see that you do nothing to draw undue attention to yourself." Her father pointed to the sign indicating the ladies' cloak room. "We'll be back." He headed in the opposite direction, removing his hat and gloves as he went.

Diana nodded but said nothing. Look her over? Like a horse at auction? Indignation clawed up her backbone, but she knew better than to say anything, especially now. Her father had been in a towering rage most of the day. Cian had cried incessantly, as if his belly ached, and her father had thrown a vase across the drawing room, shouting that someone quiet the brat or he would. Diana and the nurse had taken turns walking and rocking and patting and praying in an effort to hush the baby, but nothing had worked until he'd finally worn himself out and fallen asleep. Diana had toyed with the notion of moving the baby's nursery to the attic, farther from her father's rooms, but it was so cold up there, she worried Cian would become ill. That, and she didn't want to be so far from him. At the moment, he and Beth slept in Diana's dressing room, across the hall from her father's chambers. *Please, Lord, let him be sleeping when we get home.*

Percival had stumbled into the house after ten in the morning, much the worse for wear after yet another night out on the town. He reeked of drink and cheap perfume. Father had yelled, Percival had sniped back, and finally Father had slapped him in the face. As a result, Percival had been sullen and petty, dragging off to his rooms and not appearing until the carriage had pulled around to take them out for the evening. He was still sulking.

She handed her cloak to the attendant and received a ticket in exchange, which she tucked into her satin reticule. All around her, women chatted and laughed, admiring one another's gowns, whispering, practically vibrating with excitement. How Diana wished Catherine were there to help her, shepherd her through this evening, introduce her to potential friends, and share all the experiences. A wave of grief—grief she'd been forbidden by her father to show—crashed over her, and her eyes misted with tears.

Blinking hard, she grappled for composure. It wouldn't do at all to appear with red eyes. Checking her appearance in a wall mirror, she pinched her cheeks and touched the golden ribbon threaded through her brown curls. Her pale-yellow gown fit perfectly, and she smoothed its folds, her gloves catching a bit on the gold lace trim. The dress had been made for Catherine the previous year, and Diana had added the delicate lace at the sleeves and neckline, wanting to put her own touches on the garment to make it hers.

By the time she emerged into the foyer, her father was there tapping his foot, his mouth a hard slash in his granite face. "Come." He headed for the grand staircase, and Diana followed.

Percival had disappeared, and she didn't know whether to be grateful or suspicious. Her brother's capacity to get into trouble—already considerable—had multiplied upon their arrival in London.

The ballroom opened before them at the head of the stairs and to their left. Pale-blue walls, gilt mirrors, plaster medallions, and enormous candlelit chandeliers. At the far end, an orchestra occupied a balcony, and upon a small platform, several ladies perched on sofas.

The Patronesses. The women who decided who would and would not be admitted to their exclusive presence.

Diana stopped beside a graceful column. Someone bumped her elbow, and she turned to see a young lady who had been presented at court at the same time as she.

"Hello," the girl said.

What was her name? Surely Diana had heard it . . .

"Hello. Your dress is lovely." Diana took in the petite blonde's pale-blue gown, envying how it brought out the depth of her blue eyes. Diana had plain brown eyes, the same color as her ordinary brown hair. Catherine had possessed raven hair and velvety brown eyes, while Percival was blond. Each of the Duke of Seaton's children had favored their mother, much to his disappointment.

"Thank you. I'm so nervous I can hardly keep my knees from knocking.

And now we have to be introduced to the dragons. I hear they're stricter than the Queen herself."

Wonderful.

"I'm Emily, by the way. My father is Lord Swinley."

"Diana." She didn't mention her father. But it turned out she didn't need to.

"Diana Seaton. Yes. I met your brother at my come-out ball last week." She flushed and toyed with her fan. "He's very handsome. He said you weren't having a ball to celebrate your debut?" Her brows narrowed toward each other.

Diana shook her head. Her father had declared that paying the annual fee to Almack's, the price of private boxes at the opera and the theater, as well as for her wardrobe was more than enough without the expense of a ball to announce her arrival. Being presented at court was enough, especially since he would broker her marriage himself.

"Come, Emily." An older woman in a truly impressive turban tapped Emily's arm with her lorgnette.

"Oh dear. I'll be glad when this is over." Emily gave a small wave and trotted in the woman's wake toward the platform where the Patronesses waited.

"There you are."

Diana turned to see Lady Cathcart hurrying up.

"You were supposed to come with your father to find me." Lady Cathcart surveyed Diana, as she had done in the palace anteroom. "He's most impatient tonight. Let's make our greetings to the Patronesses and then find you a suitable dance partner." Her sponsor threaded her way through the crowd, nodding to her acquaintances, not checking to see whether Diana followed.

They waited until there was a pause in the traffic, and then Lady Cathcart stepped up. "Lady Jersey, Lady Castlereagh, Princess Esterhazy, may I present Lady Diana, daughter of the Duke of Seaton."

Diana gathered her hem and her courage and curtsied. "A pleasure."

She waited for a response, but none was forthcoming. When she straightened, the women weren't looking at her but at the entrance to the ballroom. It was her court presentation all over again.

"What is *that man* doing here?" Lady Jersey squared her shoulders as all three Patronesses stiffened, eyes narrowing.

Diana dared a look over her shoulder.

Her heart jolted, and flutters rippled over her skin.

Him.

The new Earl of Whitelock. Someone who had been frequently in her thoughts over the past several days. She'd even sneaked the newspaper up to her room and read the article related to his new status, careful to return the paper back to her father's desk before he should miss it. Ladies of proper breeding were not to read newspapers, lest they offend their delicate sensibilities—a notion Diana considered high-quality hogwash.

Mr. Haverly stood at the earl's elbow, but no one seemed to pay him any attention, all eyes being focused on the earl. After a moment's shocked silence, the assembly stirred as a murmuring buzz rippled outward.

"I shall put a stop to this, I assure you." Lady Castlereagh stood, her chin high. "He can't just stride in here like he's *somebody*. I shall have words with the doorman as well."

Lady Cathcart clasped Diana's elbow, and they retreated. "I want to see this." She pulled Diana back the way they'd come, and they arrived near the entrance in time for the confrontation.

"Lord Whitelock, Almack's is an exclusive establishment, and entry is granted by invitation only."

Diana felt for the new earl, surprised he'd even gotten as far as the ballroom without being stopped by one of the staff. After a gaffe like this, he mightn't now be invited to any social events. What was wrong with Mr. Haverly that he hadn't informed the new peer of the requirements for gaining entrance to Almack's?

"Lady Castlereagh, the earl has his invitation." Humor laced Mr. Haverly's tone. "Show her, Whitelock."

Without a word, the earl removed a small rectangle of paper from inside his tailcoat. The cloth fit him like a second skin, perfectly tailored to his broad shoulders and lean waist. His breeches matched exactly, and his linens were snowy white. He'd clearly been shopping since being named to the peerage.

Lady Castlereagh scanned the card, a flush riding her high cheekbones. Her already hawk-sharp eyes grew more intense.

Haverly smiled. "I trust there will be no problem?"

"Of course not. Welcome, Lord Whitelock." She sounded as if she had swallowed a hairbrush as she handed the card back, and the earl returned it to his inner pocket with a tight smile.

Lady Cathcart's grip fell away from Diana's arm. "I never in all my born days expected that. What can be on that card? A . . . commoner . . . just tamed a dragon."

She wasn't the only one marveling. A crackle jolted the crowd, and everyone spoke at once.

Diana looked away from the earl, not wanting to be caught staring. But she couldn't resist a few stolen glances. If she hadn't seen him in his uniform, hadn't witnessed the prince conferring the title, she would assume Whitelock had been born a gentleman. Perhaps it was his military bearing, perhaps it was the fine clothes, or perhaps it was the fearless way he refused to be cowed by someone who was so certain she was his social superior. Whatever it was, he drew admiring glances from many females.

The orchestra played a few measures, and couples lined up for a reel. Diana lost sight of the earl as people began to mingle.

"Well, I suppose we should see about finding you a dance partner. After all, your father's paying me quite a sum to chaperone you." Lady Cathcart raised herself up a bit on tiptoe.

"Might I volunteer my services?"

The suave voice slid over Diana like oil. She closed her eyes.

"We have already been formally introduced."

Please don't let it be him. Please don't let it be him.

It was him.

"Ah, Viscount Fitzroy. Perfect." Lady Cathcart nudged Diana forward. "I'll meet you back on this spot after this set."

How could she refuse gracefully? The sight of the man made her want to be ill. To have to pretend to be enjoying herself, to have to smile and curtsy and allow their hands to touch. He held out his arm, and she let her hand hover over his sleeve, not wanting to make contact.

"You look delectable tonight. That color suits you." His golden-brown eyes trailed down her gown, lingering long enough in certain places to make her cheeks flush at his boldness. "Such a nice crop of debutantes this year. I do love the start of a Season. Most diverting."

Diana trembled with the desire to slap his insolent face. He smirked and stood opposite her as the music's tempo increased. It was a simple reel, and they were one pair in two long lines, but she felt alone, exposed, and vulnerable, like a rabbit caught on open ground as a hawk swooped overhead.

He danced well, light and elegant, and acted as if he were aware of it. Every time their hands met, he smirked, inviting her to admire him.

Diana caught a glimpse of her father near the refreshment table, staring at her, and of Lady Cathcart smiling and tapping her toes to the tune. And she saw the Earl of Whitelock. He wasn't dancing. He had one hand in his pocket, looking out over the dancers with his piercing blue eyes—not that she could tell they were blue from this distance, but she remembered . . .

Would this set never end? How long must she keep this smile pressed onto her face?

Fitzroy chuckled as they promenaded down the long line, taking their turn as top couple. "You look brittle enough to snap in two. Relax, my dear. You're the envy of every woman here tonight." He had his head bent, as if they were sharing a delightful secret. She leaned away, concentrating on the steps.

At last the music ceased, and the ladies curtsied once again to their partners. She would've turned away from him, but he caught her hand and threaded it through his elbow. "Oh no, my sweet. You can't run off on your own. I'll escort you back to your keeper."

But rather than return her to Lady Cathcart's side immediately, he clamped her hand tight against his ribs, placed his other hand over hers, and pulled her in the opposite direction. In what must have been a well-rehearsed maneuver, he pivoted and placed Diana between one of the high windows and an enormous potted palm. His body shielded her from view, and he loomed over her.

"On second thought, I can't bear for you to get away, my dove. I do wish to get to know you better. We could have quite good sport together."

The scent of his pomade cloyed in her nostrils, and a quiver shot through her chest. How dare he? If they were spotted conversing this way, her reputation could suffer. Her father's rage would be palpable if she stepped even an inch out of line. She edged to the side, hoping to slip past him, but he shifted his weight to block her escape.

"I'm considered a good catch, you know. Not that I would allow myself to be caught just yet, but many girls would leap at the chance to be showered with my affections. In fact, many have."

"I am not one of those girls. Now let me by." Her lips felt stiff, and she gripped her folded fan. As weapons went, it wasn't much, but perhaps she could fend him off if necessary. The music for the next set began, and Lady Cathcart would be looking for her.

At that moment, a hand reached through the palm fronds and grasped her wrist. "I believe this is my dance."

With a tug, Diana was released from Fitzroy's custody and swirled into the arms of . . . the Earl of Whitelock. Before she could stop him, his hand was at her back, her fingers nestled in his other palm, and they were twirling to the three-quarter time of a waltz, the newest dance from the Continent, which had only arrived in Britain the previous year.

She was so stunned, she followed his lead. He wasn't as adept at the steps as her dance master at school had been, but he moved with conviction.

"I hope I haven't intruded, but you didn't appear to be enjoying the viscount's attentions."

How had she gotten into this? The earl, with the best of intentions, had rescued her from one dilemma and landed her squarely in the middle of an even greater one.

No debutante was allowed to waltz—considered by some to be a thoroughly scandalous dance because of the continual proximity of the participants—until she had been given permission by one of the Patronesses. To flaunt their authority was to commit social suicide.

Her father would kill her. Lady Cathcart would need smelling salts. Percival would probably give her a slap.

And Cian. What would her father do to the baby in retaliation for her behavior?

Her steps faltered, and the earl's arm tightened to steady her.

"What's wrong? You did want to get away from Fitzroy, right?" His breath brushed her temple and sent a shiver through her.

Oh yes, she had wanted to get away from him. Not just because he was a disgusting rake, but because she had feared she might cause a scene by smacking the leering face of Viscount Fitzroy, the man who was both her sister's seducer and Cian's father.

What was wrong with the girl? Was his dancing so terrible? He'd practiced for hours today with one of the housemaids at the Haverly townhouse until Marcus had pronounced him proficient enough to brave the ballroom. Diana moved as if made of wood, her eyes unfocused, her face pale. Or was it that Fitzroy had shocked her? If that were the case, Evan would see about calling the man outside to settle things.

She winced, and he realized his fingers had squeezed her hand too hard.

"Sorry."

"Please, we must stop." Her words, pitched low, were filled with panic.

"Are you ill?"

"No, no, but we have to stop." She pressed herself back, away from his embrace, not really struggling, but clearly distressed.

In that moment, he wondered if she thought him cut from the same cloth as Fitzroy, a *roué* who just grabbed women up against their wishes. Or had she not truly wanted to be rescued from the bounder and resented Evan's interference? Or did she consider Evan beneath her, a commoner boasting of a title he didn't deserve, not good enough to dance with a duke's daughter? These thoughts flashed through his mind, and his hold loosened. She stumbled backward, and he caught her quickly, steadying her and then letting his hands fall away.

With a stiff bow, he muttered, "My apologies. Can you find your way back to your chaperone, or do you require an escort?"

"I . . . I . . ." Her hand fluttered to her throat and then to her lips. She appeared unable to move.

He took her elbow and guided her off the dance floor toward the row of settees along the wall where most of the matrons had a good field of fire to see their charges. As they threaded their way through the crowd, people whispered, frowned, and shook their heads.

Evan gritted his teeth. He knew he didn't belong here, but they didn't have to act as if he had mange and would infect them. Scanning the area for danger, he spied Marcus angling toward him. And ahead, the Duke of Seaton stood with arms crossed, face like a blood pudding. What had jammed his rifle?

At sight of her father, Diana stopped, and a tremor went through her. She seemed to shrink a bit, become more vulnerable, and Evan wanted to put himself between her and her father, or even better, to wrap her in his arms and whisk her away. Something about the duke made the hairs on the back of Evan's neck stand up, like when he knew the enemy was lying in ambush and if he wasn't on his guard, his next step might be his last. His heartbeat increased, and hyperawareness raced along his skin.

Shaking his head at such nonsense, he took a few deep breaths, willing down the unease. What possible danger could be lurking at a fancy ball put on by a bunch of swells? Evan tightened his grip on Diana's arm.

Also on an intercept course that would bring them together all at once, Evan spied a pair of the harpies who ran this place's social register. They looked like they had just ingested spoiled mackerel.

"Why do I feel as if I'm headed to my own court-martial?"

"Because you are. Have you no idea what you've done, what you've made me do?" She looked up at him with those beautiful brown eyes, stricken with worry.

"What? Taken you away from Fitzroy? I had no idea you were enjoying his company, or I would've left you alone. I thought I was being a gentleman, but clearly I'm going to need more practice."

She stopped, staring up at him. "No, I'm grateful for the rescue, but the dance—the waltz. I'm a debutante. I don't have permission yet to waltz with anyone. Doing so without being given leave—" She shook her head, her brown curls bouncing against her smooth cheeks. "I'm ruined."

Ruined? For dancing with him? What rot. Nothing improper had occurred there in the view of all, so why the fuss?

Yet the look in her eyes, the anger simmering on her father's face, and the determined set of the jaws of the Patronesses told him there might be some substance behind her claim.

Evan, you idiot. What have you done?

"I'll explain it to them. It's my fault. I had no idea. Let me tell them what happened, and I'll take the blame."

She removed his hand from her arm and shook her head. "Sir, please. You'll only make it worse. I must insist that you leave me alone. It will be best for both of us."

Frowning, Evan took a deep breath. "Very well, but I am no coward. I will return you to your father and face whatever faux pas I've committed like a man."

Just as they reached the knot of people with judgment on their minds, a commotion at the entrance had everyone turning their heads. People stirred, and the orchestra stopped mid-measure. The couples twirling on the dance floor slowed, and into the silence, someone let out a loud gasp.

The Patronesses' mouths dropped open, and to Evan they looked like freshly landed codfish. Had the doorman let in yet another undesirable like him to tilt their axes?

Taller than most, Marcus looked over the crowd, his brows rising, and then he shot a glance at Evan.

An opening formed, and there stood the Prince Regent, resplendent in evening finery, his retinue crowding behind him. His cravat dug into his chins, and his coat was large enough to make a fine bivouac tent on the Spanish plains, but he cut a commanding figure.

To his right and left, men bowed and ladies curtsied, lowering their heads but not their eyes as they stared.

The prince strode near—was he making right for them?—and Evan bowed, mimicking Marcus, just a few steps away. Diana grabbed his arm and dipped into a low curtsy.

"Ah, two of my favorite people." The prince rubbed his hands together and then held out his palm to Diana, who took it and rose so gracefully it took Evan's breath away. "How are you, my dear? You know, you're shining everyone down around here. If you're not careful, you'll be named this Season's 'Incomparable' and have every other woman jealous." He kissed the air just over her knuckles. "And you, Whitelock, how are you faring? I can't tell you how I enjoyed conferring a title upon you." He appraised Evan from hair to boots. "You're wearing it well. I was pleased to issue your pass to Almack's. I thought I'd toddle round to see how you were making out. It's been too long since I attended an Almack's bash."

"Your Highness." Evan bowed again. "Mr. Haverly has taken it upon himself to become my mentor. I only wish I were a more apt pupil." And also that Marcus would've mentioned the prohibition against waltzing with a debutante.

"Good, good. He'll steer you right." The prince glanced up at the balcony and leaned to speak to one of his courtiers. "Tell them to play. This place is dead without music."

"Your Highness. What a pleasure to see you here." One of the Patronesses stepped forward. Lady Jersey, was that her name? "We're honored."

He nodded, his lips pursed as he studied her. The orchestra filled the room with an Austrian melody, and the prince's countenance lightened. "Ah, the waltz. I adore the waltz. My dear, would you do me the honor?" He offered his arm to Diana.

She looked from Lady Jersey to her father, who was now narrow eyed and as calculating as a miser.

"Your Highness," Diana faltered. "I haven't yet been given per—"

"She'd be delighted." The Duke of Seaton stepped forward. "I was just now receiving Lady Jersey's blessing to give Diana permission to waltz at Almack's, wasn't I, Lady Jersey?"

That lady looked as if she'd swallowed a caltrop, but she nodded. "Yes, of course. Lady Diana is a lovely dancer and of impeccable character, Your Highness. It isn't often we grant permission to a debutante her first evening here, but how could we refuse such a charming young lady?"

Evan wondered if the words choked her. Marcus appeared to be smothering laughter behind his forefinger laid along the seam of his lips.

As the prince led Diana into the center of the now-empty dance floor, Evan turned to watch their progress. The Prince Regent was a large man, with quite a girth, and he dwarfed Diana, but he moved with more grace than Evan would've imagined. Diana appeared to almost float across the gleaming wood, a half smile on her face. After a complete turn around the floor, other couples joined them, and Evan had to work harder to see her in the throng.

The Duke of Seaton and Lady Jersey were sharing some private, intense words. Behind them, wearing a smirk that made Evan's body tense, Viscount Fitzroy laughed, eyes heavy lidded as they followed Diana's every move. Percival Seaton went by with a girl in his arms, light gleaming off his golden hair. He must be quite recovered from his Salamanca injuries.

Fitzroy waited until Lady Jersey had marched off before joining the Duke of Seaton. He motioned to Diana as she twirled by in the arms of the prince. Seaton jerked his head, his brows going high. What was that bounder Fitzroy saying about her?

"You realize, my good man, that the prince saved you both from ruin, even though he has no idea?" Marcus spoke quietly, almost out of the side of his mouth. "What were you thinking, dragging her into a waltz, of all things?"

"How was I supposed to know? You might have mentioned it amongst all the other lessons you've been cramming down my craw all week." Now that he had time to mull over the situation, hot embarrassment coursed through Evan, drawing his ire. He had never asked for any of this. By rights he should be returning to his regiment and the life he knew, ready to wreak some havoc on the enemy in Spain and push the French back to France, where they belonged.

But one did not say no to the Prince Regent.

Before the dance ended, but when it appeared the Prince Regent's stamina had, he returned a flushed Diana to them. "My dear, I haven't enjoyed anything so much for years." He was red cheeked and panting slightly. "It's been awhile since I took a turn with so fair a young lady."

She curtsied. "Thank you, Your Highness." Gratitude laced her words, and Evan knew it was for more than the compliment or the dance. She knew as well as Marcus that His Highness had saved her Season and most likely her reputation.

As she straightened, the prince looked over to Evan. "I say, I have a wonderful idea. Whitelock"—he flicked his wrist, motioning to him—"as my newest nobleman, you're in need of a bride. And Diana, as my god-daughter . . ." He paused, his eyes gleaming. "Yes. What a match it would be. It would be just the thing if you two should marry. Whitelock, you should offer for the girl! She'd be perfect. In fact, I shall have to insist upon it."

Evan felt like a barrel of gunpowder with a hole in the bottom, all his insides draining out and afraid someone might light a match. Marcus let out a low whistle, and everyone within earshot went statue still.

Lady Diana's eyes collided with his, and they held as his thoughts ground to a halt and then scrambled around one another in chaotic retreat, refusing to form a line of defense to hold his position.

Marry? Lady Diana Seaton? A duke's daughter? It was one thing to pretend to be an earl, to wear the clothes and go to the parties and dances, but marry an aristocrat? Him?

And yet there was one hard and fast rule he was learning.

One did not say no to the Prince Regent.

CHAPTER 4

DIANA HAD NO choice but to hurry from the carriage and up the stairs, since her father had an iron grip on her wrist and marched ahead of her into the house. He'd not said a word on the trip home from Almack's, but his rage was such that even Percival had remained quiet.

The silence broke the moment the duke thrust Diana into the study. She staggered but managed to right herself as he strode past her to his desk. A bottle of whiskey and a glass sat ready on the blotter, and the coal brazier had been lit in the fireplace hours before and glowed a dull red, spilling heat into the room. Everything prepared by a punctilious and wary staff to make his homecoming as comfortable as possible.

And yet Diana was cold to her core. She clutched her velvet cloak around her, but it would be paltry protection from what was to come.

"How dare you?" he thundered, throwing his cane, hat, and coat to the floor like an angry child. "You had exactly one purpose tonight. Behave with comportment and not draw attention to yourself, do nothing shameful. And what do you manage to do in the course of less than an hour? Scandalize the Patronesses by waltzing, not only without permission but with that common cur who isn't fit for proper society. Not only that, but you drew the Prince Regent into the fray, and now he thinks you should marry that . . . that . . . *mushroom*." A fleck of spittle formed at the corner of his mouth. "He's nothing more than a pretender, springing up overnight, no standing, no family, nothing to recommend him."

Percival slouched by and sank into a chair, draping his leg casually over the arm, a cocky smile playing about his lips, enjoying watching Diana get a tongue-lashing.

"He did save my life, after all." Percival fingered the quizzing glass hanging from its ribbon on his waistcoat. "He has that to recommend him."

"Be quiet. If you hadn't been such a colossal fool on the Continent, you wouldn't have needed your worthless hide saved and we wouldn't be in this predicament. You should've done as you were told—kept your head down, gathered your information, and brought it back to me. Instead you went glory seeking and nearly died for your troubles." The duke turned back to Diana, whose mouth had dried to attic dust.

"You're no better than your sister was." The duke paced, stomping across the carpet and his discarded cape, red suffusing his face. "No thought to your reputation or mine. Nor to the plans I had in place. Do you have any idea the delicate negotiations I have been engaged in regarding your future?" He turned and shook his fist in her face.

She winced and leaned away from him, her knees trembling and threatening to buckle. None of this was her fault, but she couldn't even breathe a protest.

The duke grabbed a glass and poured a large helping of whiskey. Tossing it back, he grimaced and filled the glass again. When he'd gulped that one down, he growled and hurled the empty crystal tumbler at the coal brazier. Shards of glass exploded, shooting across the room. Diana ducked, but several pieces hit her cloak, tearing the cloth. She wasn't hurt, but her heart darted in her chest like a panicked hare.

"What about the money?" Percival asked, acting as if nothing had happened. "If she marries him, the inheritance becomes his the minute they say their vows. You won't see a shilling of it, just like the old lady wanted. What are we going to do? You promised me some of that money, and I made plans. I'm running low on funds, you know."

Be quiet, Percival. Diana pleaded silently, but she knew her half brother. He wanted to make things worse for her, if that were possible. He always had.

The duke fisted his hands at his sides, shaking. "I can salvage this." The words hissed from his clenched jaws. "There has to be a way."

Percival put both boots on the floor and leaned forward. "Maybe it isn't as bad as it seems. You know old Prinny. By next week he'll have forgotten about the whole thing."

A calculating gleam entered the duke's eyes. "That's it," he said, slowly. "Delay. That's what we need to do. Delay the engagement, delay any wedding. In a fortnight he'll be on to something else, and I can go ahead with my plans. I've found someone who is willing to split the inheritance with me in order to get his hands on her." He jerked his thumb toward Diana. "The more fool him. I'll send him word tomorrow that we are stalling for time so the prince can forget his ridiculous suggestion, and then we can move forward with our plans."

"What about her in the meantime?" Percival asked, as if Diana weren't even in the room.

"She will keep her mouth shut if she knows what's good for her. If she breathes so much as a whisper about the inheritance to that bounder Whitelock . . ." He paused, listening. A faint wail drifted down the stairs.

Cian.

Lord, I prayed that he would stay asleep. Why won't You answer even that simple prayer?

Diana dared to look over her shoulder at the door, wanting to go to the baby, to shush him, to comfort him, but she was rooted to the spot until her father gave her leave to move. As she turned back toward her father to gauge his reaction to hearing the baby, his hand came up and backhanded her across the cheekbone.

Stars exploded behind her eyes, and she lurched, falling and bashing her knees into the floor. She put out her hands to stop her fall, but they tangled in her cloak, and her shoulder crashed onto the rug as she twisted to catch herself. Her head followed, hitting hard, and more bright lights flashed through her skull. Tears of pain sprang to her eyes, blurring her vision further. Disoriented, she fought for breath as he towered over her, and she braced herself for another blow.

But it didn't come.

As if everything had slowed down but the pain coursing through her, he moved back, straightening, rubbing the back of his hand, as if it stung. "The child." His eyes narrowed. "That is how I shall tame you. You," he shook his finger at her, "will put the Earl of Whitelock off if he offers for you. Tell him you must consider his proposal, give it some time, since you barely know each other. In the meantime, the Prince Regent will forget his matchmaking, and things will go back to the way they should be. You will marry the man of my choosing, and I will get a large portion of your inheritance. If you don't, the child goes to the orphanage."

"No, please." She pushed herself up, the side of her face already swelling, her lips feeling stiff. She tasted blood inside her mouth where her tooth had cut her cheek. "I'll do what you say. Just don't send the baby to a foundling home."

"I'll do just as I please, and you will do as I say." He pointed to the door. "Get out of my sight, and quiet that brat. If he makes another sound, he goes tonight."

Diana pushed herself up from the floor, every muscle aching, her knees on fire and her head still ringing. Her velvet cloak tangled around her feet, and she stumbled upright, groping for the door handle and slipping out, trying to ignore Percival's laughter and snide comment about how clumsy she was.

The butler stood in the hallway, his face composed but his eyes showing pity. "I'll take your wrap, my lady."

She undid the frog closure and handed over the cloak, cold air from the foyer chilling her skin. "Thank you, Carson. Have the seamstress check it over. There might be some small tears. A glass . . . got broken."

Lifting her hem slightly, she grasped the banister and tried to hurry up the stairs, her knees still throbbing. Cian's wails had become louder, and by the time she reached her room, she could plainly hear each sob.

Beth had the baby against her shoulder, bouncing him, walking around the tufted circular ottoman in the center of the dressing room. The baby's face bobbed, knocking against her shoulder, red and wet, eyes screwed shut.

"I'm sorry, my lady. He won't leave off. He's been crying most of the evening." Her own face bore streaks of tears over her freckles as her brow bunched and her mouth trembled.

"It's all right, Beth. I'll take him. Just let me get changed, and you can take a break."

In the dim light of the dressing room, Diana hurried out of her ornate butter-yellow gown and satin slippers and into a flannel nightgown and wrapper. As she took the wailing baby from his nurse, Beth gasped. "Oh, my lady, your face."

Diana probed the inside of her cheek with the tip of her tongue, feeling the stiffness and swelling. "I'm fine." She laid Cian on the ottoman and rewrapped him tightly in his blanket. She'd learned that if she swaddled him, he soothed more easily. "Please run to the kitchen and get us a tea tray. Warm the flannel pads, and bring a cold, wet cloth."

"Yes, my lady." The girl was gone in a trice, and Diana settled into the low rocking chair by the window. She tucked Cian tightly against her shoulder, set the rocker in motion, and started the familiar *pat-pat*, rock, *pat-pat*, rock, to which he'd become accustomed. In spite of the swelling of the right side of her face and lips, she sang softly.

Hymns were Diana's favorites, mostly because they were the only songs to which she knew all the words. She had learned the songs in school, and singing had been her favorite part of the daily chapel services. She imagined Cian requesting some Isaac Watts, and smiled, brushing a kiss across his downy hair.

> O God, our help in ages past,
> our hope for years to come,
> our shelter from the stormy blast,
> and our eternal home.
>
> Under the shadow of Thy throne
> Thy saints have dwelt secure;
> sufficient is Thine arm alone,
> and our defense is sure.
>
> Before the hills in order stood,
> or earth received her frame,
> from everlasting Thou art God,
> to endless years the same.

O God, our help in ages past,
our hope for years to come,
be Thou our guard while life shall last,
and our eternal home.

By the time she started the fourth verse, Cian's cries had subsided to snuffles and hiccups, and his eyelids drooped. She sang through the song once more, and he relaxed into sleep. Beth returned with the tea tray, the warmed flannels under her arm, and a small pitcher with a damp cloth draped over the rim.

"He always quiets best for you, don't he, miss?" She poured a cup of tea and set it on the windowsill beside Diana.

Cian hadn't been asleep long enough for Diana to trust stopping the rocking and patting, so she left the tea where it was. And the compress for her face too. Time enough when the baby was deeply asleep.

"Put those warm cloths in the cradle, and cover them with the blankets. That way the bed will be warm when I lay him down."

"Did you have a nice evening, miss?" Beth sat on the ottoman, resting her elbows on her knees and her chin in her hands. "Was it as beautiful as they say, Almack's? Did all the handsome gentlemen beg you for a dance? Did anyone offer for your hand in marriage? Did you cause any duels?" She sighed, as if causing men to shoot at one another over winning her hand would be the most romantic thing imaginable.

Diana closed her eyes, resting her aching head against the rocker. "No duels. At least I don't think so." Though the consequences of this evening's work felt as dire. "Promise me, if I can't take care of Cian, you'll do your best to look after him." She lifted her head to look at the girl.

"Of course, miss." Beth raised her head and clasped her hands under her chin. "If His Grace sends our little man to the orphanage, I'll do my best to get a job there to look out for him until you can get us both out."

She said it with sincerity and such trust that Diana's eyes smarted. How could she carry such responsibility on her own? *God, do You see this? Do You hear me? I feel so alone. I pray and I pray, but nothing seems to change. At least not for the better.*

LOST LIEUTENANT

Diana sighed, laying her head back again, inhaling the sweet scent of Cian's skin, holding him tightly. She'd promised her sister that she would raise the boy as her own and love him as a mother, and she intended to keep that promise. If it meant stringing the Earl of Whitelock along, just as her father wished, she would do it. When the Prince Regent forgot about his suggestion that they marry, she would accede to her father's wishes and marry whomever he required, but she would make it a condition of the marriage that Cian's guardianship be transferred to her.

It was the only thought that made any of this bearable.

Evan stepped out of Marcus's carriage, borrowed for the morning, and looked up at the imposing edifice that was the Duke of Seaton's Mayfair home in the capital. White stucco molded to look like marble blocks, precise over-and-under windows, and a fanlight over the entrance. And a dozen steps up from the street to reach the massive black doors. Reeking of money and status.

Checking his appearance, pulling down on his waistcoat, rolling his neck against the high, tight cravat Marcus insisted he wear, Evan gathered his courage. He'd feel much more comfortable in his uniform, but Marcus had shot that idea down quickly.

"You can't propose to the daughter of a duke wearing your green woolens and pewter buttons. You're a gentleman now, and you must dress accordingly."

How, in such a short time, had he gone from simple army officer to calling on the daughter of a duke? What was God thinking? Nothing was going according to Evan's plans, and that didn't look to change anytime soon.

He patted the letter in his inside coat pocket. The Prince Regent was most serious about his suggestion of last night. The missive had arrived during breakfast, all but ordering Evan to get around to Lady Diana's home and make his proposal.

And one did not say no to the Prince Regent.

Marcus thought it a sound match. Evan and a duke's daughter. A beautiful debutante who could have her pick of men in the peerage. She wasn't likely to welcome the offer of an upstart such as him. A sound match. What a bag of moonshine.

If anyone looked out the window and saw him dithering at the curb, they might think he was scared. *Just get on with it. Maybe she'll say no and you'll escape.*

Or she might say yes. She might have to, what with the Prince Regent weighing in.

A long engagement. That was what he wanted. If they had to get married eventually, maybe she wouldn't mind being engaged for a year or two . . . or three. At least until he got used to this peerage lark. Not to mention that getting married should wait until he got his mind sorted and stopped jumping at every little noise, waking almost hourly with nightmares, and finally remembered whatever it was that had happened on the battlefield that sent him into a panic at odd intervals.

He walked up the steps, glad to move without limping at least, though the injured leg was weaker than he'd like. Still, being out of the hospital and walking had hastened his healing. Without giving himself time to rethink, he raised the brass knocker and rapped it against the strike plate.

As if he'd been waiting near the door for the summons, an immaculately liveried footman opened the door and stepped back.

Trying to remember everything Marcus had instructed before seeing him off, Evan entered, removing his hat with one hand while digging into his pocket for his crisp new calling card.

The Earl of Whitelock.

Evan felt as if he were looking at the name of a stranger. An impostor at the very least. What was he doing here?

"I'd like to speak to the Duke of Seaton, if you please."

The footman held out a little silver tray, and Evan placed his card on it.

"Very good, sir. I shall see if His Grace is at home."

Evan refrained from rolling his eyes. The man would know whether his employer was at home. Marcus had explained that this was the polite way to see if the duke was willing to talk to Evan or not. Everywhere he went amongst the peerage, pretention was labeled "good manners."

In moments, the footman returned, bowing slightly. "His Grace will see you now. May I take your things?"

Handing over coat, hat, and walking stick, Evan smoothed his hand down the front of his waistcoat, tugging it down to meet his breeches. How he missed his military trousers. Much more comfortable than this dandyish ensemble. At least Marcus had consented to his wearing boots and not buckled shoes.

The servant showed him into a parlor, rich with heavy green draperies, patterned wallpaper, and gilded frames of landscape oil paintings. Pale-green matting covered the floor, and a fire burned in the marble fireplace.

"His Grace will be in momentarily. May I bring you tea or coffee?"

"Coffee, thank you." Evan had developed quite a taste for coffee in Spain. He enjoyed the strong flavor far more than the ale most men of his regiment preferred.

Evan was left waiting for nearly half an hour, and he had no doubt the duke wanted to let him know who was superior in the relationship. But he didn't reckon for Evan, who had the patience of the Sphinx. Sharpshooters could lie motionless for hours, waiting for their quarry. Sitting in a pleasant drawing room, warm by a nice fire while it spit snow outside, drinking coffee, wasn't a bad way to pass the time.

Finally the door opened, and the duke came in. His gray hair flowed back from his forehead like a lion's mane. His eyes glinted in a face as hard as flint. Evan rose, setting his cup on the side table.

"Your Grace. Thank you for seeing me." He held out his hand, but the duke ignored it, instead seating himself in the wingback chair across from the settee and crossing his legs.

So that's how it's going to be. Evan took his seat. If the duke wanted to see who could outwait whom, he was in for a long day.

The clock on the mantel ticked softly, sleet pinged off the windowpanes, and the fire crackled. Evan held Seaton's eyes, unflinching. He might be an upstart in the peerage, but he'd dealt with numerous pompous officers, had lived through years of war, and had stared death in the face countless times. No mere duke with a bad temper would make him cower.

Eventually, the duke uncrossed his legs, sniffed, and said, "What is it you've come for?"

"I believe you know why I am here. If not, perhaps this will make my intentions plain." Evan removed the Prince Regent's missive and held it out.

The duke once more ignored the gesture. "I'm not interested."

"You should be. It's tantamount to a royal decree. I am here to make a formal proposal to your daughter, Lady Diana, the Prince Regent's god-daughter, at his request." Evan flicked the page open so the duke could see the crest at the top of the stationery.

Like a striking snake, the duke snatched the paper. "What is this tripe?" He read the page rapidly, his face going pale. "How did you do this?"

"I?" Evan's brows rose. "I had nothing to do with this. It arrived at my lodgings this morning. I'm here on the strength of it and on the strength of what happened last night at Almack's. It is my duty to offer marriage to your daughter, having unintentionally caused her some embarrassment last evening, and it is your duty, as her father, to agree, because it is the express wish of the acting ruler of the realm." Did the bounder think he'd been around to the prince's breakfast table this morning asking for the letter? Nonsense.

Red crept up beyond the duke's impeccable neckcloth, his eyes narrowing as he slowly folded the paper. He swallowed—what appeared to be a considerable amount of bile, if his expression was any indication—and placed the letter on the arm of the chair. He tented his fingers and placed them against his lips, studying Evan.

Evan wanted to roll his eyes. The man was insulting, treating him like some boot-licking social climber. "I suppose this is where I am to make promises concerning your daughter, promises to see that she is well looked after? I'll confess, as a new member of the peerage, I'm not certain how one goes about proposing to a near stranger. Where I am from, marriage bonds are forged with mutual affection and interests. I understand the aristocracy does things differently, marrying for money, titles, lands, and political alliances. However, I do assure you that your daughter will be well looked after in my care. I will see to her comfort to the best of my abilities."

The duke waved a dismissive hand, as if not really hearing Evan. Was he so little concerned for his daughter's future? His mind seemed to be elsewhere, as if working out a thorny problem. At last he came to the present.

"I will deliver your offer to my daughter." He rose, and Evan rose with him. "I will send you word of her response."

"No."

"Pardon me?" Seaton stopped on his way to the door.

"No, that won't do. I must speak to her myself. Now, if you please." Evan clasped his hands behind his back. Convenient as it might be to have his proposal handed on by someone else, that way was also cowardly. He would face the girl himself, make his offer, and hear her response. If she gave him his congé, fine. If she accepted, then he would persuade her that a long engagement was best for everyone.

"You will not see my daughter today, or for as long as I can forestall the encounter." The duke's words were clipped, clearly expecting to be obeyed.

"Your Grace." Evan almost choked on the words, since the man had no grace whatsoever. "The Prince Regent was clear in his note that he expected to hear how my interview with Lady Diana went. It is implied that I will speak with her myself. If not here, then I imagine the prince will summon both of us to Carlton House for the discussion to take place under his watchful eye."

If the duke became any more rigid, he'd snap in two. Every muscle tensed, his hands fisted, and he nodded, once, before leaving.

Evan resumed his seat, his heart thudding hard against his fancy new waistcoat. The duke might have pretended to keep an even demeanor, but the anger emanating from him had hit Evan in hot waves. Surely the duke couldn't be that upset by the Prince Regent's machinations? Marcus had explained that marriage to an earl was an acceptable match for a nonroyal duke's daughter, even if he was a recent addition to the peerage. Evan was titled, moneyed, and landed. As well as being a war hero and new favorite of the Prince Regent. Most men would stumble over themselves to have him offer for one of their marriageable daughters.

Evan had plenty of time for his nerves to settle. The butler came and cleared the tray, not meeting Evan's eyes, leaving him alone for a further quarter of an hour. Finally Lady Diana entered.

Rising, he told himself to remain calm.

Her gown, a pale blue, swished in a purely feminine way as she crossed the room, her chin down, as it had been when he'd first met her in the Queen's Drawing Room. Her brown hair curled from a knot on the back of her head. Though she kept her face turned from him, her beauty struck him afresh. Long brown lashes, creamy skin, the scent of flowers . . . roses?

"Lady Diana."

She took his hand briefly—too briefly—and sat next to him, keeping her face in profile. "My lord." She gripped her fingers together in her lap.

Now that the moment was upon him, he couldn't think of a single intelligent thing to say. She was clearly nervous, but she also seemed remote, as if her thoughts were elsewhere. An inauspicious beginning.

He rubbed his palms on his thighs, grasping for some sort of aplomb. What would Marcus do in this situation?

"Have you spoken to your father? Do you know why I am here?"

She nodded. "I was expecting you, after what the Prince Regent said last night, though perhaps not so quickly."

"I came first to apologize for my behavior last evening. I was unaware of the social etiquette regarding waltzing at Almack's, and I unduly caused you distress and embarrassment. I do hope you will accept my apologies." He kept his diction clear and modeled his speech after his father's precise way of speaking, thankful for the elocution lessons he'd received as a child. His years in the army had put some distance on his upbringing, but it came back if he worked at it.

She turned slightly his way, looking at him from the side of her left eye. "Of course."

"Thank you." He cleared his throat. "Then there is the other matter." Why wouldn't she look at him? It was disconcerting enough to propose to a woman he barely knew, but to have to propose to her ear instead of her face was putting him right off.

He took a deep breath. "Lady Diana, would you do me the honor of becoming my wife?" There, it was out.

"I am sorry."

Her chin went down, and her words hit him in the chest. She was sorry? Saying no? He didn't know if he was elated or disappointed. But she wasn't finished.

"I am sorry the Prince Regent put you in this position, where you feel you must offer for me. And I am sorry that I must follow through with his wishes and accept your proposal. I know it is not what you would've wished, but I find I have no choice in the matter." Her fingers twisted. "It appears we must both obey those in command over us."

As a promising start to an engagement, this left something to be desired. She *had* said yes, hadn't she?

The absurdity of their situation struck him, and he couldn't quell a laugh. Tilting her head oddly, she studied him out of the corner of her eye once more.

"I assure you, I'm not mad." Though his chest lurched at the thought. Perhaps he was mad. After all, he had all the symptoms. "It's just, here we are, doing something that neither of us wants or could have anticipated a month ago. A month ago I was in the hospital, recovering from war wounds and plotting how soon I could rejoin my regiment on the Continent. Where were you a month ago?"

She jerked, and to his horror, a tear formed on the lashes he could see.

"I'm sorry. It's not a laughing matter." He was an uncouth cad. What had he been thinking, trying to make light of such a serious issue?

"No, don't. It is I who should apologize." She smoothed her dress, flattening her hands on her lap.

He remembered those delicate, petite hands, how they fit like small birds into his bigger, broader mitts.

"I have been most ungracious. Though neither of us would choose this as our preferred first course of action, your offer is most gallantly made. I do accept your proposal. There is one thing I would ask, however. I would like a lengthy engagement, if you are not opposed. We scarce know one another, and a longer engagement would allow us time to become better acquainted."

He blinked. Here she was suggesting the very thing he had intended to broach. She, too, was in no rush to get leg-shackled. Happy that she should think so similarly as him, he slipped from the settee and knelt before her, taking her hands in his so he could look her in the eyes.

That was when he saw it. The right side of her face, discolored, swollen. The corner of her lip had been cut. Though she averted her gaze, turning her face, he'd seen the damage.

Cold invaded his core, even as anger burned bright in his veins. "What happened to you?" Though he suspected he knew. The mark was unmistakable.

She winced, and he realized he was gripping her hands like a blacksmith's vise. He relaxed his hold but didn't let go. "Don't lie to me. Someone struck you. Was it your father? Your brother?"

She nodded. "My father was very angry last night."

Of all things, she sounded . . . ashamed. What had she to feel sorry about? The blame lay with her worthless parent.

Guilt stabbed Evan. "Because I 'rescued' you on the dance floor." It wasn't a question. Marcus had spoken about the strict rules of London's society, but Evan, scoffing at such strictures, hadn't listened well. And it had nearly cost a young woman her reputation, and had, in truth, cost her pain and humiliation.

"I'll have a word or two with your father."

Her hands tensed in his. "No, please. It just makes things worse. There are things you don't know about, ways he has . . ."

He could almost taste her panic, and his heart slammed against his chest as his own familiar sense of panic rose up to join hers. He forced himself to remain calm, even as his breath shortened and sweat broke out on his skin.

She shrank back from him, the pulse in her throat leaping, her bottom lip disappearing as she bit it. Surely she wasn't frightened of him?

His protective nature roared to the foreground. He had it in his power to safeguard her, and he was going to do it. She was now engaged to him, betrothed. That meant something. She belonged to him. "I am afraid I won't be able to accede to your wish for a long engagement. I require that we marry a week hence." He would not be the cause of her staying any longer in this house, subject to her father's temper and abuse.

She gasped, shaking her head. "I cannot."

"As you said before, we have little choice."

"Please, I can't. I need six months . . . a year. Please."

Though her large eyes beseeched him, he knew he couldn't allow her to live in this house for a single day longer than necessary.

They would wed in one week and sort out the details later.

Chapter 5

Diana allowed the tiger to tuck the blanket over her lap as she settled into the carriage beside . . . her fiancé. How strange to think of anyone in those terms, but especially the Earl of Whitelock. She tried not to take too much room from Marcus or his mother, the Duchess of Haverly across from her. The young groom gave her a quick nod before ducking out of the carriage to take his place on the step at the back. In the two days since the earl's proposal, she'd seen nothing of him until this morning, though Carson had brought her the notice from the paper announcing their engagement.

Which made things official. Her father had raged at first, then quietly fumed, and then, as was his way, schemed how he could turn this setback to his advantage.

"Here's what you're going to do. You will say not one word of your inheritance to Whitelock. He won't have heard of it himself, or he would've brought it up when he offered for you. It's not as if I spread the news abroad when your harpy of a grandmother arranged her will. If he doesn't know about it, he can't claim it. The day after the wedding, I will arrive at your townhouse to take you for a drive. You'll come with me to the solicitor's. I'll have some documents drawn up, with Whitelock's signature forged on them, and you'll vouch that he is signing the money over to me. And you will *never* mention the funds to your husband."

He was not only prepared to cheat her—and thus her new husband—out of her inheritance but to break the law to do it. Forged documents. If he was found out, he would find himself in Newgate Prison or transported to Botany Bay. He would be disgraced.

But his actions were his own. As were hers. Cian's safety and future were most important. She had promised her sister, and she loved the baby with all her heart. She was prepared to do whatever it took to keep him safe and as far from her father's influence as possible. "If I do this, you'll sign Cian over to me?"

He grimaced at the sound of the boy's name, but he nodded once. "You can have the brat the minute you turn over the funds."

It would mean lying to her husband for the rest of her life, never telling him about the fortune he'd lost. A lie of omission. But it would also mean Cian was safe with her. That made it all right, didn't it? Her conscience bit her, but she squashed it down. Rahab lied about the spies, and God still loved her, didn't He? Surely the safety of a child was justification for not telling the truth to a man she barely knew, though he be her fiancé. Though she had prayed and prayed for some other way to be revealed, those prayers had gone unheard. She would just have to push ahead herself and hope God would forgive her.

So now she held two secrets from her betrothed. The money and a baby. How could she even broach the subject of Cian with the earl? Surely he wouldn't welcome the illegitimate child of his wife's sister into his home. Until she knew her prospective husband better, she couldn't possibly anticipate how he would react. For the time being, he mustn't know about Cian. If that meant buying the baby's freedom with her inheritance and her silence about the matter, then so be it.

Loneliness washed over her. She was trapped in her father's townhouse with all the anger and tension for a few more days with no one to advise her or care about her troubles. Her fingers went to her cheek where the bruise had faded, and she'd concealed the faint color with a little face powder. Though he had fumed and shouted, the duke had sense enough not to strike her again. Diana had the earl and his haste about the wedding to thank for that, she supposed. Her father couldn't beat her black and blue and still escort her down the aisle at St. George's in less than a week's time without raising unwanted curiosity.

"Diana?" The earl's voice jerked her out of her reverie. "I asked if you were comfortable. Here. Put your feet on this hot stone." He indicated the wrapped bundle on the floor.

"Thank you."

"Not too cold?"

"No." Though she was chilly, it was to be expected in January in London. She had so wanted to escape the townhouse, even for a short while, that when the earl's invitation for a chaperoned trip to an art exhibition arrived, not even a snow squall would've caused her to refuse.

Marcus Haverly sat across from her, next to his mother, the Duchess of Haverly. She'd come more for respectability's sake, Diana suspected, rather than any desire to appreciate fine art. The duchess wore a pinch-mouthed expression of general disapproval that kept Diana from engaging her in conversation.

Her son must be used to her moods, for he asked, "Are you comfortable, madam?"

Madam. He didn't call her Mother?

"I suppose, though it seems indecently early for such an excursion." She adjusted her fur-lined cloak. "I don't know why we had to be out and about at such an hour." Her pewter-gray hair clustered in tight curls around her face under her bonnet. She looked Diana over and gave a small nod of greeting.

Marcus had her eyes, but that was the only resemblance Diana could see.

"An early start means an early conclusion, and there are many preparations still to be made for the wedding." Marcus grinned at Diana, his eyes asking for her indulgence when it came to his abrasive parent.

The duchess sniffed. "A rushed affair. 'Marry in haste, repent at leisure.' It's not just an old saw. There's quite a bit of truth there." Her eyes flashed between the earl and Diana. "I can't help but think that if your mother were alive, she'd caution you to wait a bit. I'm surprised at Lady Cathcart for countenancing such a rushed wedding. As your sponsor, she should've been consulted."

A stab of longing went through Diana. How she wished she had a mother, or her sister, or anyone of her own to guide her, to listen to her fears, to help her. If only she had a friend to talk to, a woman who could advise her. She felt so alone, with no one to stand with her against life's blows.

"I understand you've made your curtsy to the Queen? Why didn't I read about your come-out ball?" the duchess asked.

Diana blushed. Why did she always seem to be apologizing for her father's actions? "I did not have a come-out ball, Your Grace. My father thought it an unnecessary expense."

"It appears he was correct, since you're already engaged and will be married within the week." She frowned. "It's unseemly, if you ask me. I am always suspect of a marriage performed under special license. Any marriage that can't stand to have the banns properly read falls under a cloud."

Marcus put the side of his finger along his lips, failing to hide his smile. "And after I went to all the trouble of helping Whitelock here procure that special license—and at great expense too."

"Hmph. I might have known you'd be involved. You have ever been a vexation to me. Flaunting convention and going your own way. I am told it is the custom of second-born children, but it does make you a trial." She sighed, as if bearing up under a great burden.

Diana shot Marcus a look to convey her sympathy and understanding of being publicly chided by a parent, but Marcus gave a small shake of his head and then . . . winked at her. A laugh caught her by surprise, and she quickly glanced out the window.

A pair of young ladies in riding habits passed the carriage, cantering on their beautifully turned-out mounts. A groom rode at a polite distance behind them toward Hyde Park.

"Do you ride, Diana?" the earl asked, settling back against the squabs. He had a small furrow between his brows, and his lids were narrowed, as if the weak morning light hurt his eyes.

Her suspicions rose. Had he been drinking? Was he suffering the morning aftereffects of indulging the night before?

He had a stiffness about him. Tension? Anger? Her stomach tightened, and she gripped her hands inside her fur muff. She really knew little about him. Was he a drunkard? Was he subject to tempers like her father or pettiness like her brother? Was he a rake and philanderer? A bit of panic lodged in her throat at the thought of tying herself forever to this stranger who might turn out to be anything.

She forced herself to speak calmly. "Yes, I do enjoy riding, though I do not get the opportunity as often as I would like. My father has an extensive stable, but he doesn't keep ladies' mounts. I learned to ride at school, where equitation was a required discipline." Though she hadn't sat a horse in a half a year or more, not since being summoned back to Seaton Manor and Catherine's disaster.

He nodded, and his hand came up to massage his temple. "I learned to ride as a boy. The local squire hired me to exercise his horses. He had several racehorses, and some of the best hours of my life were spent riding at a high gallop across the open fields. I missed riding when I joined the army. The Ninety-Fifth Rifles is an infantry unit. As an officer, I was eligible to ride, but as a lowly lieutenant, when mounts were in scarce supply, higher-ranking officers got first pick of the horses, and I mostly marched with the men."

The duchess sniffed and rolled her eyes. "Such plebeian work, being a common foot soldier. It's beneath the nobility, really."

"Well, madam, I was a soldier," Marcus reminded her.

"That's different. You won't hold a title like the earl here. You're a mere second son. That's why we sent you into the military. What else is to be done with a spare once the heir has reached his majority? It was either the army or the clergy, and we knew you'd be worthless to the church—you're such a rogue. Buying you a commission solved the problem."

Diana sent Marcus a compassionate look. His mother talked about him as if she didn't care about him at all. Something they shared in their parentage, evidently, since her father didn't care about her as a person, merely as his pawn to help him get what he wanted.

Marcus did not appear surprised or even hurt by his mother's words. Instead, he gave Diana attention. "You look lovely, Lady Diana. Evan is the envy of the *ton*, snapping you up so quickly."

Diana knew she blushed, and Marcus laughed. "It's true. I don't know another debutante who has made such a splash her first night at Almack's."

"I don't suppose," his mother interjected, "that you yourself made a favorable impression on any of the young ladies? It's past time that you were looking for a suitable bride. I shall have to step in and find someone if you won't put yourself out to do the job on your own."

"Now, madam, there's plenty of time. After all, as a second son, I'm not responsible for carrying on the family line. Neville's married, and I expect an announcement in the not-too-distant future that he's managed to beget an heir." Marcus's brows came down, as if her jab had gotten under his armor this time.

Again Diana felt sorry for him.

"Be that as it may, I shall have to cast about for some baronet's daughter for you. You can't really hope for someone of higher rank."

The carriage wove through traffic, passing through the fashionable Mayfair district quickly. The ground was bare, no trace of the sleet that had fallen earlier in the week. Perhaps they would have an early spring. When Diana had given thought to marriage, she had always assumed she would wed in the late spring or early summer, not the dead of winter.

She studied the earl in small glances, the man she was supposed to marry in just five days. Anxiety hammered against her breastbone. They had met all of three times before, and soon she would be his wife. And yet he had insisted upon the hasty marriage the moment he'd seen the damage her father's blow had done. She felt at once vulnerable and protected. Confusing, to be sure.

"How are the wedding plans coming?" Marcus asked.

Diana gave a small shrug. "I have no idea. My father put Lady Cathcart in charge, and I've been told nothing. A modiste has moved into the house with two assistants, and they're all working feverishly on the wedding dress. I understand invitations went out this morning. I am sure the *ton* is abuzz at the short notice."

"It will be a nine-days' wonder, I shouldn't think. A week or two after the wedding, someone else will be providing the *on dits* for the *ton* to whisper over."

"We can hope." The earl shifted, his leg brushing Diana's. "I feel as if I live in a glass box, everyone feeling free to stare in and comment. I barely recognize myself when I look in the shaving glass each morning." He rubbed his temple again, turning away from the window.

The carriage pulled to the curb. The earl didn't wait for the coach-man to open the door, grasping the handle and stepping down. He turned back to assist Diana, and she placed her gloved hand in his. His blue eyes pierced hers, and she noted the strain there. Was he really distressed by the nosiness of society? Or was it something else? Was he regretting his decision to hurry the wedding? Or was he frustrated at being boxed so neatly into a corner by the Prince Regent? If only she knew him well enough to ask. But he'd been on edge the entire journey, and she wasn't accustomed to asking anything of the men in her life, lest she get a severe setdown.

"Thank you, my lord."

Bending to whisper against her ear, he said, "I think you can stop with the 'my lord.' My name's Evan."

A shiver went through her as his breath tickled her skin.

He offered her his arm. "I'd appreciate it if you'd call me that, espe-cially when we're alone."

"Very well . . . Evan." The word tasted strange on her tongue. It wasn't a common name amongst the aristocracy, which tended to be peppered with Williams, Georges, Henrys, and Charleses. She felt shy using it. It seemed too intimate for their brief acquaintance. And yet he'd asked so nicely.

They followed Marcus and the Duchess of Haverly into the stone building, left their cloaks at the desk, and Marcus guided them to a skylit room filled with paintings and statues.

"Don't rush. This is the first time this collection has been on exhibit, and I'm looking forward to seeing it," Marcus said.

Evan offered his arm once more, and Diana placed her hand lightly on his sleeve. Pale winter sunlight cascaded from the iron and glass sky-lights onto the artworks in their massive frames. Seaton Manor had a long gallery of paintings, but they were all of Seaton ancestors, stern and sober-faced strangers Diana knew little about. Her father cared more for horses and a fine wine cellar than collecting art.

"Are you a connoisseur of oil paintings?" Evan asked. "I'll confess, I know little, and what I do know is about religious art."

"Religious art?" They stopped before a seascape. Diana thought she knew just how that little boat being tossed on the waves and at the mercy of the wind must feel.

"Did I not tell you? Though come to think of it, when would there have been time? My father is a clergyman." He stared up at the painting, his brow furrowed. "And the village schoolmaster, in order to help make ends meet, since our parish is so small."

A clergyman? No, he certainly hadn't mentioned it. "That must account for a foot soldier sounding so educated." Her hand came up to cover her mouth. She'd sounded as snobbish as the duchess. Would he be angry?

He grimaced. "Thought I'd be soundin' like a mush-mouthed peasant, then? Droppin' me haitches and rhyming me words like a Cockney?" Then he smiled, though there was still a tightness around his eyes.

Heat swirled up her cheeks, glad he wasn't angry. He patted her hand, chuckling, though he also winced and tilted his head, as if stretching a crick in his neck. "I'm only quizzing you. My father is an excellent teacher and preacher. Though I never attended university, my education would compare well to those of most of the *ton*'s elite. And I would venture to say that my Greek and Latin would stand up to scrutiny better than most, thanks to my studious parent."

Diana observed him, feeling oddly proud. A learned husband was more than she had hoped for. She was no bluestocking herself, but an ignorant husband would be unbearable. That he should be so accomplished and yet be a soldier . . . a unique individual, to be sure.

And yet for such a well-studied man, he had much to learn about the world he had now entered. He'd already proven his education was lacking in key areas.

"You mentioned that you were feeling as if you lived in a glass box with the *beau monde* looking on. That's an apt description because your every move will now be scrutinized. And the hasty wedding date is going to start rumors. You must be prepared for that." There would be those speculating that the rush to the altar was because a baby was on the way, though that was absurd, since they'd met less than a fortnight ago. That wouldn't stop tongues from wagging though. Biddies seemed to relish speculating about the worst in people. What was that old saying? Second babies took nine months, but first babies could arrive anytime? It wasn't true in her case, but the gossips never took truth into account when spreading their tales.

"I don't put much stock in rumors." He squinted as they walked through a shaft of light. "We have our own reasons for marrying quickly, and we have the blessing of the Prince Regent. Why should we care what others think?" With a sigh, he pinched the bridge of his nose. "Shall we sit?" Indicating a bench in the center of the room, he led her that way, easing down beside her and stretching one leg before him, kneading his thigh. His wound must be paining him. Perhaps that was the reason for the strain in his face.

Marcus and his mother stood at a distance, staring at a bucolic landscape and not talking. There were a few other patrons, but not many due to the early hour.

She straightened her skirts, knowing she should warn him about the severity of crossing the *ton*'s conventions and expectations. "That is something you do not seem to grasp. It is *very* important what other people think. If you break too many of the rules, you won't be received in polite society. You'll be blackballed, and then where will you be? You'll bring dishonor on your family, your title, and . . ."

"And?" He frowned.

"And me. As your countess. If you are ostracized from society, then I shall be ostracized as well."

He grunted. "From what I can see, that wouldn't be such a bad thing. Pompous, critical, strict. And what do they do with themselves all day and night but seek pleasure and approval from their own small sect?"

She recoiled, startled at the contempt in his voice. Is that what he really thought of her and her peers?

"I say, fancy running into you two here." Viscount Fitzroy's voice dripped with ennui. "Becoming an art aficionado, are you, Whitelock?"

Evan stiffened and rose slowly, his eyelids narrowed. "Fitzroy."

Diana remained seated, wishing the viscount would go away, feeling her skin crawl as he studied her under his heavy-lidded eyes. His hair had just the right amount of tousle, his linens were immaculate, and the cut of his breeches was near scandalous, just as fashion dictated, and yet he repelled her. With insolent courtesy, he lifted her hand from her lap and bent over it.

"Lady Diana. You look particularly lovely today. Dare I say your swift conquest of the newly minted earl has put the bloom in your cheeks? I have to hand it to you. I knew Seaton ladies were fast workers, but really, even I was surprised at your speed." He kissed the air over her knuckles, and she yanked her hand from his clasp. "Still, I suppose it's in the blood."

His sideswipe mention of her sister had Diana's blood heating. She gripped her hands together in her lap. How such a wretched man could've sired such a sweet baby as Cian, she would never know. And she would never reveal the baby's existence to this man. He didn't deserve to know, not after the way he had treated Catherine, trifling with her and the very next day shaming her by giving her the cut direct in front of a drawing room full of people. As if once he'd had her, she was tainted goods no longer worthy of his notice.

"I believe I'll join the duchess." Diana rose and walked away, her legs stiff, her back rigid. She had no desire to spend even a moment more of her life in Fitzroy's presence. Perhaps if she weren't within earshot, he would stop dropping his double *entendres* and veiled messages. And perhaps she wouldn't feel compelled to smack his supercilious face.

Marcus smiled at her approach, but he looked over her head. "Ah, Fitzroy. He's got a knack for turning up where you are these days, doesn't he, Lady Diana?" He narrowed his eyes, and his lips tightened.

She felt an immediate kinship with Marcus. Nothing like a common dislike to bring people together.

The duchess pulled out her lorgnette, half raising it to her eye. "He's from an impeccable family. Quite a commodity. Heir to his uncle's title. He'll be Earl of Rothwell someday. Many a matchmaking mother has her eye on him as a husband for her daughter."

"It wouldn't matter to me if he were the heir to the Persian Empire. I wouldn't have him if he were hung from top to toe with diamonds." Diana rubbed her arms, trying to ward off the shiver Fitzroy had given her.

"You show good sense." Marcus crooked his elbow, and she took it. "He seems to have plenty to say to Whitelock, doesn't he?"

Evan's and Fitzroy's voices rose.

"Oh no." Marcus's muscles tightened.

Diana turned in time to see Evan planting his fist in Fitzroy's face. The viscount staggered back, his yell echoing through the gallery and bouncing off the skylights.

"You bounder!" Fitzroy's shout was muffled behind his hands as he sought to stanch the flow of blood coming from his nose.

Evan straightened his coat and flexed his fingers, as if the blow had been nothing more than an inconvenience.

"I should call you out." Fitzroy glowered as he clapped his handkerchief to his face. "I should kill you for this." His shirt and cravat bore bright claret-red splotches.

Evan shrugged, apparently unfazed by the threat. "You can certainly try, but if you do, you'll wind up dead. I'm a soldier, don't forget. A member of the Ninety-Fifth Rifles and deft with a blade as well. You deserve more than just a single punch in the face, but I'll let you off with a warning. If I hear any more such talk, I'll thrash you to within an inch of your life."

Marcus hastened over to put himself between the two combatants, putting his hand on Evan's shoulder. But his actions didn't halt Fitzroy's threats.

"You'll pay for this, Whitelock. I have powerful friends. This isn't the end of it." Fitzroy backed up, leaving a trail of red droplets. He sped through the far door.

Diana sagged. Fighting in public? Was throwing a punch every man's answer to something he didn't like?

Evan shook his hand again and put his knuckle to his lips.

Marcus wore a worried look, and Diana's feelings mirrored his. What had Evan been thinking? Assaulting a peer in a public place? It would be a long time before the dust settled on this once word got out.

The duchess left them in no doubt as to her thoughts on the matter as she towed Diana to the two men. "What rag manners you have, Whitelock. Fisticuffs between two gentlemen . . . I take that back. One gentleman and one brawler." She pointed to Evan. "You are a peasant. Peasant born and peasant bred. A disgrace to the peerage. This is what comes of conferring titles on the unworthy." She looked as if she could bite a hatpin in two.

"Marcus, I might've anticipated you'd be the one to befriend such a scurri-lous creature. Call for the carriage. We're leaving. Come, my dear. I'm only sorry you're soon to wed this ruffian."

Diana followed, not knowing what else to do, but as she looked back, Evan gripped his temples between his fists.

Her stomach clenched. Another man with a temper. He'd struck faster than the lash of a whip, and Fitzroy had never seen it coming. Though she spared little sympathy for the viscount, she had to wonder. How long would it be before Evan turned that quick temper on her?

Evan hadn't seen Marcus angry before. Affable, accommodating, easy-going Marcus slammed his fist onto the desktop, making the inkwell jump. He dropped into the desk chair in his library and stared at Evan like a stern father.

"What were you thinking? Starting a brawl in a public place? There were ladies present. And not just any ladies. Your fiancée and my mother."

Evan rubbed his slightly swollen hand. "Fitzroy deserved it." He sank into the stuffed chair in front of the desk. The morning had been a disaster as far as getting to know his new bride better. He couldn't get over the horrified look in her eyes as she'd left the gallery with the duchess, or the way she had avoided looking at him or speaking to him on the carriage ride back to her father's townhouse. Not that she'd had an opportunity to speak. The duchess hadn't run out of words the entire journey. In fact, she was probably upstairs this minute retelling the story to her maid or her mirror. His face burned at some of the outrage she'd flung at him.

If her comments were the prevalent tenor of the peerage, he would never belong. Never be more than a rank outsider, an upstart member of the rabble, a social climber and a fraud.

And he couldn't even disagree with the assessment. He *was* a fraud. An impostor.

Marcus cleared his throat, drawing Evan's attention.

"Fitzroy might well have deserved it, but a gentleman sorts those things out in private. You'll be lucky to survive today's work. The Prince Regent wasn't there to rescue you from yourself this time. I imagine White's and Boodle's are already buzzing about it, and by tonight every soiree and dinner party will be aghast and agape, retelling it." Marcus pinched the bridge of his nose. "I shouldn't be surprised if there wasn't a mention of it in the *Times* tomorrow."

Irritation and the headache he'd been fighting all morning made Evan short tempered. "I had no choice. The man slandered Lady Diana."

Marcus looked up. "He's insufferable, I'll grant you, but you shouldn't let a few offhand remarks get under your skin like that. Just how did he slander her?"

"He told me she was quite the 'delectable morsel' and that though I had taken her away from him for a time, he was willing to wait to sample her 'delights,' as he put it. He said once she was wed and had produced the requisite 'heir and spare,' he would set about seducing her. He had it on good authority that Seaton women were … Oh, I don't even want to repeat his foul words. Trust me. He deserved more than a bloodied nose." Evan tensed as he ran the conversation through his mind again. "He should be thanking me for not dragging him out by his scruff and pounding him into a fine powder."

"He said that? He told you he plans to seduce your wife?"

"You see? I think I was quite restrained, merely punching him." The question Evan had been chewing over slipped out. "He seemed to think such behavior was typical amongst society women. Is that true?"

Marcus tugged at his cravat, yanking it off and unbuttoning his collar. "Sadly, it is not uncommon for ladies of the *ton* to find other partners after they've 'done their duty' and produced heirs. As long as they are discreet, it seems they needn't be concerned with trifling things like marriage vows and monogamy."

"That's disgraceful. You can't condone that behavior?" Evan shoved himself up out of the chair and paced before the coal fire. Surely such infidelity couldn't be acceptable in a society so strict about everyone's actions.

"Of course I don't condone it, but I also can't stop it. And not all married women betray their vows. But some do. The women justify it by saying they married for monetary or family reasons, and now that they have the freedom to choose, they can take a lover if they wish. The men justify their infidelity by whatever reasons they can come up with, if they bother to justify it at all."

Once again Evan wondered what sort of society he'd been thrust into. "I wish I was a soldier again. Getting shot at by the French was a better life than this. At least you knew the rules in the army." He planned to honor his wedding vows, as he had been taught from a boy and as he believed God wanted. But what about his bride? She'd been raised to believe that fidelity was fleeting? Did she plan to cuckold him after a couple of years? And her peers would accept this behavior as long as she kept it quiet?

He was a fraud in a society of frauds.

Chapter 6

"Are you ready?" Marcus asked as they stood outside St. George's, just off Hanover Square.

Evan would've preferred a less "fashionable" venue, but he'd had no say in the matter. He imagined the little stone church where his father had served all of Evan's life. The familiar faces of the good country parishioners who attended faithfully, his friends and family. The place he had always imagined he would marry, not this cavernous, wealthy church he'd never even been inside of before.

He'd had little say in anything since he'd awakened in the field hospital eight months ago. Soldier, patient, earl, and now bridegroom. Everything done without anyone asking his wishes.

His cravat was slowly strangling him.

This was really happening.

He was getting married.

"No." His breath hung in the frosty air. "I'm not ready."

Marcus smiled and clapped him on the shoulder. "Then you're like every other groom I've ever met. If you can't look pleased, at least try not to look pained. Lady Diana is a lovely young woman, and I think, eventually, you'll be quite content with one another."

"Easy for you to say. You've no pressure on you to marry at all, much less to someone you barely know." A trickle of sweat tracked down Evan's temple in spite of the cold January day.

Marcus laughed, and Evan scowled at him. How could he be so jovial when Evan's knees were shaking worse than on the eve of his first battle?

Restless didn't begin to describe the night past. Horrible half dreams, waking in a cold sweat, shaking, heart pounding out of his chest. Gunfire and cannon shot, screams, explosions, fire, smoke, and pure terror had stalked him every time he had closed his eyes. And when he'd opened them, he'd faced the stark reality that he would be wed in just a few short hours.

He was losing his mind. And nothing in the past month had helped the situation. He had been pitchforked into an alien land, one as perilous, it seemed, as the war he had nearly died fighting. And now he was going to be married. How on earth was he supposed to keep his wits about him *and* keep his fragile mental condition a secret from a new bride?

"Are we going in, or are you going to retreat?" Marcus went up the front steps and turned between the pillars supporting the portico. "Do I need to call for reinforcements? Your bride will be here soon, and unless you want to greet her on the steps, we should get inside and into our places."

Evan took a steadying breath—one that didn't help a bit—and followed his groomsman inside.

The altar at the front of the church looked a day's march away. He breathed in the smell of candles and furniture polish and old books, a blend familiar to him from childhood. If only his father could be here to perform the service. None of his family would be in attendance, the time frame being too compressed to allow them to travel from their parish. They would barely have received his letter explaining recent events. What would his father say? What advice would he have for Evan?

A wave of homesickness hit him. What wouldn't he give for an hour in his father's study for quiet conversation?

Evan walked up the aisle beside Marcus, his bootheels echoing on the floor. The guests had arrived, a small number, nowhere near to filling the church. Heads turned, and hands covered mouths to whisper in their neighbors' ears. Evan felt their eyes on him, gauging, studying, and no doubt passing judgment.

"You're quite the thing now, you know. Punching a viscount in a public place has made you even more of a curiosity." Marcus spoke from the side of his mouth. "The account I read in the *Times* made you out to be quite the pugilist. Though my favorite was the caricature. You look quite dashing in that one."

Evan stifled a groan. The ramifications of losing his temper had rippled outward, and he was reminded of Diana's comment that his actions in society now affected her as much as they did him. But what else was he supposed to do when someone made such vile advances toward his fiancée? Toward any woman? Fitzroy had deserved a thrashing, and he had been fortunate to have escaped with just a bloody nose.

Following Marcus's demeanor, Evan kept his eyes forward and away from those in attendance. He had no idea who was on the guest list. His own contribution had been small. One name other than Marcus.

Would he come? Evan hoped so. A familiar face, someone who had known him long before the earldom had descended upon him, long before Salamanca, when his mind had been his own, his courage tested and proven, his abilities sure. Someone who knew the real Evan Eldridge, not the Earl of Whitelock, this persona he now clanked around in like a too-large suit of armor.

Evan and Marcus stopped at the rail and turned, and Evan couldn't help scanning the faces. With his heart dropping, he looked from one to the next, until . . . There! A smile formed on his lips. He'd come.

Sergeant Shand grinned from the back row, and some of the unrest inside Evan eased. Warmth rushed through his chest, and he gave a small nod in Shand's direction.

The rector emerged from the sacristy and took his place in front of the chancel, nodding to Evan. "I've been advised that the bride's carriage has arrived."

Organ music swelled, filling the barrel-vaulted ceiling, and the massive doors opened at the far end of the aisle. Evan's heart rate tripled, and he shifted his weight, standing at attention, careful not to jostle the sword at his side. He had chosen to wear his military uniform, freshly cleaned, buttons gleaming. Marcus had raised his eyebrows but then stopped protesting when Evan had insisted. In that one small way, Evan had wanted to both recognize and remember his comrades, and to feel at least a bit like himself. The dark-green wool of jacket and pants, and the high black collar were familiar and comforting. Marcus had drawn the line at the shako, and Evan had given that one small concession. He'd go without a hat.

Marcus himself was resplendent in a forest-green coat and breeches.

His dull-gold waistcoat and shining black shoes echoed the colors in Evan's clothes.

Silhouettes appeared in the back door, a man first, then a woman.

The Duke of Seaton walked stiffly, as if being prodded from behind at every step. But Evan had eyes only for Diana. She looked small next to her imposing father, and Evan barely refrained from trotting down the aisle and inserting himself between them.

She wore a silvery dress and carried the flowers Marcus had reminded him to send that morning, a bouquet of pink hothouse roses and deep-green leaves. Her eyes locked with his, and he could read the desperate panic there, interpreting it well because it matched his own.

No maid of honor attended her, and when they reached the front of the church, her father placed her hand in Evan's without a word and stepped back. Wasn't he supposed to wait until the rector asked who gave this woman to be married? But he had abandoned Diana there, as if washing his hands of the entire proceedings. Like she was a stray puppy he needed to rid himself of with all speed. Which meant that other than Evan himself, she had no one up front to support her. Her hand was icy and slack within his grasp, as if she had entered a shocked state where she had no will of her own.

Evan frowned. This wasn't right. This wasn't the way a marriage should begin. Though he had rarely given thought to when or whom he would wed, he had always imagined it would be a natural progression—meeting a girl, making her acquaintance, courting, then after a decent interval and with a mutual feeling of regard, asking for her hand.

Nowhere in his imaginings had an unwanted title, a social faux pas, or a forced marriage entered in.

This was the Prince Regent's fault from start to finish. And the man wasn't even here to see the results of his machinations. The organ music crescendoed, and the church door slammed shut, turning every head.

Evan had time to glimpse Percival Seaton's late arrival before pain knifed through his skull and light flashed behind his eyes. He gasped, nearly buckling. Marcus grabbed his arm, and Diana's hand jerked in his. Squeezing his eyes shut, he fought a wave of nausea as cold sweat broke out across his skin. Iron bands fastened around his chest, and he couldn't draw a deep breath. Sparks erupted across his eyelids, followed by flashes of battle. *No, not now. Not now.*

"Evan?" Diana whispered. "What is it?"

Her voice seemed to pull him toward her from a long distance. He opened his eyes, trying to take in some air, and her hand came up to touch his cheek. The caress cooled his skin and seared his blood at the same time, and his gaze locked with hers, as if should he break their eye contact, he might spin off into the blood-soaked darkness of battle once more.

Slowly straightening, Evan panted, sucking in breath and swallowing. Two little furrows formed between Diana's brows as she studied him. A murmur went through the crowd, and Evan felt like an animal in the menagerie at the Tower of London, to be gawked at and whispered over.

"Evan." Marcus shook his shoulder. "Pull yourself together. This is no time for cold feet."

Diana regarded him. Was it with suspicion? Revulsion?

She would run now. Run down the aisle, get away from him as fast as she could. Any second now, Marcus would clamp his hand on Evan's wrist and shout for a doctor. He would find himself pitched into an asylum. He would never see his family again . . . what would happen to Diana? Would she think it a fortunate escape?

As if someone had doused him with cold water, he snapped back to attention. Realizing he had a death grip on her hand, he loosened his fingers, blinking and shaking his head to clear it.

"I beg your pardon. Please, sir." He nodded to the rector. "It was just a dizzy spell." *Please believe me and just get on with it.*

"Do you need to sit down?" The rector clasped his service book to his chest, pressing it against his clerical robes.

"No." Evan shook his head. "I am quite fine. Let's get this over with." He winced at the harshness of his words as Diana flinched. "I mean, let's go ahead with the ceremony."

He glanced over his shoulder to find Shand only a few feet away, his hat in his hand, ready to lend aid. Evan gave a weak smile and jerked his chin. The little sergeant nodded and stepped back, but it was a comfort to know he was there.

The rector cleared his throat, and Evan and Diana faced him. Her flowers trembled, and she still had a worried tenseness to her brow, but her chin was up, and she appeared calm.

If she can do this, so can you.

"Dearly beloved," the rector read from *The Book of Common Prayer*, "we are gathered together here in the sight of God, and in the face of this congregation, to join together this Man and this Woman in holy Matrimony; which is an honourable estate, instituted of God in the time of man's innocency, signifying unto us the mystical union that is betwixt Christ and his Church; which holy estate Christ adorned and beautified with his presence, and first miracle that he wrought, in Cana of Galilee; and is commended of Saint Paul to be honourable among all men: and therefore is not by any to be enterprised, nor taken in hand, unadvisedly, lightly, or wantonly, to satisfy men's carnal lusts and appetites, like brute beasts that have no understanding; but reverently, discreetly, advisedly, soberly, and in the fear of God; duly considering the causes for which Matrimony was ordained."

Guilt smote Evan, and for a moment he was glad his father wasn't there to see this. Not only was he about to marry a near stranger, but he was doing so without having spent time in prayer or contemplation. He wasn't motivated by a desire to love and cherish this woman, but rather at the behest of that known hedonist and womanizer, the Prince Regent.

He was a fraud and a pawn.

And what of Diana? She was a pawn as well, with no more say in whom she married than a horse at Tattersall's had in saying who purchased it. They were both well and truly trapped, and he had no business hoping that God would bless their union.

Evan started, realizing that the rector had stopped talking and was looking at him expectantly. Marcus nudged his elbow and murmured, "The ring?"

A ring? A sick feeling hit his gut. He'd forgotten to procure a wedding ring for his bride, and now the entire church was waiting. In a flash, he dropped Diana's hand and jerked his regimental ring from his finger. It was a battered bit of gold with the bugle and crown of the Ninety-Fifth pressed into the oval top, and it was miles too big and masculine for her, but it was all he had, and it was dear to him. Several of his regiment had commissioned the rings after they landed on the Peninsula at Corunna, when he was a green officer, and he'd worn it at every battle.

Diana took one look at it and pressed her lips together. Her shoulders began to shake. For a moment he thought she might be weeping, but then it hit him. She was stifling laughter.

A chuckle at the absurdity of the situation hit Evan broadside, and he bit the inside of his cheek, trying to maintain some semblance of decorum. Marcus snickering at his elbow didn't help.

The rector gave them a stern look, like a schoolmaster catching children playing a prank, and Evan tried to sober. He squeezed Diana's hand, looking at her out of the corner of his eye, and for the first time thinking that perhaps things might be looking up. There might be hope for them yet, if she could laugh.

"Forasmuch," the rector recited, "as Evan and Diana have consented together in holy wedlock, and have witnessed the same before God and this company, and thereto have given and pledged their troth either to other, and have declared the same by giving and receiving of a Ring, and by joining of hands; I pronounce that they be Man and Wife together, In the Name of the Father, and of the Son, and of the Holy Ghost. Amen."

The rector closed his prayer book and beamed at them like a benevolent grandfather.

"I present the Earl and Countess of Whitelock."

A smattering of applause went through the small crowd. The organ music swelled again. Some Handel tune?—after all, hadn't Marcus mentioned that the composer had been a parishioner at this very church half a century ago? Evan turned and offered Diana—his wife!—his arm to escort her down the aisle and out of the church. His sword clanked softly at his side, and her dress swished. He noticed for the first time that her gown had a small train and that a length of gauzy white material fell from the curls clustered at the back of her head all the way to the floor.

Pride at how pretty she was hit him in the chest. She was his. His to protect and to provide for. He'd promised her many things in the past few moments, and he'd promised those things before God. Though he had been lax in asking for God's guidance regarding the engagement, he would not make that mistake again.

At the door, Shand was there to hand him his cloak, but no one was there with a wrap for Diana.

"Where's your coat?"

She shook her head. "I left it in my father's carriage. I will be fine. Anyway, a lady never acknowledges the cold or allows it to interfere with her appearance."

"That's a load of twaddle." He swirled the cape in the manner he'd observed Marcus do, but instead of donning it himself, he settled it around her shoulders, careful not to pull on her veil. "You shouldn't have to acquire pleurisy just to be fashionable." A sense of satisfaction dropped over him as surely as the cape enveloped her.

As he handed her up into the closed carriage—borrowed again from Marcus for the purpose . . . he really would have to see to getting his own conveyance—he noticed several dozen onlookers standing along the street. They were bundled to the eyebrows, and their breath hung in frosty puffs in the January air. They appeared to be waiting for something.

"Who are those people?" he asked as he took his seat beside her and moved his sword out of the way.

"They're the well-wishers. It's become the custom amongst the peerage to throw coins to well-wishers as they drive away from the church." Diana pointed with her bouquet to a small sack on the opposite seat. "It looks as though Marcus has provided you with some."

"What do I do?"

"Lower the window and scatter the coins. They won't go to waste."

He did as she said, feeling like a fraud once again, giving away someone else's money to celebrate his wedding.

Diana handed the cloak to Carson and took back her flowers from the butler. She looked around the foyer of the townhouse. "Soon I will be free of this prison."

"Pardon?" her new husband asked.

"It's nothing. Just talking to myself. You'll think me mad, but I do tend to talk to myself rather often." *Please, Lord, let this be the last time I have to come into this house.* Even now the maids were packing her belongings, readying them to be taken to her husband's home. And tomorrow she would sign over her inheritance and take custody of Cian. Never again would they be under her father's tyranny. She just had to get through the wedding breakfast today and the visit to the solicitor on the morrow, and she—and Cian—would be free.

In this, at least, God had answered her prayers.

"What are we supposed to do at this soiree?" Evan clasped his hands behind his back, his legs braced apart, as if awaiting orders.

Did he think he was still in the army?

"When the guests arrive, we greet them and then sit down to a meal. There will be a bride cake, and perhaps some speeches, though I don't know if that will hold true in this case. I doubt my father will make an address." And perhaps just as well if he didn't.

She listened but could not hear the baby. *Thank You, Lord. Please keep him quiet while the party is going on.* Cian had been fractious since before dawn, and she'd had all she could do to keep him from being heard. She'd gotten him to sleep just in time to dress and leave for the wedding this morning, and it wouldn't do at all for him to start squalling during the breakfast. But she had better peek in, just to be sure.

"I'll just slip upstairs for a few moments. Carson, please show the earl to the ballroom."

Upstairs, she eased open her dressing room door. Amid the boxes and cases of her packed belongings, Beth sat in the rocking chair, patting the sleeping baby in her arms, an empty nursing bottle on the low table beside her.

"Oh, my lady, how did the wedding go? Is it all done?" Barely more than a child herself, Beth's eyes shone with hopeful romance.

"It's done." Diana exhaled. "The wedding was . . ." She stopped. How would she describe the ceremony? The groom had nearly fainted, and he'd completely forgotten to get her a wedding ring. Though he'd covered well, it was clear he had not come prepared. She glanced at the heavy gold ring, noting the stamp in the flat oval top. A crown, a bugle, and the number ninety-five. She had to bend her finger to keep it on at all. Later she would either return it to him or find some thread to wrap around the shank to make it fit better. Shaking her head, she cautioned Beth, "Keep him as quiet as you can. I'll try to come up to say goodbye, but I don't know if I will be able to." She bent and kissed the baby's downy head, her heart constricting at the thought of leaving him, even for one night.

A half hour later, Diana stood between her father and husband at the head of the receiving line. In keeping with his demeanor the entire week, her father radiated dissatisfaction with the situation, but he was punctilious, accepting congratulations and introducing his daughter to the *haute ton* who had attended her wedding without even knowing who she was.

Evan shook hands with everyone, but he kept shifting his weight, tightness around his eyes. Though it had been a rather small wedding by society standards, there were still many guests coming up the stairs to the first-floor ballroom. Clearly her father or Lady Cathcart had invited more people to the wedding breakfast than to the church.

Percival sauntered in, and in his wake, Viscount Fitzroy. Diana tensed. The last time she had seen the viscount, he'd been trying to stem the flow of blood from his nose, which still had a bit of a raw look to it. Her chest felt heavy, and her skin crawled at the sight of him. What had Percival been thinking, inviting him here? Had he also been at the church?

Diana caught herself edging closer to Evan and forced herself to stand still, hoping she wouldn't have to speak to Fitzroy. She needn't have worried. He and Percival bypassed the receiving line, not even glancing their way.

The Duchess of Haverly walked in, escorted by Marcus, surveying the ballroom. Large urns of flowers and ferns stood at intervals around the walls, and every sconce and chandelier had been lit. A long table covered in white cloth spanned the end of the room, and smaller tables with floral centerpieces and white chairs dotted the open space. Lady Cathcart had done a magnificent job. Diana's father had spared no expense, since it reflected well on his image of himself to spend lavishly when others were looking.

Of course, he would be using her inheritance to pay for it, so she shouldn't even be concerned with how much this might be costing him.

Finally, when all the guests had been greeted, they took their seats at the bridal table. This time Diana sat between Evan and Marcus, thankfully away from her father and brother.

"You look beautiful." Marcus raised his glass to her. "Congratulations, and I wish you every happiness."

She nodded her thanks. "Thank you. It's all happened so rapidly, I can hardly take everything in."

Eyes sobering, Marcus nodded. "You will need to have patience, but I believe you've gotten yourself a good man."

"I hope so." Did such a thing exist? A truly good man? She leaned back as a servant set a plate of food before her.

"What is this?" Evan asked softly.

"Tongue, aspic, Scotch eggs."

"The eggs I recognize. But aspic?" He poked the jellied substance with his knife.

Diana nodded. "It's quite the rage."

"Do you like it?" He looked at her doubtfully.

"No, in point of fact, I do not."

"Then why are we having it?" He set his utensils down.

"Lady Cathcart arranged the meal. And you must eat something, else you'll hurt her feelings, not to mention what you'll do to Father's cook. She's a woman of moods, and if she gets it into her head that you do not like her food, she'll be impossible to deal with for a week." In fact, she was the only one of the servants who openly stood up to her father, knowing that she would be hired in an instant elsewhere if he fired her. She was handsomely paid and ruled the roost belowstairs. Even Carson was a bit cowed by the woman.

Diana put a bite of aspic onto her fork and tasted it.

Evan laughed. "You all spend so much time doing what you think everyone else will think proper. You wear clothes you don't like, eat food you can't stomach, go places that bore you. What kind of a life is that?"

"Your life now," she reminded him, washing the bite down with a sip of punch.

Evan's fork lowered, and he made a face.

The butler appeared at Evan's elbow. "My lord, there is a person here who says he is your invited guest, but . . ." Carson's brows rose. He inclined his head toward the ballroom doors.

Evan's face lit up, and Diana followed his gaze. In a trice, the earl was out of his chair and headed toward a decidedly ordinary looking fellow who mauled his hat as he stared at every corner of the room.

"He was at the church," Marcus said. "I believe he's a former subordinate of Evan's in the army."

Eyes followed the earl, and people stopped eating and talking as he shook the man's hand, slapping him on the shoulder and drawing him into the room, weaving around the seated guests and bringing him to the head table. The man hung back, looking sheepish, but Evan would have none of it, taking his arm.

"Shand, I'd like to present my wife. Diana, this is my former sergeant, David Shand. Shand, this is Lady Diana . . . er . . . Lady Whitelock now, I suppose."

The man was twice Evan's age at least, his gray hair clipped quite short. He wore a rather shabby suit, but he'd clearly taken pains to have it cleaned and pressed. He bobbed his head. "Madam."

Diana's father snorted and pushed his chair back, but Diana rose, coming around the long table and taking Mr. Shand's hand between hers. "It is so nice to meet one of Evan's friends. Thank you for coming to the ceremony and for celebrating with us." She motioned for Carson. "Please find a place near the front table for Mr. Shand, and make sure his plate and glass remain full."

With a bit of ado, the butler seated the former soldier between the Duchess of Haverly and Lady Carter-Jones, mere feet away from the bridal party. The duchess's face pinched like she'd just stepped in something unpleasant, and Lady Carter-Jones dipped into her reticule and sniffed at her *sal volatile* as if she might faint having to be so near such a common fellow.

Evan and Diana resumed their seats, and Evan reached over and squeezed her hand. "Thank you for making him welcome. You were graciousness itself."

Warmth shot through her arm, and she knew she flushed, unused to being praised. Busying herself with her meal, she nodded, suddenly shy with this man, realizing anew that this was their wedding day and that they had a wedding night to negotiate in a few hours.

Carson and one of the footmen brought the bridal cake into the room, setting it on a round table in the center of the guests. But before he could cut it and serve the rich slices of fruitcake, another commotion drew everyone's attention.

"His Royal Highness, the Prince Regent," called a footman at the door.

Evan groaned. "What is he doing here? Hasn't he caused us enough trouble?"

"That's what you get for being his new favorite. Though"—Marcus leaned forward to speak across Diana—"this is getting a bit tedious. I've never known him to attend an earl's wedding breakfast before."

Everyone rose as the Prince Regent strutted into the room, resplendent in yellow like some overstuffed parakeet. Golden braid, lace trim, and winking buckles on his shoes, he drew everyone's attention. As he passed, men bowed and ladies curtsied. His retinue followed, while the footmen and Carson scrambled to clear a path for him.

"You should greet him," Marcus reminded Diana.

Taking her hand, Evan rounded the head table once again. "What should I do? What should I say?" he whispered.

Diana pasted a serene smile on her face as the prince approached. "Bow and wait until he speaks."

She dipped her knees into her deepest, well-practiced curtsy. Evan bowed but kept his arm strong to support her.

"My good man." The prince's voice boomed through the room. "I am delighted. Delighted, I tell you. I feel like quite the matchmaker." He glanced around, as if waiting for someone to burst into applause.

Rising carefully, Diana barely had time to let go of her hem before the prince enveloped her in a hug, squeezing her tighter than her stays. "Congratulations. Such an inspiration on my part it was, having you two marry. Whitelock, you've done well." He finally released her, and she all but gasped. He smelled of pomade and starch and bay rum, an odd combination. Clapping Evan on the shoulder, he scouted the room. "I am in time for the meal, I trust?"

"Of course, Your Highness. You will sit with us?" Diana asked. She shot a look at Marcus, who understood and vacated his spot.

A footman whisked his plate away, and though the meal was over but for the cake, a full plate arrived.

The prince ate heartily, sampling everything, having his charger refilled three times, regaling them with all the latest changes he was making to Carlton House. "You must join me there soon for dinner."

Diana nodded. Her father sat on the prince's other side, but the prince kept his attention on Diana and Evan. The duke must be fuming. To have the regent as a guest in his house and not have the opportunity to bend his ear had to gall him. Diana wished His Highness would keep his eyes properly on her face and not on the rest of her person, but in all other aspects he was a genial—if unexpected—guest.

"You're in for a delightful time, I think, Whitelock. She is a beauty. You can thank me later."

He winked, and Diana was taken aback at such a vulgar speech. He really could be an awful man.

When he finally pushed back his plate, Diana breathed a sigh. Surely he would not linger, and they could be done with this interminable breakfast. But the prince wasn't finished. He pushed himself to his feet, wincing with the effort and dabbing at his lips with his serviette. The room stilled.

"I know it is bad form to give oneself the plaudits, but I think I may be forgiven this time." He smiled, expecting everyone to agree. "As the instigator of this union—and a masterstroke it was, too—I hereby give my blessing to the Earl and Countess of Whitelock. May your nuptials be blissful, your progeny plentiful, and your happiness much." He raised his glass, and the guests followed suit with the toast.

"Also, Whitelock," the prince continued. "It might interest you to know that not only have you acquired the most beautiful rose in England..." He sent a sharp glance at Evan before tipping his head toward Diana. "But you've also snared quite a fortune in the bargain. The Home Secretary made me aware of this fact just this morning. I had no idea your grandmother had set aside such a sum for you on your wedding day, Diana."

Diana's mind stopped working. The room was completely quiet, but she didn't know if that was the true state of things or if she had lost her ability to hear along with her ability to think. What was he saying? *No, stop, you're ruining everything!* The scream echoed through her head.

"Lady Diana has an inheritance in trust, payable on her wedding day, that is now yours, Whitelock." He named the sum, causing a ripple to go through the ballroom.

The Duke of Seaton shot to his feet, knocking his chair to the floor and jarring Diana out of her stupor. Panic clawed up her chest and wrapped around her windpipe. Evan wasn't supposed to know about the money. That was the bargain she'd struck with her father. Cian's life in exchange for the inheritance. What would happen to the baby now? The urge to run from the room, to race to the nursery and gather him up, nearly overwhelmed Diana. Tears sprang to her eyes, and she gripped the edge of the table.

"Your Highness, no arrangements have been made yet," her father protested. "I have not discussed these matters with . . . my son-in-law." He stumbled on the last words, as if they nearly choked him.

"I'm sure you would've gotten around to it in a timely manner. Anyway, the sooner he knows, the better, because I am making plans myself. It's my understanding that the Whitelock property in Sussex—what is it called?—oh yes, White Haven, is in a bit of disrepair. After all, it's been vacant for many years. However, I've taken it upon myself to arrange an excursion this spring to Brighton. As you know, I've been improving my lodgings down on the coast, and I've decided to spend a bit of time there after Easter. My schedule will allow me to accept your hospitality when I am journeying to the seashore. A few days' stay at White Haven will be just the thing, especially as I know you will bring the house up to royal standards, now that you will have the funds to do so. White Haven will become an excellent stop in the future for me on my way to the Pavilion in Brighton."

Evan sucked in a breath, his eyes shutting and sweat popping out on his forehead. Diana touched the back of his hand. He couldn't cause a scene. One did not express anything other than delight at a coming Royal Visit. She squeezed his hand hard, digging her nails into his flesh. "Evan."

His eyes opened, but he didn't seem to see her. He gripped his forehead in a pinch between his thumb and fingers, as if in tremendous pain.

Diana turned to the prince, trying to forestall a social disaster. "Thank you, Your Highness. We look forward to your visit. And thank you so much for coming to our breakfast and celebrating with us. We are honored." She felt shattered, just like her father's plans, and it took all her fortitude and training to follow proper protocols.

She nudged Evan with her foot, begging him to pull himself together.

He seemed to rally. "Thank you, Your Highness. It's all a bit overwhelming."

"You've encountered much good luck recently." The prince resumed his seat. "Much of it from my hand."

"That's true, sir. You know what they say. A man can have enough luck to kill him." His voice still sounded strained.

Fortunately, the prince gave a hearty laugh. "Let's have some cake."

His wife had a fortune. He now had a fortune. And not a small one. More money than he'd ever heard of one person possessing.

Evan didn't know how to feel about that, not with his skull splitting and the word "Brighton" echoing in his head over and over. What did he know about Brighton? He'd never been there. Why should the prince's mention of the place roar through his head like a *sirocco* and make his heart thud like cannon blasts? Thankfully, his new wife carried the conversation with their royal guest while Evan struggled to master himself.

After the Prince Regent finally took his leave, the rest of the guests also departed, until only Evan, Diana, her family, Marcus, and Shand remained. Evan walked his sergeant to the door. He shook Shand's hand, thanking him again for coming.

"Been a real education, sir. Never thought I'd sit that close to old Prinny." Shand scratched the hair over his ear. "The boys wouldn't believe it of us, would they?"

"They'd take us for a couple of moonshiners, making up stories and flimflamming them. I had hoped to have more time to talk with you." Weakness radiated through his limbs, and he just wanted to sit down somewhere.

"You feeling all right, sir? You look a bit peaky."

Peaky. If only he felt that well. An idea formed in Evan's mind, and he meant to act upon it. "I'm fine. You heard what the Prince Regent said about the property in Sussex? If you're still looking for a job, I think I have one for you. How soon can you be ready to travel?"

"I'm ready any time you say, sir. Just need to stop by my brother's place and pick up my kit."

"Good. Do that and meet me back here in an hour."

"An hour?"

"If not sooner. I'll meet you on the front steps."

"Yes, sir." Shand snapped to attention and almost saluted before turning on his heel and exiting. A good man.

Evan returned to the ballroom.

The duke looked as if he could bite a tent spike in half. Diana wouldn't look Evan in the face. Percival slouched in a chair, nipping from a flask, sullen and put out for no reason Evan cared about. The man could benefit from a stint in the army to teach him what real hardship was. Though Evan had apparently rescued Percival on the battlefield of Salamanca, whatever the man had been doing there, he wasn't a soldier.

Another flash blistered his mind. A fact-finding mission? Was that it? Percival had been on one of Parliament's many fact-finding tours of war-torn areas?

Evan's heartbeat smashed against his temples. When would this torment end? Nausea gurgled through him.

"Evan?" Marcus asked. "What is it?"

Shaking his head and immediately wishing he hadn't, he said, "Nothing. A bit of a headache. Did you know about her money?"

"No. It came as quite a surprise." Marcus tapped his chin, his eyes narrowed, as if he were mentally putting pieces together to make a whole picture. "You're one of the richest men in England now if the Prince Regent has his sums correct."

It was too much. He'd never asked for any of this.

His father-in-law looked near apoplexy, and he had his head bent near Diana's, whispering fiercely. What was going on between those two? When the duke pounded the table, making the glasses and cutlery jump,

Evan headed their way. Diana had her hand over her mouth, her eyes suspiciously bright. The duke wrapped his fist around her wrist, and Evan hastened his stride, his sword clanking with every step.

"Sir, I am certain that everyone is tired. It's been quite a day." He reached for Diana's hand. "Diana, go upstairs and change into a traveling costume. I assume your bags are packed?"

She nodded, rising and stepping away from her father, fear in her eyes.

"Good. We're leaving for White Haven in an hour."

"You can't!" The duke jerked to his feet. "We haven't settled this. If you think I'm going to let a fortune walk out of this room and go to a . . . peasant like you, you've got another think coming. I want what is due me. I want that money. She promised me!" He jabbed his finger in his daughter's direction, and she flinched.

Evan's headache shortened his patience. He put on his best military officer's tone. "Sir, I don't see that you have a choice. Clearly you never intended to make me aware of Diana's inheritance. The Prince Regent stole a march on you, didn't he? The matter is settled, however unhappy you might be. I am taking my wife and we're leaving. Leaving this house, leaving London. I've got a manor house somewhere in Sussex that needs my attention, and I've a wife who obviously needs my protection, though it appears she was aware of the way you intended to defraud me. Marcus?"

"Yes?"

"I will need to either borrow your carriage or procure one. And a wagon for the baggage. Now."

"I'll see to it."

Evan couldn't wait to get on the road, to put all of this behind him and get some breathing space to decide what to do next. It wasn't deserting the field of battle so much as a strategic retreat, right?

Diana gave him one last stricken look as she left the room, as if he'd done something reprehensible. No doubt he'd committed some other societal faux pas.

Whatever it was, she could add it to the long list he was accumulating.

CHAPTER 7

"BETH, HURRY. THROW all Cian's things into this bag, and pack your things as well." Diana yanked on the veil at the back of her head, sending her hairpins scattering to the floor and her curls tumbling down. Twisting and trying to unfasten the buttons at the back of her dress, she blinked back tears.

Everything was ruined. Her father would show no mercy. He'd threatened as much in harsh whispers as the guests had departed. She could feel his fury, red hot in his eyes, iron hard in the grip he'd had on her arm.

"My lady? What's wrong?" The little nursemaid bolted from her chair, the mending falling from her lap to the floor.

"If Cian means anything to you, hurry. We have only a few minutes to get him out of the house before . . ." Diana choked on the words. "We're leaving for the country. Right now."

With the baby sleeping in his cradle, she flew about the room, gathering little gowns and blankets, wrapping the nursing bottle in a handful of clouts and pilchers, and stuffing all into a small bandbox with leather latches.

Frustrated, Diana grabbed the back yoke of her wedding gown and pulled, scattering the cloth-covered buttons and yanking the dress over her head. Her hair must look like a cast-off bird's nest, but what matter?

"My lady, I started my own packing after you came up earlier. I am ready to leave whenever you say." Without being asked, she opened one of the cases and drew out a traveling dress and half boots for Diana. She picked up the wedding gown from the floor and folded it carefully. "I think you looked very nice. I'll sew on new buttons and mend the dress as soon as I can."

"Bless you, Beth. Now, the next bit is going to be tricky. I need you to put Cian into the laundry hamper and get him out of the house without anyone seeing. We'll pile your bag with mine. There will be a wagon for the luggage, and no one will notice a couple more pieces. You will ride in the carriage with me as my abigail. We'll tell the earl you are my ladies' maid, and hopefully, he'll opt to ride his horse rather than travel in the carriage." Diana bit her lip as she tugged the last few pins from her hair and finger-combed the brown curls, separating them into hanks and braiding quickly. Things were moving so rapidly. How could she make smart decisions with no time to think?

It was one thing to lie herself, but now she was asking Beth to lie too. To basically kidnap a child. Guilt smote her, but it was nothing compared to the terror she felt for Cian if she left him in this house.

God, I don't know what to do. I'm sinning right and left here, and You're remaining silent. What should I do?

She couldn't even begin to imagine her father's rage at this turn of events, nor what he would do when he discovered Cian missing.

But would her new husband be the same? She'd seen him explode with anger at the art gallery. And when he'd learned of her inheritance, it had been all he could do not to create a scene at the reception. He'd broken out in a sweat, fists clenched, jaw tight.

How could she know what his reaction to an illegitimate child in her care would be?

"Beth, I know it is a lot to ask, but if the earl asks about the baby, I want you to say that Cian is yours."

Beth's mouth gaped. "My lady," she breathed.

"I know. I know it's wrong. And if he cuts up about me having an unwed mother as a maid, if he says he will turn you out without a character, then I will tell him the truth. I will impress upon him that it was all my idea." She winced as she pulled her hair in her haste to get it braided and pinned. "For Cian's sake, please?"

The little maid's expression firmed, though her eyes remained doubtful. "I'll do it, my lady. For Cian and for you."

Diana squeezed her hand. "Hurry now. Get the baby out of here. Keep your head down, carry the basket, and meet us around the front of the house. The earl said we'd be leaving within the hour."

Stomping her feet into the half boots, Diana gathered her cloak. Beth lifted the sleeping baby from the cradle and placed him on a stack of clean towels in the small laundry hamper.

"Cover him well. It's cold outside."

She felt as if a piece of her heart were breaking off and going into the basket with him. *Please, God, help me get him away safely.* Beth gave her a trembling smile before slipping through the doorway with her precious cargo.

Diana took up her bonnet, settling it on her hastily styled hair. Glancing in the silver-backed mirror on the wall, she wondered if her visage told her secrets.

A small knock announced the arrival of the footmen. Diana opened the dressing room door.

"My lady, the earl requests your presence in the parlor, and he instructs us to bring your things to the entryway. The carriages have arrived." The footman, in full livery of the maroon and gold of the House of Seaton, stood straight as a stair rod, his face giving away nothing.

Her new husband did not intend to linger for even the full hour. It had been less than twenty minutes since she'd raced up the stairs to change.

"Very well." She slipped her hand through the strings of her reticule. Pointing to her own personal bag and the case with the baby's things, she said, "Those are to go in the carriage with me, the rest in the luggage wagon."

"Very good, my lady."

Diana tied her bonnet ribbons as she descended the stairs. Had Beth gotten Cian out of the house through the back door? Was she even now hurrying along the mews to get to the street? Had her father thought to put anyone on watch?

Angry voices erupted from the parlor, her father's and Percival's.

"How can you let this happen? Do you know how many markers I have around town? I was counting on that money!" Percival's whine grated upon Diana's already frayed nerves.

"*You* were counting on it? Your problems are the least of my worries.

I am not to blame for your gambling debts or the gullibility of those who would take a marker from you. That money is mine. I worked for it, and I do not intend for it to escape my grasp."

"How can you get it now? Prinny blabbed before the crème of the *ton*, and now it's gone. Gone to that upstart nobody." Her brother was almost wailing.

Her eyes locked with Evan's as he waited by the door, cape around his shoulders. He pulled on his gloves, his blue eyes piercing, even from that distance. He was angry. He had to be. She had lied to him, kept her fortune a secret, aiding her father through her silence in stealing from her new husband.

Would he lash out? Would his attack be verbal or physical or both? Her knees felt like well-used dishrags.

The argument continued in the parlor. "I'll find a way. I've got a piece of leverage, but I must decide when it is the best time to use it."

Her father must've realized the parlor door was open, because she heard his heavy footsteps cross the room. The door slammed, echoing through the entryway. The heated voices went on, but muffled now.

Leverage. He intended to use Cian as leverage. She stiffened her resolve as she reached the bottom of the steps. She was doing the right thing, absconding with the baby. She must continue to tell herself that.

Marcus came in through the front doorway. "My carriage is outside. I've drawn a rudimentary map to White Haven for the coachman. You understand that I've never been there before and only have a vague notion of where it is. Somewhere near Crawley in Sussex is all I know. Are you sure you want to do this? Don't you want to wait until the morning at least? There is a suite prepared at Haverly House for you."

"And I appreciate it, but I've had enough of London for a while. I don't even feel like my own man here. I don't know if I ever will again. It's impossible to know whom to trust." He flicked a glance Diana's way, and she flinched.

The footmen passed her, laden with bags. She spied the one full of baby clothes, and guilt smote her. Evan was right not to trust her.

But she was right not to trust him too. She barely knew him, and he'd given her precious few choices since their first meeting, whether it was to waltz with him, or how long they would be engaged, or even whether they would stay in London. Instead, he'd exercised his male authority, dictating like an autocrat . . . or like an army officer.

For the moment, she would labor under the mantra that it was easier to get forgiveness than it was to get permission. She'd get the baby away and hope to keep him a secret for as long as possible.

"Let's go." Evan opened the door.

She crossed to the threshold before Marcus stopped her. "I haven't had a chance to kiss the bride yet."

Come to think of it, neither had her husband.

Marcus's eyes were kind as he bent and placed a chaste kiss on her cheek. "Take care, Diana."

"Thank you, Marcus."

"I'll wander down to see you one of these days. If there is anything you need, just send word." He squeezed her upper arms and stepped back. "The same for you, Evan. I'll turn up on your doorstep one of these days. And you're always welcome at Haverly House if you need a place to stay."

As Diana stepped out of her father's townhouse, she felt released and trapped anew at the same time. The carriage waited at the curb, and behind it a wagon loaded with luggage. Evan's former sergeant, Mr. Shand, jogged up and tossed his own rucksack on the pile and climbed aboard.

There was no sign of Beth, but Diana prayed she had reached the carriage safely. The curtains were pulled, and Diana couldn't see inside.

Evan shook hands with Marcus. "'Thank you' doesn't seem like enough for all you've done for us. I'll send the coach and horses back as soon as I can."

Marcus opened the carriage door, and Evan handed Diana inside. She ducked to avoid hitting her bonnet brim on the doorway, and her eyes locked with Beth's. On the seat beside the little maid, the hamper sat, and no noise came from it.

Beth gave an encouraging smile. "He's sleeping still," she whispered.

As Diana settled across from her, Evan grabbed the doorframe on either side and pulled himself up. He paused in the doorway, seeing the girl.

"Who is this?" He frowned.

"My maid."

He eyed the basket as he took his seat next to Diana. With his broad shoulders, Diana felt a bit crowded and sidled over to give him more room.

"Can't she ride in the other wagon? We have a few things to talk about, you know."

She could feel his anger, and she bit her lip. Just as well that Beth was here. "She cannot travel on the baggage wagon in the open air. It's much too cold. And there are no other ladies along, so it wouldn't be proper for her to be in company with a strange man alone. Aren't you going to ride your horse alongside the carriage?"

"I don't have a horse. Not yet, anyway."

To her horror, he lifted his feet and nudged the hamper aside to stretch his legs and rest his boots on the opposite seat. Beth scrambled to right the basket and keep the lid closed, as she sent a panicked gaze toward Diana.

Please, please, please. Diana prayed that the baby would stay asleep through the jostling, and for as long as possible until they were well away from her father's townhouse.

The carriage started with a jerk, and they were off. Evan leaned back, crossing his arms and closing his eyes. Beth kept her hand atop the basket, her eyes going from Diana to Evan and back again, her bottom lip hiding behind her teeth.

Diana didn't know if she drew a breath until they crossed the Battersea Bridge and put the Thames between the carriage and her father's house. She had no idea how far it was to White Haven, nor what they would meet when they arrived, but as long as the baby was quiet, they would be all right. If her father held true to form, he would most likely drink himself into oblivion this evening and, hopefully, not remember about the baby for a long time.

The carriage had barely reached the outskirts of South London when mewling cries leaked from the basket.

What was making that sound? Had an animal become trapped in the carriage somehow? Evan straightened, dropping his feet to the floor. The noise came from the basket beside the maid. Had she brought her cat with her?

The mewling changed to a cry.

Not a cat.

The maid, looking guilty, opened the basket and lifted out a squalling red-faced infant. Eyes screwed shut, mouth open, only a small triangle of its face showed, as swaddled as it was.

"Who is that?" Evan ground out the words. He had experienced too many surprises today to want another.

Diana's face gave her away. She wasn't surprised about the baby.

The maid spoke first. "My lord, the baby's mine. Please don't be angry with my lady. She's got such a kind heart. When the baby came along, she didn't throw me out without a character, like most fine ladies would. She let me keep my job and keep little Cian with me. I don't know what I would've done otherwise. I'd have had to put him in an orphanage. There wouldn't be any jobs for a girl like me with a baby and no husband, and I might've ended up walking the streets." The words tumbled out, and her blue eyes pleaded with him as her cheeks flooded with color.

Bewilderment gave way to anger, which gave way to pity. In a way, she reminded him of the young women who followed the soldiers from camp to camp. Young, trapped in a life they saw no way to escape, at the mercy of others and only trying to survive. He'd always been wary of them, while at the same time feeling sorry for their plight.

"Please don't turn me out, sir." She snuggled the child against her shoulder. "He's a good boy, he really is. And I can still do my work taking care of your lady."

He sucked in a breath as the baby wailed. "I'm not going to turn you out." His voice was rougher than he'd intended, almost a growl.

A strong look passed between the maid and Diana, and they both eased a bit. Frustration gnawed at Evan. Yet another secret his new wife had kept from him. A ladies' maid with a child.

He wondered that the Duke of Seaton had kept the young woman in his employ. He was a brutish, greedy lout, but he was also a high stickler. Maybe Diana had kept the girl's condition from him too.

A secretive woman, his new wife, and it would behoove him to remember that.

"What's wrong with him?" Evan asked as the sobs continued.

"He's hungry, my lord. And in need of a new clout, I think." The maid's cheeks grew even pinker.

Evan wanted to rub his temples, wanted to close his eyes and wake up and start this day . . . this week . . . this month over again. They were barely out of London, and they'd have to stop so she could care for the wee man. At the very least, Evan would have to climb up and ride with the coachman so she could suckle the child.

This day was getting better and better. He reached for the door handle.

"Where are you going?" Diana asked, her hand on his arm.

Did she think he would hurl himself from the carriage? "To notify the coachman that we need to stop for a bit." He opened the door, and leaning out, he shouted to the driver. Immediately, the horses slowed, and the carriage rocked to a stop. Evan climbed the rest of the way out, stepping on the wheel and pulling himself level with the coachman.

"We'll need to pull off the road for . . ." He had no idea how long it took to feed a baby. "For a while."

The horses stamped, their breath billowing in the frosty air and steam rising from their coats. "My lord, stopping now isn't good for the animals."

Evan felt a tug on his cape. Diana's face, framed by her bonnet brim, peeked out through the doorway. "Evan, we shouldn't stop here. We need to stop at the next village."

"Why? What's wrong?" The baby continued to wail, now sounding more angry than sad. Why wasn't the girl comforting him?

"We left London in such a hurry, we forgot to bring along milk for the baby."

"Milk, but wouldn't his mother . . ." While some women hired wet nurses for their babies, he would hardly think a ladies' maid would be in a position to do the same. He was in completely foreign territory here. Perhaps something was wrong with the girl, that she couldn't nurse her own child. He wasn't going to ask.

"Very well."

She ducked back into the carriage, and he nodded to the coachman. "Stop at the next inn or tavern you see."

The ride became excruciating. Though the little maid tried everything to console the child, he wailed on. Diana finally took him, crooning softly, but to no avail. Evan began to think riding aloft with the coachman would be preferable in spite of the cold.

In desperation, though he had no experience, he reached for the baby. The little face was red, eyes scrunched tight. "Young man." Evan held the infant, cradling his head since the thing seemed too large and heavy and liable to fall right off if not supported.

At the sound of his voice, the crying paused, and the eyes, a deep hazy blue that looked as if they might turn to brown eventually, opened.

"Young man, enough of this caterwauling. I know you are hungry. I'm peckish myself, but crying about it won't change anything. We've a fair bit to march yet today, and it would be best if you calmed yourself." He tucked the baby under his chin against his chest, and to his surprise, the child snuggled in and was silent.

"How did you do that, my lord?" the maid asked.

He had no idea. "It's best to be firm with new recruits." Most likely the baby had worn himself out and would sleep in spite of being hungry.

Diana worried her lower lip, but said nothing, probably as relieved as he not to have their ears blasted by sobs any longer.

The carriage swayed, and he wrapped his arms more securely around the infant, who seemed to weigh nothing at all, a scrap of humanity who was now under Evan's care. His responsibilities weighed on him more heavily than any haversack on a long, sweltering march.

A stray thought cantered through his head. Perhaps someday he would hold his own child like this. That thought hit like a sharpshooter's bullet. Him? A father? And yet he *was* married. Children were the natural result. His blood heated and his imagination fired, but he doused those thoughts with the cold water of reality.

He barely knew the bride who had been forced on him, and she barely knew him. They had much to work out before their marriage should be consummated.

The baby's downy head rested under his chin, and he cupped it, marveling at the minute size. Until he had his own skull sorted out, he would keep his distance from the new Lady Whitelock. He didn't know if he was disappointed or relieved to have made that decision.

At last they pulled into the yard of an inn.

"Stay here." Evan handed the sleeping child over to Diana and bolted from the carriage, eager to get outside, away from his thoughts. Hostlers emerged from the stable, and the coachman descended, stomping his feet and slapping his hands.

"How far to Crawley?" the man asked the nearest hostler, who held the bridles of the matched pair of bays.

"Nigh on six hours, I think, unless you get fresh horses along the way."

Six more hours?

"Would you like a change of horses, sir?" the hostler asked.

These weren't his animals. They belonged to Marcus . . . or Marcus's father, the Duke of Haverly, actually. He knew some wealthy families would send horses ahead on longer journeys and change them at frequent intervals, but Evan had made no such provision with Marcus. He had this one team, and they would need to be returned in good health. The horses, plus the baby's needs, made up his mind.

"Unharness and cool the team. We'll stay the night here and start fresh in the morning." Evan turned as the baggage wagon clattered into the yard, Shand at the lines. "Sergeant, help with the horses, and bring what we'll need for a night at this inn. Ask Dia—the countess . . ." Would he ever be used to calling her that? ". . . which bags she will need. I'll go talk to the innkeeper."

"Very good, sir." Shand snapped a salute, and Evan started.

He'd called the man *sergeant*. He rolled his eyes. It was hard to remember sometimes that they were both civilians, whether they wanted to be or not.

Stepping into the taproom was like being hit in the face with a warm, aromatic blanket. A fire roared in a huge stone fireplace, and a spit turned slowly, roasting a hunk of meat. Several men sat at tables, nursing tankards of ale, and a woman in a broad apron shoved a few more sticks into the blaze.

Behind the counter, a young man wiped down the bar, his expression indolent, not that different from the expressions of the younger men of the *ton*.

The door bumped open, and Shand entered, stepping to the side with a bag under each arm, waiting for an indication of where to take them.

"I'd like rooms for the night." Evan stepped up, aware that all conversation had ceased.

The innkeeper studied Evan's open military cloak and the wool uniform of the Ninety-Fifth Rifles underneath.

"Got a dormitory over the stables. Ye can have one of the bunks in there for you and your batman." He named the price, one he obviously thought would befit a military man needing a place for the night. "If ye have a nag, it's extra to stable it."

Before Evan could explain the misunderstanding, Shand dropped the bags to the wide-planked floor and marched to the counter.

"Mind your manners, you jackanapes. You're addressing the Earl of Whitelock, not some common foot soldier. He'll be needing a room for himself, and one for his countess, and a private room for dinner." The little sergeant slapped his hand on the counter and leaned over. "And look smart. The countess is getting chilled out in the carriage."

The woman at the fireplace gasped and dropped the poker as the innkeeper gritted his teeth and swallowed hard.

"Your pardon, my lord." Nodding to Evan, he stepped around the counter and snapped his fingers to the barmaid. "Stoke the fire in the sitting room, and make sure the linens in the courtyard rooms aren't damp." He bowed again to Evan. "I do regret my tone, my lord. Anything you need, please just ask."

"What I would like is some milk, warmed up and waiting in that sitting room as soon as possible."

The innkeeper's brows rose, but he nodded.

Shand stepped back, his mouth a straight line, and when the innkeeper wasn't looking, he gave Evan a quick wink. "Shall I bring Her Ladyship inside, my lord?"

"I'll see to it."

The child had awakened once more and was now shouting down the innyard. Evan hurried Diana and the maid into the taproom and, following the innkeeper, ushered them through a heavy curtain into a private sitting room. The baby fussed and squirmed against his little mother's cloak.

The parlor was comfortable enough, with a fire spilling light and heat into the room. Shand passed behind them on his way up the stairs with their bags, his eyes full of questions about the infant.

Diana tapped Shand on the shoulder. "I'll take that one, thank you. And thank you for driving the baggage cart and for carrying things for us."

Shand bobbed his head, handing over the small case, his eyes still full of inquiries he wasn't daring to make. "Hope the little fellow's all right."

"He will be once his tummy is full, I hope."

Evan went to the parlor window, watching the stable yard where the coachman directed the hostlers. He'd much rather be out there seeing to the horses, or having a crack with Shand in the taproom, than playing "earl" in this private room. How much did a night at a place like this cost? Then he remembered the money. Diana's inheritance, which now belonged to him. The inheritance no one had seen fit to tell him about before it was too late. He could afford to buy this inn several times over and not make even a dent in his bank balance.

He still couldn't fathom it.

His breath frosted the pane, and he turned back to the room. Diana held the baby against her traveling cloak while the maid filled a boat-shaped glass bottle from the copper pan of milk set close to the fire.

To his surprise, when the bottle was ready, Diana took it, seating herself before the fire and cradling the baby. Careful to keep the open filling spout uppermost, she put the narrow end of the glass bottle to the baby's lips.

A few drops of milk hit his tongue, and suddenly there was blessed quiet. Evan exhaled. The baby made slurping, gurgling noises, but the crying ceased.

But why hadn't the maid taken the baby to feed him? He was her son, after all. It still baffled him why she wasn't suckling him, but he was in no position to ask. At any rate, at least the infant wasn't squalling the place to rubble.

The innkeeper tapped on the doorjamb, easing the curtain aside. "I made some tea for the lady. Would my lord care for some mulled wine or some brandy? Or I could fetch you some ale." He bore a tray laden with tea paraphernalia. When he spied the baby, he paused, but then he set the tray on the low table beside Diana.

"Tea will be fine. Bring three more cups."

"Three, sir? Are you expecting guests?"

Evan stilled. He'd been counting Shand and the maid in the mix—what was the girl's name? That wasn't the done thing, he supposed. Still, he was tired of the "done thing" already, and he needed to have a conversation with Shand. Followed by one with Diana.

"Just bring the cups, please."

"Very good, sir."

The baby ate as if he hadn't seen food in a week, and Diana certainly acted as if this wasn't her first time feeding him. Evan felt surplus to requirements, but he had nowhere else to go at the moment.

"Please tell me your name."

The maid stopped rummaging around in the little case she'd taken the bottle from, and bobbed a quick curtsy. "Beth, my lord." She didn't meet his eyes, instead pulling things out of the box and folding them into neat little stacks.

It appeared that the tiny clothing had been crammed into the case in a hurry and would need some sorting. The little chap sure had a lot of garments for the son of a ladies' maid. Evan sensed Diana's generosity here.

"Beth, when your baby is done eating, perhaps you will take him upstairs. I'll see that some food is sent up for you. I'm sure you have things to see to with your mistress's belongings." That was what ladies' maids did, right? Function as a sort of batman or valet, but for girls?

The innkeeper hurried into the room with another teapot and three cups on a tray. "I've shown your valet to your rooms. At the top of the stairs on the left, my lord." And he was gone.

"Beth, pour yourself some tea, and try to get warm. It was a cold ride." She was barely more than a child herself. Fifteen or sixteen by the look of her. How had she come to be in her current situation?

Shand returned, and Evan went into the passageway with him. "I need you to sleep in the stable and keep an eye on the horses tonight."

"Yes, my lord."

Evan grimaced. "I know it's right and proper and all that, but I do wish that when we are in private, you would just call me sir, like we did when we were both soldiers and happy to be so." He pinched the bridge of his nose. "I do appreciate you stepping in back there with the innkeeper."

Rubbing his chin, Shand studied him. "But you're a proper lord now, and it wouldn't be right, me calling you anything else. And you won't get used to it if I don't."

"I don't want to get used to it. I feel like I'm wearing someone else's skin, and it doesn't fit."

Shand sent him a pull-yourself-together-and-get-on-with-it look, with which Evan was very familiar from their campaigning days.

"My lord, what about the child? Where did he come from?"

"A basket."

"My lord?"

Shand really wasn't going to let the "my lord" address go. Evan sighed. "He's the by-blow child of the maid. It appears my wife has a tender heart when it comes to turning out a young girl and her infant. It also appears she has a way of keeping secrets from me until they spring out of the underbrush like a French ambush."

The sergeant rubbed his finger across his lower lip and contemplated Evan.

"What?"

"I am no expert, but it would seem to me that there will be many things you will need to learn about your new wife. You have only known her a fortnight. I am sure she'll be discovering new things about you too."

A heavy feeling invaded Evan's chest. While he recognized the wisdom of Shand's words, he knew he was as much to blame for keeping secrets as his bride. Hers had come out, but his remained buried—and would need to continue to be kept, else he would find himself hauled off to the asylum. The nightmares, the cold sweats, the jumping at sudden noises, the headaches . . . none of those had abated, and in some cases were growing worse. And he still couldn't remember the day he was injured. The day that had ultimately brought him right to this spot. Until he sorted himself out, he would need to keep that part of himself hidden.

Dinner was . . . anticlimactic. After getting herself into a froth about spending time alone with her new husband, perhaps having to explain herself regarding the secrets she had been—and in some cases still was—keeping from him, he'd chosen to have dinner in the taproom and had left her to her own supper in solitude.

Diana nibbled at the food and talked to herself, since there was no one else to listen. "You should eat, you know. You didn't have any breakfast, nor could you face much of the wedding meal." She almost laughed. Anyone listening in would think her barmy.

"You should also be giving your thanks for finally having a prayer answered." She pushed her potatoes around on her plate. "Evan didn't throw Beth and Cian out." Instead, he'd taken the child in his arms and quieted him when no one else was up to the task.

The image of him holding the baby, speaking to the infant as if he were a tiny soldier, warmed Diana's heart. Was there a tender character inside the man somewhere? It was too soon to judge, but him not giving way to temper when learning of Cian's existence boded well.

The wooden curtain rings clacked as the drapery covering the doorway was pushed aside. Evan stood there, his cloak over his arm, the candlelight glinting off the pewter buttons on his uniform.

Her heart thudded against her stays. This man was her husband, and this was her wedding night. She had blocked the thought as best she could all day, but now she could no longer ignore the fact.

Lady Cathcart's hurried, brusque, and inadequate instructions as Diana had dressed that morning made no sense and only set her nerves to jangling even harder, so she'd pushed those out of her mind. Now she wished she'd listened better.

Too nervous to stay seated, she rose.

"Good evening, my lord."

He closed his eyes, his lips going thin. "I told you to call me Evan when we're alone. I've been 'my lorded' quite enough for one day." Stepping in, he slid the curtain across the opening, and the room suddenly felt quite small.

Her bonnet and cloak lay on the chair opposite, and she swept them up, placing them on the table beside her. "Won't you sit, my—Evan?" Her voice cracked as she corrected herself. He must think her the most gauche of schoolgirls. Where was all that refinement and decorum she'd had drilled into her?

She studied him as he took the offered seat while she perched on the edge of her chair. When she realized she was gnawing on her lower lip, she forced herself to stop, to try to relax.

"You knew, didn't you?"

Puzzlement bunched her brows. "About what?" she asked, cautious.

"About the money."

She didn't know if she was relieved he wanted to talk about her inheritance. She'd rather not speak of it at all, but it was a preferable topic to discussing Cian. Or their bridal night.

Studying her hands in her lap, she nodded. "I did." Would he yell now? Berate her? Strike her? She braced herself.

"Why?" He rubbed his palm on the back of his neck while loosening the top buttons of his tunic. He stared into the fire. "Why didn't you tell me?"

Because an infant's life was in jeopardy? Because I made a promise to my sister on her deathbed? But she couldn't tell her husband the truth, for fear he would react like her father and turn the child out.

"When was I supposed to do this? We've barely spent any time together, and none of that alone. I agree that my father should have told you, but for his own reasons, he chose not to do so."

"I heard his reasons before we left his house. He never planned to tell me. The question is, did you?" The firelight picked out his strong profile, reflecting in his eyes, making them seem warm, even though his voice had more than a touch of frost.

His hands fisted on his thighs, and Diana tensed. He seemed more tired than angry, but a man could lash out at any moment.

"My father forbade it." The words leaked through her tight lips.

"I see."

He said no more, merely studying her, and she wondered if he would demand any other explanation from her.

"My lady?" Beth's voice came from the passageway, and Diana could've hugged the girl for the interruption.

"Enter," Evan answered, his voice clipped.

The maid ducked around the curtain and dipped a quick curtsy. She crossed to Diana and kept her voice low. "My lady, I've laid out your things, but . . ." She darted a look from Evan to Diana. "I'm wondering where Cian and I are to sleep. Mr. Shand has put my lord's things in one room and your things in the other."

Diana twisted her fingers at her waist, feeling the absurdly large military ring that reminded her she was a married woman. And that he had certain rights and expectations as her husband.

"My lord?" Diana's voice barely passed her lips, and she swallowed against the nervousness in her throat.

He massaged his temples, eyes closed. "Beth, go to your lady's room. She will join you there shortly."

Beth dipped her knees and hurried from the parlor.

Evan's eyelids popped open, and something in the way he studied Diana made her blood heat, and her chest tightened. He rose, and it was all she could do to stay in one spot. Surely now he would lead her upstairs, and she would enter into a new realm as a wife. Would he be kind? Would he be so angry with her father that he would take it out on her? The butterflies in her stomach turned to ravens, buffeting her until she gripped the back of the chair and swayed.

Then he turned away. "It is late, and we've had a long day. Another beckons on the morrow. You and the maid take one room, and I will take the other. Time enough to continue our discussion at a later date."

He made her a slight bow and left the room, his footfalls sounding on the stairs.

Reprieved. At least for tonight.

CHAPTER 8

WHITE HAVEN WAS a misnomer. White Hovel would be nearer the mark. Evan alit from the carriage, which had been forced to stop at the gatehouse several hundred yards from the manor. He held on to the carriage door and stared at the Whitelock country seat of power.

This was his new home? The first piece of property he'd ever owned.

He should strike flint to steel and put it out of its misery.

Diana bumped into him as she emerged from the coach, and he realized he hadn't helped her down. Her gloved hand came up and covered her lips as she surveyed the house. Even from this range, the place was a disaster. He needed a battery of cannons and five minutes of open fire to finish what years of neglect had started.

Ivy climbed—no, dominated—the front of the structure, growing over the windows and walls in rampant fashion. Though, it might not be ivy at all. No leaves clung to the vines at this time of year. It might just be bramble. Brush and bushes, tufts of grass, and leaf detritus clogged what had once been a circular drive, and the ironwork gates here by the road hung drunkenly from their hinges, blocking the road.

The central portion of the house was several stories tall, while two lower wings poked out to the north and south of the west-facing center block.

Was that a tree growing through the roof of the north wing?

"Well, it's certainly . . . large." Diana supported her elbow on the opposite arm and propped her chin in her hand. "And the view of the hills and trees must be pleasant from the upper stories."

"It will make a glorious bonfire. High burning enough to signal ships in the channel, I would think." Evan blew out his cheeks. "I knew it would take some work, but this is worse than I imagined."

The baggage wagon pulled up, and Shand jumped down. He gave a low whistle. "Maybe we took the wrong turnoff?"

The coachman heard and sniffed. "I assure you, this is where the map and my inquiries led, my lord." He held up the piece of paper with Marcus's scrawl on it. Saying he didn't trust the hand-drawn scrap without corroboration, he'd asked at the coaching inn in Crawley and confirmed their destination.

"No. This is the correct estate." Evan gestured toward the off-kilter gates where "White" and "Haven" had been worked in the iron. When properly closed, they would form the name of the property across the top.

He'd seen post-battle buildings that looked better.

"God hates a coward," Shand said out of the corner of his mouth. It was a phrase their commanding officer in the Ninety-Fifth Rifles had said often. "We might as well advance, sir."

"Retreat is not an option." Evan repeated the standard reply of the Ninety-Fifth as well. "Help me clear the way."

Between the two of them, they managed to drag the wrought iron gates open wide enough to let the carriage and wagon through. Evan helped Diana back in the coach, but he elected to follow on foot for the rest of the way. He needed to reconcile yet another twist to his reality.

The driveway, rutted and washed out, nearly devoid of gravel, led to the front of the manor house. Gray stone walls rose three—or was it four?—stories into the air, punctuated by broken window openings, like sockets with no eyes. The brambles strangled the old building, leeching any life it might still have. Or perhaps the vines were all that held the structure together these days. The two-story extensions to either side were no better, with arched windows vacant of glass, bits of the mullions hanging, and tattered drapes blowing through the openings.

Paint peeled off the front door of the house, and the lion's-head knocker hung askew. Crisp, dead leaves crunched under Evan's boots. This time he remembered to help Diana alight from the carriage. He closed the crested door to keep the wind away from the maid and the baby, both asleep inside.

The baby had slept most of the day away. Just as well, since it seemed he'd been up most of the night in the room next door—the room where his wife slept on their wedding night.

Evan had been aware of the noise in the adjoining room because he, too, had been awake. The moment his head had hit the rather lumpy pillow, he'd fallen into the nightmare, later startling himself awake. He'd hoped no one had heard his cry.

After that, he'd feared going back to bed, since the dreams tended to cycle again and again once they started. Some way for a bridegroom to spend his wedding night. For most of the darkest hours, he'd sat in a chair before the small coal stove, dozing and waking in turns. And every time he'd jerked awake, he could almost remember . . . and a sense of panic would wash over him. Whatever it was that escaped him, it was important.

And yet the harder he tried to force it, the more elusive the images became.

"Are we going inside?" Diana's question yanked him back to the present.

"Might as well see the extent of the disaster." He grasped the doorknob, which promptly came off in his hand.

Giving vent to his frustration, he planted his boot against the latch with enough force to break it and send the door rocketing back.

A brace of doves flew up, scared from their roost in the foyer by his actions. Diana squealed and grabbed his arm, and he shielded his face as they flew past his head in a flurry of feathers and flutters.

"Zooks!" Shand exclaimed, leaping back and holding his hand to his chest, then ducking his head shamefacedly. "Your pardon, milady."

Diana panted. "What a homecoming this is turning out to be. I hope nothing else has taken up residence. Like rats . . . or . . ." Her face paled. "Bats." She clutched at her skirts, a shudder running through her.

"I'm not a fan of rodents myself. Tradition dictates that, as your bridegroom, I carry you over the threshold, but I'm afraid I would trip on the broken floor." Evan stepped up and looked inside. "It would appear that there's been a bit of a leak in the roof."

"Sir, should I bring the carriage lanterns?" Shand asked.

"Good idea." Evan turned to Diana. "Perhaps you should wait here."

"I think not. This is my new home, after all. If I'm to be mistress of such a grand estate, I should inspect it thoroughly. Just promise to save me if an unruly resident decides to scurry across the floor."

She appeared to be suppressing a giggle. How could she laugh?

Shand obtained and lit the lanterns and handed one to Evan. Bracing himself, Evan crossed into the foyer, reaching back for Diana's hand to help her over a pile of plaster and lath that had fallen from the ceiling.

Cobwebs hung everywhere, and in the weak light, dust motes danced in the air, stirred up by their passage. Heavy drapes, rotted by the elements, hung in tatters from the large windows, blocking most of the light but letting some rays of the late-afternoon sun in.

A massive sweeping staircase led to the first floor, and doors stood half open on both sides of the central passageway. Diana swept aside a bit of debris with her foot. "Look, parquet floors. These must've been lovely once upon a time."

Evan bent to inspect the floors. Small pieces, lots of them, inter-joined. "This must've taken forever to lay." He didn't mention the obvious signs of rodent infestation also littering the floor. Delightful.

Shand nodded. "White oak, I think."

"Can it be restored?" Diana asked. She held her cloak tightly around her.

Was it possible that it was colder inside than out, or was it just his imagination?

"Maybe." Shand shrugged. "How much money do you want to spend?"

Evan glanced at Diana, but she was carefully not looking at him. Money, and the fact that she hadn't told him about how much was coming to her upon her marriage, sat between them like a boulder. Her explanation that her father had forbidden her to mention it rang true, and if the bruise he had seen on her cheek the day he went to propose was any indication, she had probably feared more of the same if she didn't obey.

It made him want to visit his father-in-law with a bit of retribution.

But the truth still remained. By marrying her, he had become a very wealthy man. It felt wrong. Distasteful. The man was supposed to provide for the woman, not the other way around. But everything had been turned upside down and backward in his life for weeks. He should be accustomed to it by now.

Diana peered into one of the rooms on the right. "Oh my. Look at that."

He joined her while Shand explored the other side of the house. A long, dusty table sat in the center of the space, so he assumed it was the dining room, but Diana was looking up. A massive chandelier hung from the center of a plaster medallion of what looked like fruit and flower shapes, and though covered in dust and cobwebs, the many crystals winked back the faint light making its way through the vines covering the windows.

"Are those cherubs?" he asked.

Peeking through the grime on the vaulted ceiling were fat little winged babies tumbling and peering from behind clouds.

"They're adorable."

"They're . . . unsettling. How could you eat with all those faces watching you?"

She laughed aloud, the first time he'd heard her do so, and it had an odd effect upon him, as if something inside him that had been tensed for a long time eased a bit. As if a warm breeze had whispered in a cold, dark place.

And wasn't that fanciful thinking? But her face was more relaxed and open than he'd seen it before. Unguarded as she gazed up at the water-stained mural.

She was beautiful. Like some fine statue or painting, but real. And she was his.

"Evan." Diana did a slow turn and then touched the marble mantelpiece. "I know the place looks a bit of a disaster now, but it's got . . . potential. I really think we can make something fine here."

"She's right, sir. Cleaned up and repaired, it could be a cracker of a good house." Shand crossed the foyer again, holding his lantern aloft.

Evan stared at the pair of them. How could a veteran campaigner and a girl who had been sheltered by a father so possessive and domineering as to be qualified as a jailer have such a positive view of the world that they could see a diamond in the midst of all this rubble?

And why did it make him, who had seen too much of war and destruction to follow flights of fancy, want to embrace that view?

A familiar metallic click sent a cold shaft of iron from the top of his head to his heels. Someone had pulled back the hammer on a gun, and in that instant, Evan went from civilian to soldier.

"Who are ye, and why are ye here?"

The voice ricocheted off the walls, and Diana turned toward it.

Panic clawed up Evan's chest, and the need to protect her overwhelmed him. His hands felt empty without his rifle. His only weapon was a knife, and that had been tucked into his boot. Where was his gear? What kind of soldier went into battle so poorly armed? Gripping the chair in front of him, in one movement he lifted it and spun, slinging it toward the door, where a man aimed a blunderbuss at him. At the last instant, Evan swiped upward with the chair, knocking the gun skyward.

A gout of flame, a roar, and pellets hit the ceiling, massacring cherubs and shattering crystals. Somewhere behind him, Diana screamed. The gunman toppled backward from the force of the blast, and Evan leapt after him, pinning him down, yanking the gun from his hand, and hurling it into the hallway.

He had the man by the coat front, shoving him onto the floor, straddling him, and raising one fist, when an iron grip wrapped around his wrist. He pivoted, bringing his other hand up for an undercut to the gut to this fresh assailant.

Barely in time, he pulled his punch. Shand shoved him backward, letting go of the wrap he had on Evan's arm. "Sir, stand down!"

He pointed to the man on the floor, a man whose hat had fallen off and revealed a shock of white hair. Wrinkles seamed his face, and he cowered, his faded-blue eyes red rimmed and streaming tears.

Evan's chest heaved as he fought the rage that possessed him. His skin itched and twitched, and he clasped and unclasped his fists, staggering to his feet. For a moment it was as if he had been back on the battlefield, fighting for his life. The smell of gunpowder hung in the air, burnt sulfur and saltpeter stinging his nose. He gulped, tremors trickling outward from his core. He bore down in his mind, trying to put the monster back in the cupboard, afraid of losing control completely.

What was happening to him? Why couldn't he quell the panic? Why was he torn between the past and the present, unsure at any moment when something would pull the door open and let the fear and anger out?

"My lady?" Shand asked.

Evan jerked. Diana. She'd screamed. Had she been hit? How could he forget about her? He whirled again and almost struck her. She'd come up behind him unheard. Jumping back to avoid his hand, she squeaked.

Dust covered her hair and shoulders, and bits of ceiling plaster clung to her cloak. But it was the fear in her eyes, the way she had thrown her hands up to ward off a blow that whipped a cold, sober wind through his thoughts, chasing away the last of the battlefield mind-set.

He reached for her, but she skittered backward, putting space between them, just as she had last night in the inn parlor.

"Let me help you, sir." Shand reached down and pulled the old man up from the floor.

Evan noticed for the first time that his former sergeant was armed.

Shand tucked a pistol into the back of his trousers, pulling his coat down to cover the weapon. "Are you hurt?"

Seeing the man's hunched back, his tottering balance, shame seeped into Evan. He'd attacked a feeble old man?

Still, the stranger had held a gun on them. Evan went into the hallway and picked up the weapon. Weighing it in his hands, he grimaced. Amazing that the thing had fired at all. Rust encrusted the trigger, the hammer, and the pan. It had to be nearly a hundred years old, a Dutch blunderbuss by the look of it, a swan-neck barrel that flared at the muzzle, a pitted and chipped stock. The thing had probably been new around the time the Spanish Armada sank.

"Who are you?" Evan asked.

The old man glared, the question putting some starch in his spine. "I could ask the same. What do ye mean coming in here where ye've no right?"

"I have every right. I own this house and property. Now, I'll ask again. Who are you?"

"That's a lie. This house belongs to Himself, the Earl of Whitelock. He put me in charge, and I'm his steward. Have been since Himself inherited the title. He's away just now, but when Himself comes back, he'll toss ye out like the mongrels ye are." The man swiped his hand under his rather bulbous nose and glared at Evan.

"You're waiting for the Earl of Whitelock to return?" Evan wanted to quit the old man, for he was clearly deranged. There were fences to mend with his wife, but she stayed on the other side of the table, as far from him as possible while he tried to make sense of the "steward's" words.

"Aye, and he'll sort you lot out."

From what Marcus had said, the former Earl of Whitelock had died more than twenty years ago and the house had been vacant since then. Had the old man been waiting more than two decades for his master? He was daft. Surely someone, somewhere along the way, had mentioned the former earl's demise?

Evan felt even worse. Not only had he attacked an old man, but one who was demented. "Sir, please sit down." The "steward" tottered, as if a slight gust might knock him over. Evan pulled out one of the chairs from the dining table and turned it.

Shand guided the man to the seat and knelt before him. "What is your name, sir?"

"Greville?" He scratched the hair over his ear, asking rather than telling. "Yes, Greville Monroe. Steward of White Haven." He sounded more confident now.

Footsteps pounded from the back of the house, coming toward them, and Shand rose, pulling his pistol as Evan stepped between the door and Diana. His heart kicked up again, but he fought to remain calm.

A woman skidded to a halt in the doorway, slipping on the debris. "Grandfather, are you hurt? I heard a shot."

Shand put out his hand to steady her. "He's not hurt, madam. Does he belong to you? He really shouldn't have a gun. He's a danger to himself and others carrying that old relic around."

The woman jerked away from him, her white cap slipping back to reveal dark-red hair. "Who are you people? What have you done to my grandfather?"

Puzzlement clouded Shand's eyes. "We've not done anything, madam."

"A likely story, trespassing as you are. Get out of here, or I'll have to call for the magistrate." She knelt before her grandfather, touching his knee. "It's monstrous to treat an old man this way."

He was covered in dirt from rolling on the floor, and his hands trembled.

Shand had clearly reached the end of his patience. "Madam, may I present to you the Earl and Countess of Whitelock? They have every right to be in this home, since they own it. If your grandfather was once in the employ of the former earl, that situation ended long ago. I admire his willingness to protect the property, but he's in no condition to be wandering around with a loaded gun and pointing it at his betters."

The woman rocked back on her heels, her cap tumbling to the floor, and Evan realized she was past the first blush of youth. Perhaps mid-thirties?

"You're the earl?"

She was looking at him, and he felt an impostor. He wanted to say no. To say he was just a simple soldier, a clergyman's son, plain old Evan Eldridge.

But that bridge had been crossed . . . and burned. He couldn't go back. "I am."

"We'd heard there was a new Whitelock, but no one mentioned you'd be coming here. My grandfather . . ." She lowered her voice. "His mind wanders sometimes, and he thinks he's a young steward again. I do apologize, my lord. Please don't punish him. He wouldn't understand." She sidled on her knees until she could put her arm around the old man.

"I don't intend to punish him. I'm sorry for . . ." Evan spread his hands. "He shouldn't have that gun."

"I'll take it from him. I promise."

"Best let Shand keep it. It's so old, it's a miracle that it fired at all. Next time it could explode. It doesn't appear to have been cleaned in a long time."

She frowned at the sergeant but said nothing.

"I assume you live somewhere on the property?"

"Yes." Pushing herself up, she curtsied quickly. "Here at the back of the house. When the housekeeper left, we took over her rooms."

"When did she leave?" Evan glanced at the dirt and debris.

"I was a child of twelve. All the staff left about that time. And most of the tenants. The land's been fallow all this time. The magistrate, Mr. Jones, asked Grandfather to stay on and protect the house. For a while, he also protected the grounds, but it was too much for him. Now it's all he can do to keep thieves and vagrants out of the manor proper. The crofters' cottages are full of squatters and the like." She kept her hand on her grandfather's shoulder as he muttered and twisted his gnarled hands in his lap. "I get work sometimes at the inn or taking in mending or washing, but it's been hard going the last few years."

So Evan had a house that was falling down, land that had lain fallow for twenty years, and squatters in the cottages. How could he turn White Haven into a profitable estate? He knew nothing of estate management, carpentry, farming. He had none of the skills necessary to be a landowner.

And in ten or twelve weeks, he would be hosting the Prince Regent and his retinue.

Diana removed her cloak and handed it to Beth, surveying the small room. The coaching inn at Crawley would be their home for the foreseeable future, and as there was no private parlor available, this room at the head of the stairs would have to do. She bent over the laundry basket that served as Cian's crib, checking that he was still covered.

She didn't want to stay at the inn at all, but there was nowhere else. White Haven was uninhabitable at the moment, especially for a baby. Would her father send someone after the child? If he did, would those men look first at the inn? How could she protect the baby? She had no rights to him, none that a court would listen to, anyway. It didn't matter that Catherine had put her son into Diana's keeping. Her father was his legal guardian.

Somehow, she felt that if she could just get the baby to the estate, he would be safe. He would be surrounded by servants, under her watch constantly. But here at the inn, he seemed vulnerable. The place would be full of unfamiliar people, travelers . . . or men sent by her father.

If only she could trust her new husband to protect the child, but she didn't know him well enough. He'd been gentle with the baby on the trip here, but that was only for a little while. Her promise to Catherine was forever. To raise Cian as her son. How could she do that and keep his identity a secret?

The first item on the agenda was to provide a safe place for him to live, which meant getting to work as soon as possible to make White Haven habitable.

Mr. Shand carried in another load of baggage. "His Lordship will be up soon. Where would you like me to put things?"

Where indeed? With such a tiny room and so much luggage, it would be a squeeze.

"Beth, run downstairs and fetch me ink, pen, and paper. If there is none to be had, take a coin from my purse and find the closest stationer. I'll help Mr. Shand get the luggage sorted, and then we can get to work. Also, see if the inn has a milking cow. If not, we'll have to find someone who does and purchase milk."

"The earl has already inquired, my lady. The cook here will keep you supplied." Shand shifted a valise from one hand to the other.

Warmth hit Diana's chest. Evan had already asked about food for the baby? He was such a puzzle to her. At turns he was kind and then volatile. Not above using his fists at the slightest provocation, and yet he'd been patient and considerate when it came to Cian.

And herself too. Though he acted swiftly, and sometimes physically, he had never directed his anger or his fists at her.

He tapped on the open door and came in, surveying the room. "This place is so small, you'll have to step outside to change your mind."

Diana nodded and pushed aside a bandbox. "Still, it won't be much for housekeeping. The innkeeper said this was where the coach driver usually sleeps, but since you've rented the entire floor, we can use it as a bit of an office or sitting room."

"Where's your maid?" He noted Cian's basket on the small writing desk.

"I sent her for writing implements. We're going to need a great many lists."

"Lists?" He moved a hatbox from a chair and sat down.

"Of all the things to do, the supplies, the servants and workmen we'll need."

He leaned back and put his hands over his eyes. "Do you think it's even possible? I fancy a good fire would solve all our problems. We can send our regrets to the prince and tell him the place is a pile of ashes. Then we wouldn't have to host a Royal Visit. At least not until we could build."

"He's invited himself for a visit to White Haven, and it is incumbent upon us to make the place ready. One does not say no to the Prince Regent." She set Cian's basket near the little coal stove and sat at the desk.

"Don't I have cause to know it?" He sounded rueful and a little bitter, and she flushed.

Why did he have to remind her that he had been forced into this marriage? She was rowing in the same boat, but she didn't continue to cast that fact up before him.

Beth came in clutching a handful of paper, ink, and a quill. "The innkeeper says this is all he has, but he'll send for more if you need it."

"Thank you. Take the baby into the next room and unpack. Close the door please."

"Yes, my lady."

When they were alone, Diana uncapped the ink, frowned at the quill, and held it out to Evan. "Have you a knife? This nib is shredded."

He pulled a dagger from his boot, and she blinked. Once again she was reminded that he'd spent a great deal of his life as a soldier. With two quick strokes, he sharpened the pen and cut a nice slit in the end. "Not as good as if I could harden it in some hot sand, but it should do for now."

"Thank you. Now, the lists."

"Where do we even start?" He pulled his chair away from the wall, lifting it over a packing crate, and set it beside her.

As he sat, his thigh and his shoulder brushed hers, and she was very aware of how much larger he was than she. His face was so close to hers, she could see the clear blue of his eyes and how they were a bit darker around the pupils. He had high cheekbones and a narrow-bridged nose. His bottom lip was fuller than the top, and for a moment, she wondered if his kiss would be soft and gentle or masterful.

"Diana?"

"Yes?" She blinked, looking at the paper, praying he would never know where her thoughts had been taking her, heat rising up her throat and into her cheeks.

"Can you not think where to start either?"

She tried to remember what they had been speaking of as she inhaled the scent of his shaving soap. "Help first, I should imagine. Servants, skilled labor, and estate workers. Should we start from the top and work our way down?"

"The top? You mean the attics?"

She frowned. "No, start with the highest-ranking servant, the steward, and work your way down to the bootboy." Did he know nothing about domestic help?

He nodded. "Oh, like the army. Field marshal to private?"

"Exactly." She dipped the pen and wiped it on the edge of the inkwell. "Will Mr. Shand be your steward or is he your valet?"

"Can't he be both?"

"For a time perhaps, but you're going to want to hire someone who can oversee the estate, especially when you're away, and that man can't also spend time being in charge of your clothes and toiletries. The steward will stay on the estate, and your valet travels with you."

"I see. Well, for now I can dress myself, and Shand can help me around the property. What else do we need?" He propped his elbow on the desk and his chin in his hand, studying her.

Her face warmed under his scrutiny, and she had to wonder what he saw and whether it pleased him.

"Once the house is habitable, we'll need a butler, a housekeeper, a cook. Beth is my lady's maid, and you'll need the aforementioned valet. Those are the upper staff. Then for the lower staff, we'll need a scullery maid or two, upstairs and downstairs maids, a parlor maid, footmen, kitchen maid, laundress, and a bootboy. Those are just the inside help." She wrote as she talked. The paper wasn't of the highest quality, but it would do until she could buy better. "Outside you'll need a coachman, a gardener, a gamekeeper, a gatekeeper, groundskeepers. Depending upon whether you intend to keep a large stable, there will be grooms and stable boys. Beyond that, you will have the tenant farmers who will work the land for you in exchange for proper housing and a portion of the crops or the money they bring."

With every new item on her list, his expression grew bleaker.

"That is a lot of people who will be dependent on us . . . on me."

"Being a nobleman brings responsibility. It isn't all riding around in fine carriages and attending *ton* functions. *Noblesse oblige* isn't just an idle notion."

"I'm learning that."

"To fix the house is going to take a lot of work. Skilled workers. You'll have to send to London for them, most likely, and they will need a place to stay while they work. This inn"—she waved toward the small room—"will never hold them."

"Do you have any ideas?"

Diana nodded, pleased that he would ask her opinion, since no man had ever done so before. "One thing you will have to do is roust the squatters from the cottages and see what condition the crofts' barns are in. If they are like the house, they're going to need work. Re-thatching at the very least."

"How many cottages are there?" He scrubbed his hand down his cheek and tapped his lower lip, drawing her gaze.

She swallowed. "It depends upon the size of the estate. There could be five, or there could be fifty."

"I don't know the acreage. I suppose I'll have to ride over it to find the boundaries."

"From the little we saw at the manor house, you're going to need carpenters, painters, plasterers, masons, glaziers, and laborers. Something will have to be done with the thicket that is growing on the front of the house, and the driveway will need to be dragged and graveled. I can make a guess at what the kitchen gardens and formal gardens must look like. If we're to have the house ready for a Royal Visit, we're going to have to focus our attention on those areas the Prince Regent is likely to see, and wait on the rest. Though you won't want to wait too long on the cottages, because spring will arrive, and you need to get fields planted. Without proper housing, you will find it difficult to get anyone to work for you."

"I doubt we will at any rate. You're talking about . . ." He paused. "A hundred people to hire? Maybe more? I don't even know where to look for them. I'm sure skilled workers aren't just to be plucked off of the hedges. It will take weeks to even find the right people."

She nodded, her shoulders sagging. "It is a daunting task."

Evan leaned a bit closer. "How is it you know all these things? About the servants and the workers and such? I suppose it was living on your father's estate?"

She ran the barbs of the goose-feather quill through her fingers. "I was sent away to school when I was seven, and I have not spent much time at Seaton Manor. But I was raised for this. I was groomed to marry a landed gentleman and to run a house, to be the mistress of an estate." Though no one had prepared her for the condition of the particular estate of which she was now the mistress. Nor being the wife of the Earl of Whitelock, late of His Majesty's army.

She looked up and found he was so close, she could see the many shades of blue that made up the irises in his eyes. One could almost imagine plunging into them as if into the sea. His hand reached out and captured her hands, stilling their movements with the feather. Warmth seeped from his skin to hers, and the roughness of his hand, the size of it, bespoke their differences. She leaned in toward him, almost as if being tugged . . .

Thick, dark lashes fringed his eyes, and he had a clear shadow along his jaw. Would his whiskers be rough in the morning? Her hand itched to investigate, to skim her fingers along his sharp cheekbone. What would his hair look like, tousled from sleep? Was it coarse and springy or soft and silky?

They were mere inches apart, and Diana moistened her lips, swallowing as the distance between them closed in tiny increments. His eyes flared at the movement of her tongue across her lips, and . . .

A knock sounded at the open door, and Evan straightened sharply, breaking the threads that had pulled them closer. "Come." He spoke toward the door, his voice sounding deep, gravelly, sending a shiver across her skin.

Mr. Shand entered and paused. "Your pardon. I didn't realize . . ."

Diana sought to regain her composure, smoothing her hair and then her collar, feeling a sense of loss and . . . longing . . . that surprised her. And a touch of irritation that they had been interrupted.

"Come in." Evan waved him farther in, his voice sounding more normal. "We're having a council of war, and I'm realizing what an asset Diana is going to be."

The little sergeant stood almost at attention, his eyes shifting between Evan and Diana, and she knew what it must've looked like, what it almost had been . . . which only made her cheeks heat even more.

"Please, sit." Diana motioned to the settee. "We value your input as we . . . plot our strategy? Is that the right term?"

"Yes, ma'am." Shand perched on the edge of the piece of furniture, his hands on his knees. "I came up to see if you wished me to send the carriage and horses back to London, sir."

Evan picked up one of her lists and cleared his throat. "The carriage will certainly be going back to London, but it won't go empty. I'm beginning to see what an immense task bringing this estate up to scratch is going to be and that I was much too hasty bringing you here, Diana. I propose to return with you to London, see you installed in lodgings there, and set about hiring the required workmen."

"Oh no, please." She dropped the pen on the desk, splattering ink, but uncaring. Reaching out, she grasped his sleeve. "Don't send us back. We'd much rather stay with you here." She couldn't go back to London. If her father got word, and he surely would, he'd come for Cian, and she would be alone, powerless to stop him. It would be too good an opportunity to miss to punish her for letting her inheritance slip away from his grasp. Here at White Haven, the baby might be too far away to bother with, but right in the city? "Please." She swallowed, blushing hard. "I don't want to be parted from you."

Though she was pleading with Evan for Cian's sake, she realized the words were true for herself too. The baby's safety was paramount, but her reputation would be at risk as well. If he sent her back to the city and left her there alone while he returned to Sussex, tongues would wag. And she might find herself the recipient of Viscount Fitzroy's unwanted attentions again. Then there was the fact that in spite of herself, she was beginning to like her husband. The way he saw to her comforts, the way he protected her from perceived danger, the way he asked her opinion. Her fingers slipped down his sleeve to his hand.

He looked down at their entwined fingers, at his military ring on her finger, and returned the pressure. "This inn is no fit place for a lady of your quality. It will be weeks before the house will be ready. When I go back to London, I'll have to request an audience with the Prince Regent, and I'll have to be frank with him about the condition of the estate. We won't be in a position to offer him hospitality this year. Perhaps next spring."

She shook her head. "You cannot. That would be social ruin. Many peers wait their entire lives for a Royal Visit to their estates, and very few have the privilege. To refuse . . ." Her mind boggled at the notion. "Put that out of your head. The house and grounds will be ready when he comes. There is no other option. Even if it takes an army of workers and every last shilling you own."

Evan's hand went slack in hers for a moment, and then tightened. "What did you say?"

"I said you cannot refuse the Prince Regent."

"No, not that. You said, 'even if it takes an army of workers.'"

"Yes. The expense doesn't matter, not with so much at stake."

Suddenly, his lips parted in a broad smile, and her heart felt as if it had stopped.

"You're brilliant." He leaned forward, gripping her upper arms, and planted a loud kiss on her forehead. "Shand, get the carriage ready. We're heading to London, you and I, and we're going to raise an army."

CHAPTER 9

EVAN SMOOTHED HIS uniform tunic and headed up the steps to the offices of Coles, Franks, and Moody. He and Shand had turned up on Marcus's doorstep too late last night to visit his solicitors and get things sorted out, but Marcus had assured him that morning was soon enough. After a rocky night's sleep, Evan had laid plans and strategized with his friend in the breakfast room of Haverly House. Marcus was extremely helpful, but also puzzled.

"What I don't understand though, is why you didn't bring Diana back with you." Marcus had stabbed a piece of ham on his plate. "You whisk her out of town for one night and then leave her in the country to come haring back here?"

"She wanted to stay." Guilt hit him in the gut. She had insisted that it would be best for her to remain at the inn. Her little maid and the baby were tired out from their travels already, and it wouldn't be good for the little tyke to go out in the cold air again so soon. Diana would be fine, and she could perfect some of her lists. He wasn't to worry.

But he did worry. She was his wife.

His mind shot back to that moment when he had almost kissed her. The depth of her chocolaty eyes, her rosy lips, the scent of flowers that clung to her. His mouth went dry.

Evan looked up from his breakfast plate to catch Marcus contemplating him with a speculative look. Dropping his knife and fork onto his plate, Evan pushed the half-finished breakfast away and stood. "I've dispatched Shand on his assignments."

Marcus nodded and held up his slip of paper. "And I've got my marching orders. Not that I will be able to accomplish all this in just a day or two. What I can't finish before you leave, I'll either send or bring down to you as soon as I can."

"Thank you, friend. I don't know what I would've done without you since entering into this aristocratic fracas." Evan took his leave, his own errands weighing on his mind.

Though the lawyers' office building was unassuming at street level, the reception room was elegant and refined. Potted ferns, restrained landscapes, and a hush that said there was no need for ostentation.

A slender young man with glasses, thinning hair, and a truly impressive moustache looked up from his desk—a different secretary than when Evan had visited the place with Marcus nearly a month ago. "Do you have an appointment?" His eyes drifted over Evan's travel-stained cloak, green uniform, and no-longer-well-shined boots, and went back to his papers, as if not caring about the answer to his question.

Evan's mouth tightened. His uniform wasn't proper gentleman's attire, he knew, but it was comfortable and familiar. If clothes truly did make the man, then why wasn't he afforded respect based upon his military service? If he dressed like an idle dilettante, people would jump to do his bidding.

"The Earl of Whitelock to see his solicitors." He put one of his cards on the desk, snapping the corner as he did so.

The young man's neck jerked straight, and he almost leapt from his chair. "Lord Whitelock, of course." He gulped. "Please, take a seat. Would you like a cup of tea? I'll just nip into the office and see which of the gentlemen is available to meet with you." He scuttled from the room like his coattails were smoldering and without waiting for an answer about the tea.

Evan yanked off his gloves, tucked them in his cloak pocket, and removed the heavy garment. With so many capes on the shoulders, it was certainly warm, but this style made him think of wearing his military pack, it was so weighty.

He took a seat and picked up a newspaper neatly laid out on a small table. His name leapt off the crisp pages. "Whitelock Nuptial Celebration Graced with Royal Visit." All the details of the ceremony and reception were there, including the Prince Regent's arrival and announcement of Diana's inheritance. The newspaper expressed surprise that the couple had reportedly left the city so quickly, especially with such a fortune now at their disposal. "The Earl and Countess of Whitelock will surely be the most sought-after guests at upcoming social events this Season, and it is hoped they will return from their wedding trip quickly, though with a rumored Royal Visit this spring, perhaps they would stay in the country preparing for the big event." The article finished by commenting that Lady Whitelock, because of her great beauty, her father's title, and the inheritance, would've been named "The Incomparable" of this Season, and wasn't it quick work by the new earl to snap her up before others could ply their suits?

Evan felt like a fortune hunter. He'd barely had time to toss the paper onto the table in disgust when the secretary returned. "My lord, won't you please come with me. You may leave your cloak here." The man practically genuflected, clasping his hands together and hunching his shoulders in an effort to please.

The inner office was even more richly appointed than the reception room, with walnut paneling, thick woolen carpeting, and golden drapes at the windows. Leather-bound tomes ranked on shelves, looking as if they had never been opened, and green-shaded lamps stood on the corners of a massive desk.

"A pleasure to see you again, my lord." Mr. Moody, the lawyer Evan and Marcus had met with the day after Evan's first audience with the Prince Regent, stretched out his hand, his chin jutting and his eyes gleaming behind his square-framed glasses. "Please, won't you sit down and tell me how I may be of assistance to you. Anthony, bring tea. Unless you'd prefer something stronger?" He raised bushy eyebrows toward Evan.

At ten in the morning? "No, thank you." He took the chair offered, the leather butter soft under his hands.

The lawyer took his seat, rested his forearms on his desk, and laced his fingers. "What can I do for you?"

Evan tamped down his true feelings and kept his voice businesslike. "It's about the matter of my wife's inheritance. I understand the Home Secretary was going to see to the transfer of ownership from a trust to me."

"Oh yes. And so he has done. I have the paperwork here." He slid open a drawer and withdrew a folder. "The money is in the account we opened for you at the Bank of London when we transferred the remainder of the Whitelock funds into it." Flipping open the file, he scanned a ledger page. "I have taken care of certain bills that arrived here before your marriage—a tailor, a haberdasher, a boot maker. I had thought there would be more expenses, but you've been most frugal up to now." His finger followed a line of neat entries, and then his eyes rose to peruse Evan's uniform. "Should I expect more debits on the account? More tailoring, perhaps?"

Evan nodded. "There will be many new draws on the account, and I am sure tailoring will be somewhere amongst the invoices." He would need some sturdy working clothes and some riding attire. Perhaps he could order them, have them sent to White Haven, and get by with his uniforms until they arrived.

"Of course. With such an impressive sum, and coming from . . ." He hesitated, then must've decided to be quite frank, and plunged on. ". . . such pedestrian origins, you must want to really splash on some things. Horses? Club memberships? Carriages? Once you have entrance to White's or Boodle's, your marker will be good at the tables, so may I assume there will be wagering debts? And if you have a mistress to set up in a house of her own, I assure you, I handle such matters for my clients with the utmost discretion. You'll want to experience some of the finer things in life now that you have the means. I am a bit of a wine connoisseur myself and would be happy to help you lay down a nice cellar."

Was the man aware that he was rubbing his thumb across his fingertips as if he could feel the money in his hands? The solicitor spoke of buying horses and carriages, clothes and shoes, alongside mistresses, drinking, and gambling, as if they were all legitimate, common expenses for a gentleman of means.

"Not at this time, thank you." Evan was aware that his tone was dry, and the lawyer's brows came down. "I've been to White Haven, my new estate, and the manor is in need of some improvements." Which was stating things rather lightly. "I am in town to find workers and to procure the supplies I will need to start the repairs. I will instruct the vendors to send all invoices here, but I will also require that copies be sent to Mr. Marcus Haverly, who will be acting as my proxy here in London while I return to White Haven to begin the work."

Moody sat back in his chair and stroked his beard with one hand while drumming his fingers on his desk top with the other. "You're going to be in the country overseeing the work yourself? Wouldn't it be better to hire someone to do that? A *gentleman* would send an architect and a builder and would hire a decorator and a steward to accomplish his wishes while he stayed in the capital to enjoy the pleasures of the Season. You can certainly afford it. No true gentleman would sully his hands with such trivial things as . . . home maintenance."

The frown on the older man's face irritated Evan, as did his reference to Evan not acting like a gentleman. He was tired of pretending to be something he was not. And yet there was no escape from the charade. He was an earl, and he would continue being an earl whether he—or the *haute ton*—liked it or not.

"I prefer to have charge of the repairs myself. All I require is that you inspect the invoices and pay them in a timely manner. If you cannot do that, I am sure there are other law firms who would be eager for the opportunity."

By the time Evan left Coles, Franks, and Moody, the solicitor had practically been tripping over himself to accede to Evan's every wish.

The bank was just as accommodating, though they did suggest a guard accompany Evan on his way back to Haverly House, considering the amount of money he'd withdrawn for immediate expenses and purchases. Evan declined, since he'd arranged to meet Marcus on the bank steps at midday, and he would have the carriage.

It was the first of many long days in London for Evan.

All week, as he went from lumberyard to bricklayer to ironmonger, Evan spent money he hadn't earned. He bought materials and tools, and along with Shand, gathered a workforce. With his own townhouse rented for the rest of the Season, he continued to lodge with Marcus, heading back to Mayfair every evening with his mind and his list of things to do still full.

He was eager to get back to White Haven and get work started. This assembling of an army, of having a battle plan, energized him in ways he hadn't felt since Spain. And if he was honest, he wanted to get back to Diana. He missed her, which surprised him. She'd been part of his life for such a short time, and yet she'd begun to feel integral. Not only that, but it was his job to look after her, to protect her and see that she was provided for. He couldn't do that when they were apart.

As he had so many times since returning to London, he unrolled the blueprints of White Haven, which Marcus had procured from the architectural firm that had built the house sixty years before. Thankfully, they were still in business, and had also done the renovations thirty years ago when the previous earl had inherited. Evan ran his finger over the legend for the ground floor. Entry, parlor, dining, breakfast, library, music rooms. Then on the first-floor, bedrooms, dressing rooms, ladies' sitting room, sewing room. And in one wing, rooms labeled "The Royal Apartments." Rooms kept on the chance that a royal personage would grace the house with his or her presence. What a waste. The top floor and cellars were less ornate, with room for the nursery, schoolroom, servants' quarters, kitchens, storerooms, and more. In all, over fifty rooms made up the house. There was no way they could refurbish and repair fifty rooms before Easter. Impossible. They'd have to work on the various areas in some sort of order to prepare for the Prince Regent's visit.

Evan's attention returned to the master suite. Two large sleeping quarters separated by adjoining his-and-her dressing rooms. An entire room each to store clothing in and to dress? And separate bedrooms for the master and mistress. His parents had never had the luxury of separate bedrooms, living as they did in the manse of whatever parish in which his father served, but even if they had the option, Evan doubted they would've used it. Would Diana, raised to be a lady, prefer sleeping apart once they moved into the house? Would the servants expect it of the master and mistress? Living as a family but with so many other people in the house felt like an ordeal he might never get used to. His own mother had never employed so much as a charwoman before, and he was supposed to hire more than a dozen people just to work in his house, never mind all the employees who would toil on the estate?

How thankful he was that he had Diana to help. When it came to estate management, he was as raw as a new recruit. God might have pitch-forked him into this unfamiliar and daunting new arena of the gentry, but perhaps He'd also thrown Evan a lifeline in Diana for a helpmeet.

On the evening of his last day in London, with a caravan of wagons loaded and ready for an early departure, and all the workers housed at an inn on the south side of the river, Evan held his hands to the fire in the study at Haverly House, wondering what he'd forgotten.

"You've accomplished a mountain of work in a very short time." Marcus leaned back in his chair and propped his feet up on the desk. "I wish you'd brought Diana with you though. Word is out now that you're in town without her, and the biddies are clucking about it. I even heard a rumor that you married Diana to get her money, took her off in the carriage, and when you were crossing the Thames, you pitched her in." He grinned. "Now you're back to spend her money, and the Bow Street Runners should be knocking on the door at any moment."

Evan clenched his fists. "That's excellent. I'm a usurper of a title I don't deserve, a fortune hunter, and now a murderer?"

"It was said in jest, I'm sure. The fellow who voiced it was half in his cups at the club." Marcus stopped smiling. "Speaking of which, I met your father-in-law coming out of Boodle's this afternoon. I was walking by, and he crashed into me. The man was completely foxed, and the doorman at the club was not best pleased when the duke appeared ready to bring up his most recent meal onto the steps of the establishment. Seaton's been imbibing rather heavily since your wedding, it seems."

"He's in mourning for his lost fortune, I expect. I am having a difficult time feeling sorry for him, considering everything." Evan took the poker and stirred the fire. "The fact that he kept the inheritance a secret . . . Considering what I know of the man, I shouldn't be surprised, but he forced Diana to keep it a secret too. To lie to me. No doubt she feared what he would do. He'd struck her in the face the night of the Almack's bash. And I don't for a moment believe it was the first time. I won't soon forget he laid hands on Diana." He jabbed at the logs, reducing them to a pile of coals and ash.

"Oh, I'm not feeling sorry for him. Just wondering what will become of him if he continues down his current path. He's got a reputation for scheming, and things tend to work out the way he wants because he doesn't give up. I believe you're probably the first man to ever thwart him and get away with it. But just because he hasn't taken action yet, doesn't mean he won't. He's got the cunning of a Spanish viper." Marcus laced his fingers across his waistcoat. "You might want to be careful. He's a vengeful man as well as a conniver. He won't take lightly your marrying his daughter, but even less the loss of all that money. He might be drunk as an old wheelbarrow at the moment, but you can wager he is hatching some plan to get his hands on at least part of that money."

"What can he do? His daughter is my . . . bride." Evan shouldn't really be calling her his wife, not without them having consummated the marriage. He had thought he was protecting Diana by giving her time to get used to him, to get to know him, before sharing her bed, but perhaps it would be better to make her his wife now. Her father couldn't call for an annulment that way. "And the money is residing in my bank account, where the duke can't get at it. He can drink and rage and scheme all he wants, but what real harm can he do?"

"If I were the duke, I'd think about killing you," Marcus muttered.

Evan turned. "What?"

"I'd kill you. Or have you killed. And soon." He stared at his hands. "Follow my reasoning. His daughter is set to inherit a fortune when she marries. Under British law, the instant she is married, the money belongs to her husband. However, should the husband die before producing an heir, the money would then belong to his daughter, and Seaton would move all the bricks of St. Paul's Cathedral by hand if he had to in order to get her back under his control if she didn't have a husband to protect her."

A shiver went through Evan, but he wasn't sure if it was internal or external. Kill him? For an inheritance? "That's a bit extreme, isn't it? Murder?"

"I'm sure he would make it appear to be an accident. Just be careful, won't you?" Marcus tapped his laced fingers on the backs of his hands. "There's Percival to consider too. Word about town is that he's accrued quite a few gambling debts, pacifying his creditors with promises of money to come. Now his creditors have come calling. He's gone to ground somewhere, though I haven't been able to track him down just yet."

Evan considered Marcus in the glow of the firelight. He looked the picture of relaxation, idle wealth in fine clothing, and yet he seemed to know much about the comings and goings of a lot of people. Was it just that London society was fairly small—a few hundred families at most—or was it something more? He seemed to be interested in knowing what many people were getting up to.

"Why care where Percival has gone? He's not out to kill me, too, is he?" Thoughts of such an ineffectual man as Percival Seaton didn't raise any fear in Evan.

"Not that I've heard, but as I said, I haven't been able to locate him this week. However, death threats aside, I would think *you* would care, having saved his life and all. And now he's your brother-in-law. Saving his life made you a hero, and then an earl, in the first place. What prompted you to run out on that battlefield like that?"

The abrupt change in topic startled Evan. In an instant, the room seemed to close in around him as his mind rocketed from the chilly London study to the summer heat of Salamanca. What had prompted him to race into danger in Spain? Though he could hear the sounds of cannon and rifle, the screams of horses and men, though he could smell the smoke and blood and dirt, he couldn't bring the battle action into focus. He clenched the arms of the chair, his eyes narrowing. Pain radiated from the back of his neck up across the top of his head. He took a deep breath, in through his nose, out through his mouth, trying to stay calm. A flash of an image, then another . . .

"I was running down a slope. I needed a horse quickly because I had to get back behind the lines to our command post . . ." The words came out as if he recited the story of another man. "I had a message for my commanding officer . . ." His voice trailed off as he stared into the fire, concentrating so hard, sweat popped out on his brow.

"What message?" Though Marcus asked in a soft voice, there was something in his tone that said he was anything but asking casually.

"It was vital." Evan wracked his memories, feeling as if he stood in a pool of light in an otherwise darkened room as images and bits and sounds and thoughts whirled around him. He closed his eyes, grabbing at the wispy tail of memory. "I intercepted a spy—"

The door crashed open, and the Duchess of Haverly swept in. "Marcus, get your feet off that desk and behave like the gentleman I raised you to be."

The memory snapped from Evan's mental grasp and evaporated. Weakness radiated from his core, seeping through him like water across a stone floor. Slamming his eyes shut, he searched his head for the memory, but it was gone. He breathed hard, as if he'd run a great distance. He wanted to shout at the duchess for interrupting. He'd been on the cusp of remembering. But what?

A spy? He'd intercepted a spy?

He had been running down a hill. Toward the battle . . . but from the French side? That couldn't be right. In the normal course of events, he would've had his rifle and been perched on some high ground, picking off the enemy's officers one by one. But there had been a message to deliver? Another oddity, because he was a lieutenant, and if he had word for his commander, he would've sent an enlisted man instead of leaving his post to deliver it himself. He only would've relayed the message himself if it had been of the utmost urgency and secrecy. He opened his eyes.

The duchess shot him a hard look. He'd been so preoccupied with his memories, he'd forgotten to rise at her entrance. He pushed himself upright. "Good evening, Your Grace." This was his first encounter with the duchess since returning to London, and he was not sorry.

"Hmm. The butler tells me you'll be leaving tomorrow?" She wore a green frock, diamonds draped about her creped throat and ostrich feathers wafting above her iron-gray curls. "It's all over town that you shunted your bride off to the country and left her there. Shameful, that's what it is. How you can expect to be accepted into London society when you behave like a"—she waved her beringed hand, as if searching for the right descriptor, only to shrug, as if it exceeded her vocabulary to describe him—"man of no breeding, is beyond me. You should be making your appearances at the opera, the theater, dinner parties. And you should bring your bride and show everyone how happy you are." She sniffed and fingered the quizzing glass hanging from a ribbon around her neck. "Marcus, your sister will be arriving tomorrow, and I expect you to be here to greet her. She's created one excuse after another why she should stay in the country, but

I've lost my patience. Sophie might be engaged and no longer needing the Marriage Mart, but she won't do herself any favors pining away in the country until her fiancé returns. Why you men get delusions of grandeur and head off to war is beyond me. Baron Richardson should be here, and we should be preparing for the wedding of the Season."

Marcus rolled his eyes.

"Sophie's never much cared for town, and Rich is doing his duty as a Royal Marine. You'd be better to blame old Boney for prolonging this war than the brave men who have been and are still fighting it." Marcus's tone had a bit of bite to it, unusual when he spoke of or to his mother.

She scowled. "I might know you'd take the opposite side from my views. Marcus, why must you always vex me so?" She sailed out of the room as abruptly as she'd arrived, closing the door with vigor.

Evan massaged his temples. Maybe if he tried, he could remember . . .

"You said you'd encountered a spy?" Marcus returned to the topic. "How? What did you learn?" He leaned forward, one fist on the desk.

What could Evan say? That he didn't remember? That he couldn't recall much of anything from that day? That would lead to more questions he couldn't answer. He chose to treat the situation lightly, at least until more of his memory returned—if it ever did.

"And look what it got me. I ran onto the battlefield, wound up rescuing the Prince Regent's godson, and I have to dress up and play the fine gentleman for the rest of my life. I really can't talk about military secrets. I've told you too much already." He pressed his hands against his thighs and pushed himself upright, stretching and faking a yawn, praying Marcus wouldn't ask him anything more. "I've got an early start in the morning, so I'd best head to bed. Thank you again for your hospitality and help."

Marcus eyed him, creases forming between his brows. "I'll continue on with the other things you've left for me to do, and I'll be down to White Haven soon." He rose, started to say something and thought better of it, then rubbed his palm against the back of his neck beneath his longish hair. "I know your estate seems a long way from London, but be careful all the same. Watch over Diana, and don't underestimate Seaton.

He won't accept this without a fight, and when he does fight, he won't play fair."

Evan firmed his resolve. "If it's a fight he wants, I'd say I have more experience. Perhaps he should be wary of me."

"Do you think it will be today?"

Diana gave a small sigh. The maid had asked the same question every day for the last week. Glancing at her homemade calendar on the desk, Diana didn't need to count to know Evan had been gone for eleven days.

In some ways the time had gone quickly, and in others the days had stretched out to feel like a hundred.

Eleven days at this inn lavishing attention on Cian, cuddling, singing, rocking, admiring his sweet smiles that came with more frequency. Eleven days without fear of an angry outburst from her father, a sly dig or slap from her brother. But also eleven days of worrying and wondering if the duke would send someone for the baby, and she would be powerless to stop him. Eleven days—and nights—of wondering about her new husband, about where he was, what he was doing. Eleven days of remembering that almost kiss and being filled with an odd longing and regret that it hadn't happened. Wondering if they could be happy together and wondering when he would choose to exercise his marital rights.

Evan had been in a rush to make her his bride, but not to make her his wife. How was she supposed to fulfill her duty of providing him with an heir if they never shared a marriage bed? Certainly the flight from London and his quick return to the city had interrupted things, but beyond that near kiss, he'd made no advances of a romantic nature.

Which did little for a girl's confidence.

Perhaps when he returned they would sort things out.

"I hope he gets here soon. Time is getting away from us." She'd circled the eighteenth of April as the date by which she hoped they would have the major repairs finished. The eighteenth was Easter Sunday, which the prince would surely observe in London. He was the current titular head of the Church of England, after all. Following Easter, he would venture to Brighton and could arrive here as soon as the nineteenth, though she hoped he would wait until the beginning of May before heading south.

If only the prince had specified a day, and a duration, for his stay, she could arrange things better. She didn't care if plans changed, but she needed to know there was one in the first place. Strategizing gave her a sense of security and control, something she'd had precious little of in her life.

Diana rose from the desk and gathered her papers, butting them into a neat pile and slipping them into the leather folder that had become her constant companion. Pencils went into loops inside, and she gathered her reticule. "I'm going to the manor. I'm not sure what time I will return, but it will be before dark."

Beth nodded. A snuffling cry came from the adjoining room. "He'll be wanting a feed and a cuddle, I expect." She hopped up from her chair, her cap slipping on her head.

Torn between wanting to stay with Cian and needing to get on with her work, Diana wrapped her cloak around herself and donned her riding gloves. "I must fly. I've finished the ground floor, and today I'll be working upstairs."

The local vicar had generously made his gig and horse available for her use, and when she reached the taproom, the innkeeper sent one of the hostlers out to hitch up for her.

"Good morning, my lady." He'd certainly been helpful and deferential, especially when he realized they would be his guests for an extended period, guarantee custom in his best rooms, and make weekly payments faithfully.

Diana had but to ask, and he tripped over himself to fulfill her request. "Good morning. Would you see that there is plenty of coal for our fires? And that a can of hot water is ready for when I return? And please tell the cook how much I enjoyed breakfast." She tied the strings of her bonnet. "I'll be away until evening."

Hooves clopped on the cobbles outside, and she glanced up from threading her wrist through her reticule strings. The hostler had been quick.

But it wasn't her gig waiting. It was a carriage. The Duke of Haverly's crest gleamed on the door, and the matched grays steamed gently in the midmorning sun.

Her heart thudded, and her breath caught when the door opened and Evan's dark head, hatless, emerged. He wore a many-caped cloak that parted as he moved, showing his uniform beneath. He turned his broad shoulders sideways to get through the carriage door, hopped down, not bothering with the step, and strode toward the inn, his tall black boots gleaming. Gone was the hesitancy and any favoring of his leg, as he had done at his investiture. He looked lithe and athletic, bursting with vitality.

And he was her husband.

The thought sent a tremor through her as she reacquainted herself with his face and form.

Mr. Shand jumped down behind him.

Diana stepped onto the stoop as Evan approached. "Welcome back, my lord."

He stopped, looking her over from hem to hair. She wore her most serviceable boots, dark-blue dress, and brown cloak. Her hair was pulled back into an ordinary knot, and her bonnet had no adornment beyond a ribbon tie. As he stared, she became self-conscious of her plain attire, wishing she'd opted for something more attractive to wear for his arrival.

With a half smile, he closed the distance between them, his hands spread as if he might embrace her, but at the last minute, he stopped. "Good morning."

Diana was aware of Shand's eyes on her and the innkeeper behind her, but mostly of the deep blue of Evan's eyes, so close to hers. Then he bent and bussed her cheek with a quick kiss.

Her skin tingled.

"You're going out?"

"P-pardon?" She tried to gather her wits and not appear a simple-minded miss knocked off center by her handsome man's attention.

The parson's gig arrived, with the placid piebald mare in the traces and the hostler holding the reins.

He motioned to her bag and folder. "You were going out?"

"Oh yes." A bustle of noise and voices drew her attention. Behind the carriage a row of wagons came down the road, full of people and cargo. "What is all this?"

He grinned, and her stomach swooped. Two deep creases formed in his cheeks. Had she ever seen him smile so broadly?

"Remember how you said it would take an army of workers to get the estate repaired?" With a broad flourish, he waved toward the oncoming wagons. "This is that army."

Men climbed down, some gray haired, some missing limbs or eyes or carrying canes. The halt and the lame. Diana looked from the growing crowd to Evan and back again. "Who are they?" *And how on earth are they going to help us fix White Haven? Some of them can barely walk.*

"Veterans. Either wounded in battle or mustered out because of age. Some came from St. Bart's, where I was hospitalized, and the rest came from other places in the city. Shand seems to have an entire network of contacts, and when he sent word, they arrived in droves."

His smile wasn't dimmed as the men gathered around. "We made quite the caravan leaving the city, didn't we, men?"

Those closest nodded and grinned, and several dragged their hats from their heads, staring at Diana. Her cheeks warmed at the scrutiny.

"Men, this is Lady Whitelock. You can call her my lady or ma'am. She will be your mistress and your countess, so treat her with respect." Evan's voice had taken on a challenging tone, but his eyes twinkled. "You're as rapscallion a bunch as I've ever seen, but I know you'll serve your lady well." There was a hint of steel, a warning perhaps? Or possessiveness?

Diana nodded to those nearby, and was rewarded with shy bows and tugged forelocks.

"There are some skilled workmen in the bunch too. I simply had to hire experts for some of the repairs, but not many. Oh, and lest I forget, there are a few women in the bunch. Most of these men are married, but until we have proper lodgings for their families, they've come alone. But I thought there would be some need of ladies to help you right away." Evan motioned to Shand, who brought four women to meet Diana.

"Mrs. Bradford, Mrs. Halcott, Mrs. Reedscome, and her daughter, Daisy."

The women bobbed curtsies as Diana took in their shawls, caps, and red cheeks. "Please, go into the taproom and warm yourselves. What a cold journey you've had in those open wagons."

"Sergeant Bradford!" Evan raised his voice.

"Yes, sir." A stout man with a bristle of gray whiskers on his chin came forward. He snapped his heels together and stood at attention. His left sleeve had been folded up to the elbow and pinned to cover the missing forearm.

"I'm placing you in charge here at the inn. Find billets for all the men and the ladies. We'll probably have to take over the stable loft here and possibly spill over to another inn if there is one in town. Tell the innkeeper he'll be well compensated. Shand, bring the tradesmen with us, and the supplies. We pressed on at dawn so as not to waste time, and I know the men are eager to get to work."

Evan had no trouble issuing orders, and Diana could see him in command of soldiers on the battlefield.

He turned to her. "I'm sorry to rush away when I've only just gotten back, but everything took longer than I anticipated in London. As it is, I wasn't able to accomplish everything. Marcus is seeing to some things."

Her brows rose. "I'll come with you. I was going to the estate, in any case." She indicated the open gig. "I haven't been idle in your absence."

"Haven't you now?" He opened the carriage door. "What have you been up to?"

"Wait and see." She apologized to the hostler for the inconvenience, and he turned the vicar's gig around and headed toward the stables.

Shand joined them in the carriage, and the talk was of which men would be best suited to which tasks, and who had skills and who would need training. Diana listened, seeing a new side to her husband as he laid his plans. Since she'd met him, it seemed as if either she or Marcus had been guiding him in the ways of the peerage, but now he was confident, as if finally on solid ground, directing men, making plans. His conversation gave her a chance to study him, admiring the way his cheeks had filled out some since she'd first met him and how his skin didn't look as finely drawn. As the carriage jostled, his thigh brushed hers, and their shoulders bumped from time to time, and Diana didn't try to stop it from happening. She found the contact pleasant, exciting even.

The still-broken gates to White Haven stood open, and as they passed through, Diana's stomach clenched. Would he approve of the work she'd had done? Or would he think her place was back at the inn, waiting until it was time to pick out paint colors or wallpaper or china patterns? Or would he take care of that himself too? Hire someone to come in and decorate? He had such a commanding air about him. Would he resent any intrusion on her part? She wished she knew him better so she could anticipate his reactions.

The house looked the same from the outside, being swallowed by brambles and vines, windows staring out like blank eyes. Evan strode to the front door, grasped the doorknob, and paused. "You had it fixed?"

Diana nodded, clutching her folder over her chest. "The local blacksmith repaired the latch, and he sent his apprentice to install it."

He swung the door open. It still squealed on its hinges, but it no longer dragged the floor. This time no birds flew up in alarm. Instead, the front hall was empty of plaster and debris. Cobwebs had been brushed away and the worst dust removed. Though the floor needed repair in some places, it had been swept clean. A sturdy ladder stood in the center of the hall. Only yesterday Diana had been atop it with a broom, brushing down the walls to remove the worst of the dirt.

Shand gave a low whistle from the doorway.

Gaping, Evan stepped inside and turned a slow circle. "How did this happen?"

Diana couldn't tell if he was pleased or just surprised. She rushed to explain. "I knew the first thing we would have to do would be clean. We can't even evaluate what needs repairs until we clear out the mess. So Louisa, Greville, and several ladies from the town have been coming daily to make things as tidy as possible. You remember Louisa Monroe and Greville, her grandfather?"

"How could I forget?" He rubbed his hand along the back of his neck. "He almost shot me."

She nodded. "He doesn't even remember that. Bits of his memory elude him. He's losing his mind, but he's harmless . . . without the gun."

Evan's head came up, and his gaze sharpened. "He doesn't remember pointing a gun at me?"

"He truly doesn't. In all my encounters with him, he's never mentioned it. In fact, there are days when I have to remind him again who I am and that the old earl is dead."

"I'm not doubting you. I've heard of people losing their memories before."

He had a wry twist to his lips, and Diana wondered if one or more of the men he'd brought with him were suffering the same issues as Mr. Monroe. There had been quite a few older men in the work crew, though none so old as Greville.

The door in the far wall opened, and Louisa came through, a basket under her arm. She'd tied her hair up under a kerchief, and her apron bore signs that she'd already been hard at work. She halted, staring at Shand before turning her attention to Diana and Evan.

"Oh my. I didn't know you were here." She bent her knees slightly. "My lady, the kitchens are nearly cleared out. Grandfather's been sweeping out the scullery and the larder. What would you like him to do next?"

Diana shook her head. In her efforts to prove that her grandfather was still useful, Louisa had been keeping him busy.

"Make sure he rests and that he stays warm. Then he can help you in the laundry rooms. The earl has brought many workers back with him, so please prepare your grandfather. I don't want him to be startled when they start hammering and the like."

"Yes, ma'am." She bowed her head quickly to Evan, sent a sharp look Shand's way, and disappeared to the back of the house once more.

"There's so much to be done." Evan clasped his hands behind his back. "But at least we can begin the work properly now."

Suddenly shy, unsure, Diana toyed with the edge of her folder as she held it with crossed arms to her chest. "There are a few things I'd like to talk to you about, if you have the time. You and Mr. Shand, since I assume he's going to take over the role of steward?"

Shand looked out the open doorway at the wagons pulling into the still-weedy and rutted drive. "Sir, the men are here and raring to go."

"Get them started hauling in the supplies and materials, and then join us in the dining room for another council of war."

Evan put his hand at the small of Diana's back to guide her into the next room, and she felt the pressure there, aware of how infrequently he had touched her. His kiss still lingered on her cheek, and her fingertips brushed the spot.

The dining room, though in need of much work, looked a different place than the last time he had seen it, and she watched his reaction. All the plaster blown off the ceiling by the gunshot had been swept away, and the chairs had been placed around the clean table.

"Won't you sit? I'd like to show you how I've been spending some of my time." She set her folder on the table and untied the cloth tapes holding it shut.

He turned one of the chairs beside her and straddled it, crossing his arms on the back and resting his chin on his wrists. She'd never seen a gentleman sit that way before, and she was sure it wasn't proper. Perhaps it was a soldier's mannerism and perfectly acceptable for a military man.

Sounds of movement came from the foyer as the men carted in supplies. Shand didn't believe in letting the grass grow under his feet, did he? When Evan gave an order, it was done.

With trembling fingers, she laid out the pages into neat stacks. "I thought a systematic approach might be best. I know there are structural issues to consider, such as mending the staircase and repairing the roof, but I went room by room and made lists of what will need to be replaced, what can be repaired, and what should be altered. I've included lists of furnishings, rugs, lamps, and the like, as well as some possible color schemes." She spoke quickly, wanting to get it all out before he passed judgment.

Would he think she'd assumed too much? Would he look on her work as the mere jottings of a woman, not to be considered?

Shand cleared his throat behind them. "Sir, I believe you've spliced yourself to a real gem here, if you don't mind me saying so. She's done a heap of work for us."

Diana's heart glowed a bit at the sergeant's praise, but she waited for what her husband would say. She kept back the most personal pages, the sketches she'd done of how she hoped the house would look someday. Her father had sneered at what he called "her little drawings," considering them of no account. Diana had forsaken showing anyone her artwork, for fear of further scorn. She loved to draw and to design, but she knew better than to put her work forward. Lists were one thing. Revealing her heart by showing her drawings was another thing altogether.

Evan picked up one page after another, reading here and there, fanning the papers out. Finally, he sat up. "These are excellent. I couldn't have done it better myself."

She let out a breath, trying to quell the smile that *would* break through. His words pleased her far more than they ought, but she treasured them anyway.

Loud noises came from the foyer, and they watched as man after man, some with crutches, some with wooden legs or hooks, carried in lumber, crates of nails, and boxes of tools. Diana was amazed at how they got on with the work despite their wounds, but doubts crept in. Cheerful and willing they might be, but how could this ragtag bunch ever complete all the repairs the house needed? And in a short time?

Evan still couldn't quite grasp all the work his wife had accomplished in his absence, and with little help and no direction from him. Every room on the lower floor had been swept out and cleared. Most of the furniture that was still useable had been brought to the drawing room on the main floor, one of the few rooms where the windows were still intact.

And her lists. The job he'd been least looking forward to was now well on the way to being finished. She wrote with a beautiful hand, much better than the claw marks his own writing resembled. Lists of furnishings, lists of measurements for draperies and wall coverings and trim, lists of linens and household goods, china, cookware, cleaning supplies, room by room she'd gone through the entire house.

Even now she bent over the stacks of pages, organizing, searching for something. "Ah, here it is. My list of lists." She held up the paper, triumph in her eyes.

"You have a list of your lists?" Evan couldn't keep the amusement from his voice, but regretted it as she slowly lowered the paper and uncertainty clouded her eyes. "That's most industrious of you. I wouldn't have thought of that."

She nodded, glancing away. Sunshine from the window lit her profile, and he drew a deep breath.

He'd missed her, which was odd, since she had been in his life such a short time. But when he'd seen her on the stoop of the inn, he'd almost put his arms around her then and there. He could smell her scent, flowers and soap and femininity. And the rustle of her skirts, the way she tucked her hair behind her ear, the way she pinched her lower lip when she wasn't sure about something. For all his adult life, he'd lived in a male-dominated universe. To have the care and companionship of a woman such as Diana both scared and fascinated him. Everything about her was foreign and yet intriguing.

He could still feel the softness of her cheek against his lips, the tickle of the hair at her temple as it brushed his nose, and the fineness of her skin, translucent and smooth. Evan swallowed and clenched and unclenched his fists.

Diana tapped her papers into a pile and returned them to the leather folder, leaving the "list of lists" on the top as she gathered everything. They went into the entry hall, where the men moved back and forth with their loads.

He could read the doubts in her face as she watched his cobbled-together workforce. They wouldn't win any prizes for beauty, but what she didn't know was the courage that dwelt behind the scars. These men had seen battle and survived. They had done without, endured, and overcome in situations she couldn't even dream of. Learning carpentry, gardening, farming, horsemanship . . . these would be nothing. They deserved better than to be cast off from the army as unnecessary.

While he was proud of them, shame hollowed out his chest. If only he could count himself amongst them. He had seen battle, he had recovered from his wounds . . . outwardly. But inside, in his mind and heart, he was still bleeding, still shattered. The nightmares stalked him, the sense of impending doom, the panic he tried to lock away but that swarmed over him like a breach in the line every time he let down his guard.

He'd captured a spy? Had he been able to get any information out of the man? Had he been able to convey the information to his superiors? Or was he imagining things? He couldn't bring the prisoner's face into focus.

Was he making things up, or did he really know something important? The house began to close in around him, his collar began to tighten, and his breath to come faster. He needed to return to the present, to focus on the tasks before him.

"Shand, find those you think best suited to the outdoor work, and assemble them on the drive. Set them to clearing all that rubbish off the front of the house so we can see if the stonework is still intact." He offered his arm to Diana. "I'm going to walk the exterior. Would you like to come with me on the inspection? I would value your input."

Her bow of a mouth opened, and surprise hit her brown eyes. Had no one ever said that to her before? Evan considered what he knew of her father and brother. Most likely not.

Would her father really try to kill Evan? It seemed so absurd and far-fetched. Especially given the "gentility" of the aristocracy. Nobles talked and talked, but what did they actually do? Seaton had shown his true colors, a drunkard, a liar, and not above hitting a woman, but he was too much of a coward to come after a man. Evan didn't fear cowards.

Diana hesitated as she raised her hand to his elbow, and he realized he was frowning. He smoothed his expression into one more cordial. Thoughts of her family always made him frown. How could someone so sweet have come from a scoundrel like Seaton? He led her outside, grateful to breathe the fresh air and push away lingering memories of the battlefield.

Studying the facade, he scowled. "What a mess. Bracken and brambles everywhere."

"But graceful lines. I love the proportions and the symmetry of the windows. Once the glass is replaced and the woodwork painted bright white, they will be beautiful." Diana tilted her head to look into one of the broken panes. "I love how the center of the house is tall and spare, but the wings either side are lower and spreading. The ballroom is here on the north end. Can't you see it, well lit, great golden blocks of lamplight spilling out as the dancers turn and sway and music fills the air?"

Evan helped her down a pair of steps, puzzling over the layout of the grounds and the way the broken path seemed to turn back on itself in the midst of the weeds and high grass. "What did this area even used to be? There are flagstones here, but they don't lead anywhere."

"These are the parterre gardens. Imagine these box hedges and yews trimmed down to knee height, with flowers planted within the borders. Formal, geometric plantings. That gnarled tree in the center is probably an apple tree, which will flower in the spring. Can't you just see it?" She removed her arm from his and turned in a half circle. "A fountain at the far end and an arbor with a bench beneath it. Climbing roses and clematis and wallflowers on trellises." She pointed to a brick enclosure. "Behind that wall is the space for the kitchen gardens. And next to that, you won't believe it. There's an orangery."

"A what?" He followed her gaze to a tall, many-windowed building perhaps fifty yards away.

"An orangery. At one time, when it was properly heated, it held more than two dozen orange trees, lemon trees, and maybe some banana palms too. It seems the previous earl was quite a botanist. Either that or he really enjoyed tropical fruit. Can you imagine having oranges whenever you wanted?"

"We did once, in Spain." He narrowed his eyes, remembering. "At one point, that was all our troop had to eat. The supply chain had been cut off, and we bivouacked in an orange grove. For nearly a week, it was nothing but oranges, morning and night. I was never so glad to see salted beef and oat porridge in my life as when the supply wagons rolled in." He could still remember the Spaniard who'd protested them eating his crop. But war was like that, and they lived off the land as much as they could. Even if it was someone else's land. Now he wondered how he would've reacted if it was his property that had been overrun, his crop that had been devoured. Guilt settled into his middle.

They reached the edge of a glade that sloped away from the back of the house, and Evan paused. Stacked stone fences crumbled here and there, and hedges had grown wild, with unwanted species of trees forcing their way up through what had once been neatly laid-out fields. What had grown here? Wheat? Barley? Oats? Hops? Or had this been pastureland for cattle and sheep?

"Greville Monroe, if his memory can be trusted, tells me the estate runs to more than three thousand hectares. Two thousand of those used to be under production, crops, cattle, and orchards, with another thousand of woodland and the lake. There is a succession house where plants are started and seeds stored. And granaries, barns, and farmyards. Someday we can create quite the ramble through the woods, and there is a boathouse somewhere along the shore and a summer pavilion for parties. White Haven will become one of the most beautiful properties in England if we do it right."

Evan stared at her, and she stopped talking, the words dying to silence.

"I'm sorry. I have overstepped." She tucked her chin, her arms tightening around the folder. "You know what is best for the estate. I'll keep my thoughts to myself."

"No, it isn't that. I'm just wondering if all women are like you."

Her head came up, eyes questioning.

"Everywhere I look, I see overgrown, broken-down shambles. But when you look at it, you see graceful lines, serene paths, blooming flowers, and possibilities." He pointed to her folder. "You can see the parlor furnished and the dining room with the cherubs restored. I'll admit that I don't have much experience with women, but I had imagined you'd be in despair at the monumental task of bringing this place up to scratch, and here you are already seeing the finished results in your mind."

He took the folder from her grasp and threaded her arm through his elbow. "And don't keep your thoughts to yourself. I find them refreshing and encouraging."

When they reached the stable block, south of the west-facing house, he stopped. The stone building spread wide, with an opening in the middle to drive carriages through to the inner yard. Slate tiles had broken off the roof, leaving gaps, and weeds grew almost to the barred windows, but above all rose a beautiful clock tower. Though missing the hands, the clock faces looked austerely out over the property from each side of the cupola.

"I was out here taking inventory yesterday." Diana took back the folder and riffled through it, pulling out a page and consulting one of her lists. "There are boxes for forty horses, and quarters for coachmen and grooms above the stables. A carriage house, harness room, feed rooms. It takes a lot of horses to run an estate this size." She peered over one of the open half doors in the stable yard. "Can you imagine all these boxes filled?"

For the first time, Evan felt he had caught her vision, the way she could see a positive future when she looked at the house and grounds. "I *can* imagine it." He went from one box to the next. The stables had fared better than the house, and it wouldn't take much to have them ready for occupants. The thought that had been niggling at the back of his mind for some time blossomed. "But . . ."

"But what?"

"You'll think me daft."

Her delicately arched brows rose, and her eyes filled with questions.

"Perhaps I already do." A saucy grin touched her lips. "After all, you married me without so much as a courtship and brought me to this grand estate with undue haste, so quickly that we're now living in an inn." She waved her hand at the wreckage that was their property. "Perhaps you're as daft as a duck."

Which hit rather close to home, though she didn't know it. He hesitated, knowing what he wanted would be considered sheer folly to people of her class. It would be sheer folly to most anyone, except perhaps a military man.

"What are you thinking?" she asked. "And I promise not to laugh."

He took a deep breath and then plunged.

"That first week, after I was made an earl"—it still sounded strange—"Marcus was showing me around town and getting me kitted out like a gentleman. He took me to Tattersall's to look for suitable carriage and riding horses—which I still don't have." He remembered the encounter with Fitzroy and Diana's brother, Percival, and their invitation to visit the high-class prostitutes of King's Place, and his collar grew tight. "In the back of the stables at Tattersall's, they kept a pen of horses that didn't have a very bright future ahead of them."

She tilted her head, listening, toying with her lower lip, drawing his attention. "What kind of horses?"

"Military horses. Cavalry and artillery horses no longer useful to the army. In some cases they'd been wounded. In others they'd just become old or lame. Or they could no longer face the guns, the sounds and smells and sights of the battlefield. Surprising that they were even shipped home." He pressed his lips together. "The army tries to recoup some of their investment by selling them, mostly as cart or hackney coach horses. Those that do not sell wind up at the knacker's yard. I know we would need suitable carriage horses for traveling to London, and perhaps mounts for riding and hunting, but what would you say if I told you I wanted to bring cast-off army horses here to White Haven and either rehabilitate them into useful animals or give them an easy retirement?"

She stopped pinching her lip and instead tucked it behind her teeth, all levity gone. He stood still, waiting, knowing she would think him a soft-headed buffoon.

"Why would you ask me? You are the earl. You can do as you wish."

Though he had known they would need to speak of it at some future date, he hadn't anticipated doing so in the chilly, broken-down stable yard. How to broach the subject? Candor was best. After all, they couldn't go their entire lives without speaking of the subject.

"It's the money." The money that was making all this possible but which he wished had never existed. That newspaper article that made him out to be a tuft-hunter, lining his pockets with someone else's gold, had sat heavily on his mind for days. Several of the merchants he had spoken to in London had hinted that he'd only married Diana because she brought such riches with her. One slyboots had even declared that he was astonished at the speed with which Evan was spending his wife's money. It had stuck in Evan's craw.

"While in my head I can justify spending your inheritance on the house, because we have no choice but to prepare for a Royal Visit, and because you need a fit place to live, in my heart it is harder to reconcile. Pensioning off derelict army horses, that would be my own idea, not something you would ever need or the prince would ever see. Yet, I would need your inheritance money to make it happen. Though the law says that money is mine to spend as I wish, it rightly belongs to you. Spending it on things that benefit you is right and good. Spending it on something selfish for my own pleasure doesn't sit well."

Raising her gloved fingers to her lips, she shook her head. "You're a strange man."

"I have heard that said before." He shoved his hands into his pockets, uncomfortable to be the subject of such study, frustration at his London encounters boiling up, frustration at the entire situation and being helpless to change it. "I feel like a kept man, living on someone else's money. It's one thing to receive the capital from the former earl's estate. That was a kind of reward, I suppose, for what happened at Salamanca." Not that he deserved that either. He hadn't even known he was saving Percival Seaton's life, much less that he was the godson of the Prince Regent.

Flashes of the battlefield crashed through his mind, and he could feel the panic strangling his airway, the thud of his heart as it raced. His fears of being inadequate to the task of being an earl warred with his already battle-weary mind. He kicked a pile of leaves, the words bursting out. "I'm thrust into this farce, where I am supposed to pretend to be something I'm not. Nothing is mine. Nothing is me. I'm a soldier. I'm a common man." He pounded his chest with his fist, trying to draw in a decent breath as his mind lurched through the smoke and cannon fire, searching for the memory that eluded him, the thing that felt so urgent that sweat broke out on his skin. "I didn't ask for any of this. Not the title, not the lands, not the money, not the wife. I feel as if God has played some awful joke on me."

Her face went gray, and she flinched, as if he'd struck her.

Then he realized what he'd said, but it was too late to call back the words. Angry with himself, angry at the futility of his memory and his inability to control his chaotic thoughts, he whirled and slammed his open hand against the top half of one of the doors, crashing it shut so hard it splintered and fell to the cobbles.

Diana leapt back, and he shook his hand, the pain radiating up his arm. Why had he done that? What was happening to him? He wasn't given to displays of temper, and yet he could barely control the rage misting his vision with red.

"The money was never mine. It was never meant to be mine." She stood stiffly, her folder held like armor, frost riming her words. "My grandmother left that money in trust because she knew if she left it to me, my father would find a way to seize control of it. He nearly purloined it anyway, first by planning to sell me as a bride to one of his cronies and then by forcing me to keep it a secret from you, hoping to forge your signature and steal it." She looked away, not meeting his eyes. "I have always known it would never be mine. Grandmother used it as a way to exact revenge on my father. I was just the means to her end."

Erica Vetsch

She blinked hard, and when he saw the flash of silvery tears on her lashes, the anger dissipated, bleeding off slowly.

Her lips trembled. "You say you had no choice in your circumstances, but I would charge that you had more say than I will ever have."

She left him standing in the stable yard as dead leaves skittered over the cobbles.

167

CHAPTER 10

"MY LORD, IF you have a moment?" The innkeeper stood in the doorway as the maid cleared away the remains of breakfast.

Evan scrubbed his hands down his face. In the week since he'd returned from London, he'd done nothing but make decisions and solve problems. Except the problem of repairing the damage he had done to his fragile relationship with his bride.

He didn't seem to be gaining any ground on that front.

"I'll leave you alone." Diana pushed her chair back.

Evan shook his head. "No, stay, please. What is it?" he asked the innkeeper. Perhaps, if the innkeeper made it quick, there would be time to at least talk to Diana before the responsibilities of the day crowded in.

"My lord, it's . . . your men." He throttled his bar towel.

"Are they causing trouble?" Sergeant Bradford was a strict man, and he hadn't reported any of the men getting out of line.

"Oh no, my lord, it's just that they're filling up every corner of the inn and stables. My kitchen is overstretched, and the bill for the victuals is substantial. You're being most generous, my lord," he hurried to assure, "but my help is beginning to protest the workload." He shifted his weight. "I don't mean to tell you your business, but would it not be less expensive to house them in the estate cottages? Or are you already considering that?"

Evan closed his eyes, leaning back. The estate cottages. He'd forgotten all about them. In the rush of work on the manor house and grounds, the tenant cottages had slipped his mind. He hadn't even inspected them.

"Thank you. I'll look into it." He grimaced. What had he come to, needing to be reminded of his obligations by an innkeeper?

"Very good, sir."

Diana rubbed her fingertip across her lower lip in that way that was becoming familiar to him. It meant she was thinking hard.

"I suppose you should get out your paper. We're going to need more lists."

She reached behind her for the folder on the desk and slipped out a page. In a trice, she set the paper before him.

"'Cottage Repairs and Supplies.' You remembered the tenant houses? Why didn't you say anything?" But he knew why. Ever since his tantrum in the stable yard, she had kept herself aloof. Helpful, courteous, but remote. And she hadn't voiced her opinion voluntarily. If he asked, she would tell him what she thought, but she was wary of him.

Which only made him feel more ashamed. He should apologize, but how could he without revealing the turmoil behind his words and actions? His lack of control over his memory, his emotions, his reactions? If he couldn't stop it happening over and over, his apologies would carry no weight.

"I thought you would get to them when you could. I haven't been round them, but I spoke with Louisa and Greville, and she drew a map of the estate and where the cottages are and their sizes. I made a preliminary list of things such as thatching, mortar, furnishings, and firing that will most likely be needed." She sorted out another page with a rough-drawn map. In the center was the large shape of the house and stables, and dotted over the property were squares that represented cottages. He counted a score and more.

Responsibility settled heavily around his shoulders.

He ran his eye down the line of items jotted on the list. It was as neat and well thought out as everything she did. "Would you like to come on the inspection tour? You could polish this list and make it more accurate." Which wasn't much of a selling point, but he couldn't think of another way to let her know he wanted her with him. "We could ride. It would be a good way to see the rest of the estate. There are horses for livery here."

For the first time in days, light shone in her eyes, and he took heart that he had pleased her. Perhaps his suggestion would act as a peace offering, an olive branch of sorts.

"I would enjoy that."

He pushed himself out of his chair. "Excellent. You can change and meet me in the stable yard."

Shand was not enamored of the idea of riding horseback. "I'm infantry, sir." He eyed with suspicion the shaggy beast before him that looked like he'd rather be taking a nap than crossing the countryside. "And enlisted, at that. Enlisted infantry doesn't ride."

Evan stroked the animal's nose. "If you're going to be the estate steward, you're going to have to get used to traveling on horseback. Someday, hopefully before I shuffle off this mortal coil, White Haven will be a prosperous, self-supporting estate, and you will need to know every inch of it. We'll start today."

His former sergeant grumbled but stopped mid-complaint, his jaw dropping. Evan turned to where he was looking.

Would he ever get used to her beauty? Diana came toward them, clothed in a riding habit of deepest blue, a cunning hat on her head, with a short veil that ended just below her chin. She carried a riding crop and looked a picture.

And she was his. Again he felt the overwhelming desire to protect her. From her father, and . . . from himself. He couldn't let his temper and anxiety affect her. He would do better.

The groom came out leading two more horses, these sleeker and more nimble-looking than Shand's. "They're both good horses, my lord. Either would be suitable for the lady, but I saddled the mare for the countess. There's a mounting block too."

"Thank you." Evan took the reins of the chestnut gelding, and the groom looped the bay's reins over her head.

When Evan swung into the saddle, his head whirled, and the images flashed again behind his eyelids. He'd been racing down a hill on foot, dodging and weaving to present a difficult target to anyone aiming his way. *Faster, he must go faster.* A bullet whizzed by his head, and he took a misstep, tumbling down the slope. Scrambling, Evan tried to get to his feet, disoriented from the fall. Bullets whistled through the air and thwacked the ground around him, kicking up gouts of sandy dirt. Dodging, weaving, he looked for cover. He couldn't stop. The information he carried was too precious. It had to do with the spy, he was sure . . .

But what was it? What was the message he knew was so important but couldn't remember?

The feel of the horse beneath him . . . through the smoke and dust, he'd spied the horse tethered to an artillery wagon, his teammate down and still. The living horse plunged and bucked, trying to escape the screaming bullets and the advancing soldiers, but he was trapped. If Evan could get to him . . .

Was any of this a true memory, or only his mind filling in the scene he'd read about in the newspaper?

"Evan?" Diana's voice sliced through the fog, pulling him back. She sat atop her horse, gathering her reins, and looking at him quizzically. "Shall we go?"

"Yes." He tried to loosen the knots in his shoulders as his horse side-stepped. "Let's go."

They set off south on the road that ran past the inn, Evan at her side and Shand coming along behind. According to the map Louisa had drawn, the tenant houses were scattered over the property at regular intervals, but a cluster of cottages sat near the wooded part of the estate. They would start there.

Within a quarter mile, Evan knew that Diana was a more than competent rider. She handled her mount with confidence, secure in her side-saddle, hands steady on the reins. Shand continued grumbling under his breath as he bounced in the saddle. Evan shifted in his own seat, feeling a twinge or two in the leg where he had been wounded. It had been so long since he'd ridden, he'd probably have to take his dinner off the mantel-piece tonight. His thigh, where the scar tissue had healed, twinged and stung, stretching in ways it had not been called upon to do thus far.

A cart track veered off the main road, and Diana turned onto it. Trees arched overhead, cutting off much of the light, and grass and weeds grew down the center of the path. Ahead, a clearing opened, and within it, in a circle with a well in the center, sat six stone cottages. Smoke trickled weakly from a few chimneys, and broken tools and scraggly chickens were scattered about the yards. A massive black hog with wicked-looking tusks rooted around one of the foundations. The place smelled of rotting straw, pig effluent, and woodsmoke.

Shand dropped off his horse. "Hello, the house!" he bellowed.

A chill went up Evan's arms, and his legs tightened, causing his horse to sidle. "Stay on your horse," he warned Diana. His senses were on alert, senses he had learned to trust through years of soldiering. Something dangerous lived here, and he wished in that moment he'd brought more men with him.

A large, filthy man with a long beard and tattered clothes stepped out of a cottage on their left, rubbing the hilt of a skinning knife down his cheek. "Who are ye, and what do ye want barging in here and yelling like ye are?"

Three other men emerged from the falling-down houses, dirty, with a feral look about them. How many more lurked behind the broken shutters and half-open doors?

"Stay behind me," Evan cautioned Diana, keeping his voice low. He'd been remiss not to have scouted the area before riding in. The English countryside was turning out to be not that different than the Peninsular War. He reached under his cloak and wrapped his hand around the butt of his pistol, tucked into his waistband. At least he'd had the foresight to come armed. His senses were sharp, and he never let his eyes linger long in one place.

"What ye hidin' there?" The big man stepped to the side to get a better view. "Well, ain't that a pretty morsel?" He eyed Diana and then spit into the long grass. "Ye folks seem to have lost yer way. Ye want to pass through here, ye'll have to pay a tax."

"You're addressing the Earl of Whitelock and his countess, so you'll keep a civil tongue in your head. You're squatters, and you'll clear out of these houses within the week, or you'll be thrown out." Shand slapped his reins against his boot top. Evan's former sergeant had faced cannon fire without flinching, and he would not back down from a band of ruffians. "He'll pay no tax for crossing his own land."

The mountain of a man's eyes narrowed and shifted to his fellow squatters and then back again. "The earl, is he? How do we know? Any dandy could ride in here and say he was a lord. If he's the earl, then he's fallen down on his duties. Even if he is the earl, I say we don't clear out. I say we've earned the right to stay. Squatter's rights. Haven't we, men? Maybe we'll just take your horses, your purses, and that fancy bit of goods with the big eyes. Maybe we'll tar and feather ye and send ye packing back to the big house like a whipped cur while we amuse ourselves with the lady." He motioned toward Diana with his knife and stepped forward, two of his friends closing ranks, the other two spreading to the sides in what must be a practiced maneuver. It was the way road agents would deploy when robbing a carriage.

Evan's blood leapt, ready for battle. How he wished to answer their challenge, to take them on, to turf them out and settle the matter, just he and Shand, as they had done many times before.

But there was Diana to consider.

And he was a lord, who shouldn't descend to fighting without exploring other options. If he let loose the soldier within, he would further alienate his sensitive bride. He would try diplomacy first. Force later, if need be.

Shand drew in a deep breath, but Evan nudged his horse forward before he could speak. "I have a proposition. And this is the only time I will make this offer. You are welcome to stay here, in these houses, as tenants of the Whitelock holdings under the condition that you will work and be profitable to the estate. The cottages will be repaired, tasks will be assigned, and you will be expected to fulfill them. Food will be supplied, and firing, and tools for the work. You will be amiable to others who work the estate, and you will not cause embarrassment to the Whitelock name. Mr. Shand here will be your supervisor, and you will answer to him and thus to me. Should you violate this agreement, you will be expelled from the property. Should you choose not to take up this offer, you will leave by this time two days hence. Stealing is prohibited, unlawful behavior will not be tolerated, and respect will be shown to those in authority over you—and you will never again refer to your mistress as a 'pretty morsel' or 'a fancy bit of goods.' Is that understood?"

Before the biggest man could speak, Evan whipped out his pistol and aimed it at the man on his right, who had been inching forward with his hand raised to grab Diana's bridle. "One more step and I will perforate your head."

The man froze, white showing around his eyes, stark in his dirty face. Evan didn't look back at the leader, trusting Shand to keep watch.

"What say you, men? Stay and abide by my laws, or go?" He kept the pistol leveled on the nearer man.

"What if we want to think about it?" the big man asked.

"I require my answer now. I don't have time to waste. It is a fair offer. By rights I could evict you all without notice. I'm willing to work with you if you're willing to work with me. But I will not be taken advantage of. Choose your path." Evan raised his voice. "That goes for everyone in these cottages."

Heads poked out of doors and windows—men, women, children.

"How many of you are there?" Shand asked.

The big man scratched his cheek with the hilt of the knife again. "'Bout twenty."

"How have you been living?" Evan noted the deerskin boots and the leather pants. He'd probably been poaching deer and fowl and fish and anything else he could hunt.

"We get by," he evaded.

"Are you a hunter? I am in need of a gamekeeper. And an assistant gamekeeper." Those positions were somewhere on the list of employees Diana had written up. "If you can manage the game on the estate without poaching, and see that no one else poaches, you can have the job and choose your assistant from your compatriots here."

Light entered the man's eyes, the light of hope, but it was a guarded hope.

"Why? You don't even know me."

"I'm willing to give a man a chance. You'll report to Mr. Shand here, and he'll report to me." Evan lowered the gun, resting it on his thigh. "If you're not up to the task, or if you steal from me, I'll toss you off the place myself."

"You're really the earl?"

Lord help me, I am.

Evan forbade Diana from accompanying them to visit the other cottages. "Not until we know what we might encounter. I apologize for putting you in jeopardy, and I won't run the risk of doing it again. We'll head back now."

She was still reeling from their encounter with the squatters and how quickly her husband had produced that gun. He'd leapt to protect her, and he'd done it without anger. He'd been more than fair with the squatters, offering employment in return for honest labor, but leaving no doubt that he would go to great lengths to protect what was his, be it land, buildings, or his wife.

Did that mean he was accepting his role as the earl and as her husband? His words in the stable yard the other day about having no choice in whom he married had cut deeply, and she'd held the hurt close, using it as a barrier for her growing feelings for him.

They returned to the inn, and Evan reached up for her, lifting her from the saddle, his hands spanning her waist, her palms braced on his shoulders. When her feet touched the cobbles, her hands slid down to rest on his chest, and he held her still, staring into her eyes. His own were the same pure blue as the sky over his head.

"I am sorry. It was a foolish mistake, not reconnoitering before taking you with me. Something I have done twice now. I took you to White Haven, where we were nearly shot, and now to the cottages, where we were nearly set upon by scoundrels. I have promised to protect you and been derelict in my duties again and again."

His hands on her waist distracted her. They were firm, keeping her in place, but not harsh, and she felt no fear of him. Instead she relished their closeness, the breadth of his chest, the width of his shoulders, the strength of him, the maleness, so different from herself.

"I did not feel unprotected, my lord . . ." He quirked his eyebrow, and she corrected herself. "Evan. You have taken very good care of me, and today was no exception. I did not know you carried a pistol."

"I didn't think I would need it in the English countryside, but there you are. I learned my lesson when Greville and his blunderbuss entered the fray."

Was he aware that he still held her? And that the courtyard of the inn was a very public place? If they had been alone, she might even dare to step closer, to rest her cheek against his chest and hope that his arms would come around her to hold her securely. His desire to protect her roused in her the desire to be protected by him. To shelter in his arms and know she was safe. Which was such an odd sensation, since she'd never felt safe with any man in her life before.

"My lord?" The innkeeper stood to the side, and Diana let her hands drop from Evan's chest.

He released his hold on her, a frown darkening his face. "Yes?"

"You have visitors. I put the gentleman in your private parlor."

Diana tensed. Was it her father? Or someone he had sent to fetch the baby? Where was Cian? Was he safe?

Evan's expression smoothed, and he offered Diana his arm. "Perhaps Marcus has arrived. He said he would visit as soon as he could."

That would be it. Diana calmed her fluttering heart. Marcus Haverly, come to assess their progress and possibly bring some of the items that had been ordered for the house. She shouldn't shy at shadows.

But when Evan parted the curtains to enter the parlor, it wasn't Marcus or her father, and if this was a henchman intent upon taking a baby, he was the kindest-looking henchman imaginable.

Evan followed her into the room, and stopped. The man rose from the chair beside the fire. Thin, with sparse gray hair, his faded-blue eyes reminded her of someone.

"Dad?"

Diana paused, her hands raised to unpin her hat. His father?

"Son. I received your letter, and several people sent me clippings from the newspapers of London. I thought it high time I came to check on you again, though you are not easy to find." He shook his son's hand and pulled him in for a hug. "A man named Marcus Haverly gave me your direction."

"It's so good to see you." Evan stood back but kept his hands on his father's shoulders. "Is Mother with you? How long can you stay?"

"Only a few days. It's difficult for a preacher to be away from his church for too long. Your mother is here too, but . . ." He shrugged. "When we arrived, there was a young woman with a darling infant, and the little fellow has brought out all her mothering instincts. She and the maid have retired upstairs to coo and fuss over the child." He raised his eyebrows, looking from Diana to Evan.

"Oh, pardon my manners. Diana, this is my father, the Reverend William Eldridge. Dad, this is my . . ." He swallowed. "My wife, Diana."

The reverend put out his hands, and Diana found herself brought forward, inspected, and kissed on the cheek. "Welcome to the family, Diana. You're quite as beautiful as Mr. Haverly told us you would be. He also informs me that your character is even sweeter than your looks."

Diana knew she was coloring.

A grin split Evan's face. "He's a silver-tongued rascal, my dad. You should hear his sermons."

"The question is, has he passed any of that loquacity to his son?" Diana gave his fingers a squeeze. "Won't you sit down? Have you had tea? And was your journey pleasant, sir?"

"Please, call me William, or, when you feel comfortable, Father or Dad. We've been so eager to meet the woman who captured Evan's attention so quickly."

She couldn't stop from locking eyes with Evan. Did his father think this a love match? A whirlwind romance?

Unpinning her hat, she laid it and the net veil aside and took the place beside her new father-in-law. Evan tossed off his cloak and sat opposite.

"You're still wearing your uniform?" William asked.

Evan shrugged. "It's comfortable. I'm used to it."

"My boy, slippers and dressing gowns are comfortable, but I hardly think appropriate for me to wear in the pulpit. There's a time and place for your uniform, but I think that time has passed, don't you? You are now a gentleman, and you'll be expected to be attired appropriately."

A sigh was Evan's only answer. Diana had wondered at his continued use of his uniform, but now she saw it for what it was, an effort to hold on to his past and the man he had been before all this had been thrust upon him—including her.

"Evan." A tiny woman bustled into the room, holding Cian in one arm and opening the other to her son.

She was nearly a head shorter than Diana and comfortably rounded without being heavy. Her brown dress and quick movements reminded Diana of a sparrow.

"Oh, my son. It is so good to see you. I wanted so badly to come to

London when you were in hospital, but I'd been laid low with a chest cold, and your father thought it best I stay behind and get well, lest I bring the sickness to you and delay your recovery." She stepped back and appraised him. "You've healed well?"

"Yes, Mother. I'm fighting fit now." He held out his arms and stepped back so she could see all of him. "The leg's near perfect."

Her eyes, the color of hot cocoa, appraised her son. "Let's have no more talk of you being fighting fit. Your fighting days are over. You're still too thin. And what about the headaches? Your father said the doctor was concerned. Have they abated?"

"For the most part. Nothing to worry about." He brushed her concerns aside.

Diana frowned. Headaches? He'd never once mentioned a painful head, though she did recall him rubbing his temples from time to time and a certain strained look in his eyes. She had thought he was exasperated or angry, but was it possible that it hadn't been temper but an aching head that caused his ill humors?

Cian squawked, and Mrs. Eldridge fussed over him. "Isn't he beautiful?"

Evan gave the baby his finger to hold, and Cian's eyes focused on his face. "Hello, little man."

Diana's heart squeezed. The baby's mouth opened, and one corner quirked up in one of his rare smiles. He gave a little gurgling coo that melted her heart.

"Look at that. He knows you." Mrs. Eldridge handed the baby to her son, who took Cian and nestled the baby in his arms.

Evan had the right touch with the infant, even being able to soothe his evening fussiness better than Diana or Beth, much to their chagrin.

"A lovely child. Diana, dear, I hope you don't mind or consider me interfering. His young mother was looking so tired, I said I would watch the baby while she took a nap. I understand he's not the best sleeper in the world."

Poor Beth. She had to be exhausted, and Diana felt guilty that she was encouraging this charade about Cian's parentage, putting so much of the baby's care on her maid. But what else could she do? Evan might send the baby right back to her father if she revealed that Cian was her nephew and that she'd stolen him. She had to continue the lie in order to keep her promise to Catherine.

Yet watching Evan look down at the baby he held so carefully, she wondered. Could she trust him with her secrets? With Cian's future? With her heart? If she told him, would she betray her promise to her sister?

"I just love his little face," Mrs. Eldridge continued. "His eyes are so hazy and dark, they'll be turning brown any day now. Alas, I had hoped for a brown-eyed boy, but Evan got his father's eyes. Just goes to show you. Cian's mother's eyes are so blue and her hair so red, but he looks more like you with his coloring than Beth, Diana."

Uneasiness rippled through Diana. Cian's mother had possessed beautiful brown eyes, but Catherine was dead. Fitzroy had golden eyes, like a cat's. Cian definitely favored his mother . . . and his aunt . . .

The baby began to fuss, and Evan raised the infant to his shoulder, patting his small back and talking softly to him. Quickly, the cries subsided.

"There you are, Evan. You're a natural. And now that you've married, we can expect grandchildren soon." Mrs. Eldridge propped her chin on her clasped hands. "I've always thought that being a grandmother is the loveliest work. There were times when I wondered if I would ever get the opportunity. But God spared your life and brought you home, and He's given you a lovely bride."

Desperation rose in Diana's chest, and her eyes sought Evan's. They had nothing on which to hang his mother's hopes of becoming a grandmother. They were not even sharing sleeping quarters. When you had secrets, meeting your in-laws was fraught with peril.

They spent a delightful evening dining and talking, and Diana began to relax. Perhaps they wouldn't come a cropper, tripped up by an awkward question here or there. She was fascinated by the relationship Evan had with his parents. They were kind, cordial, warm, not a harsh word or criticism amongst them. Oh, they teased one another, and they laughed, but none of their humor was mean-spirited. And all the while, they passed the baby from one set of arms to another, something her father never would've countenanced—never even thought of doing, keeping a child with adults during dinner.

Was this what family was supposed to be? Harmonious, enjoyable, safe? Diana hoped the evening wouldn't end.

When it came time to climb the steps to the bedrooms, Evan held Diana back with his hand on her arm. As soon as his parents—his mother still cuddling the now-sleeping Cian—turned the corner of the staircase, he lowered his voice. "I had the innkeeper put my folks' things in my room and make up a cot in the room we've been using as an office for Beth and the baby. I know it's a cheek, but I've had my things moved into your room."

Her mouth dried to dust. They would sleep in the same room tonight?

His blue eyes glittered in the light of the candle he carried, and her heart knocked against her ribs. She struggled for some aplomb, but no words came.

"If you don't care for the idea, I can bivouac with the men in the stable loft."

He wore a grimace, and she knew he would lose face when it became known that he wasn't sleeping inside the inn.

"Of course you must stay in my room." Her breath hitched, and she was thankful for the low light. "Our room."

She led the way up the stairs, her mind whirling, unable to grasp any thought for long. He followed closely with the candle, and he opened the door for her. Sure enough, his cases had been moved in, and Beth's and Cian's moved out.

Lighting a brace of candles on the table, he said, "I'll head outside for a few minutes so you can ready yourself for sleep."

Grateful for a few moments' reprieve, but afraid he would come back before she was prepared, she hurried out of the dress she'd changed into before dinner and into a nightgown. She sat at the small dressing table, staring at her reflection in the candlelight. Her eyes looked too big for her face, dark pools in her pale skin. With chilly fingers, she pulled the pins from her hair, letting it tumble down over her shoulders.

A light tap sounded on the door, and Evan stepped inside. She met his eyes in the mirror and rose, too restless to stay seated.

He crossed the small room and took her chilly hands in his. "Diana, I had wanted to give you time to get to know me better and for me to get to know you, but circumstances have arisen that have changed my mind about when we should consummate our marriage."

She nodded, head down. What circumstances?

"I thought to give you my reasons, and after you've heard them, you can agree or refuse."

He squeezed her hands, and she raised her chin to look him in the eyes, testing his sincerity. She had a choice? She could agree or disagree? Some of her nervousness fled with the knowledge that she at least had some say in what was going to happen to her.

"First, I believe we should have our bridal night because it is one of the purposes of marriage, and it is right in the eyes of God, the church, and mankind. We are to be fruitful and multiply."

Diana had no argument with that logic. She understood her duty to be a wife to him in that sense, and to provide him with an heir.

"Second, Marcus informed me that your father could very well be scheming even now for a way to annul the marriage and get his hands on your fortune. If we consummate our union, he will not be able to have the marriage dissolved on that count."

An icy hand gripped her heart and squeezed. She could not go back to her father, and she could not take Cian into that house again. If lying with her husband would forestall that happening, she would not protest.

"And third . . ." His voice deepened. "Because I want to. I find you very beautiful, sweet, and desirable. I am blessed to be your husband."

Her breath quickened at the intensity of his gaze. So he *did* desire her. Her confidence blossomed, and she returned the pressure of his hands.

"And yet I must confess, I am . . . reluctant to share this room with you, for . . ." He closed his eyes and took a deep breath. "I suffer from the occasional nightmare." His eyes popped open. "I would not have you think me disturbed. It is just that I have seen much in battle, and sometimes my mind, while I am asleep, returns to the skirmishes and conflicts. If I should begin to stir in sleep or even to mumble, please do not be alarmed, and do not be afraid to wake me."

He looked so vulnerable, even . . . ashamed? Was that the real reason he had delayed so long?

"I have been known to have the occasional bad dream myself."

"The choice is yours, Diana. Do you want me to stay, knowing that if I do, we will be man and wife before dawn?"

A sense of calm came over her, and all because he had given her a choice. For that alone she would have done nearly anything for him. But there was a remnant of shyness, and she couldn't speak the words. She nodded.

His expression softened, and his hands came up to cup her shoulders, drawing her to him slowly. With infinite patience, he lowered his head, giving her plenty of time to lean away if she chose.

But she did not so choose. It was time, and she raised her face. His lips skimmed her forehead, her cheek, and then her mouth. Heat spiraled through her middle, and her eyes closed on a sigh. His hands moved from her shoulders to frame her cheeks, warm and large, holding her still, but she didn't feel trapped.

Everything about this felt new, exciting, and . . . right, because it was this man. Her husband. Evan deepened the kiss, his arms coming around her waist and his hand spreading on her back. Her arms drifted up about his neck, and she surrendered herself into his keeping.

Slowly withdrawing, his eyes ardent, he eased his hold on her long enough to bend to blow out the candles on the dressing table and plunge the room into darkness.

Hours later, she lay awake beside her husband. His steady breathing told her he was asleep, but Diana couldn't find slumber.

She was different now. Everything that had been forbidden her just weeks ago was now right and good. She could never go back to not knowing.

She listened to his even breaths, turning as gently as she could onto her side to study his faint profile in the darkness. They were husband and wife now.

Did that mean she could trust him? He had been nothing but kind to her, providing, protecting, concerning himself with her wants and needs. And he had approved of her input on the house.

His protection and provision had extended to Cian, seeing that he had food and warmth and comfort, even though Evan believed him to be the illegitimate son of her maid. He hadn't banished the child or the "mother."

Would he be as accepting if he knew that Cian was her nephew and that she had stolen him out of her father's house and had been deceiving him right along about who the child really was?

He had been willing to protect her from the possibility that her father would annul the marriage. She would trust him, in the morning, with her secret. *Thank You, Lord, for putting me into this man's care. I prayed for an escape from my father's control, and You provided one.*

For the first time in a long while, she felt as if God had heard her prayers and answered them. At last enough peace seeped into her that she felt she could sleep

Evan stirred, and she froze. Slamming her eyes shut, she feigned sleep lest he think she was lying awake fretting . . . or staring.

His legs moved restlessly, and he flung his hand up over his head.

"Get back," he muttered.

She started before she realized he wasn't talking to her. This was one of the dreams he'd mentioned. He'd said to wake him, but her hand hovered in the air over his shoulder.

His head twisted on the pillow. "It's Arthur Bracken, I tell you. Get out of my way."

At the words "Arthur Bracken," ice entered Diana's veins. What did he know of that name? Of that man?

"I have to find him." Thrusting his hands into the darkness, he swept right and left, nearly clipping Diana with his right arm. "No!" He jerked upright in the bed, panting, dragging the blankets.

She touched his shoulder. "Evan?"

His chest heaved, and he gulped in air. A fine sheen of sweat coated his skin.

"Diana?"

"Are you all right?"

He wiped his hands down his face. "Yes. I'm sorry I woke you. Go back to sleep. I'm fine."

Diana turned her back to him to lie on her other side, clutching her pillow. He had nightmares about Arthur Bracken?

So did she.

Cold radiated from her middle, and her peace scattered like mist in a high wind. Her confidence that she could confide in and trust Evan shrank, and her certainty that God had brought them together on purpose did likewise.

Arthur Bracken was the given name of the odious Viscount Fitzroy, Catherine's seducer and Cian's father.

CHAPTER 11

EVAN STOOD ON the horseshoe drive in front of White Haven, hands on hips, eyes narrowed. The arrival of March had brought with it warmer temperatures and a greening of the countryside. With the brambles removed and the stone scrubbed, White Haven had taken on the look of a proper estate house.

New glass gleamed in the windows, and just yesterday the workers had finished applying a fresh coat of white paint to the mullions and frames. The front doors had been sanded, stained, and varnished, and all the hardware re-blacked.

He moved out of the way as a team of draft horses plodded around the drive, dragging a blade, smoothing and leveling the gravel that had been arriving by wagon from a distant quarry for the past few days. Putting his hands into his pockets, Evan backed onto the close-cut grass of the front lawn. His coat was tight across his shoulders, but he had been assured that it was properly made and measured, that fitted jackets were *au courant* for today's gentleman. At least his Hessians were comfortable. He still missed his uniform, but his father had been correct, as he most often was. It was past time for Evan to embrace his role as an earl and dress accordingly.

Diana had been a great help with that, complimenting his attire often. She had a flair for adding a special touch here or there to her own dress that made it unique, and he'd noticed the same with designing the décor in the house. Her stamp was all over the house and grounds, and he was discovering more about her through her choices. She preferred rich colors in the house, and dark woods. Her tastes ran more to florals than geometrics, and she was quite sentimental, wanting to refurbish and hang on to older pieces rather than chuck the lot and start new. The finished rooms were inviting and soothing.

None of the work at White Haven would have been done as well without her influence, nor would he be adjusting to life as an earl with any degree of ease if she hadn't been dropped into his life. She was his adviser, guide, helper, and complement.

Which was as God intended a husband and wife to be, was it not? The wife was a helper fit for her husband? His better half?

On the north end of the manor, where the parterre gardens lay, Diana directed a group of workers, holding a sheet of paper—one of her many lists, no doubt. She wore a pale-pink gown and a spencer in a deeper hue of the same color, and a bonnet that hid her face from him, but he watched her anyway. She had blossomed over the past couple of weeks, her movements less jerky, as if no longer expecting to be slapped down if she gave her opinion or disagreed with something he said. He hoped that he—and the changes to their marriage—had something to do with the changes in her, in the rise in her confidence. She'd certainly wrought changes in him.

Even his parents had noticed, though their stay had been all too brief. When his mother had kissed his cheek before climbing into the post chaise, she had looked deeply into his eyes with that familiar expression—the one that made him feel as if she knew all his secrets, and she'd smiled. "I'm so happy for you, son. You'll make a good fist of being an earl because you're making a good fist of being a husband. God bless you both."

One of the workers held up a potted plant to Diana with a questioning look, and whatever she said made him chuckle. She joined him, her laughter making Evan's heart feel light. Though he sensed she still kept some part of herself hidden from him, perhaps in time she would trust him with that as well. It was enough that they'd made progress, that they were finding their way together as husband and wife. His father had cautioned him that a marriage was built day by day, and Evan was content with the way his was going.

"She's looking quite grand, isn't she, sir?" Shand came to stand beside him.

"Pardon me?" Evan swung around, ready to take umbrage at his sergeant for making such a comment about his mistress.

"The house. She's coming into shape, isn't she?" Shand eyed the structure.

"Oh yes." Evan coughed to cover his embarrassment. "We've made great headway. Did you get the latest shipment of furnishings unloaded?" Wagons came almost daily from London: rugs, draperies, china, lamps, bedding, things he'd ordered when he'd been in the city, things Marcus had ordered from lists sent by Diana, things Evan didn't know even existed or that he needed until they arrived and were installed.

"The cottages are finished as well. I'll confess, I had my doubts as to the wisdom of keeping that band of riffraff on the place, but they've done nearly all the work on the cottages themselves, using what you've supplied. They've turned into good laborers. Most of them, anyway. I did have to run off that pair of scoundrels who stole the new tools and tried to sell them in Crawley."

Evan's gaze returned often to his wife as they talked. "It was a risk, keeping them on, but it seemed the right thing to do, to give them a chance. Something my father would've done." How many times, growing up, had he seen his father give someone another chance, show mercy where the world clamored for justice? "I couldn't have done any of this without you, Sergeant."

Shand shifted his weight, spreading his hands. "It isn't much different from the army, I'm finding. Men are men, and leading is leading. A good plan and the discipline to follow it go a long ways."

"You've got everyone moved out of the inns now?"

"Everyone except you and my lady. Bradfords and Halcotts are moving your things into the main house today. They're bringing Beth and the baby with them."

They would spend their first night in the new house. In those separate bedrooms. Evan and Diana had continued to share their room at the inn even after his parents had returned to their home, letting Beth and her son keep Evan's former room. But that would all change today when they took up residence at White Haven for the first time. Separate rooms, because they were in the peerage and it was expected.

He had assumed the maid and the baby would be moved into the servants' quarters on the third floor, but Diana had other plans. It was too cold up there for an infant, and his crying might keep the other servants awake. They needed their sleep in order to fulfill their duties, and anyway, there was a lovely south-facing room that just begged to be made into a nursery. It would receive sunlight nearly all day, and there were enough windows to provide proper ventilation . . . By the time she had finished extolling the virtues of the room, Evan realized he agreed with everything she said. The woman had some strange power over him—he found himself wanting to please her in things great and small.

Louisa Monroe came from the back of the house and headed toward Diana and the gardeners. Shand stiffened. "That woman."

"Who, Miss Monroe?"

"Yes. I've never met anyone like her. She would make an excellent artillery gunner. Barking orders and taking charge. The entire house staff is afraid of her." Shand scratched the hair over his ear, his eyes never leaving the housekeeper.

"Are you afraid of her?" Evan teased.

Affronted, Shand almost reared up on his tiptoes. "I am not. And I won't have her interfering with my stewardship. Someone needs to remind her that I don't work for her, nor do I answer to her."

Evan hid his amusement. His steward and his housekeeper had been at daggers drawn since the moment they met. Whenever they encountered one another, Miss Monroe did plenty of head tossing and skirt twitching, and Shand did his share of belligerent glaring and harrumphing.

Shand continued to stare after Louisa, but he changed the subject. "Plowing will start tomorrow. The men have burned off the fields. That seemed the easiest way to get rid of the overgrowth. I'll say this for that old tartar Greville Monroe. He kept excellent records back in the day, and he remembers everything that happened to him that is more than twenty years old. Can't remember that we've had a conversation earlier in the day, but ask him something about this estate from 1790, and he knows every detail." Shand tucked his thumbs into his waistband. "Never seen the like."

"The mind is a strange thing." And didn't Evan have cause to know it? His own mental frailties continued to disappoint. He remembered bits of the day in question only in snatches, and those bits he wasn't sure were reliable. He and Greville were two of a kind.

"I came to see if you wanted to visit the stables, sir? The first horses have arrived."

"I promised my wife I would tour the Royal Apartments with her first. I'll meet you at the stables later." Evan sketched a low wave to his steward and headed toward the gardens.

Edging around men clipping the box hedges and men raking leaves and men forking over the flower beds, he finally reached her. So many workers swarmed over the place, it was impossible to get her to himself when the men were here.

"The pinks and the columbine go in those beds, and the roses will line the walk over there. Laburnum, daisies, and sweetbriar will fill in the bare patches." Diana pointed and directed, sounding so confident. At his approach, she turned and smiled. "Do you like it?"

He studied her rather than the gardens. Her cheeks were flushed, or just reddened by the fresh spring air, and her eyes were as deeply hued and velvety as the pansies she held. "Yes, I do."

Unable to help himself, he grinned as her flush deepened, and she ducked her chin.

"I thought we might walk through the house. Things are coming along nicely, but there is that one wing that needs help." He held out his arm, and she set the flowerpot on the verge and slipped her hand through his elbow.

How different from the first time they had walked up to the front door of White Haven. Evan was tempted to do as he'd teased then and scoop her up in his arms to carry her over the threshold. But there were too many workers around, and he didn't want to embarrass her to the point of being awkward with him.

The front hall rose grandly to a coffered ceiling, the stairs had been repaired and re-carpeted, and the banister gleamed from many coats of polish. Light slanted in through the rear windows upstairs, bathing the gallery in a warm glow. To left and right, parlor and formal dining rooms were clean and furnished. The house smelled of fresh paint, beeswax, and lamp oil. Not a speck of dust or a cobweb to be found.

"I can't believe the transformation only a few weeks have made."

"There's still plenty to do, but it's shaping up nicely." She kept hold of his arm as they mounted the stairs.

"That's due to you. I still don't know the first thing about furnishing and decorating a manor house. I'm better with the fields and the stable. Shand says the first horses have arrived. I'm meeting him at the stables after this. We can wander that way once we're finished here. If you like." He was careful to give her the option to refuse. He'd noticed that if he gave her a choice, she was more relaxed. If he was forgetful and made a choice for her, she tensed and withdrew. Even though her confidence had grown over the past weeks, she still checked every decision with him, asking his permission to implement her ideas.

Just as it was taking time for him to be comfortable as an earl, it was taking time for her to feel that her ideas would not be ridiculed, that she was safe with him in every respect.

They turned left at the top of the stairs, and at the end of the hall, he opened the double doors wide into an area of the house they hadn't touched yet.

The Royal Apartments.

At least in this part of the manor, the furniture had been draped with dust covers, though these were tattered and moth-eaten.

"How much will it take to get them up to scratch for the prince's visit?" Evan lifted the edge of a cover, revealing a chair with a pale-blue upholstered seat and slender, curved legs. It looked too spindly to support the prince's bulk. Diana had assured him weeks ago that the Royal Apartments could wait until later, because they were not in as precarious a shape as the rest of the house. The repairs would be cosmetic. So he had followed her lead and left these until last.

Diana drew aside the drapes at one of the tall windows, releasing a cloud of dust. The workmen had replaced all the broken panes, and the light shone in strongly, revealing the neglected look of the place. "I have a list downstairs."

"Why am I not surprised?" he teased. "So I've looked at the original blueprints, but none of these rooms were labeled other than 'Royal Apartments.' What is the function of each space?"

"This will be the receiving room, and there will be a smaller parlor next door. Beyond that are the royal bedrooms, one for the prince and one for . . . well, it's supposed to be for his wife. But since it's well known that the Prince and Princess of Wales have no affection for one another, I would not expect her to travel with him. There are separate dressing rooms, as well as a bathing room." She put her hands on her hips, silhouetted by the window. "I peeked under these dust covers, and there are some really lovely pieces. I know the prince is a stickler for fashion, but I don't see why we should buy new when we have beautiful furnishings that just need a bit of care." She frowned. "The real challenge will be the royal bed. Whoever looked after these chambers in the past took all the draperies from the bed. They've either been stored somewhere that we haven't unearthed—and I would suspect they were now moth-eaten if that is the case—or they were stolen or sold. That canopy is a good twelve feet high, and it would've been draped with damask or silk or brocade fabrics. We'll have to order new. And we should have new wallpaper and paint. The floors are sound, so a bit of wax should bring them back up."

Evan was distracted by what a pretty picture she made with the sunlight behind her, barely paying attention to what she said.

Her hands dropped to her sides, and she shifted away from the window. Her bottom lip disappeared, and her brows headed toward one another. "Were you thinking of doing something else in here? Would you prefer to clear everything out and start new? Or are you concerned about how much all this is costing?"

"No." How quickly her confidence could disappear. "I don't know the prince's taste, but yours is impeccable. Don't worry about the money. Spend what you need to do the place up right." Though they had been spending at a remarkable rate, they could pinch pennies once this Royal Visit was out of the way if they had to. "I think you should have a free hand here. Once the repairs to the rooms are finished, the plaster, the woodwork, and the like, you will be in sole charge of the furnishing and decorating. I won't even walk through these rooms until you're done. No oversight, no permissions needed. Make everything exactly as you want, and when you're finished, show me."

She regarded him warily at first, and then her sweet smile appeared, making his heart kick like a colt.

"You're sure?"

"Of course. I trust you." The words came out easily, and he realized that he did trust her. Though he knew he had awakened her with his bad dreams and restless sleep on more than one occasion, she had never said a word about it. And as the days and nights had passed, his nightmares had diminished. Was it because she was nearby and that he felt such peace when he could reach out and know she was there every time a dream woke him? Was his mind and spirit healing from the horrors of war because of her presence in his life?

He still couldn't remember much of that day. The bits he could piece together made little sense, and he wasn't sure what was real and what wasn't. If he had captured a spy at Salamanca, wouldn't someone from his regiment know? If he had raced off to inform his superiors, wouldn't he have left the spy in someone's custody? Presumably Shand's, but when Evan had asked him about his sergeant's part in the battle, Shand had mentioned nothing about a prisoner, nor the fact that Evan had left his post to get to headquarters.

But with all the work on White Haven, and with his new marriage taking much of his time, the horrors and questions were receding. Evan was learning to make peace with not knowing, with perhaps never knowing. His attacks of anxiety and panic had lessened, and with each day, he felt more like himself. Perhaps he would even trust his fears to Diana, tell her the reasons behind the nightmares, tell her about the gaps in his memory.

"You trust me?"

Diana's words drew him back to the present. "I trust you." He spoke carefully, and he stepped closer. He had never kissed her in the daylight, never expressed physical affection for her outside their darkened bedroom. But he very much wanted to right now. How would she react?

She stood still as he raised his hands to her cheeks, warm and smooth and soft. With a wee smile, he bent his head to avoid her bonnet brim and brushed his lips across hers once, twice. Not wanting to scare her, he resisted the urge to deepen the kiss, and he stepped back, letting his hands trail over her shoulders, down to her fingers. "It's what husbands and wives should do, trust each other. You trust me, right?"

Her hands stiffened in his, and her breath caught a bit in her throat. Her eyes broke with his, and she looked down and to the side.

Puzzled, Evan let go of her fingers. Trying not to be hurt, trying to remember that she had little reason to trust the men in her life up to now, he sighed. *Be patient, Evan. As patient as you would be with a wounded bird. She'll come to trust you if you take it slowly.*

The sound of a baby's cry echoed faintly from downstairs, and Diana's chin came up, her eyes lighting. "They're here."

She raised her hem and hurried from the room, leaving him staring after her. She certainly put a lot of store in her maid's child. Even Evan's mother had remarked upon it. Again, he wondered why. Was it just that she had a tender heart?

He wandered the rooms, pulling off the holland covers, peeking into cupboards and drawers. Eight rooms, kept and furnished with the sole hope that some royal personage would grace the estate with a visit.

"Woolgathering, are we?"

Evan looked up. Marcus grinned at him from the doorway.

"I didn't know you were coming today." His heart lightened at the sight of his friend.

"And I come bearing more gifts. Well, not gifts exactly, since you're paying for them, but still more furnishings and furbelows for your new domicile." He crossed the room and shook Evan's hand. "The place is looking grand."

"Except for this wing." Evan waved to the covered furniture, the faded rugs, and the dust. "Though from what Diana said, she intends to keep the furnishings, which should help the exchequer a bit."

"Not to worry on that score. I've been going over the accounts with your lawyer, and even he's amazed at how little you've spent." Marcus ran his finger over the rosewood veneer of a side table, leaving a clear track in the dust that had accumulated in spite of the furniture covers.

"That's because I don't gamble, and I don't have a mistress, and I haven't bought any racehorses or the like. Almost every shilling has been spent on the estate, and I don't know what my lawyer considers a little money, because the amount I've spent on this place is enough to equip and supply a regiment for the rest of the war. Come. Let me show you the house." He clapped Marcus on the shoulder. "Did you pass Diana downstairs? We're getting moved into the manor today, and her maid had just arrived."

"I saw her briefly." Marcus nodded. "She looks happy. Marriage must agree with her. She told me where you were and that she would see me in a bit. In quite a hurry, she was."

"It's the maid's baby. You'd think she hadn't seen the child in weeks, not just since this morning. She's got quite an attachment to the little fellow. Not that I blame her. I quite like him myself."

At Marcus's sober expression, Evan hurried to explain. "I know it's unorthodox, but she kept her maid on even after she bore a child out of wedlock. Diana was so worried about what I would think—afraid I might dismiss the girl—she tried to keep it a secret, but it's hard to keep an infant quiet when you're all confined in the same carriage." He scratched his chin, remembering his surprise when cries had come from the basket. "And Diana loves fussing over the boy, helping take care of him. I think"— he was in uncharted waters here—"maybe growing up as she did, in that awful household, Diana needed someone safe to love who would return her affection without conditions, and she chose the baby."

Marcus said nothing, his piercing eyes thoughtful.

"Anyway, enough about that. Let's find Diana and go see my new project out in the stables. If my accounts start hemorrhaging money, it will be because I can't say no to a war horse—or my wife."

Diana inhaled the scent of spring on the breeze, contentment settling over her as she and Marcus strolled the gravel path between the house and the stables, following Evan.

"How are you coping with all this, Diana?" Marcus asked.

Their feet crunched on the newly leveled gravel, and she glanced through the iron gates into the freshly dug kitchen garden, where rows of vegetables had been planted.

Evan strode ahead, so eager, he reminded Diana of a child at Christmas. He hurried under the archway beneath the belvedere clock tower, his coattails flapping. He always seemed to be on the move, overseeing, ordering, and organizing, very much in command these days. He'd settled into being the master of the estate much easier than he had London society.

"Better as time goes on. The place really was a disaster when we arrived, but Evan has worked wonders. He's so driven and focused. And he handles the men wonderfully. So much has been accomplished so quickly because he knows how to direct and lead."

"He's a good man." Marcus clasped his hands behind his back. "He's coped well with everything that has been lobbed his way."

"Including me?" Diana asked. Evan *had* coped well with her. For the most part. Though he still had an unpredictable temperament upon occasion, she now wondered if it had more to do with what he had seen on the battlefield, his injuries, and the nightmares that disturbed his sleep. Evan didn't want to talk about those things, so they must bother him, else why not discuss them? And those episodes had grown less frequent the more time he spent at White Haven.

Men were more complicated creatures than she'd ever assumed. Her father and Percival were simple enough. Angry, arrogant, and greedy. But her husband was a cat of a different color, one she was just beginning to know and might never fully understand.

"Well, you must admit," Marcus said, "you were, shall we say, an unexpected blessing." He smiled, but his eyes were piercing, as if taking her measure. "But you've worked wonders here. And you have excellent taste. Your orders have been arriving steadily in London, and between the lawyers and myself, we've overseen the purchases. Even my mother and sister, when I showed them your sketches and color choices, think your designs are flawless, and my mother is not often pleased by anything."

Diana hugged that bit of rare praise to her heart, remembering the duchess's caustic tongue. "She is a bit of a Tartar, isn't she?"

"I think the Prince Regent should put her in charge of the troops on the Peninsula. She'd have the French routed—horse, foot, and artillery—within a month. Never seen such a bossy female."

Diana stole a look at him from under her bonnet brim and noted that he had a rather indulgent look about his mouth and eyes now. For all his mother's carping, he did seem to hold her in some affection. Which was generous of him, since the woman seemed to feel he was unimportant, being merely a second son.

They walked under the stable's arched entrance into the cobblestone yard. Evan stood with one of the grooms, running his hand down the foreleg of an underweight chestnut that tossed his head and jerked on his lead. Other equine noses poked over the half doors of the stalls, and Diana counted six occupants, not including the chestnut.

"Walk him around for me." Evan stood back and made a circular movement with his finger, totally engrossed. The groom—one of the men they had encountered at the cottages in the woods—led the horse away at a walk.

"So this is the pet project." Marcus crossed his arms and studied the animal. "There's some work to be done there."

The chestnut's head bobbed low every time he put his left foreleg on the ground.

"There's time. Once the paddock fences are properly repaired, these fellows can be turned out to graze and laze in the sunshine and hopefully come right again." Evan followed the horse's halting gait. "They need time to recuperate, some peace and quiet. When they've rested and put on some weight, we'll start gentling them again. They're not useless, just a little banged up." He leaned and bent to keep his eyes on the horse's walk.

Diana watched her husband's face, seeing the determination there, the fire in his blue eyes. Did he see his comrades in these horses? Was that why he had hired so many former soldiers, so many halt and lame, and given them jobs and a place to live and a purpose? Her heart warmed.

Nobility had more to do with character than birth. There were many who called themselves noble because of their family tree, but Evan had nobility stamped all over him because of his character.

Not for the first time, she wondered if she should trust him with her secret. But what did he know of Arthur Bracken? He'd never spoken the name aloud again, not waking or dreaming, but she feared what he might do, what connection he might make between Bracken and Cian.

"My lady." Marcus turned to her and offered his arm. "I can see your husband will be engaged here for a while. Perhaps you would like to show me the orangery? I've heard it was once legendary. I'd love to know your plans for the place."

She took his arm. "Evan, you don't mind? We'll return shortly." She
didn't want to take any of Evan's joy with his new stable inhabitants away,
but he was totally engrossed in diagnosing the chestnut's limp with the
groom and didn't seem to need her help.

"Fine. I'll see you up at the house." Evan ran his hand down the foreleg again.

Diana smiled at Marcus. "I hope you're up for a bit of a trek. Not much
work has been done on the orangery or the path to get there yet."

The track was rutted and overgrown, and Marcus held back tree
branches and Diana ducked under them, raising her hem so it wouldn't
snag on the weeds that encroached along the trail.

The orangery, with its symmetrical, tall arched windows and pale
stone walls, rose above the brambles. Here the workman had just begun
replacing the broken glass and repairing the flat roof. "We don't plan to
stock it just yet. There are so many other things that need tending, not
to mention laying in fuel to keep it heated enough to grow fruit." Diana
stood back and let Marcus open the glass-paned doors.

The dead trees and bushes had been sawn up and hauled away, and
the flagstones swept. Here and there, an iron bench stood along the center aisle, but beyond that, the building was empty. Cold and soulless for
the moment, but if Diana closed her eyes, she could almost smell the delicate fragrance of orange blossoms and taste the fresh tang of citrus on her
tongue.

"Someday." She raised her eyes to the ceiling thirty feet above. "We'll
have oranges and lemons for sure, and maybe some palms, just because I
love the look of them. Down at the far end, we'll have seedbeds, to sup-
plement the succession house for starting new plants for the gardens and
wintering over more delicate things."

Marcus led her to the closest bench. "Diana, I didn't bring you down
here to talk about plants. I wished to speak to you in private."

His voice held such gravity, Diana's chest squeezed tight. "What is it?"

He didn't sit, clasping his hands behind his back and pacing the
uneven slate floor. "It's your father."

Her hands fisted in her lap. She worked some moisture into her mouth.
"What about him?"

"Two nights ago, as I was coming home from the opera, my carriage nearly ran him down in the street. He staggered out of a tavern, so drunk he couldn't have hit the ground with his hat—if he knew where his hat was." Marcus stopped pacing. "It has been his constant condition since your marriage."

Gratitude that she wasn't in London to bear the brunt of his drunken temper washed over Diana. "I'm sorry to hear that." What else was she supposed to say?

"I had my coachmen pick him up, and I took him home. This isn't the first time. But this time, he was very . . . talkative."

Talkative? Cold invaded her core.

"Diana, he told me . . ." Marcus pressed his lips together, breathing in through his nose. "He said a lot of things, but interspersed amongst all of it, he said that his daughter had disgraced him by having a child. A boy. And that the boy was now missing from his house."

She felt as if she were falling through darkness. Air refused to enter her lungs, and all she wanted to do was run. Run to the house and snatch up Cian, protect him, protect her sister's memory. Without realizing it, she had gotten to her feet.

Marcus put his hands on her upper arms. She shrank from him, trying to pull away, all her fears of men rushing back to collide with her fears for her nephew.

"Diana, is it true? Is the baby your maid is claiming as her own your child?"

Her eyes clashed with his. "What?" He thought Cian belonged to her, was her son? She sifted back through what he'd said, forcing herself to be clearheaded.

"Evan said you hold the child in unusual affection, and now I know why." His voice held an edge. "He's my friend. I can't stand by and let him be defrauded. He deserves to know."

Guilt smote her. Evan did deserve to know the truth. The real truth, not what Marcus surmised and not the lie she'd told.

But what would he do? Marcus's anger at what he thought was her duplicity was evident. Would Evan react likewise?

"Tell me the truth." His grip tightened. "Is that child yours?"

"No. And yes."

"Speak plainly, woman. I've been going around in circles trying to make sense of it. I followed your trail from boarding school, and I can find no one who knows anything, nor will they say."

"Followed my trail?" Why would he do that? "Who are you to investigate me?"

"Never mind. Tell me about the baby."

"Promise me you won't tell Evan." She needed to tell him herself. If he found out another way ... It didn't bear thinking about.

"I can't make that promise. Tell me the truth."

Diana sagged, and he let her go, easing her down to the bench. She put her face in her hands. It would be such a relief to tell someone, but it should be her husband.

"Diana."

"His name is Cian, and he's my ... nephew." The last word came out a whisper.

"Percival's by-blow?" Marcus's voice went high.

"No, my sister, Catherine's, child." The moment the words were out, she wanted to call them back. Voicing them was a betrayal of her promise to her sister. And yet what choice did she have?

"Your sister? I didn't know you had a sister." Marcus perched on the arm of the bench.

"Percival is the oldest, from my father's first marriage. Then came Catherine, from his second. She is—was—two years older than I. Father's second marriage didn't last long. And he married my mother soon after his second wife's death. Last year, Catherine had her debut Season, but she was sent home because ..."

"She was with child?" He said this gently, which encouraged Diana to continue.

"Yes. My father was furious, of course. He had been negotiating her marriage, and she'd ruined herself. He banished her to the country, withdrew me from school to stay with her, and refused to allow her a midwife or *accoucheur* to attend the birth. Cian was born just before the new year, and she died the same day." Diana looked up at him. "But not before I gave her my word to raise him as my own, to love him and care for him and protect him from my father." She straightened her back, firming her chin. "My father forbade anyone to ever mention Catherine again, continually threatened to discard Cian in a foundling home, and he used the baby to bring me to heel. He had plans to marry me to a man of his choosing, one with whom he could negotiate to get his hands on at least a portion of my inheritance. I was willing to go along with his schemes because when the inheritance was handed over, he would give me custody of Cian. But everything went wrong. The Prince Regent wanted me to marry Evan, and then he told everyone at the wedding breakfast about the inheritance. Though he didn't mean to, the prince foiled all of my father's plans, and he put Cian's life in danger."

"So you stole the child and had your maid pose as his mother."

Diana nodded. "I had no choice. I couldn't leave him in my father's care. I promised Catherine I would keep the baby safe. I know it's wrong to have Beth masquerade as his mother, but I told her if Evan wanted to dismiss her as a result, I would tell him the truth."

"You should've told him long since." Marcus rubbed his palm against the back of his neck.

"Are you going to?" Trembles radiated from her middle. All her worst fears about the trustworthiness of men rose up and coiled around her.

He sighed. "I don't know. By law, your father has legal custody of the child. And by rights, your husband should know that the child is his wife's nephew. But I wouldn't wish anyone to be under the control of the Duke of Seaton, and I can see why you didn't tell Evan right away."

Diana waited. She was at his mercy now that he had confirmed the truth.

"I wasn't in London last Season, and I never met your sister. No one speaks of her, even to wonder where she is now." He pushed himself upright and walked a few paces away.

"My father probably told people that he married her to a Scot or an American to explain her absence."

"Who is the baby's father?"

She shook her head. "That I will not tell you. It makes no difference to the situation, and I promised Catherine I wouldn't ever breathe a word of it to anyone. Suffice it to say that Cian's father would not be interested in his son and that he would be no better a guardian than my father."

"Is he Irish?"

The question was so random, it sidetracked her thoughts. "What? No. Why would you ask that?"

"His name. Cian is as Irish as they come."

A weak laugh escaped her stiff lips. "It was Catherine's choice. We had a gardener named Cian when we were little. He was an Irishman, and he was kind to us. And perhaps she chose the name so people would think just as you did, that his father was Irish."

"My other question . . . is your brother blackmailing you? Threatening to reveal your sister's secret, and yours, if you don't pay him?"

The question seemed to be drawn from thin air. "Percival? Blackmail? No, of course not." Though she wouldn't put it past him. "I haven't heard from my brother—or my father—since I left London. Why?"

"Percival seems to have plenty of money at the moment, when a few weeks ago, he had none." Marcus frowned. "I'd like to know the source. He disappeared for a while, running from his creditors, and now he's popped up flush with cash."

Diana rubbed her lower lip. Marcus certainly seemed to have a lot of information, and to be seeking more. Was it idle curiosity or something else?

"What are you going to do?" she asked. "About what I've told you. Are you going to tell Evan?"

"You need to tell him yourself before he finds out some other way. He deserves to know." Marcus held out his hand to help her to her feet. "He's a good man, and he'll do the right thing."

Diana's fingers curled, and she withdrew them from his grasp. What if Evan thought the right thing was turning the child over to his legal guardian? What if Evan was furious with her for lying to him?

God, give me courage.

CHAPTER 12

THE FIRST NIGHT in their new home should have been a joyous occasion, but Diana was so preoccupied with what Marcus had told her, she could barely keep her mind on hosting dinner. The food was excellent, mostly because Marcus had brought with him a chef, properly interviewed in London by his mother and passed as acceptable. Tomorrow Diana would meet with the new cook to plan menus for the week and begin preparations for the Royal Visit, but for today she would be thankful he was proving as capable as his references suggested.

Awash in candlelight, the dining room showed to wonderful advantage. Fresh paint, the murals restored, gleaming china and silver, everything perfect. Evan sat at the head of the polished table, with Marcus and Diana on either side.

Even the cherubs overhead seemed to be happy with the improvements. Though they didn't have her worries.

"I still can't believe the mountain of work you've accomplished." Marcus eyed the massive gilt mirror over the fireplace. "You would never know the house was an abandoned wreck just a few short weeks ago. Once you finish the Royal Apartments, you'll be ready for His Highness's visit."

"There's still a fair bit to do before the estate is self-sufficient." Evan poked the duck breast in cherry sauce on his plate. "I don't know that I will ever grow accustomed to this fancy food. Not after years of dried peas and salted beef in the army."

Diana pushed her food around her plate. The chef was essential for hosting the Royal Visit, and she was grateful for the Duchess of Haverly seeing to finding one for White Haven, but Diana, too, had grown accustomed to the plainer fare of the inn.

Marcus studied her across the table, but she didn't meet his eyes. Would he tell Evan her secret? Would he feel compelled to tell her father?

Perhaps tonight, when everyone had retired, she would find the courage to tell Evan, to beg him for help in protecting Cian.

One of the footmen, a retired soldier with a dashing eye patch, removed her plate. Bending close, he murmured, "My lady, your maid needs you upstairs."

"Now?" Diana took her napkin from her lap.

"Yes, ma'am. It's something to do with the child. She's in your bedchamber."

Marcus watched her, and she swallowed. Dare she leave him alone with Evan? But Cian needed her. She placed her napkin beside her goblet and rose.

Evan and Marcus got to their feet, her husband's brows rising.

"Excuse me, please, gentlemen. Something needs my attention." She followed the footman out of the dining room, casting one last glance back at Marcus, hoping he would hold his tongue in her absence.

Upstairs, Beth paced Diana's bedroom, Cian against her shoulder. A flush rode the baby's cheeks, and his eyes were dull.

"What is it?" Diana rushed forward, hands outstretched for the boy.

"He's feverish, ma'am. And his breathing is queer." The girl handed Cian over, worry screwing up her features. "It came on sudden-like. He's had a bit of a heavy chest and a sniffle the past couple of days, but it got worse quickly. He's off his feed, and I can't seem to liven him up."

Diana touched Cian's tiny hand, alarmed at the heat radiating from his skin. His narrow chest rose and fell rapidly, but it was the lack of interest in his eyes that scared her most.

"Get me some cool water, and have Miss Monroe bring me a sugar cone." Perhaps he was just wearing too many blankets. She would perk him up with a bit of sugar water, and maybe he'd be fine. Diana laid the baby on the satin bedcover and unwrapped one of the blankets Beth had swaddled him in.

Beth scurried from the room, and Diana lifted the listless baby into her arms, cradling him and pacing. Normally at this time of the evening, Cian was fussy, ready for his bottle and bedtime. At the inn, Diana had worried that his crying every evening would upset the patrons of the taproom downstairs. Now she wished he *would* cry a little bit.

Was it just a feverish cold? Or something more? Should she send for a doctor? How could she know? The thick rug cushioned her footsteps, and a fire chased the early spring chill from the room, but gooseflesh appeared on Diana's arms, and her feet felt like lead. The room was beautifully appointed with pale-green satins and ormolu furnishings, but she ignored all of it in favor of the dark-eyed child.

Please, Lord, You can heal. You can help. I need Your help now. Was He listening? Did He know how much she loved this baby? How much she needed him? *Please, let me know You hear me.*

Beth returned with the water, and Louisa followed with a paper-wrapped sugar cone from the safe in the butler's pantry.

"My lady?" the housekeeper asked, the keys on her chatelaine jingling softly. "What's wrong with the wee sprout?"

She didn't wait for an answer, coming forward and cupping his head, listening to his breathing. "I don't like the sound of that chest."

There was a bit of a rasp each time Cian inhaled. Diana realized she was breathing harder, as if she could help him.

"What should we do?"

"Let's try to get him cooled off and see what happens. Fevers rise quickly in little ones, and they can drop just as fast. Many's the village child I've treated. It's probably nothing to worry about."

The housekeeper's bustling, assured manner gave Diana confidence. "You don't think we need to send for the doctor?"

"I wouldn't let that man treat a sick cat. He's got no more notion of how to cure patients than a doorstop would." Her mouth pinched. "He'd probably prescribe blister packs and whiskey for the child. Now, let's see that young man."

Though they bathed Cian, and he did seem some cooler, his breathing didn't ease. If anything, it grew worse over the next hour. Each intake brought a rattle, and each exhale sounded like a tiny bark. What was happening to him? He took only a few teaspoons of the sugar water, too exhausted for more.

Louisa's brusque tongue and hearty manner faded, and her face grew grim. Diana worried anew, pacing with Cian in her arms, glancing at the clock every time she passed it, praying without forming words in her head.

Finally the housekeeper motioned to Beth, as if coming to a decision. "Go and get Mr. Shand. And bring some coal and a kettle. Have one of the footmen bring cans of water. Hurry, girl."

"What are you doing? Why do you need Mr. Shand?" Diana's arms tightened around Cian. "Do you know what this sickness is?"

"We'll try a few remedies and see what helps." Louisa opened the cupboard under the washstand and withdrew a stack of cloths. She dipped one in the fresh water Beth had just brought and drew it down Cian's cheek. The baby squeaked and snuffled, then went back to concentrating on breathing.

"What is it?" Diana was afraid to ask, but she had to know.

"Most likely he's a bit croupy."

"Croup?" How did one treat that?

"Aye, I'm hoping that's all it is."

Shand tapped on the open door. "What can I do for you, my lady?"

Louisa addressed him without looking up. "I need a few things from the apothecary in town. Camphor oil, yarrow powder, and some cloves. Hurry, man. Don't stand there like a garden statue."

"My lady?" he asked Diana. Ignoring Louisa, he clearly didn't wish to take orders from the housekeeper.

Those two got along like oil and water, but Diana had no time for their antics at the moment. "Please get everything she needs. And ask the earl to come to my room." Evan would want to know. And she wanted him to be with her.

Shand glared at Louisa, then bowed quickly and was gone.

The one-eyed footman reappeared with a coal hod and a can of water.

Louisa directed him. "Bring several of those tall-backed chairs from the hall and two new bed sheets and some blankets."

Diana continued to hold Cian. Evan strode into the room, concern reflected in his blue eyes. "What's going on?"

Cian coughed, his little chest wheezing and his face going red. Diana looked up at her husband. "He's sick. It came on suddenly."

Evan's large hand came out to cradle the baby's head, and her heart squeezed. Just having him there comforted her.

Marcus came into the room, his hands in his pockets, his expression sober. "Is there anything I can do to help?"

"Shand is going into town to get some things for Louisa. She's got a plan."

"I could use your help." The housekeeper stoked the fire. "Help me arrange some furniture if you will, sir."

Marcus and the footman arranged four ladder-backed chairs in a square, and Louisa shook out a bed sheet, draping it over the chairs. "Steam will help him breathe easier. We'll boil some water and hold him under the tent to trap the steam in with him."

"What about his fever?" Evan asked. "Won't the steam heat him up?"

"It won't matter if he can't breathe. We'll deal with the fever later." She poured a boiling kettle of water into a basin. "Whenever that man gets back with the camphor oil, we'll add that to the water. Hope he doesn't take his sweet time."

She reached for Cian, but Diana shook her head. "I'll keep him. Just tell me what to do."

"It's no job for a lady. Let me sit under the tent with him."

"No." She couldn't turn loose of him. Evan's brows arrowed together, and he looked from Beth to Diana. The maid looked concerned but not panicked, not the way she would if Cian were really her son.

Not the way Diana felt. But there was no time for explanations, not now.

Evan held the sheet up, and she ducked under with the baby in her arms, seating herself on the square of carpet in the center of the chairs. Louisa pushed the basin in beside her, and Diana put Cian in her lap, loosening his blankets. He would be warm enough without them.

Steam rose from the porcelain basin, and Diana's skin became damp. Cian continued to wheeze and bark, working hard to get air. The skin on his fingers and around his lips became blue.

Louisa changed the water, and a fresh batch of steam rolled up. Diana's dress, so carefully chosen for tonight's dinner, stuck to her skin. Cian's brown eyes closed, and she wanted to cry. Her every attention was on the rise and fall of his little chest, the sound of his raspy breaths.

A commotion at the bedroom door drew her attention.

"You took long enough," Louisa snapped.

"I had to rouse the apothecary. Here." Paper rustled. "I went as fast as I could."

Evan raised the sheet to check on Diana. "Medicine's here."

Louisa edged around him, reaching into the steam tent to let a few drops fall from a small bottle into the water. Immediately Diana could feel her own sinuses clear as the pungent aroma of camphor filled the small space.

"That should help." Louisa stoppered the bottle. "We'll refresh it often."

Cian lay in Diana's lap, arms and legs lax, as if he had no strength for anything but trying to breathe. While her eyes watered at the almost noxious strength of the camphor, he appeared unaffected. If anything, the baby seemed to grow worse, almost choking.

After an eternity, Louisa threw back the sheets. "It's not working. We'll have to try something else."

"What?"

"His throat is full of phlegm. We have to make him choke it up."

Panic made her arms shake. "How? Will that work?"

"We don't have a choice." Louisa rummaged through the bottles Shand had brought. "You," she barked at the steward. "Cut a rock of sugar off that cone."

Evan put his arm around Diana, and she leaned into him, cradling Cian against her chest.

Quickly, Louisa took the chunk of sugar, popped it onto a spoon, and let a few drops fall out of a medicine bottle onto the sugar, which melted into a grainy slush.

"This will make him vomit, so be ready. I won't use much, because he's so small."

She tipped Cian back in Diana's arms, pushed down his chin, and poured the contents of the spoon into his mouth.

Within seconds Cian began to drool, and his breathing worsened.

"He's choking. What did you give him?" Diana almost screamed, holding the baby forward over her arm, letting the drool spill to the floor.

Louisa reached for the basin to catch the spittle.

Then he erupted. And continued to do so for several minutes.

But when he finally stopped retching, he began to cry.

The most beautiful cry Diana had ever heard, clear and indignant. Before, he had been trying so hard to breathe that he'd had no air for crying. Now his wails filled the room as tears filled her eyes. *God, You hear me. Thank You. Thank You for saving him. Thank You for sending Louisa. Thank You, thank You, thank You.* The words echoed through her head in a steady stream as she cuddled Cian close.

"He's coughed up the phlegm." Louisa sank into a chair, putting her face in her hands. "Thank the Lord."

"Amen." Evan sagged onto the blanket chest at the foot of the bed, his hands braced on his knees.

Diana realized he must have been praying as hard as she.

Taking a cool cloth, Diana bathed Cian's little face, which made him mad. She laid him on the bed and changed his gown, and when she wrapped him tight and put him against her shoulder to cuddle him, he quieted and fell asleep.

"My sweet boy. I don't know what I would've done if I'd lost you," she murmured against his neck.

As Louisa, Shand, and the footman cleaned things up, Evan put his hand on Diana's arm. "Perhaps you can give Cian back to his *mother* now?" His voice was dry, brittle as the brambles that had covered White Haven such a short time ago. "If she *is* his mother. If I didn't know better, I'd say Cian belonged to you."

Beth, who had been sitting in the corner of the room throughout the evening, jolted, and everyone in the room stilled.

Diana's eyes clashed with Marcus's. The time of reckoning had come.

"I didn't tell him." Marcus spread his hands. "But he has a right to know."

He did have the right. She only wished she had told him before he'd guessed.

"Evan, could we speak in private please?" She had a sense of stepping off a cliff, knowing there would be no turning back.

Evan led the way into his new bedroom and closed the door behind Diana, who still held the sleeping baby. His gut was tight, especially looking at his wife's face. Was it fear, or was it guilt?

"Cian doesn't belong to Beth, does he?" Evan went on the offensive, afraid of what she was going to tell him and wanting to take it head on. "I should've known. You've been playing me for a fool this entire time, haven't you? Even my mother suspected. She commented on how the baby looked like he could be more yours than the maid's. When I look at him, he favors you. Same brown eyes, same curling brown hair. I suppose everyone knew about it but me?"

Diana's hair clung to her forehead and temples in damp ringlets, and the steam had made her dress limp. A flush rode her cheeks, and she looked broken, vulnerable, and scared. He steeled himself against her.

"Tell me the truth. Is that Beth's son you're holding?"

"No." Tears formed on her lashes, but he was beyond caring.

He'd been duped. Her gentle, virginal air had been a sham. She had tricked him in more than just this. How had he not known? No wonder she'd been so eager to marry, hadn't even complained when he'd rushed her to the altar.

"Explain."

She gulped. "Cian isn't Beth's child. He's mine."

The words cut another wound in Evan's heart.

"When were you going to tell me? And what else have you been lying about? You know what? Don't explain. You've lied so much, I will never be able to trust what you say."

"Evan, please." Her hand reached out, entreating him. "Just listen."

He crossed his arms. "I'll listen, and then we will never speak of this again. You know, I was of two minds whether we needed separate bedrooms after all we've shared, but now I'm glad."

She flinched, as if he'd struck her.

"Cian is my son because I promised his mother I would raise him as my own." Her chin came up, and the color drained from her cheeks. "His mother was my dear sister, who died giving birth to her son. And before you ask, no, she wasn't married. She went to London for her debut Season, and she was seduced by a scoundrel. She came home in disgrace, though no one in London knew. My father kept her a prisoner in the country, and when she was dying, I promised to look after her baby." Her arms tightened around Cian. "And you might as well know that I stole him from my father's house. By law, my father is his guardian, but Catherine never wanted that. My father tried to use Cian as leverage to get me to obey him, to sell him back to me if I would sign over my inheritance to him without your knowledge. When the prince foiled his plans, I knew I had to get Cian out of the house to keep him safe." She blinked hard, refusing to let the tears fall. "I should have told you sooner, but I was afraid. I barely knew you. How could I know you wouldn't threaten the same as my father, to abandon Cian in a foundling home at the first opportunity? Or return him to my father's house, which would amount to the same thing?"

Evan's arms fell to his sides. The baby wasn't hers . . . and yet he was. The by-blow of her sister and some London rake.

"What about the baby's father?"

"He doesn't know about him, nor would he care. He would be worse than my own father, if such a thing is possible."

"Who is he?"

She shook her head, her mouth setting in a firm line. "I promised Catherine I would never tell."

Evan turned and went to the window, drawing aside the heavy drapes and looking out on the night. For long moments, his mind whirled with what he'd learned.

The conclusion of his thoughts was always the same.

His wife had lied to him. Here he had been thinking that God had brought her into his life to help him, to complete him, and she'd been deceiving him from the moment they met. Some blessing she was turning out to be. A bad joke, more like.

A searing pain jerked from the nape of his neck to his brow, and he grabbed his temples.

"What are you going to do?" Diana asked.

He couldn't think, not with the pain taking away his breath.

"Just go."

The door closed softly, and he pressed hard on his head. When would he be free of this torment?

CHAPTER 13

DIANA FELT SHE walked on soap bubbles. Marcus had departed for London with the final list of furnishings and fabrics for the Royal Apartment, kissing her cheek and squeezing her hand.

"It will come right. Give him some time. It's been a shock."

She'd nodded, but she didn't believe him. Together, she and Evan had been building something precious, something that boded well for their future. She had begun to trust him, to believe that when she told him about Cian, he would side with her, perhaps even be proud of her courage in secreting the baby out of her father's house. She had hoped he would want to throw his mantle of protection around her and the baby, accept Cian as . . . if not his son, at least his ward.

But now, several weeks after Evan had learned the truth, he still regarded her with mistrust. As if she were the villainess in the play, not her father, not her sister's seducer. He avoided her during the day, finding reasons to be busy elsewhere. Mealtimes were taken in near silence, the only safe topic of conversation the latest improvements and changes to the estate.

And he stayed alone in his own room each night.

The one thing that remained the same was the work that continued at a frantic pace. The hastily ordered appointments for the prince's rooms had arrived, and Diana spent most of her time overseeing the cleaning, repairs, and installations in the royal wing, paying attention to every detail. Her reputation as a hostess would be made or broken by this visit, and she intended to be a credit to her status in the peerage. Perhaps, if she performed well, Evan would value her as he once had and they could rebuild the trust that had been broken.

Now she stood on the back terrace in the May sunshine, looking out over the sloping lawns and gardens, catching a glimpse of sunlight off the lake below. Easter had come and gone, and the prince could arrive at any moment. Everything was as ready as they could make it, and there was nothing to do but wait.

A warm breeze teased her cheeks, and she smelled the loamy, fresh scent of spring. The distant trees wore a mist of pale green as new leaves unfurled, and the daffodils and crocus, long neglected but now weeded, were thriving along the garden borders.

Near the kitchen gardens, the tang of smoke hung in the air. A handful of outdoor workers burned the last of the bracken and garden clippings. The ashes would be spread under the shrubs, food for new growth.

Yes, everything was coming along. Workmen had begun repairing the boathouse and the outbuildings, and Evan had spoken of stocking the orangery and succession houses this season rather than next. Diana couldn't contemplate next year. Or next month. If only they could get the prince's visit behind them.

Behind her, Louisa opened the glass doors and stepped onto the terrace. "My lady, we have visitors."

Diana turned, noting the sour expression on her housekeeper's face. Never the most genial of women, Louisa looked as if she'd just drunk pure vinegar. "Is it the vicar?" He'd mentioned on Sunday the possibility of paying a call during the week.

"No, two men. One says he's your brother, my lady."

Cold chills raced along her skin. Her brother? Had he come with her father? Or had he been sent? Diana's first instinct was to find Cian, to make sure he was safe. But the baby was in the new nursery with Beth, where he had been recuperating from his sickness. Though he seemed fully recovered, Diana had instructed Beth to keep him indoors and quiet.

"Where are they? And who is the other gentleman?"

"They're in the drawing room. The other gentleman didn't give his name, ma'am. The footman is seeing to their baggage. Should I put them in the south wing?"

"No!"

Louisa jerked, and Diana realized she'd shouted. Modulating her voice, she strove to sound composed. But the south wing would never do. The nursery was in the south wing, the room chosen to take advantage of the sunshine all day. The farther she kept Percival from the nursery, the better for her peace of mind.

"Please, put them in the east-facing guest rooms near the Royal Apartments."

"Yes, ma'am." She lifted her hem to return to the house, but Diana stopped her.

"Do you know where the earl is at the moment?" she asked.

"A new batch of horses arrived, and I believe he went down to the stables."

She didn't want to greet her brother on her own, especially if their father was with him, but would Evan be her ally or her foe if he joined her? Should she send for him or brazen it out alone?

The decision was taken from her hands as Percival nearly collided with Louisa in the doorway.

"I say, the view's not bad." He slouched onto the terrace, insolent as always.

Diana tensed, but she held her ground. Percival might have bullied and tyrannized her while she lived in her father's house, but he wouldn't be allowed such privilege at White Haven.

"What are you doing here?" She kept her voice neutral and flat.

"Thought it was high time I saw where you were hiding yourself. Rumor had it you wouldn't be ready for the prince's visit. Some bookmakers were laying odds, in fact." He tapped the head of his cane into his palm. "I guess I lost a bet. The place looks shipshape now. Must have cost you a packet." Percival sized up the back of the house, with pristine masonry and shining glass, not a bramble or cobweb to be seen.

"You found her."

Diana started as another visitor strolled through the French doors. Her heart constricted. It wasn't her father after all. She should've known who would be her brother's companion. The two had been inseparable in London.

Viscount Fitzroy gave her a mocking bow. Tousled hair just right, Hessians polished to a shine, rust-colored waistcoat under a pale-jade jacket, and indecently tight breeches of deerskin. Up-to-the-minute fashion and suave charisma.

He repelled her like finding a garden slug in her lettuce. At the same time, she felt dismay. She turned back to her brother lest Fitzroy see her disgust. Cian's father, in her house.

"Lady Whitelock."

She didn't respond. She well remembered his coarse and inappropriate comments to her in the art gallery, and the way he looked at her now said he was still of the same mind.

Concentrating her attention on Percival, she said, "My finances are none of your concern, if you remember, so how much we spent on the house is no business of yours."

"We'll see about that when Father arrives, won't we?"

"He's coming?" She couldn't keep the dismay from her voice, but regretted not having better control when Percival grinned a wicked grin.

Her brother fingered the diamond-studded quizzing glass on a gold chain hanging from his lapel. Where had he gotten that expensive bauble?

"He's coming with the Prince Regent. Two days from now. That's why we're here. We were sent as town criers, if you will, bringing you the news. I was with the prince this week, and I told him we'd let you know." Percival preened, clearly expecting her to be impressed by his access to the Regent's inner circle. "I have enjoyed quite a bit of Prinny's company since you got married. Helps being his godson, of course, and the brother-in-law of his new favorite earl."

Fitzroy took a seat on one of the stone benches, crossing his legs elegantly and leaning back. "There are many enjoyments to be experienced when one is close to the prince, aren't there? He knows how to have a good time, I'll give him that." He flicked his wrist. "Too bad your housekeeper is such a cow. Too old and vitriol-tongued. Perhaps there are some prettier maids on your staff? I could use a bit of easy company."

Her hands fisted. "If you trifle with my employees, I'll have you thrown out like old dishwater."

"Tut-tut, my dear. Such a temper. It wouldn't do to go chucking the prince's friends out of the house on the eve of his arrival, would it?" Fitzroy smirked. "What would the prince say?"

His smugness galled her. Diana would like nothing more than to show them the door, but she had no choice. They would be staying while the prince was here, because the Regent wished it.

But they'd better watch their steps.

She took a grip on her frustration and forced herself to say, "I'm sure your luggage is in your rooms, if you'd like to freshen up. I'll notify the cook we'll be four for dinner." The thought of sitting down to a meal with these two made her stomach churn.

Percival wandered back inside, but Fitzroy approached her, crowding her. She stepped back, her skirts brushing an urn of flower seedlings behind her, cutting off her escape.

"Leave me alone. You've no right to accost me, especially not in my own home."

He laughed, and anger burned her throat.

"Accost you? My dear, I've done nothing of the sort. I just wanted to remind you of a few things." He touched her cheek.

She flinched. "I want to hear nothing from you."

"And yet you must. First, I wanted to remind you that my offer remains. When you tire of Whitelock, I'll be waiting for you. You'll soon realize that though you can try to dress up mutton, it will forever just be a sheep. Evan is and always will be common as dirt. When you're ready for a real gentleman, a true-born gentleman, I'm here."

"My husband might be a commoner by birth, but he's more of a gentleman than you'll ever be." She wanted to forget her status and smack his face. It wouldn't be ladylike in the least, but it would relieve her feelings. "I despise you, and I don't care who knows it."

"Ah, but that brings us to the second thing of which I must remind you. I hold power over you, and I intend to wield it. If you let your—shall we say, disdain—of me show, even for an instant during the prince's visit, I will let it slip that not only did I manage to seduce your naïve older sister but that I've bedded you as well." He leaned forward to drip his oily whisper into her ear.

Aghast, she shuddered. How dare he? She'd kept silent about Catherine, to the detriment of her marriage, and here he was threatening to throw tinder on that fire by claiming he'd seduced both sisters? Her hand rose to slap his impertinent face, but he grabbed her wrist, twisting it behind her back, wrenching her toward him so that she crashed against his chest.

A man cleared his throat, and Fitzroy froze, slowly backing away and letting go his hold on her arm. His brow resembled a thundercloud, and his eyes promised trouble.

"My lady, is everything all right?" Shand bowed and stepped forward, his eyes sharp. "His Lordship sent me to fetch you. There's something he wants to show you in the stable yard."

Relief poured over Diana, both for the escape from Fitzroy and that Evan had sent for her. It was the first time in weeks that he had expressed a desire for her company, and she needed them to be in harmony now more than ever, as there were enemies within their gates.

"I'll come right away." She fussed with her hair and dress, hoping she would look pleasing to her husband, that she could hide the disquiet in her heart at Fitzroy's threats. "Do go inside, sir. I'm sure your rooms are ready."

Fitzroy leered and sneered, but there was little else he could do with the steward there. "Remember what I said." He marched into the house.

Diana breathed again. "Thank you, Shand."

"My lady." He looked after the viscount, his eyes troubled. "Was that man causing you trouble? I remember him from the wedding."

She forced a smile. "You said the earl wanted me?" Again, her spirit leapt with hope at the thought.

Shand gnawed his lower lip. "I do beg your pardon. His Lordship didn't send for you. It was the first thing I could think of to get you away from that man, if that was your desire." His brows lifted in question.

"Oh, I see." One shouldn't feel so desolate, but she couldn't help it. "I appreciate you rescuing me. Some guests can be quite tiresome, can't they?"

"True, ma'am. The earl might not have sent for you, but there are some new horses at the stables, and I would be happy to escort you down to see them."

"Thank you, Shand." She started along the paved walk with the steward two steps behind. How would Evan react to the arrival of these particular guests?

Evan studied the new animals, but his mind wasn't on horses. What was he going to do?

His wife had lied to him, and in his astonishment and sense of betrayal, he'd responded scathingly. And he'd been punishing her ever since. With silence. With isolation. While he tried to make sense of things, to decide what he was going to do.

The wound was still raw, and he couldn't resist probing it. All the warning signs had been there, but he had refused to see them.

As if lying to him weren't enough, Diana had drawn him into caring for the child too. He'd taken much satisfaction in being the one who could soothe the baby when he got fussy in the evenings, spending the time after dinner holding the child against his chest, patting the tiny back and murmuring to him. Evan had been able to draw the biggest smiles from him too, toothless, drooling, delighted smiles.

And he'd felt good doing so, since the child belonged to a lady's maid and he'd felt sorry for the girl. Doing her a kindness hadn't taxed him overly.

But now he didn't know how to feel. The infant was his wife's nephew, his relation by marriage now. That made him responsible for the child in a tangible way. Not only that, but he was responsible for his wife's actions, and she'd deceived him, but worse, she'd stolen a child from his guardian. How was he supposed to protect her from the consequences?

Diana.

He might be angry with her for lying, but he couldn't fault her compassion in secreting Cian away from her father's house. But why hadn't she told him? Why lie to him? Perhaps in the beginning when they hadn't known each other well, but why continue the deception once they had become . . . close?

He missed her. He missed being with her, talking with her, hearing her laughter, watching her blossom with newfound confidence. Since the night of Cian's illness, she'd retreated once more into her shell, protecting herself from his surliness in the same way he'd seen her protect herself from her father.

Had his reaction to her secret undone all the good living here at White Haven had accomplished?

She was the one who had lied to him. So why did he feel so guilty? It wasn't fair.

God, how can this be Your plan? It seems every time I think I'm finding my footing, You fire something else at me. The earldom, a wife, a manor house, and now a helpless ward? Why? Why didn't You just let me stay a soldier?

His thoughts tumbled like water over a mill wheel, turning and splashing. Absently, he approached a rangy bay with white socks and a wide white blaze. The animal was no beauty, with feet like dinner plates and a mane as wild as bracken. He snorted and stomped, his hoof ringing on the cobbles. White ringed his eye, and he wrenched his head away from Evan's hand.

Wheeling on the end of his rope, the bay dragged the groom a few paces. Down his left flank, he bore a long scar. A saber slash. No other weapon could cause such a wound.

Recognition arrived at the same time as a memory flashed across his mind.

Men shouting, smoke, cannon fire, flying dirt, and concussion. He was running, zigzagging across the battlefield, racing toward a wagon where one horse had been shot. The other had tried to run, but the dead weight of his teammate had prevented his escape.

Evan's breath came quickly, and his skin prickled with sweat. Hot pain seared through his head, and he squinted as the sunlight stabbed his eyes. His episodes had been so infrequent lately, this one caught him broadside, staggering him with its intensity.

Commodore. The name flitted across his mind. That was the beast's name. Commodore.

This horse had been at Salamanca. And other battles as well, one of the animals that had hauled provision wagons for the Ninety-Fifth Rifles. The very animal who had carried Evan to safety behind the lines, dragging a wagon with Percival Seaton hiding inside. The fateful action that had started Evan down his current road.

Evan took several deep breaths, reminding himself that he was in Sussex, not Spain, that war was a thing of the past for him, that he was safe.

And yet terrible urgency swept over him again. A spy. He had to get to his commanding officers.

Frustration burned in his throat. Why couldn't he remember? Why couldn't he forget?

"Sir?" the groom asked. "Is something amiss?"

He shook his head, unable to speak as the pain and panic pursued him. *Calm down. Deep breaths. Don't let him see your distress, or he'll call the bailiffs and they'll cart you away to the asylum.*

The groom's face screwed up in concern and not a little alarm. "Should I call someone, my lord?"

Fighting to dispel the panic and shards of memory, Evan focused his attention on the lad's face. He hadn't had an attack this bad for weeks. When he finally spoke, his voice croaked, and he cleared his throat to try again.

"The other horses can go into the paddock once you've checked them over, but keep this fellow here. In fact, I'll see to him. You look after the others." Taking the lead rope, Evan nodded to the groom, who bowed before instructing the stable lads to move out with the seven other new arrivals. Evan's hand shook on the rough hemp, his palms sweating.

When he was finally alone in the yard, Evan turned back to Commodore. He examined the rough reddish-brown coat. Somewhere along the way, the horse had suffered a terrible injury. Was it in those terrifying moments at Salamanca as he had saved Evan's life? Or had it happened later in another battle? Evan had been shot, hanging over Commodore's neck, gripping his mane, telling himself over and over that he mustn't fall off, that he had to get to the British line. Once he'd reached relative safety, he'd crashed to the ground, and that was all he could remember before waking up aboard a ship, being transported back to England to recover.

The horse's wound had been stitched badly, and the scar was jagged and rough. Amazing he'd survived, that someone hadn't put him out of his misery rather than treat him.

"Easy, boy. Easy." He slowly shortened the lead rope. With a few snorts and stamps, the gelding let Evan touch his neck, his hide twitching and his tail swishing.

What a strange twist, that the very animal who had saved Evan's life should arrive at White Haven. The Lord moved in mysterious ways.

"Sir?" Shand came under the archway into the stable yard. The horse skittered. "They've arrived then?"

"Yes, eight new ones today. Look at this, Sergeant. Remember this animal?" Evan turned, full of enthusiasm, but he froze when he saw Diana behind his steward. Lines of strain marred her beautiful face.

He felt a cad for his treatment of her, even as his righteous indignation rose up to justify his behavior.

"Why, sir, it's old Commodore himself." Shand kept his hands and his voice low, coming up on the horse's off side. "I sure do remember you, old son. Look, my lady. It's one of the horses from our old unit."

Diana hung back, twisting her fingers at her waist, her teeth worrying her lower lip. Sunlight glinted off his military ring, the ring she still wore because he hadn't gotten around to getting her something more suitable.

She looked as ready to flee as Commodore.

Shand stopped admiring the horse to look from Evan to Diana. The silence lengthened to the point of awkwardness, and Evan's former sergeant turned steward rolled his eyes.

"Sir, my lady has news for you. I'll take Commodore so you two can speak in private." His tone bore a hint of censure, which only made Evan feel guiltier, and as a result, angrier. He wasn't the one who'd lied, and yet he felt everyone was waiting for him to apologize.

Leading the big horse across the yard to one of the open boxes, Shand looked back once over his shoulder. His expression plainly said he thought Evan and Diana were both being foolish.

Evan's neck felt stiff and his face warm as he walked toward his wife. With the easing of cold weather, she'd taken to wearing lighter gowns, and this one today, in pale lavender, picked out the golden flecks in her eyes and showed off her delicate neck and shoulders. As he approached, she looked everywhere but at his face. She was as tense as a fawn caught out in the open.

He stopped before her, studying the way the sunlight raced along her brown curls, at how the whiteness of the part down the center of her head made her look vulnerable. Several curls brushed her brow and cheeks, and he remembered how silky her hair was, entwined around his fingers. "Shand said you have news?" His voice was rough.

"Yes."

Her tongue darted out to moisten her lips, and his eyes were drawn to the movement. Those sweet lips, so kissable . . . And yet they had lied to him, he reminded himself.

"Well?" he asked when she didn't continue.

She swallowed. "Messengers have come from London. The prince and his retinue will be here in two days."

Two days. He didn't know whether to be glad or anxious. For weeks now, the visit had been the focus of nearly every decision, every purchase, every effort. And now it was upon them.

"There's more." She wrung her hands. "The messengers are my brother and Viscount Fitzroy. They're at the house, and they claim they are staying through the prince's visit."

"In my house?" His voice rose, and his fists clenched. Diana flinched, and he realized what he'd said. "My house" instead of "our house."

Percival and Fitzroy. He'd made it abundantly clear that he had no desire to see either of them again, and they were taking up residence in his—their—home?

Diana spread her hands. "What was I supposed to do? I'm not strong enough to throw them out. And they were sent by the prince."

"I *am* strong enough to throw them out, the lot of them." And angry enough to do it.

"Wait. Please."

Her hand touched his arm, and he looked down at it, disconcerted that even that mild contact was enough to stir him.

"I need to know what you're planning to do about Cian. Because I don't know how much Percival and Fitzroy know. I mean, Percival knows about Cian of course, but I don't know if he knows the baby is here with me. And Fitzroy doesn't know about the baby, but he does know that Catherine fled London, and I don't want him putting the pieces together. He'll spread the news like a plague, and all of London will know. Even sparing that, both of them would tell my father, or else try to return the baby to him, expecting to be rewarded, I'm sure."

Bleakness crossed her face and her tone. She looked up at him with those big brown eyes. She wasn't begging, but she wasn't far from it. What kind of man did she think he was? He might be upset with her for not telling the truth, but he wasn't a monster. He wouldn't give a dog he didn't like to the Duke of Seaton, much less an innocent child.

Diana blinked hard. "Percival is sure to want money if he finds Cian is here. Money from you to keep it quiet or money from my father for bringing the baby back. Or possibly both, if he tries to play both ends against the middle."

Money.

The word left a bad taste in Evan's mouth. Before he had any money beyond his officer's pay, his problems had been simple. Try not to get shot or blown up or bayoneted. Survive until tomorrow. Now that he was rich, his life was so complex he didn't even know who he was anymore.

His troubles seemed to begin and end with the Seaton family. And Lord help him, he was married to one of them. And yet he didn't really see her as a Seaton, not anymore. She was a Whitelock. He had thought she was beginning to feel like an Eldridge, but that had been a fantasy. He was an Eldridge, his parents were Eldrigdes, but Diana was an aristocrat, something he wasn't and would never be. She could be Diana, Countess of Whitelock, but she'd never be just plain old Diana Eldridge.

"Let's go greet our 'guests,' shall we?" He offered her his elbow, a temporary cease-fire of sorts. It wasn't a capitulation, an admission of wrong, or a return to their previous accord, but he could pretend. He'd been doing it for so long now, pretending to be a gentleman, an estate owner, a member of the peerage, what was one more pretense thrown on the pile?

When they entered the house, Fitzroy strolled out of the drawing room, a glass in his hand.

It wasn't Christian of Evan to feel such antagonism, and yet he couldn't help it. He truly disliked the man. Diana must've felt the same, because her hand tightened on his arm and she sucked in a breath. At least they were reading from the same map in this, if nothing else.

Fitzroy raised his glass, the amber liquid reflecting the light from the large windows. "Cheers, and congratulations. I didn't get to properly greet the bride at your wedding. But better late than never."

He eyed Diana in a way that made Evan's blood run hot. The bounder. He remembered the satisfaction of punching Fitzroy in the nose at the art exhibition, drawing claret, and he had to force himself not to repeat the action.

"I don't remember issuing you an invitation to White Haven, Fitzroy."

A self-indulgent smile crossed the viscount's face. "Oh, you didn't have to. The Prince Regent did that for me. I'm sort of an envoy, making sure everything is in readiness for His Highness's visit."

The mantra that had been driving Evan's life for months reared its head once more.

One does not say no to the Prince Regent.

Though the country and the man himself might be better if someone did every once in a while. Much as he would love to chuck this interloper out on his ear, if he was here in an official capacity, they'd have to suffer him.

Contemplating the soaring foyer, Fitzroy sucked in a breath through his teeth. "It will have to do, won't it? Though it all feels a bit rustic. Still, what else can you expect in the country? I suppose the prince can bivouac for a few days." Condescension dripped from his voice. "Though it won't be up to his high taste."

Diana glared. "You wouldn't know good taste if you ran over it in the street." Her words were like arrows. "I'm sure the prince will have no complaints with our hospitality."

Evan wanted to cheer her on. She was a magnificent sight when riled.

Fitzroy must've thought the same, for his gaze focused on her once more, and he bowed, as if awarding her a point in a duel.

Percival slouched into the entryway. He glanced at Evan and Diana and grinned. "Hello, Whitelock. Surprised to see us?"

"Fairly."

"I know. It's an awful cheek to just barge in, but you'll have to make the best of it. When you're invited to accompany your ruling monarch on a trip to the seaside, you don't say no, do you?"

Something about Percival was subtly different from the last time Evan had seen him. He wasn't pouting or petulant. He had a fizz to him, some sort of inner excitement that gave him more personality than his former behavior implied.

Marcus had mentioned that Percival was throwing money about, money that had come from some source unknown to Marcus. Was this new confidence a result of having plenty of blunt?

Evan fisted his hands. They had him in a forked stick, and everyone in the room knew it. He couldn't throw them out, and he couldn't stomach them.

If the prince got wind of any of their difficulties, he would forever regret making Evan a member of the peerage.

Evan certainly regretted it.

CHAPTER 14

EVAN STOOD WITH Diana on the front steps of White Haven, watching the parade of coaches and wagons approach down the curving gravel drive from the gate house a quarter mile away. He lost count as they disappeared behind the trees and reappeared closer.

"How many do you think there are?" he asked as the staff at White Haven lined up, women on one side of the entrance, men on the other, all carefully pressed and presented.

Even old Greville Monroe, bent over his cane, looked respectable now that he wasn't trying to blow anyone's head off with an antique blunderbuss. Louisa and Shand eyed one another like always, scowl for scowl. Evan rolled his eyes, returning to the immediate situation.

"Did you know there would be such an army?"

Diana shook her head. "I had no idea. I thought maybe twenty, but look at all those coaches."

The house would never hold them all. Would it be considered bad form to shelter them on the lawn in tents? They could set up a mess tent and parade ground and call it Camp Whitelock.

"At least there will be one friendly face." Diana raised her hand to Marcus, who rode near the front of the caravan.

Grooms stood ready to take the horses and carriages to the stables, while the footmen would manage the baggage. The staff had been drilled in their duties, and even Louisa promised to hold her tongue.

But it was up to Evan and Diana to manage the guests, to entertain them and see that everyone was well tended. His heart thudded against his waistcoat. He wasn't ready for this.

Percival and Fitzroy stood on the steps behind him, and as the prince's carriage rolled to a stop, they crowded forward, to the point of edging past Evan and Diana and usurping their position as hosts.

Let them, the sycophants. He stood still, keeping Diana's hand through his arm. They would present a united front—though it might be a pretense—and be dignified.

Marcus swung out of the saddle, handing off the reins and ignoring Percival and Fitzroy in favor of greeting Diana. He smiled, and he held out both hands. "Lady Whitelock, you look enchanting." He planted a kiss on her raised cheek before shaking Evan's hand.

Diana did look enchanting. Her pale-green dress touched her in all the right places, making her look womanly and elegant, and she'd woven a golden ribbon through her curls that matched the trim on the gown and highlighted her beautiful eyes. Grace and breeding in every inch of her. But her renewed grip on his arm said while she might look composed, she was nervous.

The Prince Regent took quite a while to descend from his gilded ornate carriage, his face red with the effort. When his gold-buckled, red-heeled shoe touched the step, he winced.

"Oh dear," Diana murmured. "It must be his gout acting up."

Evan wanted to laugh at the sight of Percival and Fitzroy, one on either side of the prince, trying to gauge where best to grab him to assist him to the ground.

Finally, the prince batted their hands away, flapping the lace at his cuffs and stepping onto the gravel. He stood still, looking at the house for a moment, before his florid face broke into a wide smile when he spied them. "Whitelock."

Evan bowed deeply, and Diana sank into a low curtsy.

"Welcome to White Haven, Your Highness. It's an honor to have you here."

The prince looked satisfied, as if he agreed. "The place looks magnificent. You've done well. I hope the inside is as lovely as the outside."

When he glanced left and right at the long rows of servants, they bowed and curtsied as well. Behind him, chaos reigned as people emerged from carriages, horses whinnied and stamped, and baggage rattled.

Diana sucked in a breath, and Evan followed her gaze. Emerging from a black carriage, her father hunched and lowered himself before straightening. The Duke of Seaton was a shadow of his former self. He'd lost weight, and his clothes hung on his frame. His dark eyes were dull, and his nose red. Cracked blood vessels spidered his cheeks, and his hair, usually impeccably smooth, was rough and overlong.

Marcus had said the duke had been drinking heavily, but now Evan could see the effects himself. The only thing that appeared the same was the hooded quality of his eyes and the hardness of his mouth. The duke moved Percival aside with a glare and placed himself beside the prince as if it were his rightful spot.

The prince ignored Diana's father and brother, instead offering her his arm. "It was a brutal journey. I could use some refreshment and a comfortable chair."

"Of course, Your Highness. Please do come in." She looked back over her shoulder, sending Evan a pleading look.

While he would much rather stay outside and organize things, he sighed and followed them inside, motioning for Marcus to come too. Shand could see to the carriages and horses, and Louisa and the house staff would see to the luggage and room assignments.

Over the next hour, his wife amazed him. She was elegance personified. The prince settled into the overstuffed chair she'd had made especially for him, and his foot was placed onto an ottoman with plenty of cushions. Evan sat with Marcus on the settee to his left, and Diana was on his right. She offered His Highness an array of drinks and cakes and savories, and he took some of everything, claiming each was a personal favorite of his, and how had she known?

Evan intercepted a wry look between Diana and Marcus, and he suspected that everything was the prince's favorite and that both his wife and his friend, and probably everyone else in the *ton*, were well aware of it and couldn't go wrong with the food offered as long as it was plentiful.

Finally, the prince leaned back, dabbing his lips with a serviette. "Precisely what I needed, my dear. I can see that this respite, halfway between London and Brighton, could quickly become my favorite stop." He ran his hands over the brocade upholstery and squirmed himself a bit farther into the cushions. "This room is delightful. Who was your designer?"

Evan spoke up. "Lady Whitelock designed the rooms herself, Your Highness."

The prince's brows rose. "Such talent. This room is restful and exhibits excellent taste, Diana." He puffed up his chest. "And to think, you're my godchild."

Across the room, the Duke of Seaton glowered, shifting in his seat, crossing and recrossing his legs, drumming his fingers on the arm of his chair. Evan was no protocol expert, but the duke's actions bordered on the improper, showing such impatience in the presence of the prince. Diana kept casting her father worried glances when she thought no one was looking.

Marcus leaned over and whispered, "You're a blessed man. Diana's doing splendidly. The prince is quite taken with her, and the house looks well. I trust she got the Royal Apartments sorted?"

Evan nodded.

"What about between you two? Things weren't so amicable when I left."

Before Evan could answer, the prince was getting to his feet. Everyone in the room rose, and Diana took the prince's arm.

"Of course. Please let me show you to your rooms." Diana looked every bit the lady she was as she glided along beside the portly prince.

The moment they left the room, with several others following, Marcus held Evan back. "A moment, if you please? We need to talk."

"Let's go into the library. It will be quiet there." Evan led Marcus to the back of the house, to the dark-paneled, cozy library, one of his favorite rooms in the manor. Most of the books had been destroyed through neglect, rats chewing on the leather covers, mildew foxing the pages. But Diana had chosen replacements, and the room now smelled of furniture polish and paper, leather and beeswax.

Marcus admired the room with his eyes and expression before sobering. "Percival and Fitzroy have been here for the past few days?"

"Yes. They showed up, sent by the prince to make sure all was in readiness."

"Hmm." Skepticism coated the sound. "Is that what they said?"

"You mean the prince didn't send them?"

"If he did, it would be the first time. The prince expects everything to be perfect for him no matter when he arrives, no advanced troops necessary. No, your brother-in-law and the viscount came on their own hook, which means they have their own agenda."

"Other than being bothersome? What?"

"I don't know. I think it has something to do with where Percival has suddenly gotten a source of income." Marcus rapped his knuckles on the desk. "I think it has something to do with his time in Spain last year, but I can't seem to run it down."

Evan studied his friend. "Why are you so curious? Is it so odd that he has money? Maybe he's been winning at the tables, or maybe he came into an inheritance the same way Diana did."

"Let's just say, I've been asked to look into it by someone very senior. He's got questions, and he thinks I can find the answers. Has he said anything that would indicate where the money is coming from or why he came to White Haven early?"

Scratching his cheek, Evan thought back over the past two days. "Frankly, I've done my best to avoid both of them. But I did notice that Percival seemed different . . . more . . . powerful maybe? Less petulant for sure. Like he has a newfound confidence. It might be money. Money makes you aristocrats do strange things." He grinned, but he didn't feel funny.

Marcus had been asked to look into something by someone "very senior." In Evan's experience, that could mean a lot of things. Marcus's father was "very senior" in rank and influence. Perhaps he was doing his father's bidding. Or perhaps a senior ranking officer in his old unit had some questions.

"In any case, keep an ear out. If he says or does anything odd, let me know, will you?" Marcus shot his cuffs. "You didn't answer my question about how things were going between you and Diana. Did you get things sorted about the baby?"

The ever-present heaviness swelled in Evan's chest. "Let's just say we're flying the flag of truce until the prince's visit is over. We'll talk about what we're going to do afterward."

"She did the only thing she could, if you think about it."

"No, she could've told me the truth. Married people shouldn't keep secrets from each other, especially not ones of this magnitude."

Marcus tilted his head, one eyebrow rising. "Really? Have you been totally honest with Diana? About your headaches, the nightmares, the panic that you can't control?"

Startled, Evan shot up from where he'd been leaning on the desk. "How do you know about that?"

"You're not the only soldier to come back from the wars. I've had my share of nightmares. And I've watched you. Your outer wounds have healed, but the inner ones? Have you remembered anything more about that day? And have you told Diana about your memory loss?"

Evan hated it when the truth rose up and smacked him in his face. He hated it even more when an accusation of hypocrisy in his thinking was true. Diana had kept an important secret from him because she was afraid of what he would do with the information.

And he'd done the same to her.

"Not a great feeling to be hoist with your own petard, is it?" Marcus gave him a compassionate look. "I've been there myself. No one ever actually died from having to apologize, and I'm sure she'll be gracious when you tell her."

Evan rubbed his palm on the back of his neck. "You're right. She probably will be, and I'll feel even more of a heel."

Clapping him on the back, Marcus grinned. "Not that I have any experience, but I believe that's not an uncommon feeling for a married man."

The clock on the mantelpiece chimed. "I suppose we'd best go dress for dinner. Diana has put you in the south wing since you already know about Cian. You're next to the nursery. Hopefully, the little blighter won't keep you awake at night."

With much on his mind, Evan entered the master bedroom. His valet, a former batman in a Northumberland regiment, had hung a freshly ironed shirt and Evan's dinner clothes in the dressing room, but the man wasn't to be found. Probably fetching hot shaving water.

The door connecting his dressing room to Diana's stood open an inch or two, and he could hear rustling. She was probably dressing for dinner too. He heaved a sigh. He should knock and go in, make a clean breast of it, tell her what he needed to, and ask her forgiveness.

But knowing what he should do and doing it were two different things. He hated being wrong. And he really hated being wrong in front of someone he cared about, whose opinion he valued.

A thump sounded from her dressing room, and a gasp.

"Don't think I've forgotten how you abandoned me, nor how you stole my money. You'll give me some funds or else." The Duke of Seaton.

"Or else what?" Diana's voice, and he could hear both defiance, which made him proud, and fear, which made him mad. No one should strike fear into her heart.

Evan went to the door, his hand on the knob ready to wrench it open and protect his wife.

"Or else I'll tell the Prince Regent about you stealing that baseborn brat of your sister's out of my house. I've bided my time, but I won't wait much longer. You'll regret trying to cut a sham with me."

"If you do, I'll tell him of your threat to put Cian into a foundling home. You saw the prince today. Whom do you believe he will side with?"

She had spirit, he'd give her that. But it was time Evan intervened.

Pulling the door open, he saw the duke raise his hand. Quick as a hawk, Evan intercepted the blow, the duke's fist smacking Evan's palm.

He gripped it, forcing the man back, interposing his body in front of Diana. "You've made a serious misjudgment here, Seaton. For years Diana had no one of her own to stand up to your bullying ways, but that is no longer the case." He squeezed the fist, and the duke's red eyes watered. "I realize you are here as part of the prince's retinue, and as such I must suffer your presence in my house for a few more days. However, if you come anywhere near my family, and that includes Cian, I will throw you out of this house with a maximum of fanfare and attention, the Prince of Wales notwithstanding. You will keep to yourself, you will cease your threats, and you will walk small when you are around me. If I find out you're working some devious plan in the background, I'll expose you for the rotter you are. Am I making myself understood?"

The older man's knees shook, and he sank a few inches under the pressure of Evan's grip.

"I asked you a question."

"I understand."

"Then get out of here."

He released his grip, and Seaton almost fell. He gave them both a black look, cradling his bruised hand against his middle as he escaped.

When the bedroom door crashed shut, Evan turned to Diana, cupping her shoulders. "Are you all right? He didn't hurt you?"

She shook her head, brown eyes blinking fast.

Then he was kissing her. Her lips, her eyelids, her hair, her temples. He really should stop and apologize, say all the things that needed saying between them, but he couldn't seem to make himself. Especially when her arms went around his neck, her fingers tunneled into his hair, and she kissed him back as if she, too, had missed this.

"Ahem." A discreet tap at the connecting door. His valet. "My lord, your shaving water is ready."

I must not yell at this interruption. I must not yell at this interruption. Evan loosened his hold on his wife and turned to the nearly closed door.

"I'll be there in a moment. Shut the door."

With a snick, they were alone again.

"Diana, there's a lot I need to say to you and a few things I need to hear, and there's no time. We're hosting the Prince of Wales for dinner." He shook his head, wishing he could lock all the doors and take her into his bedroom, where they could settle things in a grand making up.

Her eyes were bright as candle flames and her lips rosy and slightly swollen from his kisses. Unable to resist, he kissed her again. "Tonight. We'll talk tonight."

Bemused, she smiled and nodded.

Evan went to dress, his heart lighter than it had been in months.

How Diana performed her hostess duties, she would never know. Every time she caught Evan's eye, she found herself smiling, her imagination wrapped in a world of two, where no one else could intrude. How she longed for the evening's end, when they could be alone to say what was on their hearts and heal the breach between them.

The way he had fronted her father on her behalf made her want to soar right up with the birds. Not only had he thrown a ring of protection around her, but he'd included Cian.

A true gentleman in every sense of the word.

"I know it's the wrong time of year, but how is the shooting here at White Haven?" the prince asked Evan.

Evan thought for a moment. "From the little I've ridden over the property, there is plenty of game. I have a new gamekeeper who would know more than I. Deer, waterfowl, doves. I'm told there are foxes too."

"Too bad it's early spring. Otherwise we could organize a hunting party." The prince waited expectantly.

Diana held her breath.

"Perhaps you would be able to return in the fall?" Evan asked.

She exhaled. Though neither of them really wanted another Royal Visit, not to offer would've been the height of bad manners.

"An excellent idea. Ratcliffe, make a note." The prince motioned to one of his courtiers. "We'll have to make plans. I've a very busy schedule, as you know, but a hunting weekend in Sussex? Excellent."

Several guests smirked, and Diana couldn't decide if they were being derisive because the prince would never again ride to hounds or take a strenuous walk through the fields with a fowling piece, or that they were smugly anticipating another vacation in the country come autumn.

"I understand," Viscount Fitzroy said suavely, "that Whitelock here was a crack shot in the Ninety-Fifth Rifles. Perhaps we can organize some target shooting on the morrow for a bit of amusement? I'm not a bad shot myself. Perhaps a contest?"

The prince nodded. "That sounds like an excellent amusement. I wouldn't mind a bit of a flutter." He rubbed his pudgy hands together. "How much should I wager, and on whom?"

"I'll join in." Percival leaned forward from midway down the table. "The shooting and the wagering. We can bet on ourselves, can we not?"

There were fourteen men at the table, and twelve of them put their names in for the contest. Diana mentally organized hampers of food, tables, chairs, and how to make the prince comfortable out of doors for an afternoon. She needed pen and paper to make a list. And what to do with the ladies? She'd planned a trip to a nearby abbey to study the architecture and beautiful stained glass. Perhaps they could postpone that until the following day and join the men in the field.

Diana caught Evan's eye and knew right away that something was bothering him. Did he not want to shoot? Marcus wore a less-than-thrilled expression too. Was something amiss?

She glanced down the long table to where her father sat, noticing that the footman was filling his wineglass yet again. The duke would bear watching. Drink had always made him irascible. She signaled the footman with a shake of her head, and he left the glass only half full, bowing slightly in her direction that he understood.

Courses were removed and courses were set, conversation swirled around Diana, and she did her best to follow along, especially on the prince's discourses. At least no one would go away hungry. It was proper protocol to stop eating when the prince laid aside his fork, but he didn't, putting away a prodigious amount of food, while Diana pushed hers around her plate. Would this dinner never end?

A jovial holiday atmosphere hung over the party. Eventually Diana shepherded the ladies across the hall into the drawing room for tea and gossip, while Evan stayed behind with the prince and the rest of the gentlemen for port and gossip.

As she paused in the doorway, she looked back. Percival and Fitzroy had their heads together, whispering. Her father looked longingly at the decanters the footmen carried in, and Marcus listened to something the prince was saying.

But Evan looked at her. An intense, private, we'll-be-alone-soon-to-sort-things-out look that sent a frisson up her spine and made her heart thud against her stays.

As she turned away, Fitzroy caught her eye. His sneer was insolent, yes, but something else lurked there. Something dangerous, malicious. His threats echoed in her ears. Threats to not only divulge his conquest of Catherine but to claim the same of her.

She rubbed her upper arms, though the house was warm enough. She vowed to tell Evan everything, promises to her dead sister or not. Cian's safety and hers must come first.

After an age, Evan mounted the stairs to the master suite. As an early riser, the social timetable of the *ton* was exhausting. It was well past midnight, and the guests were finally in their rooms. Shand took care of seeing that everything was secure, putting up the fire screens, and blowing out candles and lamps. Louisa loitered in the foyer, as if checking up that the steward was doing his job properly. Evan sighed as he climbed the steps. At least all their jibes and jabs kept the pair on their toes and ensured everything was done properly. He'd seen such competitiveness in the army, but he hadn't imagined it taking place in his own home.

He only hoped Diana, who had retired more than an hour ago, wasn't fast asleep. He'd been anticipating their private conversation all night and had even caught himself losing track of what his guests were saying as he stared at her across the drawing room or the dining table.

He needn't have worried about her being asleep. She wasn't in her room. And when he checked, she wasn't in his either. Disappointment poked him.

There was one place to try before he roused the house looking for her, and he went silently down the lushly carpeted hall to the south wing. He opened the nursery door and discovered his wife. She nestled in the corner of a settee before the low fire, Cian asleep against her shoulder. His head lay just under her chin, and his pink bow of a mouth pursed and relaxed. One fist rested against her collarbone, like a small seashell.

The smile she sent him over the baby's head made his insides warm. Without a word, she patted the upholstery next to her.

"Is he sick again?" Evan whispered as he sat.

"No, just fussy. I came to check on him before I went to bed, and he was grousing a bit. Beth was exhausted. I told her I'd take him for a while, and he finally fell asleep. You don't need to whisper. He's hard to get to sleep, but once he's succumbed, your entire regiment could march through the room with fife and drum and he wouldn't notice." She spoke indulgently, lovingly. In nightgown and wrapper, with her hair lying in a braid on her shoulder, she looked cuddly and ready for sleep herself. She'd kicked off her slippers and drawn her feet up, tucking them under her hem for warmth.

"Can you put him in his cot now?"

"I can, but . . . can we talk here? I don't want to let him go just yet."

Evan didn't let his disappointment show. He'd like to sweep her up into his arms and carry her back to his room and settle all their differences there, but if she wanted to talk here, he could be patient. For now.

"All right, but you're too far away over there. Come here." He held out his arm, inviting her to snuggle against his side. When they were situated, she in his embrace and Cian in hers, he sighed. "I'm proud of you, you know that?"

She leaned back to see his face. "Why?"

The temptation was too great. Though he'd promised himself they would talk first, he couldn't resist brushing a kiss on her lips. "So many reasons. I don't know another woman who could have taken on the task of fixing this house to meet royal standards in just three months the way you have, especially with a crew of former soldiers and squatters as her staff. You've accepted and trained them and showed that you care about them, a group of people that society often overlooks. You've won their loyalty and their respect.

"You've utterly charmed the Prince Regent, and Marcus claims that an invitation to White Haven or our house in London next Season will be the most coveted of the social calendar. But . . ." He squeezed her gently, reaching across her and Cian to envelop them further. "I'm most proud of you for how you love this child and would do anything to protect him." He swallowed his vanity and said what he should have a long time ago. "I understand why you didn't tell me the truth about Cian belonging to your sister. And why you stole him out of your father's house. I was wrong to be angry with you or to treat you so shabbily ever since I found out. That wasn't very noble of me."

Diana reached up and caressed his face. "If I had known you then as I do now, I would've had no reservations in telling you. I would've begged for your help instead of trying to conceal the truth. I should have told you long before I did."

He swallowed another chunk of his pride. "The thing is, I blamed you and treated you shamefully for keeping a secret from me, when all the time I've been keeping one from you."

She sat up, holding Cian to her shoulder. "What?" Firelight reflected in her brown eyes, and her hand cupped the baby's head.

This was his Rubicon. Once he crossed it, he was committed. He would give her knowledge she could use against him if she so chose. He would be vulnerable. All his military training said if you ever gave someone the opportunity to best you, you gave them a weapon to use against you.

This was what love did to you. Made you vulnerable because the person you loved had enough of your heart to break it. He'd never trusted someone like that before, but now he needed to. Wanted to, even.

Because he loved her. It was as simple as that. Love was more than regard, more than trust, more than companionship. It was giving everything without reservation, without secrets.

"It's about my injuries." Evan wasn't sure how to begin. "And the lasting effects."

"What's wrong? Is it serious? Why didn't you tell me?" She patted his arms, his chest, his leg.

He wanted to laugh at her show of care, but he stilled her hands.

"Are you in pain anywhere?" she asked.

"I'm fine. Well, nearly so. It's the wound to my head." He raised her fingers to touch the scar that ran just over his right ear, now well covered with hair. "The doctor says it was a bullet or a piece of shrapnel, and that I was very lucky. I don't think it was luck. God saved my life on that battlefield, though there were times when I wished He hadn't."

Her bottom lip disappeared behind her teeth. "Oh, Evan."

"The thing is, I don't remember how it happened or anything much about that day. Nothing reliable, anyway. And I don't know if I can trust those flashes of memory I do have. Anything can bring them on, a sound, a word, a smell even. That new horse in the yard, Commodore? He was at the Battle of Salamanca, where I was wounded. When I saw him, it was as if I were back in Spain, with bullets flying and cannons roaring." Even speaking of it had his heart racing and his skin prickling with sweat. He drew in a deep breath that scudded in his throat. "I think I was racing back toward the British lines with news of a spy that I'd captured, but I don't know. I can't remember." He pressed his hand to his temple as a pain shot through his head. Was it a real pain or only a result of trying to remember? A phantom pain like amputees experienced? It felt real enough.

She brushed his brow with her fingers, light as a bird. "That explains so much. The headaches . . . the nightmares?"

Heat prickled across his flesh. "I sometimes think I'm losing my reason. I was afraid to tell you, lest you think me insane and seek to have me put into an asylum."

Her chin dipped, and she looked at him through her upper lashes. "You cannot have seriously contemplated that thought. An asylum? Because you have bad dreams?" She looked at him as if he were a simpleton.

He felt like one. "It is the common treatment for this ailment. I've seen it before, many times. In the wake of a campaign, there are many wounded, and the sights and sounds and fear are terrible in the thick of battle. Some men's minds break, they lose their reason, and some become demented, harming themselves and others. Some men just go quiet, not speaking, not hearing, just staring into space . . ." He swallowed. For months now he'd feared he would slide into that mental oblivion, that his unreliable mind would finally snap. "The French have a term for it. *Vent du boulet*. It means wind of the bullet. Referring to men hearing bullets whistling by even when they're not being shot at. They shake and sweat and jolt at the slightest noise. Hopeless in battle after that, and often as not, put into an asylum. If I had only been having a few bad dreams, I wouldn't have worried. It was the memory loss, the panic that attacked out of nowhere, the loss of control. Even rage. I've never been a man of quick temper before, but it was as if I couldn't master my feelings. I know you've lived in fear of your father's temper all your life, and I didn't want you to be afraid of me." He brushed a few stray wisps of hair off her cheek. "I never want you to be afraid of me."

She leaned into his touch like a kitten, and he stroked her cheek with the back of his fingers.

"How do you feel now?" she asked. "Are you still suffering?"

"It's better but not gone, and I still have very few memories of that day. I wish I could recall why I was where I was, what I was doing, and whether the spy is a thing of my imagination or a real danger. I have no recollection of saving your brother's life. Did I mean to, or was it an accident? The papers say I ran across the open ground to get to the horse still tethered to the wagon. I cut the horse loose from his dead teammate, and I hopped on his back, racing toward the British line . . . and Percival was in the wagon. And then I was in the hospital, the Home Secretary came to visit, and the prince made me an earl. All for doing something I can't remember. I feel like such a fraud. All I wanted was to heal sufficiently to return to my regiment, but God had other plans." The familiar feelings of inadequacy roared up. "I hope that with time I'll return to normal and that even if I never recover my memory, I can be at peace with it." He smiled, leaning over to kiss her hair, inhaling the scent of her. "Having you and Cian and White Haven has certainly been an excellent distraction."

She pillowed her head on his arm. "I had no idea you were suffering like this. I wish you had told me sooner. I wish we had both been honest with each other from the start. We've wasted so much time worrying about what might happen if the other one knew the truth, and none of those things turned out to be accurate."

They sat in silence for a time.

"What are we going to do about Cian?" she finally asked. "You heard my father. He wants what he considers his due, or he'll raise a commotion. Then there's Percival, who knows about Cian and Catherine. I can't believe he hasn't asked for money, though at the moment he appears to have plenty. Marcus asked me if Percival was blackmailing me, but I told him no. I hadn't heard from anyone in my family since we left London."

"Do you know where Percival got his money?"

"No. He's terrible with funds, always running short. He and Father have the most awful rows about it, his gambling and womanizing and spending. Perhaps he's been winning at the gaming tables?"

Evan wrapped his arms around his little family. "Maybe. If so, it won't last. Gamblers never win in the long run. But about your father. I suggest we make him a bargain. We sign over a portion of our remaining funds, and he signs over custody of Cian."

Again she straightened, holding her hand against the baby's back to keep him on her shoulder. "Are you sure? You would do that?" Joy and incredulity dueled on her face.

"It seems the simplest solution, doesn't it? A onetime payment, and he leaves us alone forever."

"I don't like giving in to his demands, but if it means Cian is safe, then we must consider it." She worried her lower lip again. "There is one thing you don't know. About Cian." Her arms tightened around the baby, as if to protect him. "When she was dying, my sister told me who his father was. And she made me promise never to tell anyone. I don't want to break my word to her, even though she would never know."

Evan thought about it. If he had fathered a child, he would want to know. Then again, he would never father a child with anyone but his wife. But the *ton* was different. Their attitude toward these things was lax. Promiscuity seemed to occupy them constantly, and by-blows seemed to be common. What did he owe the man who had seduced his wife's sister?

He reached out and put his thumb against her lip, drawing it out from behind her teeth and rubbing it gently. They had discussed enough for the time being. When the house was empty of guests and Cian's future was settled, she could tell the rest of the story. Leaning forward, he brushed a kiss on Cian's downy dark head. "You don't need to tell me tonight. Now, put that young master in his cot where he belongs and come to bed. I have a few other things to say to you, but they don't require words."

CHAPTER 15

EVAN STOOD WITH Shand, watching the spectacle. "All of Wellington's army doesn't take this much provisioning and maneuvering." Just getting everyone from the house to the spot chosen for the contest had required more than an hour and most of his staff.

The prince himself sat on a plush chair, his foot on a pillowed stool, refreshments within reach, his every action fawned over by several servants and courtiers.

"Sir, the Ninety-Fifth would never let you live this down if they could see it. Entertaining pampered princes and the like after facing the guns at Salamanca." Shand put his hands on his hips. "We're scarcely a quarter mile from the house, but they've brought enough equipment for a six-month siege."

"It seems to be the theme with this caravan, excess baggage and 'necessities.' Forty carriages, twenty servants just for the prince, plus courtiers, secretaries, and various hangers-on. Not to mention all the friends he invited along. And every one of them with luggage and servants." Evan noted another wagon rumbling up, this one with more chairs and tables for the guests. His staff, the veterans and their wives, were working nearly around the clock to satisfy their guests' needs and wants. Evan would have to find a suitable way to reward them once the royal carnival moved on to Brighton.

Marcus strolled over, thumbs in his waistcoat pockets. "Do you think we'll ever actually get to the target shooting?"

"You mean before I'm in my dotage?" Evan asked.

Percival's loud laugh caught their attention. Evan's brother-in-law stood in a circle of young bucks, writing names in a small notebook while Fitzroy took money.

"Those boys would gamble on their grandmothers' coffins." Shand kicked a tuft of grass. "I thought soldiers were bad, but aristocrats will bet on anything. Viscount Fitzroy cornered me this morning to find out just how good a shot you were, sir. I gather he fancies himself quite a hand with a long gun and wanted to know what his chances were."

"What did you say?"

"That you were a veteran of more than a dozen battles and that you were still alive, so that should tell him something." Shand grinned.

Evan took note of the grooms leading several horses down the slope from the stables. At dinner the night before, he'd shared with the prince about his efforts to rehabilitate both veterans and military horses here at White Haven. Though he hadn't thought the prince all that interested at the time, this morning His Highness had asked to see some of the horses after the shooting competition. Evan's head groom had chosen the most promising from amongst them, as well as Commodore, at Evan's request. He thought the prince might like to see the animal who had saved Evan's and Percival's lives and as a result brought them all to this place and time.

He'd instructed the grooms to saddle several of the most suitable, in case the Prince took it into his head that he'd like to ride a war horse. Evan hoped not, but he wanted to be prepared. After all, one did not say no to the Prince Regent.

Though the horses would be kept well to the side, Evan thought the exposure to light arms gunfire from a distance would be a good reintroduction for the horses to help them get over their fears and nervousness.

Here by the lake, on the level ground, Shand and the gardeners had set up wooden markers paced off at varying distances. A dozen contestants had thrown their names into the mix to compete, and the prince had offered a prize, a silver coffee service engraved with the winner's name. One of his attendants would be dispatched back to London to commission the work when the contest concluded.

The excess and expectations shouldn't have surprised Evan, but they did. An impromptu friendly competition now needed a prize worth many pounds? Had he really existed on poor rations and scavenged oranges while deployed, while the aristocracy squandered their money on such frivolous things?

He said as much to Marcus, who as a veteran of combat himself, would understand. "I can't help but think of our fellow soldiers still in Spain while I'm here playing games."

"I received word this morning," Marcus said, his voice low. "Wellington has set out from his winter base in Portugal, and he intends to march north with part of his army, while sending another part south in a pincers movement, in an effort to cut Marshal Jourdan off from a retreat to France. With Napoleon still licking his wounds after he had to flee from Russia, Wellington feels now is the time to strike and settle the war for the Peninsula at least. Once that's done, he'll form his plan to march on Paris."

Evan nodded. Where Marcus got his information was a mystery, but Evan didn't doubt its truth. It was the spring of the year and time for armies to be on the move. All winter Wellington would have been strategizing and provisioning and building up, as had the French. A renewal of the fighting was inevitable.

And Evan would be there now if not for the Prince Regent.

"Do you miss it?" he asked Marcus.

"The call of the bugle? I admit I don't miss the mud, the stink of unwashed soldiers, or the constant danger, but part of me misses the men, the camaraderie, the conviction that we were doing something important that would be remembered for generations. Though there are many ways of serving your country beyond carrying a rifle. Wasn't it Milton who said, 'They also serve who only stand and wait'?"

"Yes, though I don't think he was speaking of serving the British army, but rather God." Evan smiled at Marcus's expression. "I don't look like much of a student of the classics, do I? But a classical education isn't the sole purview of the upper classes. My father was a dedicated schoolmaster."

"Ah, of course. You were blessed to have your minister-father as your teacher. I had rather more stern educators." He rubbed the seat of his pants with a knowing grin. "But I did learn my Milton."

"Sirs, I think I should get this soiree started, or we'll still be standing around until dinnertime." Shand sketched a bow and headed to the area he'd marked off for the shooters.

"Gentlemen, if you please." He held up his hands, beckoning the contestants.

"Are you sure you won't join in?" Evan asked as he shrugged out of his tight jacket and put it in Marcus's offered hand.

"Blades are my weapon of choice, so I'll leave it to you lot. I've been commandeered by your steward to serve as a judge. I vowed to be impartial, so make sure you win on your own merits." He grinned.

"You haven't placed a bet with Percival, have you?"

"No, I'm not a betting man, and as a judge, it wouldn't be right for me to wager on the outcome. I just want to see you put him and Fitzroy into their places. They're both acting strange. Pompous and secretive and whispering away like a pair of debutantes at their first ball." He kept his eyes on them as they strode down to the line. "Watch out for them. I get the feeling they're up to something."

"That's not strange behavior for them. They've always been pompous and secretive, and it seems they're always planning something." Evan slapped Marcus on the shoulder. "See you afterward."

"Gentlemen." Shand addressed the ones who would take part as they lined up. "The contest will be held in rounds. Everyone will shoot in the first round, and the top six will move to the next round as determined by the judges, Mr. Haverly and myself. If a third judge is required, His Highness has offered to fill that role." Shand waved his hand up the slope to where the spectators sat under the sunshades and parasols. Even the ladies of the house had foregone some excursion that Diana had planned in favor of watching the target shoot.

Evan picked out his wife, seated next to the prince, her sky-blue dress easy to spot. For a brief moment he allowed his mind to drift back to the previous night, and he smiled, thankful they had reconciled and for once in their married life were in accord and honest with one another.

He was a blessed man with a lovely bride and now a . . . son. Because he had determined he would raise Cian as his own. If God should bless his marriage with more children, the law dictated that his firstborn son would be his heir, but Cian would never know want of love and family and a place at White Haven while Evan was alive.

The Duke of Seaton sat aloof. Evan would deal with him this evening, offering him a onetime payment for custody of the baby and inviting him to leave White Haven for good. After that, he would have a word with Percival and hasten him and Fitzroy on their way as well. They could be "advance envoys" for the Prince Regent in Brighton.

"In the first round, each man will stand and shoot once at the closest, then the middle, and then the farthest target. In the second round, those that move on will shoot from a kneeling position. And in the last round, the shooters will be prone."

Shand spoke so all could hear, and Evan was reminded of how his sergeant had chastened and harried many a new recruit with that booming voice. He'd chastened and harried his officers, too.

Evan rolled his head to loosen his neck and shoulder muscles. He hadn't held a rifle in more than half a year. Would his old talent return? Did he want it to? At one point in his life, he'd thought being a crack shot was the only thing he was really good at, but over the past few months, he'd discovered other abilities, talents that had overlaid the past. Talents that had more to do with building up than tearing down.

One by one, the men took their turns. Some were proficient and some woefully inadequate. When the first shot cracked, Evan flinched, inhaling the smell of gunpowder, blinking as a flash of memory exploded in his head, a memory of an unnamed battle. He closed his eyes and took a deep breath, flexing his fingers and reminding himself that he was in the peaceful Sussex countryside, not the war-torn Continent.

Another crack of rifle fire. This time his eyes popped open, and he swayed, bumping into one of the guests.

"Your pardon," he murmured. Why hadn't he thought? Anticipated that the commotion of gunfire might bring his struggles to the forefront? Had anyone noticed? What if he had held his secret for all this time only to have it broadcast to the crème of the *ton* at this late date? Sweat popped out at his temples, and his hands trembled.

But he couldn't resign from the competition now. Shaking his head, he strove for resolve. He would buckle down and shoot, and perhaps he could put an end to these episodes, somehow prove to himself that there was nothing to panic about.

He felt like one of the war horses being reconditioned to loud noises.

Glancing toward where the grooms held the mounts, he took courage from the animals. None of them were panicked. Several had their heads up, and one chestnut fellow looked eager, as if ready to charge into the fray.

If they could face it, so could he.

When it was Evan's turn, he stepped up to the table to receive his ammunition and select a rifle.

"Sir, not one of those." Shand bent and retrieved a long burlap-wrapped bundle from beneath the table. "You'll want this one."

Puzzled, Evan took the object and let the rough cloth fall away. His throat tightened, and his eyes sought Shand's. "Soldier? Where did you get this?"

His hand brushed the satin smoothness of the walnut stock, grazed the dull brass plate with his name engraved upon it, and hefted the bulk. His Baker 1800-model rifle. It felt like an old friend.

"I retrieved it after the battle, sir. I knew you'd want it back for the next skirmish, but when I tried to return it to you, they said you'd been wounded and taken to Vitoria and the hospital ships. When I found you at St. Bart's in London, I thought I'd just keep it until you got back to your old self, sir."

Shand's look spoke volumes, and Evan didn't know what to say. Did his sergeant know how he'd suffered after the battle with both his physical and mental wounds? Had Evan only been fooling himself that he'd kept his secret well?

"Thank you, Sergeant."

"Do the Ninety-Fifth proud, sir."

Evan looked at the rifle he held, his companion and partner in many a campaign. Considering what they had been through together, a friendly target shoot should be nothing. At least no one would be shooting back this time.

He loaded the weapon, not even needing to think about what he was doing, his hands performing the familiar task with ease. By the time he had finished, the paper targets had been replaced on the stands.

Wrapping the shoulder strap around his left hand, he nestled the butt of the rifle into his right shoulder. The sight at the end of the rifle glinted in the sunlight, still polished and shiny, the way he liked it. One long breath to steady his muscles, exhale halfway and hold it, squeeze the trigger.

Lower the rifle, breathe quickly, and reload. In less than thirty seconds he was ready to shoot again, this time at the middle target.

By the time he'd loosed the third bullet, he knew he had scored comfortably well, enough to move on to the second round but nowhere near what he'd been at his peak.

Six competitors moved on, and this time they knelt to shoot. The betting increased, and Fitzroy and Percival were both amongst the second-round lot. Percival missed the third target entirely, but he wasn't alone. Fitzroy just clipped the edge of the paper to get him into the final three with Evan and a courtier named Ratcliffe.

With every shot, Evan relaxed a bit more. He was able to stay in the present and not be yanked into the past. He didn't start with each explosion or sweat as the scent of gunpowder filled the air. Perhaps this was exactly what he needed to lay those ghosts to rest.

"Sirs, this is the final round. Each of you will be prone to shoot." Shand pointed to a canvas sheet laid on the grass to protect their clothing. "The score will be aggregate, as in the other rounds."

Fitzroy shot first, and though he hit the bull on the first target, he missed the second and third. Ruefully, he rose, brushing off his waistcoat and shaking his head.

Percival snickered. "It's looking good for me. I might be out of the competition, but I'm going to win either way." He checked his notebook. "You're going to wind up owing me money, Fitz."

Ratcliffe, a man of few words and intense eyes, took up his position and fared better, hitting all three targets, but only one inside the rings.

When Shand handed Evan his rifle, calm seeped over him. As a Green Jacket marksman, Evan had done most of his shooting in a prone position, creeping as close as he could to enemy lines and trying to take out artillery men as they loaded cannons. His favorite tactic had been to get near enough to shoot the limber stationed behind the cannon and hopefully blow up the ammunition stored there.

He imagined himself on his belly in some tall grass, as he'd done a thousand times before. Beginning with his shoulder and neck, he purposely relaxed each muscle, down his back, his arms, his legs. Conscious of his entire being, he closed his eyes and steadied his breathing.

"I think he's gone to sleep," Percival snickered.

Evan opened his eyes, grasping his rifle lightly, sighting down the barrel at the closest target. Careful not to jerk the trigger, he pulled back gently, trying not to anticipate the shot or brace for the recoil. Thwack. The familiar kick of the gun went through his shoulder, and he exhaled.

"A bull!" Shand announced.

Rising, Evan reloaded, aware that the crowd on the hill and his fellow competitors ranged in a half circle behind him had all fallen silent.

He took his time with the second shot as well, blanking out the people around him, until the only things that existed were himself, his rifle, and the target. Just like old times. He raised the barrel a fraction of an inch to account for the distance. He squeezed the trigger, absorbed the recoil, and stood all in one fluid motion. Shand raised his field glass. "Another bull!"

The crowd on the hill burst into applause. On points, all Evan had to do was hit the third target, and he would win the competition. Satisfaction flowed over him, and he grinned. He still had the old talent. Deliberately, he reloaded, assessing his feelings. Though he had been reluctant to shoot at first, he somehow felt it had done him good.

"One more target, sir." Shand sent him a steady look. "Finish it."

He resumed his position, the sun warming his back. Calm flowed over him, making him feel as if, once he fired this last shot, he would banish the final remnants of frustration and guilt at not being able to remember the day he was wounded. He would let it go, focus on his new life and responsibilities, and trust that God had not made a mistake bringing him to White Haven as the earl.

The third target was somewhere near a hundred yards away, well below the maximum distance for the Baker rifle, but farther than most casual hunters would shoot. Though he was rusty, he was confident in his ability to hit inside the rings at least.

Before he thought about it, he was standing up once more, accepting slaps on the back. By his previous standards, the last shot, hitting four inches outside the bull, wasn't good, but it had been sufficient.

"Well done, sir." Shand reached for the rifle, and they both laughed.

Evan was nearly finished reloading, though the competition was over. He shoved the ramrod down the barrel one last time and slotted it into its place.

"Old habits. Reload before you do anything else." Evan laughed. "How many times did you say that to new recruits, Shand?"

"More often than I can count, sir."

As a group, the contestants climbed the slope to where the guests were arranged under their awnings.

The Prince Regent lifted his glass. "Most amusing. Good shooting." He sipped the champagne. "Your bride has been extolling your virtues, Whitelock. To hear her tell it, you must be the finest shot in all of Britain."

Evan sought Diana's eyes and noted her blush. She had been boasting about him?

"I am a blessed man, thanks to your generosity, Your Highness." He went to Diana's side and put his hand on her shoulder.

The prince wore a smug expression, but since he always seemed smug to Evan, it was hard to tell if he was pleased at the praise or merely taking it as his due.

"You owe me fifty pounds, Fitzroy." Percival's petulant voice drifted over the buzz of the guests. "You bet on yourself, and you lost."

Evan wanted to roll his eyes. Why did those two ever become friends? They squabbled like fishwives.

Viscount Fitzroy reddened and thrust Percival's hand off his arm. "I said I would pay you, and I will."

"You had better, or I'll spread it around that you wager and run." Percival's voice held something sharper than usual, and heads turned.

Fitzroy reared up like an angry badger. "How dare you? Arthur Bracken does not renege on his bets."

Arthur Bracken.

Lightning cracked inside Evan's head, and his hand tightened on Diana's shoulder. She winced, and he let go, raising his hand to his head.

Arthur Bracken.

"What is it?" Diana rose, touching his arm. Her pale collarbone bore the marks of his fingers, and a fleeting regret dashed across his heart.

But it was quickly overlaid with images, sounds of battle, himself crouching under an outcropping of rock on one of the many hills that dotted the landscape. He'd crossed into enemy territory, stealthy and lethal, scaling to the high ground where the French artillery had set up a battery. But he'd misjudged his position during the climb. He'd arrived beneath a small encampment. Had he stumbled upon the battery command post? Salamanca lay in the distance across the Tormes River behind the British line. He was much too far from his own army for comfort. If he should be discovered, there would be no one to rescue him. He gripped his rifle and listened intently to two French soldiers above him and out of sight. His French wasn't as good as his Latin, but he could make out what they were saying.

Arthur Bracken. A spy. An assassination attempt on the Prince Regent. Brighton.

The memory echoed in Evan's head, pieces falling into place like a parquet floor, tight and smooth. The relief at finally remembering made him light-headed, and he opened his eyes, grabbing the sunshade's support pole for balance.

Everything rushed back, clear as clean glass.

He hadn't *captured* a spy at Salamanca—he'd learned the name of one. He had been racing back to the British line to tell his superiors that the Prince Regent's life was in danger from someone named Arthur Bracken, when he'd been shot.

Arthur Bracken, who was also Viscount Fitzroy?

"It's you." He stared. "You're Arthur Bracken."

Fitzroy struggled into his tight jacket, a look of contempt on his face. "Of course. Bracken is my given name. But I am properly addressed by my title."

Diana had gone pale as milk. "Just as your name is Evan Eldridge, but people address you by your title, Whitelock." She gripped her hands hard at her waist, hard enough that they shook. "What do you know of Fitzroy's given name?"

Marcus gave Evan a hard stare. "What's going on? Have you remembered something?"

"The spy. The spy I thought I had captured at Salamanca. I didn't capture him. I merely learned of his existence—and his identity. That's what

I was trying to get back to safety to tell the commanders. The two Frenchmen I overheard said that Arthur Bracken would try to assassinate the Prince Regent when he made his annual trip to Brighton." Which must be why the word "Brighton" had struck him so hard at the wedding breakfast. It all made sense now.

"What's this?" The Prince Regent began to rise from his chair, a lengthy process that he didn't get near to accomplishing. "Someone's trying to kill me?"

Before anyone could move, his face a crazed mask, Fitzroy reached down and drew a dagger from his boot top, made a wild swipe at the Prince Regent, and leapt away. A woman screamed, and blood gushed from a slash on the prince's upper arm. The prince gasped, clutching at the wound, while dumbfounded guests stood looking on in horror.

Marcus grabbed a serviette from the side table and clapped it on the gash. He yanked on Diana's hand, pressing it over the cloth. "Hold pressure on that cut."

"Grab him! He tried to kill the prince!" Shouts echoed down the slope. Several guests started after Fitzroy as he ran toward the lake. On the way, he shoved a groom aside and took one of the war horses that stood waiting patiently for their portion of the proceedings. Swinging aboard, Fitzroy galloped away. The guests who had chased on foot stopped in confusion.

Evan still had the rifle in his hands, and he set out after them, Shand at his side, Marcus at his heels.

"He's making for the woods. If he gets there, we'll lose him. That place is a bramble," Shand yelled.

"Shoot him if you have to. We can't let him get away!" Marcus added.

Reaching the horses that were snorting and jerking on their reins, Evan threw himself on Commodore's back, scrabbling and clutching the animal's mane, kicking him into a gallop before he was fully settled in the saddle. He didn't wait to see if Shand and Marcus followed. They would be behind him as soon as they could.

He assessed the distance and changed his angle, hoping to cut off some time in the pursuit. The horse the viscount had chosen had been a cavalry officer's charger and was fleet of foot.

Commodore had been an all-purpose horse, big and rangy, used for hauling and as a saddle horse when needed. He might not be the fastest animal, but he had stamina and determination. He seemed to understand that his job was to chase, and he threw his entire being into the task. His stride ate up the ground, and Evan bent low over his neck.

Don't let him make the woods. Shoot him if you have to. Marcus's orders echoed in his head.

When he thought he had closed the gap enough, Evan pulled on the reins to slow Commodore. But the horse was full of run, nearly wild. It took strength and determination to pull him out of his gallop. As soon as it was safe to do so, but not waiting until the horse had stopped completely, Evan slid to the ground, his momentum causing him to stagger. It was now or never.

Fitzroy looked back over his shoulder, and he must've thought Evan had given up the chase, because Evan saw a flash of a grin.

Dropping to his knee, Evan braced his elbow on his thigh. His breath came in gusts, and he forced himself to calm. He would only get one shot. Gauging the distance, he sighted. He raised the barrel and led his target slightly. The bullet needed to arrive in a specific space at the same time as his quarry.

Fitzroy stood in the stirrups, bent over his horse's neck, presenting a tricky target. He was perhaps twenty yards from the tree line, and he must be certain of his escape.

The viscount never made it to the woods. A split second after the explosion of gunpowder and the muzzle flash, he toppled from the saddle into the dirt, raising a cloud of dust. His horse continued on, wheeling in a circle at the edge of the trees and turning back, wild-eyed and skittish.

Evan leapt to his feet as hoofbeats sounded behind him. Shand and Marcus arrived. With his gun in one hand, aware he hadn't taken time to reload, Evan jogged toward Fitzroy. He held the gun like a club in case Fitzroy was still able to fight.

When he reached the viscount, he knew he needn't worry. Fitzroy lay sprawled on the ground, blood pouring from a wound in the center of his chest. If his fancy waistcoat had been the target, Evan would've hit the bull.

Marcus knelt beside him. "Who sent you? Who gave you orders to kill the Prince Regent?"

Fitzroy smiled, teeth stained with blood. He coughed and sputtered.

Marcus grabbed his shoulder and shook it. "Who sent you? Who is your commander?"

Fitzroy stared at Marcus for a long moment, defiant and malicious. Then like snuffing a lamp, the light went out of the viscount's eyes, and he went limp.

Marcus rose, his face grim. "I was so close. I've been trying to expose the assassin for months now." He pounded his fist against his thigh.

"How did you know? How could you? I didn't know myself until I heard his name and it all came rushing back. I couldn't remember anything certain of that day until just a few moments ago." Evan looked from Marcus to Shand. Shand didn't seem surprised at Evan's lack of memory. The sergeant was a shrewd one, for sure.

"We'll talk about it later." Marcus brushed aside the questions, totally in command. "Shand, bring the body. For now I want to speak with Percival Seaton."

Chapter 16

Diana took charge of the Prince Regent, since no one around her seemed capable of sense. Marcus had grabbed her hand and pressed it onto the serviette over the wound before charging down the hill in pursuit of her husband.

Please, God, keep Evan safe. And Marcus and Shand. Help me know what to do with the prince. Everything had happened so quickly. She would never forget the slash of the knife, her intense shock, or how quickly Evan had taken off. Nor the fact that her husband seemed to have regained his memory.

Or that Arthur Bracken, Viscount Fitzroy, her sister's seducer and her nephew's father, was also an assassin.

But for now her task was the prince.

"Your Highness, you'll be all right. Keep still. Hold my hand."

Chaos reigned around her. People milled and women swooned and men shouted. This would never do. Where was their stoicism? She wanted to yell at them to pull themselves together and behave like Britons.

Louisa appeared at her side. "What can I do, my lady?"

Diana's mind raced, creating a list in her head. "Get these people away from here. Find six of the biggest men and have them take a door off its hinges at the house and bring it here. We need to get His Highness to his rooms, where he can be tended. And pour me a brandy." She motioned to the decanter on a side table, her fingers stained with the prince's blood.

On his part, the prince didn't complain, merely gritting his teeth, his normally florid face as pale as his linens.

"Hold fast, Your Highness," she murmured. "I'm sure the tale of your bravery in the face of an assassin will be told far and wide. You're a credit to Britain." A little flattery would be better than sympathy, she judged.

He nodded, his jaw tight.

Someone poured a decent amount of the brandy into a tumbler, and she held it to his lips as Louisa ordered people to step back. "You gormless nits, you're no help at all. Get away with you. You're as useful as a glass hammer, you are." She shooed with her apron, and well-titled gentlemen and ladies scurried out of her path.

"That woman's tongue is as sharp as Fitzroy's knife," the prince grumbled.

"She is a bit caustic, but she does get things done." Diana smiled.

Several footmen arrived, toting one of the doors from White Haven. As gently as possible, with Diana maintaining pressure on his wound, they got the corpulent prince onto the makeshift stretcher. It took all six men a considerable amount of effort to carry him up the hill, into the house, and up the stairs to the Royal Apartments, endeavoring to keep him level the whole way.

"Fetch hot water, towels, and my sewing basket," Louisa barked to one of the footmen as they brought the prince into his boudoir.

Several people had followed the procession into the room, crowding around the royal bed. Diana's arms ached.

"You are not going to take a needle to me, woman." The prince raised his head. "Bring a proper doctor from town."

Louisa put her hands on her hips and stared at him as if he had cotton wool for brains. "If you had ever met the town doctor, you'd be begging for my services. He's a drunk and a lout and wouldn't know a knife wound from a bullet hole if he had an instruction manual and a spyglass. Now, all of you clear out. I can't work in this crowd." She flapped her hands, as if herding geese.

After a verbal standoff that the prince had to settle, four courtiers were allowed to remain, but they all stood warily, as if afraid of what the housekeeper would say next.

Diana bit her lip to keep from laughing. Was there anyone Louisa was afraid to dress down?

A maid arrived with a steaming kettle, and a footman carried a stack of snowy towels and Louisa's sewing basket, which usually resided next to her rocking chair in the servants' dining hall.

"Now, lie still and don't whine. It isn't regal to snivel." Louisa hiked her skirt and sat on the edge of the bed. Strands of red hair escaped from her lace cap, but she was swift and gentle as she took over for Diana.

The prince was properly chastened, probably for the first time in his life. Without another word, he let the housekeeper get about her business.

Which left Diana time to wonder what had happened to her husband.

Arthur Bracken, Viscount Fitzroy and Cian's father, was a spy and an assassin. A failed assassin, thank the Lord.

And Evan had remembered.

She recalled how he'd once shouted the name *Bracken* in his sleep, and she hadn't asked him about it for fear that he knew something about Bracken being Cian's father. And when she'd had the opportunity to tell him who Cian's father was, she'd hesitated out of loyalty to her sister and the promise she'd made.

If she had told Evan last night, would he have remembered then? Could all of this have been avoided? She raised her hands to her face, only to realize they were bloodied.

"Louisa, I need to find out what happened to Evan. I'll return as soon as I can." She snatched up one of the clean towels, scrubbing her hands as she hurried out of the room. Ducking into her bedroom, she washed at the basin, frowning at the pink water and the evidence left on the finger towels.

Making her way downstairs, she encountered her still-bewildered guests. The house buzzed like a kicked-over hornet's nest, people gathered in clumps. Several men helped women enter through the glass doors at the rear of the house, but Diana had no time for those who had fainted or pretended to faint. They would be fine, sniffing their vinaigrettes and moaning over the shock of it all, while plotting how to make the most of the golden firsthand gossip they now possessed.

Where was her husband? He'd raced after Fitzroy as if fired from his rifle. She took comfort in the fact that he hadn't gone alone. Shand and Marcus were with him. When she reached the terrace, she held her hands beside her eyes to help her focus on the long distance down to the lake and the woods beyond.

Were they returning?

Two figures rode toward the house, and behind them a third rider leading a horse with a burden thrown across the saddle. Her heart leapt into her throat. One of them was dead. But who? Had they shot Fitzroy, or had Fitzroy managed to kill one of them before being captured?

Who was that draped over the saddle?

Unable to move, she waited, watching, trying to pray but unable to form any words.

As the riders grew closer, she recognized Evan in front. He rode that immense bay with the white blaze, and his rifle lay across his thighs. She let out her breath, her feet coming unstuck from the pavers.

A proper lady would no doubt have waited on the terrace, but she decided she must not be a proper lady. She picked up her skirts and started down the slope as fast as she could go. Past the chairs and tables where the guests had observed the contest and almost to the place where the targets still stood upright like wooden soldiers.

She came to a stop as Evan pulled his horse to a walk.

Marcus kept on toward the house, while Evan slung his rifle strap over his head and one arm, slipping the rifle onto his back in what must be a well-practiced maneuver. Without his horse breaking stride, Evan leaned over and wrapped one arm around Diana and hoisted her up side-saddle in front of him. Her legs draped over his thigh, and she flung her arms around him, assessing his health, seeing that he had no cuts or holes. The horse tossed his head, and Evan legged the animal back into a canter. She gloried in her husband's strength and stability. With his arms firmly around her, she felt safe and secure.

"How is the prince? Is he alive?" Evan asked.

"Yes, but he's cut quite badly. He's being brave, though it's costing him. Louisa is tending him, and by tending, I mean breathing fire."

She expected him to laugh, but he didn't.

"What happened to Fitzroy?" she asked.

"I shot him. He's dead." His voice was flat, matter of fact. "Where is Percival?"

Raising her head, she frowned. "Why? What's he done?"

"We need to know how much he knows about this. He was at Salamanca, he is friends with Fitzroy, and he's suddenly got money when before he had none."

Her heart went cold. Percival was a bully and a dilettante, but a spy? A potential assassin or conspirator? Surely not.

When they reached the terrace, Marcus was already off his horse and striding into the house. Evan let Diana slip to the ground before dismounting himself. His rifle stuck up at an angle behind his shoulder, but he seemed not to be aware it was there. He followed his friend into the house, and Diana set off in his wake.

How she wished the manor was empty of guests as she threaded her way amongst the people clustered in the front hall. They were looking away from her toward the drawing room door, where Marcus and Evan had gone, and she hurried there, determined to be present when they questioned her half brother.

Marcus and Evan were lifting Percival from a chair, one on each side, when she arrived. "Come with us," Marcus said.

"I'm not going anywhere with you. Unhand me." Percival struggled, red blotches appearing on his cheeks as he took the measure of those looking on.

"What is all this?" Diana's father asked. "Take your hands off my son."

"Sir . . ." Evan paused. "Stay out of this. I'll deal with you later."

"You can't speak to me that way." The duke tottered as he rose to his feet.

"Father, sit down." Diana spoke to him sharply. "Your turn will come, but for now it's Percival who has some questions to answer."

Her father's mouth fell open, his eyes blinking. She had never dared to stand up to him, to rebuke him publicly. Diana didn't give him another glance. He had no power over her any longer.

"I say, let me go!" Percival kicked out, and while he missed Marcus's leg, he managed to hit a table, upsetting a vase and toppling it to the floor with a crash.

"We can do this here in front of everyone, or you can come quietly with us to the library. It is your choice." Marcus twisted Percival's arm up behind his back and marched him through the hall toward the rear of the house. Evan hurried after them.

By the time Diana reached the library, Percival had been put into a deep armchair, and Evan was just closing the door. She held her palm against it. Evan looked as if he intended to refuse her entry, then he capitulated with a nod.

When she'd slipped inside, he turned the key in the lock. Diana went to the window seat while Evan stayed by the door, his arms crossed as he leaned against the portal.

"Now is the time, if you want to avoid a noose. Tell me what you know." Marcus leaned over her brother.

Diana was amazed. The normally genial Marcus seemed a different man, focused, intent, and not a little frightening.

"I don't know anything," Percival exclaimed. "What do you mean, accusing me? I had nothing to do with this madness. That's what it must be, a momentary madness on the part of Fitzroy. Where is he? He can tell you I had nothing to do with any plot to kill the prince."

"No one is going to believe that. How could you not know? You've been thick with Fitzroy for more than a year now. You were in Spain and had ample opportunity to cross paths with a French spy to courier a message to Fitzroy. How did you get on that envoy to Spain in the first place? What were you doing on the battlefield, where you had no business being? What did Fitzroy tell you about who ordered the assassination? Where did your sudden influx of money come from?" The interrogation came so thick and fast Percival had no time to answer.

But he didn't look guilty, only confused. When the questions stopped, he spread his hands. "I don't know. Fitz mentioned the trip to Spain and thought it might be a lark, something to alleviate boredom. We were supposed to go together. When my father heard about it, he thought it a good idea, and he used his influence to get me added to the envoy. He thought it would give me some experience and perhaps further my stocks with some of the power brokers in the City."

"But Fitzroy didn't go on the expedition," Marcus observed.

"No. He pulled out at the last minute. I don't know why. He just said he couldn't go and to leave it alone. But he said he expected a full report when I got home. Especially about those Spanish girls we'd heard so much about." Percival rubbed his hands on his thighs, darting a look at Diana.

Typical. The lecher. She looked away.

"How did you get trapped on the battlefield? You were supposed to be miles behind the lines." Marcus leaned against the desk, crossing his arms, looking like an avenging judge.

"We were so far from the battle, we could hardly hear the guns. The man I was supposed to be aiding, Peters, wanted to see the fighting, so we loaded up in a wagon and headed toward the front. He said he wanted real information to bring back to Parliament, not some secondhand drivel fed to us by the commanders. We went to the high ground, well back from a battery of Portuguese artillery, but Peters wasn't satisfied. He got out of the wagon and went to argue with the colonel in charge that we be allowed closer, and the driver went with him because the driver spoke Portuguese.

"I was alone in the wagon, and a shell hit nearby. It came out of the clear blue sky. All I could think was that I was going to die, and I wanted to get out of there. I climbed onto the wagon seat, and when I grabbed the reins, the horses took off. They raced straight down the hill. There wasn't even a road. I couldn't stop them. Before I knew it, we were in the thick of the fighting. The front lines were charging one another." Percival's eyes were stark, reliving his terrifying experience. He gulped and continued.

"I was yanking on the reins, but the horses wouldn't stop. I could barely see, there was so much smoke. I had no idea where I was, whether on the British side or the French. I just knew I wanted to get out of there. Then I got shot, and when I looked down, my foot was bleeding. I guess I might have fainted. When I came to, I had fallen backward into the wagon, and there were bullets flying everywhere and shells exploding. I thought I was going to die."

Evan straightened from leaning back on the door. "Those were war horses, trained to run into battle. When the shell detonated close by and you picked up the reins, they ran."

"Stupid beasts. It was like I wasn't even there hauling on the reins. I stayed in the back of the wagon, trying to hide, but the wagon box must've made a fine target. Bullets were whistling by. It was like the air was full of lead. Then you were there, cutting the dead horse loose, climbing on the live one, and we were racing back the way we'd come. My foot was hurting like—" He broke off, glancing at Diana. "Hurting a lot, and just as we reached the base of the hill where the British troops were assembling for another charge, you were shot and knocked off the horse. But there were plenty of British and Portuguese soldiers about, and they hauled us back to the hospital tents."

"What did you tell Fitzroy when you got back? Had anyone tried to give you a message for him? A letter?" Marcus pressed his palms into the desk, leaning forward.

"No. I tell you I knew nothing about what he was planning. He never breathed a word of it. I wouldn't have gone along with it if he had. I'm no traitor." Percival spread his hands, fingers wide, palms up. "Nobody gave me any messages for him. Nobody in Spain even mentioned him to me."

"Where did you get your money? You've paid your debts all over London, and you've spent lavishly. Everyone knows you were counting on getting part of Diana's inheritance, and when you didn't you were strapped for cash. So where did your money come from all of a sudden?"

Percival scrubbed his hands down his handsome face. "This is going to sound bad, but the money came from Fitzroy."

Diana's heart sank.

"Why would he give you money?"

Hesitating, Percival looked from Evan to Diana and back. "It was because of Diana," he mumbled.

She straightened. "What?"

Percival shrank in his chair. "You keep him off me, and I'll tell you. But you have to keep him off me." He pointed to Evan.

Marcus glared. "Tell me what you know, or Whitelock is going to be the least of your worries."

"Ask Fitzroy all these questions. He'll tell you."

"Fiztroy is dead. He was a traitor and an assassin, and he was shot trying to escape." Marcus's tone blew coldly through the room.

Diana crossed her arms, hugging herself.

Sweat broke out on Percival's brow, and he dug in his waistcoat pocket for a handkerchief. "He's dead?" He looked as if he were trying to work some moisture into his mouth. "You're sure?"

"I'm sure. He can't help you now. Why did Fitzroy pay you, and what does it have to do with Diana?"

The news of the viscount's death seemed to split Percival open like a bag of seed. "Fitzroy paid me a handsome sum to get him into White Haven. We weren't part of the official royal party, and no matter how we wheedled and sidled up to the prince, he just wouldn't issue an invitation. Fitzroy was desperate to be included, and when I asked him why, he said it was because of Diana. He wanted her." Percival swallowed hard, sending a fearful look at Evan.

Evan's fists bunched, and he shot a hot look at Percival.

"It wasn't my fault. He had an obsession about her. And he promised that if I helped engineer a situation where he could get his hands on her, he'd pay me even more."

Diana was on her feet in a flash, crossing the room. Trembling with rage and betrayal, she stood before her half brother. "It isn't the earl you should be worried about. You thought you could sell me? Sell my virtue? Do you have any idea what he planned to do when he 'got his hands on me'? He threatened not only to tell everyone in society that he'd seduced and compromised our sister but that he had done the same to me. And the price of his silence was that I must submit to his wishes and give myself to him."

Freezing in his chair, Percival took in what she had said. "You mean Fitz was the one who bedded Catherine? Is he the brat's father?"

Diana realized what she had revealed, and her hand went to her mouth. But she had been going to tell Evan anyway. She glanced across the room at her husband, her heart sinking at his granite expression. She turned back to her worthless brother.

"That's right. He fathered a child on your sister and abandoned her. Now she's dead. And you helped him worm his way into our house so he could attempt to kill the Prince Regent. You might not have known about his ultimate plan, but you brought him here knowing he would try to assault me or blackmail me into submitting to his wishes." Her stomach lurched, and she thought she might be sick all over him. Turning away, she found herself face to chest with her husband.

His hands came up and bracketed her shoulders, and he gently put her behind him, shielding her from her half brother. She rested her hands high on his back and her forehead on her hands, grateful for his protection and strength.

"Percival, you make me regret saving your miserable hide," Evan said.

"You have no idea who told Fitzroy to try to kill the prince?" Marcus asked.

"No. I didn't know he was going to try. I don't know anything more than I've told you. I'm a victim here."

Evan tensed under her hands, and she grabbed him from behind. "Don't kill him. Please." It would be too much to explain, and she had no desire to see her husband go to the gallows, not for the likes of her worthless relative.

Marcus narrowed his eyes, disgust etching his features.

"Get out." Evan's voice cut the air like a razor. "Get out of my house and never come back. If we are ever at the same function in the future, you will not speak to us, you will not acknowledge us in any way, and you will never try to contact us. If you do, I won't be responsible for my actions. Do you understand?"

Percival nodded and scrambled to his feet.

"And what's more," Marcus said, his voice equally deadly. "Know that you will be watched every day for the rest of your miserable life. I'll know where you go, who you are with, and why. If you put so much as a buckled shoe wrong, you'll find yourself either standing in the dock or on a boat to Botany Bay."

Evan went to the door, unlocked it, and held it open. "Don't even stop to pack your bags. We'll send your belongings back with your father. Get out."

Scuttle wasn't too strong a word for what Percival did, head down, shoulders bent, feet churning.

Marcus followed him. "I'll make sure he leaves." He closed the door behind him, leaving Evan and Diana alone.

She stood there, feeling ashamed and uncertain and guilty. She came from a family of rotters. There was no denying her corrupt relations. She wouldn't blame him if he wanted to cast her out too.

And then Evan did exactly the right thing.

He opened his arms.

She didn't need a second invitation. Tears burning her eyes, she went into his embrace, pressing her cheek to his chest and wrapping her arms around his waist. He stroked her hair, her shoulders, her back, squeezing her tight and resting his chin on her head. Finally, she raised her head to look at him.

"Diana. Why didn't you tell me what Fitzroy threatened?" He cradled her face in his hands.

The anguish in his eyes drove deeply into her heart. She blinked, and two tears tracked down her cheeks. "I was afraid for such a long time. I had promised Catherine I wouldn't tell her secret. And Fitzroy . . ." She gulped, his name stumbling out of her mouth. "He said the prince had sent him, and I knew if I told you, you would quite possibly beat him to mush and toss him off the estate. I didn't want to cause trouble between you and the prince, especially if the prince expected Fitzroy and Percival to be here. And if you remember, we were out of countenance with one another when they arrived. I didn't know if you would ever listen to me again, you were so angry about Cian."

She shook her head. "I'm so sorry. If I had been honest with you from the start, you could have protected Cian, protected me, and none of this would've happened. I should've asked you, that first night we spent together, when a nightmare awoke you. You shouted the name 'Bracken.' I knew Fitzroy's given name, but I was afraid for Cian. I couldn't think how you knew or what you knew. If I had spoken up then, perhaps your memory would've returned sooner and we and the prince would've been spared all this."

Where she expected censure, felt she deserved it, he surprised her. Softness entered his piercing blue eyes, and he raised her chin as he lowered his lips to hers. Brushing gently across her mouth at first, he tightened his embrace and took possession of her, searing her to her toes, washing away the hurt and fear and secrets. She melted into him, entwining her arms around his neck, kissing him back as her tears lent a salty flavor.

"I love you, Diana Eldridge, Lady Whitelock," he whispered against her skin, sending gooseflesh coursing down her arms. "I think I loved you the moment I first saw you in that ridiculous court dress and ostrich feathers."

He had never said those words to her before. He loved her. Which gave her the freedom to say aloud what she felt for him.

"I love you, Evan Eldridge. I think I fell in love with you when you first held Cian in the carriage, even though you thought he was a nobody child of an unwed maid." She nuzzled her temple against his chin, feeling the slight rasp of whiskers, inhaling the scent of his soap and tang of gunpowder that clung to him.

He kissed her again and again, holding her against him as if he never wanted to let her go. Joy burst like rockets behind her eyelids. He loved her. She loved him. She, who had never been loved, was loved by a good man. If she ever needed proof that God heard her prayers, this was it.

Finally he withdrew by increments, coming back for shorter kisses as if loathe to stop. He rested his forehead against hers. "I wish we didn't have a houseful of important guests. I'd sweep you up into my arms and march to our room and lock the door. I wouldn't care if we didn't leave it for at least a week." He sighed.

Diana thought that a wonderful proposition.

"But we should at least see how the prince is doing and apprise him of developments, don't you think?"

Smiling, blinking hard, she nodded, trying to come back to reality. "I suppose it's what a good host and hostess would do. Oh my, I must look a fright." She patted her hair, aware that it was mussed. Her eyes were probably red and her cheeks blotchy too.

"You look like you've just been thoroughly kissed." He grinned. "You look perfect to me, but we can stop by your room on the way to the Royal Apartments so you can tidy up."

As they left the library, they heard raised voices from the back hallway. "What now?" Evan asked.

He pressed his hand to the green baize-covered door that separated the front of the house from that area dominated by the domestics, and Diana put her fingers to her lips.

Shand and Louisa stood face to face in the back entryway, silhouetted in the light from the open door. "Woman, I tell you, I'm not hurt. His Lordship shot the man from two hundred yards away. He died quick. This blood isn't mine. It's the viscount's. I had to load him onto a horse to bring him back."

Louisa's face crumpled, and she launched herself into his arms, sobbing on his shoulder. "I feared you were hurt. Anything can happen when there are scoundrels about." The words came out muffled and distorted by crying, but the meaning was plain.

Diana met Evan's eyes, clapping her hand over her mouth to stifle a giggle of surprise.

Shand put his arms around Louisa, hugging her tight. "Silly woman. I don't know where you get your notions. A lesser man would be insulted that you thought so little of his abilities."

"Don't you call me silly. I was right to worry . . ."

Evan softly closed the door, drawing Diana away with him toward the front hall.

"Well, if that doesn't take the biscuit. Did you suspect those two?" he asked in a whisper.

"No. I'm still not sure that I saw what I think I just saw." She wanted to burst into laughter. "White Haven has a strange effect on people, doesn't it?"

"Not White Haven." He squeezed her waist as they mounted the stairs, ignoring all their guests. "Love. Love has a strange effect on people."

When Diana had changed and redressed her hair, Evan escorted her to the Royal Apartments. She looked so beautiful, her dress rustling, her floral scent pleasing him, so feminine and pretty . . . and his. Truly his now, for he had not just her hand in marriage but her heart.

As she had his.

And right at this moment, none of it felt like a mistake. He was exactly where he was meant to be, doing exactly what he was meant to do.

God hadn't led him astray or sent him on a ridiculous error-strewn path outside His will.

What had started out looking like a curse had become blessing upon blessing.

He shook his head as he tapped on the door to the prince's chambers. It had taken him much too long to come to that conclusion.

"Are you ready?" he asked.

Diana nodded, gifting him a brilliant smile.

A servant opened the door and stood back. "His Highness is expecting you. This way."

They followed the liveried man through the sitting rooms and into the bedchamber. Marcus stood at the foot of the canopied bed, his hands clasped behind his back. The prince reclined upon a mountain of pillows, his arm wrapped in so many bandages it resembled a leg of mutton. Lines of pain and strain etched his face, his pallor the color of the bed linens.

He spotted Evan and Diana.

"Come."

Marcus stepped to the side, giving Diana an encouraging smile. "I've just been making my report to His Highness."

"So he has. This is a rum day's work. An assassin right here in the house with me? What sort of security are the Home Secretary and the Royal Horse Guards running when assassins and spies are allowed to roam freely with unfettered access to their quarry? And not just any quarry but the ruling monarch?"

He scowled in a heads-will-roll humor that had Evan wishing they'd never come to check on him. Were they all going to pay the price for Fitzroy's villainy? He'd never seen the prince so ill-humored.

Shifting his weight, the prince grimaced. Diana left Evan and went to his side, helping him adjust the pillows to a more comfortable angle. When she would've stepped back, he grasped her hand. "My dear, stay and comfort me. Looking at pretty things makes me feel better, and you're by far the prettiest thing to come through those doors today. I'm surrounded by incompetents. Only you and that spike-tongued housekeeper of yours have shown any sense."

She glanced over her shoulder at Evan, her eyes eloquent, and he covered his amusement with a nod.

"Your Highness, you have been so brave. Such an example to your subjects. I wouldn't be surprised if ballads weren't written in your honor. You must rest and rebuild your strength. I prescribe some calf's foot jelly and some beef tea. You lost quite a bit of blood, and you mustn't strain yourself. I know you planned to leave for Brighton in a few days, but you must not jeopardize your health by venturing out too soon. The nation is depending upon you."

How did she do it? Evan marveled at her ability to turn him from surly granite to pliable clay in an instant. The Prince Regent practically purred under her fussing.

"You're quite right, my dear. It has been harrowing, and I will need time to recuperate."

She continued to hold his pudgy hand between her palms. "I'm sure we will do everything we can to make you comfortable. You're a robust man, and I am certain this won't set you back much. And think how you will climb in the people's regard."

Evan and Marcus shared a look. The people had not much good to say about old Prinny, assassination survivor or not. Surely she didn't believe what she was saying? Then Diana turned her face away from the prince, catching Evan's eye and giving him a slow, deliberate wink.

Marcus guffawed, quickly changing to a cough to cover his amusement. And Evan averted his gaze to stare out the window. The minx. She knew exactly what she was doing.

"You there." The prince indicated the courtiers hovering around the perimeter of the room. "Clear out. I want a private word with the earl and countess. You're all useless anyway. I've been in agony for hours, and none of you has lifted a finger, like the countess has in just a few minutes, to make me feel better."

When Marcus made to leave, the prince said, "You stay, Haverly."

"Of course, Your Highness." Marcus bowed and returned to his post at the foot of the bed.

"Come to this side, Whitelock, and sit. I don't want to have to crane my neck to see you properly." The prince beckoned to the other side of the feather mattresses from where Diana sat.

Evan picked up a spindly chair and brought it to the bedside. When he was seated, he asked, "Your Highness?"

The prince pursed his lips, his eyes intent. "Haverly here tells me that I have you to thank for dispatching my would-be assassin."

"I did what any man would do under the circumstances." Evan didn't know what to say. He was embarrassed to be praised for taking a man's life. He had drawn no pleasure in the act. Doing what was required by decent men didn't need to be rewarded.

"So you say, but you were the man to do it when there were many others present who did not, including those who are being paid to see to my protection. I assure you, this will not pass unnoticed. How shall I reward you? I've made you an earl. Should I give you a dukedom?"

Evan straightened. "Oh no, Your Highness. Not that." He had barely gotten used to the idea of being an earl.

"Then what? The Crown cannot appear ungrateful."

He wanted nothing. He had everything he needed in Diana . . . and Cian. And then it dawned on him what to say.

"Your Highness, there is one thing I would seek, and you are the only man who can grant it." Evan wished he was the one holding Diana's hand instead of the prince.

"Make your request then, and if I am able, I will fulfill it."

Evan looked into Diana's eyes rather than the prince's when he spoke. "To explain my desire, I must first tell you a story. A story about a brave girl who cares more for others than she does for herself. A girl who is loyal and courageous and good. This girl had a sister she loved very much, a sister who fell under the power of a bad man with ill intent. As a result, the sister's virtue was compromised. She was forced to leave London society, and in near isolation in the country, she gave birth to a son. Sadly, she did not survive her confinement, and on her deathbed she begged this girl to take the baby, raise it as her own, and never reveal the secret of the child's father."

Diana's bottom lip disappeared, and moisture formed on her lashes. He wanted to go to her, and hold her, and remind her of how brave she was, and assure her she didn't have to carry this burden alone anymore. The width of this ridiculously opulent bed was too much separation, but he forced himself to remain in his chair.

"The girl and baby were virtual prisoners in the house of her father, who was not a good man. He had no love for the girl or the child, and he constantly used the child as a weapon to subdue the brave girl. When he desired to marry the girl to a man of his choosing and for his own advantage, she agreed because he promised to give her the child if she obeyed."

The prince listened, his mouth open a bit, his brows raised.

"But before he could marry her off, the Prince Regent stepped in and gave the girl in marriage to another man, along with the fortune that the girl would inherit upon her wedding day. The prince gave his blessing on the marriage, even attending their wedding breakfast and assuring the couple that he would visit their country home in the coming months."

The prince's eyes snapped from Evan to Diana and back again as realization dawned.

"But the girl was torn. What about the child? Her new husband insisted upon leaving the city immediately. If she left the baby behind, her father had threatened to abandon him to a foundling home. But how could she take the baby with her into the home of her husband, a stranger who might not appreciate having an illegitimate child brought into his household? What if this man, too, decided to cast the child out? So she cleverly disguised the baby's identity and secreted him out of her father's house, claiming that the child was the offspring of a ladies' maid that she had compassion on and wanted to help."

Evan studied his hands in his lap. "Eventually the girl came to trust her new husband enough to reveal the baby's parentage and her promise to her sister. The husband was surprised, and at first he struggled to come to terms with the information, but he finally realized that his wife had not deceived him out of any malicious intent but only to ensure the baby's safety. He promised to protect the child as well, but even with the husband's protection, the danger wasn't totally averted for the infant. The girl's father is outraged that his plans have been foiled to get his hands on the girl's inheritance, and he has bided his time, scheming how to get his revenge. Legally he has custody of the child, but morally he is bankrupt. He has threatened the girl and her husband. They must pay him, or he will take the child. If they try to keep the child, he will tell the Prince Regent and have them in court for kidnapping."

Letting the last sentence hang in the air for a moment, Evan took a deep breath and braced his hands on his thighs. "You ask me what reward I would have for bringing to justice the man who tried to kill you? I ask a life for a life. I ask for the life of Cian Seaton, son of Catherine Seaton. I ask for custody to be transferred from the duke to myself and my wife. We plan to raise Cian as our own son, see to his needs both physical and spiritual, and give him the love he deserves." His voice grew rough as the tears that had formed in Diana's eyes tumbled down her cheeks.

For a moment, Evan felt like the prophet Nathan, coming before his ruler, delivering information through the power of a story. But how would the prince, who was no King David, respond?

"This is true?" the prince asked. "There is really a child, and the Duke of Seaton is using him to extort money from you?"

Marcus spoke from the foot of the bed. "I can verify this account, Your Highness."

Letting go of Diana's hand, the prince made a fist, then pointed his plump finger at Marcus. "Bring the Duke of Seaton here now."

With a small bow, Marcus left.

"I will hear from his own lips what he intends to do with the child."

Diana rose from the bedside, wiped her tears with the backs of her hands, and went to the table, pouring a small helping of brandy into a glass and bringing it to the prince. The restorative put color back in his pale cheeks. When he returned the empty glass to her, she put it on the table and circled the bed to stand beside Evan's chair. Her hand rested on his shoulder, and he reached up and covered her fingers with his own, squeezing them gently.

The duke entered the room with Marcus just steps behind. Eagerly Diana's father approached. "I'm honored that you summoned me, Your Highness." He wore a smug smile, but he slanted a hot glare at Diana and Evan.

Evan felt her stiffen, and he increased his grip on her hand, rising and circling her waist with his arm. "It will be all right."

"What if he sides with my father?" she whispered, her lips brushing his ear. "The prince is most mercurial in nature."

"Then we'll find another way. Trust me." He hugged her hard into his side.

The prince glared at Seaton. "I have just been told the most disturbing story by your son-in-law and daughter, and that story has been verified by Mr. Haverly. I have asked you here to defend yourself."

Her father's complexion went ashen and then livid. "What lies have they been telling you? My daughter is not trustworthy, Your Highness."

"I see." The prince studied Seaton. "Perhaps we had best continue this conversation in private. Whitelock, Haverly, all of you, step outside. I'll send for you if I need you."

"Your Highness, would you like me to stay as a witness? Perhaps as protection? There has already been one attempt upon your life today. It would be most reckless not to take precautions." Marcus stayed at the foot of the bed.

"Hmph. Perhaps you are right. Stay, Haverly."

The duke snarled. "Are you suggesting that I would try to . . . That's absurd."

Evan took Diana's icy hand in his and led her from the room. In the anteroom to the bedchamber, Diana sank onto a chair, as if her legs wouldn't hold her a second longer, and Evan paced.

The double doors did little to stop the sound of the heated exchange within, but they couldn't make out the words. They didn't have to wait long, but it felt like an eternity. The doors flew open and the duke stomped out. He strode with his fists at his sides, his movements stiff, his face blanched.

"Whitelock?" the prince called.

They returned to his bedside, and Evan noted the flush riding his cheeks and the fire in his eyes.

"You may rest assured that the child known to you as Cian Seaton will remain in your custody. And that the duke will never trouble you again regarding his well-being." With satisfaction, he let his head fall to the pillows.

Diana rushed to his side, kneeling by the bed and taking his hand. "Thank you, Your Highness. Thank you."

Evan inhaled sharply. "We are in your debt, Your Highness."

"You know, I take much criticism for investing titles on those some of the *ton* deem unworthy. But look at this case. A bred-and-born duke acting like a scoundrel, and a common-born soldier behaving with nobility. I don't think I made a mistake in your case, Whitelock."

With a rueful smile, Evan shook his head. "There was a time when I was certain you had. I didn't know the first thing about being an earl or a husband. I'm still not sure I know much, but I'll learn."

Diana nodded. "I think he's finally realized that nobility starts in the heart, not in the pedigree. It's a matter of action, not standing."

The prince patted her hand. "I'm tired. Send in that housekeeper with some of that beef tea you promised." He sighed, as if suddenly weak, shooing them away.

Marcus remained, but he grinned and nodded to them as they went.

When they were once more on the other side of the prince's bedroom doors, Evan hugged Diana and swung her in a circle. She tilted her head back and laughed, gripping his shoulders.

"You were wonderful." He gave her a resounding kiss.

"Cian is ours. No more danger, no more threat, no more fears. I can't wait. Let's go see him and tell him the good news." She took his hand, tugging him toward the nursery.

Later that week, Evan walked along the upstairs hallway. Wall sconces lit the way, creating pockets of light in the passageway. The guests had all gone on to Brighton, including the Prince Regent, who had recovered more quickly than anyone had anticipated. The prince swore it was the dedicated nursing of Louisa Monroe and the beautifully appointed and restful rooms created by Diana that had him on his feet so soon.

Evan secretly believed it was because the cut on his arm, though painful, wasn't really that serious.

He regretted that Marcus couldn't stay longer. That had been his plan initially, but earlier that day a messenger had arrived from his family home in Oxford. Marcus hadn't shared the nature of the dispatch, but the bleak expression in his eyes worried Evan. For a duke's second son, Marcus had incredible access to the Prince Regent and to information from many sources. Evan respected his friend's privacy, so he didn't ask, but he had a feeling Marcus was more than an idle bachelor of the *ton*. Perhaps someday Evan would know more, but for now he was content to call Marcus Haverly his friend. He prayed whatever was amiss in Oxford could be resolved quickly.

He traced Diana to where he thought she would be, in the nursery, snuggled on the couch with Cian in her arms. Every night of the last week, she'd come here just before bedtime, as if she couldn't quite believe he was really theirs and always would be.

This time, though, Cian wasn't asleep. He leaned back against her, clacking a string of spools and babbling.

"He's decided now is a good time to play?" Evan sat beside his wife, holding his finger out to the boy. With a toothless grin, Cian grabbed the finger and tried to shove it into his mouth.

Contentment settled around Evan, something that over the past several months he thought he'd never feel again.

"Say, I have something for you, Diana." He fished in his pocket. "It's long overdue, I'm afraid." He made a fist over the small object and drew it out.

"What is it?" She readjusted the baby in her lap. "A present?"

She looked so eager, he felt a stab of guilt. He was still learning things about her. Evidently presents were high on her list of good things. He'd have to scatter them through her life with more regularity.

"You remember that the prince awarded a prize, a silver set, to the winner of the shooting contest?"

She nodded.

"When His Highness dispatched the courtier to procure the prize from a London jeweler's shop, I sent my own private order along with the man." He took her left hand in his. "For months you've been wearing this ring, a regimental ring clearly masculine and military and wildly inappropriate for a wedding band, because your husband was such a dolt that he didn't buy you a proper ring for your wedding day." He slipped the heavy gold ring from her finger. "I thought it high time you had that proper ring."

Setting his regimental ring on the upholstery beside him, he opened his other hand. "Where that ring brings reminders of battle and comrades and campaigns, this one reminds me of you and our union, our promises before God." He slipped the band onto her finger, where it fit perfectly.

She raised it to the light, her perfect mouth opening slightly and her eyes sparkling with what he hoped was delight. "It's beautiful." She turned the band, an intricate design in pierced gold of leaves and flowers. At the center of each flower, a tiny diamond winked and sparkled.

"You certainly are."

Later, with Cian now asleep on his shoulder and Diana tucked into his side, he sighed. "I wish I could hold on to this moment, this time. I don't want anything to change. We're so happy now. The house is done. The Royal Visit is over. The servants and tenants and horses have settled in. Cian's happy and growing like a well-watered weed." He brushed the boy's dark hair, marveling at its softness. "I wish I could stop time."

Diana's brows arched. "Hmm, I don't think that's possible. Anyway, I don't want to stop time at all."

He frowned, a bit stung that she hadn't joined in his sentiments. "Don't you?"

"Well, there are always new adventures ahead, aren't there? And I want to share them all with you."

He relaxed at her explanation. That made sense.

"There's one adventure we've embarked on that I'm particularly excited about." She wriggled a bit tighter against him.

"And what's that?" Evan laid his head on the back of the settee and stretched his legs out, crossing his boots at the ankles. "Being parents to Cian?"

"Cian and the new baby."

Silence reigned for a long moment, and Evan felt as if time truly had stopped. He lifted his head.

"The what?"

"The new baby. Possibly the new heir to White Haven." She sat up to look at him, and his eyes dropped to her middle. "Or possibly our first daughter, you never know."

Waves of happiness burst over him, and he wrapped his arms around his little family. "When?"

"Around Christmastime, I think." Her joyous smile went straight to his heart.

How much more blessing could one man take?

"You know the Prince Regent will insist upon being the new baby's godfather, don't you?" she asked.

With a chuckle, he kissed her temple.

"If he asks, we'll have to say yes. You don't say no to the Prince Regent."

SERENDIPITY & SECRETS

The GENTLEMAN SPY

ERICA VETSCH

KREGEL
PUBLICATIONS

Chapter 1

Haverly Manor
Oxfordshire, England
January 1, 1814

HE SUPPOSED THAT someday he would have to forgive the child for being a girl.

Marcus Haverly took one look at the squirming pink bundle in the nurse's arms and sighed, the weight of the world threatening to push him into the ornate rug beneath his Hessians. He set down the book he'd been reading, his appetite for the written word evaporating as reality set in.

His mother dragged into the study, her shoulders slumped, her hands lax.

Who was more disappointed? He would hate to have to live on the difference. He rose, put his hands into the pockets of his breeches, and went to stand before the window, staring out into the night. Frost rimed the edges of the panes, and in the distance, black trees lifted skeletal arms toward the moon.

"How is Cilla?" he asked.

"The *accoucheur* has just gone. He says everything went well but that she needs rest." Mother's voice sounded as if she spoke from the bottom of a pit. "I can't bear it. A girl."

Marcus glanced over his shoulder in time to see her sink into a chair, the very picture of despair. The poor woman. All her hopes dashed in a split second.

The child squeaked and snuffled, drawing his attention. He should at least go and look at his niece. After all, he'd been anticipating the birth for months.

The birth that was supposed to set him free.

She had a tuft of dark hair atop her round head. An impossibly tiny hand lay next to her full cheek, the nails minute and faintly blue. Sparse lines of color indicated where her eyebrows would be someday.

He didn't know if he'd ever met a baby as fresh as this one. Though he searched her features, he could find no resemblance to either of her parents. Overall, she looked a bit like an old man. Though he would never say so to Cilla. She was much too frail a flower to accept even the mildest of teasing.

Looking at the baby's helpless little face, as innocent as a person could be, he felt a stirring somewhere in his heart. He would do his duty by her. He owed that much to Neville.

"Take her to the nursery. See that she has everything she needs." He nodded to the nurse, a woman nearly twice his age, thoroughly interviewed and scrutinized by his mother a month ago and passed as acceptable.

When she had departed, Marcus went to the desk . . . his desk now, he supposed. It was all his. The desk, the study, the house, the grounds . . . and the responsibilities. What a way to start the new year.

"What are we going to do now?" Mother eyed him from under the black lace trim on her black cap, her iron-gray curls clustered about her face. Lines of strain showed around her eyes and mouth. "This is an unmitigated disaster."

Marcus jammed his thumb and forefinger into his eyes at the bridge of his nose and breathed in. Why was there no air in this place? A cannonball lodged in his chest, cold and heavy. First his father and brother, and now this? Every event bound him to his burdens with more chains and hawsers than a frigate to the dock.

Mother sniffed, and he lowered his hand, digging for his handkerchief. He needn't have bothered. She had one and dabbed her eyes with the black scrap of linen.

I'm surprised there's a dry square of cloth left in the house. The amount of weeping that has gone on this last six months would fill the Serpentine in Hyde Park.

He chided himself for being unfeeling. She had suffered both great loss and now a great calamity. He should make allowances.

Though it seemed he'd been making allowances for the woman for most of his life.

Her dress seemed to swallow the light from the fireplace and wall sconces. Still wearing black bombazine from head to foot, though the time of deepest mourning had passed months ago. He continued to wear a black coat out of deference to her feelings, but much to his mother's dislike, he'd taken to wearing his buff deerskin breeches and a gray waistcoat. Every time she noticed he'd had his tailor remove the black cloth-covered buttons on his jackets and return the brass originals, she would pucker her lips and let a pair of tears form on her lower lashes.

"I suppose I have no choice but to accept it, but it seems God has been most cruel to me. I feel as if I am Naomi from the Bible. You might as well call me Mara." More sniffs and eye wiping. "That's what she said, wasn't it? When everything had been taken from her . . . that her name now meant 'bitter'? I'm just empty. How can this be happening? I didn't plan for any of this." Her voice vacillated, as if she didn't know whether to feel angry or just victimized.

"A son with higher expectations than mine of his relationship with his mother might take offense. You lost your husband and your eldest, but I still remain, and your daughter, and your widowed daughter-in-law. Not to mention a new grandchild." Marcus kept his voice bland, as he always strove to do in her presence. He was who he was, no more, no less, born in the order God had chosen. As a second son, he no longer resented the affection lavished on his elder brother. Though his parents had three children, only one had mattered when it came to the succession. Sophie, his younger sister, had been attended and sponsored and chaperoned, but his father had purchased a major's commission for Marcus the moment he'd earned his sheepskin from Oxford. He was the spare, not the heir.

He had ceased to let it rankle years ago.

For the most part.

"I have a grandchild, yes, but not a grand*son*." Mother sat up. "I wanted a grand*son*."

"And I wanted you to have one, but God had other plans."

And God's plans had put paid to Marcus's own. Life would be so much easier if God would stay confined to Sunday worship and evening prayers instead of encroaching on Marcus's carefully laid arrangements.

"God has abandoned our family. Or He's punishing me for something. Why else would He treat me this way?" She put her hand to her throat, the tears thickening her voice. "Oh, it's all such a mess. Still, I suppose we'll have to move forward. We have no choice. Tomorrow we'll begin packing for London."

"London?"

"Of course. Now that your circumstances have changed, we must begin the search." A fortifying breath lifted her shoulders.

"The search?" He sounded like a parrot. "For what?"

"Well, for a suitable bride for you. I made inquiries last Season, but I wasn't aiming high enough, I suppose. I was looking for a baronet's daughter, or a squire's, but now I'll have to start over."

The hawsers tightened around his chest. "I'm in no rush. After all, it's only been a few months since our bereavement and barely an hour since it all became official." A wife was the furthest thing from his mind right now. His life up to this point had been carefully ordered, everything divided, kept separate, and tidy. Work, society, family, God. Adding the responsibilities of a dukedom left little room for a wife.

"You might not be in a rush. In fact, I've never known a time when you were, but I am. We've learned, much to our regret, how quickly circumstances can change. You must marry soon and set up your nursery. It's your duty to this family and to the memory of those we've lost." Her backbone stiffened, and for the first time in months, a gleam entered her eyes. "I shall make a list and begin my inquiries . . . or . . ."

"Or?" He was doing it again, mimicking her.

"Or you could marry Cilla."

She said the words slowly, as if only now thinking of them, but he wondered. Had this been her plan for months now, should the infant be a female?

"That would solve a multitude of issues. She's in need of a husband. She's of noble birth. And she's obviously fertile."

A shudder racked down Marcus's spine.

Cilla was a nice woman, but she was also timid, sensitive, and, if he was honest, boring. She had suited his staid, proper, and dutiful brother right down to the ground, but Marcus couldn't imagine himself married to her. Of course, he couldn't imagine himself married to anyone. At least not yet.

"It's too soon to make a decision like that. And it's too late at night. Go to bed, madam. We'll no doubt talk about it in the morning."

She rose, gathering her dignity around her like a coronation robe. If there was a silver lining to the dark clouds hanging over his life, it was that at least a hunt for a suitable bride would give her something else to think about than her bereavement. Of course he would have the final say, but her quest would keep her occupied and out of his hair for a while. For the first time in recent memory, she swept from the room with an echo of her former imperious manner.

The fire popped and the mantel clock ticked, the only sounds in the room. What was he supposed to do now? He needed to send word to London, ask for direction. Partridge would take the message.

He would have to wait for a return missive to come from Sir Noel. His superior would know what to do. Though if his mother was serious about leaving for the city right away, he might wait and speak with Sir Noel in person.

Sir Noel would answer the question foremost in Marcus's mind, the question he'd wrestled with ever since he'd received word that his father, the duke, and his brother, the heir, had been killed in a carriage accident almost seven months ago.

If Marcus was now forced to become the Duke of Haverly, could he still continue his work for the Crown?

London, England
February 1, 1814

"This is your last chance, Charlotte. If you don't find a husband this Season, you're finished. Your father won't impoverish himself further, and I can't say I blame him. Three Seasons on the Marriage Mart really is the outside limit."

Lady Charlotte Tiptree looked up, one tendril of hair twined around her index finger. Her concentration broken, she tucked a slip of paper into her book on Roman history to mark her place and forced herself to return to the nineteenth century. "I'm sorry, Mother. Were you speaking to me?"

"You're the only other person in the drawing room, are you not? Please put that down and pay attention. Why must I always drag your nose out of some tome or other? If your father catches you reading again, I don't know what he'll do." Mother shook her head, her hands fluttering. Mother's hands always fluttered, especially when she was agitated. "And sit up like a proper lady. I don't know what your posture will become if you continue to lounge like a sultan. It's as if we didn't go to great expense to see you become a lady. What did they teach you at that finishing school?"

Refraining from rolling her eyes—another gesture that would get her a scolding—Charlotte pulled her legs off the arm of the deep chair and put her feet on the floor. It had taken an age to get into a comfortable reading position, and now all that effort was wasted. She smoothed her plain gray skirt. The dress was serviceable and chaste, covering her from neck to ankles, but nothing about it was pretty. None of her clothes were really pretty, her father feeling such fripperies an unnecessary expense. He could pinch a shilling until the King's profile cried. And as for the finishing school, it was more of a prison on a barren wasteland in Dartmoor. Run by an impoverished gentlewoman with no sense of humor, the Hitchin's School for Young Ladies was an academy so obscure, Charlotte had been one of only a handful of students, and none of those with social aspirations or titled family.

It had been less expensive than sending her to Switzerland with other girls of her rank.

Plastering a pleasant, slightly vacant expression on her face—the aspect Mother thought all young ladies should wear—Charlotte put her feet primly together and straightened her shoulders. "What is it you'd like to speak about?" Though she knew. It had been the topic of many a tedious conversation throughout the summer, the fall, and over the interminable holidays.

Mother exhaled, her features relaxing into kinder lines. "I don't mean to nag, but you must face the truth. If you don't change your ways, you're going to wind up a spinster. You're nearly there now. Your father has spent all the money he intends to in order to see you prepared to take your place in society. What kind of a thank-you will it be if you squander your last opportunity? You're not getting any younger, and there will be many fresh faces in the *ton* again this year. If you don't put yourself out to be agreeable, to be the sort of woman a peer is looking for in a wife . . ." She gripped her fingers in her lap.

Something hovered on her lips, and Charlotte tensed. Mother rarely hesitated when Father wasn't present, so whatever it was must be momentous.

Mother took a deep breath, as if fortifying herself. "Your father has instructed me to inform you that if you are not engaged to be married before Easter Sunday, he will have no choice but to send you to live at Aunt Philomena's in Yorkshire." Tugging her handkerchief from her sleeve, she waved it as she talked, the scent of her lavender sachets filling the air. "Philomena broached the subject herself, and he's latched on to the idea. I tried to talk him out of it, but he's adamant. He says your lack of a husband is your own fault and that becoming Aunt Philomena's companion would be fitting punishment for your behavior over the last two years."

Charlotte's mind went blank. This was a new twist. Father had occasionally made vague statements as to her future, but nothing this definite . . . or dire.

Aunt Philomena. She winced.

To be accurate, she was Charlotte's great-aunt on her father's side. Having just endured the Christmas holidays with her at the Tiptree estate in Essex, the thought of a life sentence as her companion drained the blood from Charlotte's head.

Surely this was an idle threat? Her father couldn't be so unfeeling, could he?

Aunt Philomena complained about everything. Nothing suited or satisfied her, and her voice could crack glass. She must go through a half dozen paid companions every year because none of them could abide her for more than a few weeks—either that or she fired them for any of a hundred petty reasons.

But as a relative, Charlotte would not be allowed to quit, and Aunt Philomena would be delighted to have a servant who couldn't give her notice no matter how poorly she treated her. No wonder she'd planted the seeds of the notion for Father to consider. And Father would surely jump at the chance to fob Charlotte and the expense of keeping her off on someone else.

But Aunt Philomena?

Philomena smelled perpetually of naphtha soap, vegetable tonic, and ceaseless discontent.

But . . . Charlotte's only escape would be to find a husband?

Was there no other answer? No way to avoid either fate?

It wasn't that she was averse to having a husband and a family, but the men of the *ton* were all so boring or boorish, or both. Self-absorbed, idle, lightweight . . . None of them seemed to *do* anything constructive or important with their lives.

Mother put on a brave, encouraging face. "You're not unpleasant to look at, you are the daughter of an earl, and you have a proper education and training in deportment. You would be an acceptable bride if you'd only try. All it requires is that you exert yourself, perhaps use a bit of flattery, a bit of coquettishness. Make a man feel good about himself. Show an interest in something other than your books, and perhaps flirt a little."

Flirt. Act like an empty-headed miss who couldn't cross a ballroom unless a man gave her directions and lent his arm for her to lean upon.

"Don't make that face at me, young lady. It's not wrong to be smart, but it is wrong to assume that everyone else is stupid compared to you. If you continue to make potential suitors look foolish with your sharp tongue, you're destined for Yorkshire and the life of a lady's companion, and you might as well forgo this Season and head to Aunt Philomena's now." Her mother's voice had sharpened, and her shaft hit true.

Charlotte nodded, letting her chin drop, knowing she had been guilty of handing out setdowns when she lost her patience with the shallowness of conversations at balls and dinners. But how could she possibly marry a man who bored her to sawdust? If only she could meet someone who actually *did* something with his life, who could claim to have read *any* book in the last year, who did more than talk about his haberdashery or his driving skill with a coach-and-four. Someone who wasn't looking for a bit of fluff to admire him and remind him how wonderful he was. Someone who might actually be capable of fidelity and genuine love and soul-nurturing conversation.

Perhaps someone who could see behind the plain dresses and severe hairstyle, prescribed by her parents, to the person she was inside.

"Now," her mother said, brisk and businesslike as she rose from her chair. "Put that book away and get your cloak. We're going to start as we mean to go on. I've received an invitation to meet some friends at the Frost Festival. It opens today, and there will be lots of people there with whom to mingle. All the most fashionable persons will turn out for the occasion. I will expect you to be polite to those we meet. In fact, say as little as possible, and you'll be fine. Dress warmly. I can't remember a winter this cold, and it's bound to be worse on the river."

Charlotte had about as much experience holding her tongue as she did flirting. She set her jaw mutinously, but she obeyed, taking the book along with her to her room, lest her father come across it and confiscate it.

An hour later when Charlotte stepped out of the carriage at the top of the steps leading down to the Thames, her mother's claims of cold seemed an understatement. Icy wind scudded over the cobbles and whipped at her bonnet ties. For the first time in years, the weather had been so bitterly cold that the river had frozen completely. Enterprising souls had used this phenomenon to revive the Frost Festival, and crowds had gathered for the entertainment.

"Come. I've arranged to meet someone on the quay." Her mother gathered her woolen cloak about her, her cheeks already pink with cold but her eyes bright and eager. Mother, like the rest of the *ton*, loved any reason to socialize, and the temperature wouldn't daunt her if it meant a chance to gather with friends.

Charlotte burrowed her hands into her knitted muff and followed Mother down the steps, careful where she placed her feet on the uneven stone. All around her, people laughed and called, vendors hawked their wares, and children wove and dove between the revelers.

Smoke from braziers and campfires whipped around, propelled by the stiff breeze, and the aromas of cooking meat and yeasty ale enticed investigation.

A small city had sprung up on the solid surface of the river—booths, tents, shacks. Straw had been strewn in paths to make impromptu "streets." Standing as they were above the icy surface on the pier, Charlotte observed a juggler entertaining a crescent of onlookers, and she spied a thin urchin dipping into the pocket of one jovial man while he was distracted.

She checked that her reticule was secured around her wrist and nestled deep into her muff. All summer long she had been saving to purchase a subscription to a lending library for the time she would be in London. Her father rarely turned any money over to her, and she'd had to hoard and scrape to purchase each of the treasured books in her collection. She couldn't afford to be robbed if she was to have new reading material this Season. A subscription would allow her to read as much as she wanted of books she could never afford to purchase.

"There they are." Mother took Charlotte's elbow and tugged her toward the end of the pier. "And they've brought Dudley."

A groan worked its way up Charlotte's throat, and her shoulders sagged. They were meeting the Bosworths? Dudley Bosworth? Mother hurried toward her friends while speaking in a low tone. "If you won't take care of the matter of finding a husband yourself, I'm going to have to intervene. Now, be nice."

All too soon Dudley was bowing over her hand, his rounded face parting in a reluctant smile. "H . . . hello, Lady Charlotte."

Was his face red from cold, or was he blushing?

Remembering her mother's admonition to keep her mouth shut, Charlotte said nothing, only nodding to him. He'd paid some court to her last Season, probably pushed into it by his mother, for he suffered greatly from awkwardness around girls. Charlotte hadn't been interested then. She wasn't interested now. Dudley was nice enough, she supposed, but he was about as exciting as blancmange.

"Charlotte was just telling me how eager she was to see you again. She couldn't wait to come to the festival, knowing you'd be here," Mother said, sending a warning glance Charlotte's way, forbidding any contradiction to this bald-faced lie.

"We were delighted to know you were coming, my dear." Mrs. Bosworth looked fondly from her son to Charlotte. "Dudley was most anxious to see you too." She inclined her head a little, as if encouraging Dudley to say something. He shot a startled glance at his mother and then covered it up by nodding vigorously.

So that was the direction in which the land lay. Ambushed by their parents. Charlotte turned away under the guise of dealing with the wind wrapping her plain woolen cloak around her, and a bookseller's stall caught her eye below. If only she could escape to that little oasis in the crowd.

"Let's take in some of the festivities, shall we?" Mr. Bosworth clapped his gloved hands together and then rubbed his palms against one another, as if anticipating all he would see and do.

Dudley stood between Charlotte and her mother, shifting his weight. He half offered his arm to Charlotte, and the other to her mother, then stilled.

His father solved the dilemma. "You escort Charlotte, my boy." He held out both elbows to his wife and Mother, and they strolled back along the length of the pier, leaving Dudley and Charlotte to come along behind.

Taking his arm meant removing her hand from her muff, a proposition she didn't relish. She was more than capable of walking without support, and her hand would freeze through her glove. Still, proprieties. Reluctantly, she placed her hand in the crook of his elbow.

"It . . . it's good to see you again," Dudley said. "I hope you had a pleasant Christmas."

"Yes, thank you," she lied, remembering the strident irritation of Aunt Philomena's petulance. She would be good. She wouldn't say or do anything to embarrass her mother or Dudley. She would hold her tongue. She would not be packed off to Yorkshire like a naughty child.

She hoped she was up to the task.

People jostled and pushed in around them, and Charlotte felt her muscles tightening. She didn't like crowds. Her eyes darted, looking for avenues of escape amongst the throng.

The descent from the pier to river level brought a new perspective. She now looked up the embankment at the street, a view she'd never had before. Dudley proved useful, guiding her through the shoppers and revelers to one of the straw-strewn paths. Her mother and the Bosworths had stopped at a cart to admire a display of silk shawls, but Charlotte pulled gently on Dudley's arm in the direction of the bookseller she'd spied from above. If she had to be here, she was going to see something she liked.

The man minding the bookstall doffed his cap and blew on his hands. His gloves had no fingertips, possibly to make him more adept at picking up and leafing through his merchandise, and as a consequence, his fingers were red as cherries.

"Sir, you look like a scholar. Are you hoping to stock your library? I've several impressive volumes that would look magnificent on your shelves." He spoke to Dudley, ignoring Charlotte.

Dudley shook his head, sputtering. "No, no, sir. I'm not looking for books."

A pity.

Charlotte touched the spines of a tray of books set at an angle to display their titles. She loved everything about books—the beautiful bindings, the mesmeric endpapers, the heft, the smell. And that was not even counting the words and worlds they held. Her own small library of getting on for a dozen volumes was her most precious possession, each book carefully saved for, pored over, and treasured.

"Ma'am, the novels are over here. I've a nice selection." He directed her to a shelf to the right of the booth.

Charlotte enjoyed a good novel, but at the moment she was interested in something more scholarly to sink her teeth into. "Do you have anything on Greek history?" She'd love to read a few pages, snatch a few moments, a few words and paragraphs to savor later.

The bookseller put on a patronizing grin. "Are you buying for a gentleman friend? Surely a mere woman wouldn't be interested in something as taxing as Greek history?" He shook his head, winking at Dudley. "I have some manuals on home management and a few recipe books here somewhere that might suit a lady like you."

Frustration burned its way up her chest.

"What utter twaddle. I may be a 'mere woman,' but I am certainly capable of comprehending a history book for my own education and enjoyment. Women aren't relegated to only perusing recipes and fiction, you know." The words flew out in a torrent, and her voice rose. "Of all the idiotic—" Charlotte broke off when she became aware she was drawing attention.

The merchant held out his hands as if to plead innocence, glancing at the audience that had stopped to see what the fuss was about, and Dudley hunched his shoulders under his many-caped cloak, as if he wanted to disappear.

She pressed her lips together. *So much for holding my tongue. When are you going to learn?* She should apologize, but righteous indignation clamped her throat tight. It wasn't the bookseller's fault, not really. It was society . . . and the women who played along and perpetuated the notion that no female could have a thought deeper than a finger bowl. The vendor had merely voiced what most people assumed, and by doing so, carried the trope further.

"Charlotte Tiptree." Her mother's low voice cut across the ice. "Come with me, please. There's something I wish to show you." Her hand came up and clamped on Charlotte's arm, drawing her away from the books. "Excuse us for a moment, Dudley."

When they were a few yards away, in a blind alley between two vendors, Mother gripped Charlotte by the shoulders and gave her a little shake. "You haven't heard a word I said today, have you? I leave you for one minute, and you start spouting like a broken vessel. You're embarrassing yourself. I've a mind to send you home so you can do no more damage to the Tiptree reputation. We have generations of prestige and good standing in London society, and I'll be blessed if I'll let you and your unblunted tongue ruin it for us."

If she weren't so cold, Charlotte would've been able to feel the blood rush to her cheeks. She'd done it again. Let her feelings get the better of her and take the restraint off her tongue.

She saw a long future with Aunt Philomena stretching ahead of her.

"Now, you'll stay close to me, and if I hear you say more than 'yes, ma'am' or 'no, sir' the rest of the afternoon, I'll put you on the first coach to Yorkshire myself. I intend to enjoy myself today, and you will do nothing more to prevent that. Do you hear me?" She gave Charlotte one more shake, her voice never rising above a harsh whisper, all the more piercing for it.

"Yes, ma'am," Charlotte muttered past her clenched teeth.

She followed her mother over to the Bosworths, keeping her head bent, determined to walk small. Before they moved on, she stopped before the bookseller. He stiffened, as if bracing for her next onslaught.

"My apologies, sir." She kept her voice low, but she met his eyes. "I spoke out of turn. You have beautiful books here. I hope the festival brings you great success."

He nodded sharply but said nothing, no doubt fearful of incurring her wrath once again.

With a weight in her chest, she hurried to catch up to her mother before her absence was noted.

Booth after booth, stall after stall, they moved up and down, watching the entertainers, listening to music, admiring the wares. Dudley bought Charlotte a cup of hot chocolate and a Scotch egg served in heavy paper to catch the grease. The chocolate warmed her temporarily, but her toes were numb, and her cheeks stung in the stiff breeze. If only her clothing allowance would stretch to a fur-lined cloak like those other women in society wore . . . How long must they stay?

At last Mother declared they would have to depart, and Charlotte barely stifled an exclamation of relief. She'd adhered strictly to her mother's mandate and said nothing most of the afternoon. Being so vigilant exhausted her.

At the base of the embankment stairs, Mrs. Bosworth embraced Mother, kissing her cheek. "Verona, it was a pleasure, as always." She looked over Mother's shoulder at Charlotte, her eyes clouded with indecision. Perhaps she was rethinking trying to matchmake for her son, at least where Charlotte was concerned.

Dudley shook Charlotte's hand, formal and stiff, and Mr. Bosworth did the same. "Very nice to see you, Lady Charlotte. Lady Tiptree."

"Lady Tiptree?" A woman in several layers of shabby clothing nearly stumbled to a halt on the ice near them. "Are you the countess?"

She must've been a handsome woman in her prime, but now she looked gaunt and thin. A streak of dirt decorated her cheek, and she clutched her cloak about her, no gloves on her hands. Her head was bare, her raven hair streaked with silver and clutched into a knot, drawing attention to her sharp cheekbones and her dark brown eyes.

Mother frowned. "Yes, I am the countess. My husband is the Earl of Tiptree. Who are you?"

The woman reared up, her eyes sparking. "Who am I? Who am I?" Her voice ricocheted off the stone steps leading up to street level, and it seemed everyone in a wide radius stopped to hear. "I'm the woman who kept your husband satisfied and happy for twenty years before he abandoned me. I'm the woman who bore Joseph Tiptree, the earl himself, a daughter only to see him turn his back on us and put us out on the street—that's who I am." Her hands came up, bare fingers curled like claws, and fisted at her temples, as if her outrage consumed her.

Charlotte inhaled icy air that froze her lungs. The woman swayed, and people drew back, as if getting too close might contaminate them. Mother stood rooted to the spot, the color draining from her face.

A whirl of questions roared through Charlotte's mind. Was this woman telling the truth? Her father had kept a mistress? Or was she a lunatic, raving nonsense? But the woman had known her father's name. His name and his title. Of course she could've learned them from anywhere. Was she only looking to force money from the Tiptrees? Or was she being honest?

"Aye, that's right." The woman spun around to glare, spitting the words to the onlookers. "Back away. Act like I'm not good enough to wipe your shoes."

"Madam, this is neither the time nor the place." Mr. Bosworth frowned at her, his side-whiskers bristling.

"When is the time then? Joe dumped me in the street, after I was loyal to him for years. Turned me out of the house he kept me in. He won't see me. He won't return my letters. And now Pippa, our daughter, is forced to make her own way." Her body quivered as a gasp went up from the onlookers and many heads bent to whisper behind their gloves. "After he promised me he'd take care of us forever. That he'd see Pippa had a good life. I'm trapped in St. Giles trying to keep body and soul together, and my daughter is . . . has become . . ." She covered her face for a moment, but then her chin rose. "I just wanted you to know what kind of man you are married to. You have everything you need, and your daughter here will never have to worry about having food or warmth or a roof over her head, thanks to her father. But my girl, his second daughter, is forced to sell herself, something I vowed she would never have to do—" A sob cut off her voice.

"Verona, let's go." Mrs. Bosworth grabbed Mother's arm. She looked the woman over, her eyes sharp enough to draw blood. "Whoever you are, get away from us. You're no better than you should be and have no one to blame for your circumstances but yourself. Accosting your betters in public like this. Go back to the rookery, where you belong."

Mrs. Bosworth hustled Mother up the steps to the street, but Charlotte didn't follow. Instead she yanked off her muff, tucking it under her arm, and peeled off her gloves. Dudley hovered nearby, shifting his weight, too much of a gentleman to leave without Charlotte but clearly uneasy.

"Here, take these." Charlotte held the gloves out to the woman. "What's your name?"

The woman studied her skeptically. Her cold-reddened hand trembled as she took the woolen gloves from Charlotte's fingers. "You look like your father. Same coloring." She stuck her hands into the gloves. Did she think Charlotte would snatch them back? "My name is Amelia Cashel. Former mistress of the Earl of Tiptree." She almost sneered, her words bitter and hurt.

"Charlotte, come here at once." Mother's voice shot down the steps.

"Please, you say you have a daughter? How old is she?" Charlotte dug in her reticule and pulled out her entire savings, meager as it was, forcing down any remorse for the library subscription she had hoped to purchase.

"Her name's Pippa, and she's nineteen."

Pressing the coins into the woman's hand, Charlotte nodded. Her mind raced but felt stunned into immobility at the same time as she hurried up the steps, Dudley coming along behind like a faithful hound.

She had a sister.

"Charlotte Tiptree, this might be the most foolish thing you've done in your entire life," she whispered to herself as she hurried down the street, head bent, lugging a basket that bumped against her thigh with every step.

Ice coated the gutters and glazed the cobbles, and she had to watch her step lest she fall. The darkness didn't help. She'd left behind the lighted braziers and streetlamps a few blocks ago. "At least you can be thankful that the moon is nearly full." Though the moonlight seemed to do little good. The stars were mere pinpricks, and the buildings created shadows deep enough for a horde of miscreants to shelter in.

Having given every cent in her purse to that woman, Charlotte had none for hiring a coach, and her father had taken the carriage out tonight. She was forced to walk. It might be less than two miles from Mayfair to St.

Giles in distance, but it was leagues in social standing and safety. Block by block along the Tottenham Court Road, the houses dwindled in size, the side streets narrowed, and her tension increased.

Her hands ached with cold. She hoped her gloves were even now warming Amelia Cashel's hands . . . or Pippa's. Charlotte had no second pair, and she couldn't carry the basket and use her muff, so cold hands it was.

She'd never been to one of London's rookeries, much less one as extensive as St. Giles. If she wasn't wont to snaffle her father's newspapers and read them in secret, she wouldn't even know what a rookery was, much less where to find one. According to the broadsheets, the rookeries teemed with villains and ne'er-do-wells, women of low morals and men of evil intent.

Which made tonight's gambit seem foolish indeed as she bumped along, head bent, trying to keep a grip on both her imagination and her courage lest the one get out of control and the other flee entirely.

As Charlotte saw it, she had two major obstacles: finding Amelia Cashel's residence in a warren of tenements and squatters' flats, and getting back to Mayfair safely. All without her parents any the wiser.

If her mother knew where her daughter was and what she was doing, she'd grab Charlotte by the cloak and drag her to Aunt Philomena's on foot, bouncing her every step of the way.

Dinner tonight had been a nightmare. Her mother had sat as still as a Roman statue. Father presided over the meal as if nothing untoward had occurred. Had Mother even told him? He'd surely find out soon enough, London gossip being what it was. Charlotte toyed with her food, her mind consumed with the knowledge that her father was a philanderer and liar and that she had a sister. Well, a half sister, but a sibling nonetheless.

Pippa.

Pippa Cashel. Nineteen years old. Which made her two years or so younger than Charlotte. All her life she'd wished for, prayed for, longed for a sibling, a sister, someone to share things with, to talk with, to laugh with. She knew her parents were disappointed that they had been unable to produce more children, in particular a son, but Charlotte shared that disappointment.

She had grown up lonely, and a sister would have banished loneliness.

Charlotte glanced at her father. He looked the same as always, perfectly barbered, impeccably if plainly clothed, his features sharp, his coloring, as

Amelia Cashel had said, fairish like her own. She glanced around the dining room, taking in the papered walls, high ceiling, a single candelabra on the table, but high overhead a chandelier that could be lit when company came over and her father wanted to impress. A fire in the coal stove had warmed the room, and the food, while plain, had been plentiful.

But no one had spoken a word during dinner.

Now, as Charlotte hurried farther from her home in Mayfair, cold, scared, on a mission of mercy that might not even be wanted, guilt smote her. Her sister had none of what Charlotte took for granted every day. Pippa's mother hadn't even owned a pair of gloves.

If Amelia Cashel was to be believed, her daughter, Pippa, was now a doxy? As proper and sheltered as Charlotte had been, she knew what a prostitute was, what happened during the transaction. She had science and medical books to thank for her knowledge, since her mother would never speak of such an intimate subject as relations between a man and woman. If either of her parents knew she read about anatomy and physiology, they would be horrified.

But the idea of any woman being forced to be employed as a prostitute . . . Most women of society seemed to believe that a woman who sold her favors did so because she wanted to, because some fatal flaw in her character that she couldn't overcome made her behave so poorly.

Was that true?

Were the Cashels merely subject to their sinful natures?

If so, what did that make her father, who had kept a mistress for two decades? Who had turned them out without any means of support when he tired of them?

Shame writhed through her middle, and she gripped the handle of the basket until the wood bit into her hands.

The air stank. Trash gusted along the street, and the buildings loomed overhead, the upper stories cantilevering out over the ground floors, cutting off the faint moonlight. Lamplight showed around tattered curtains or crooked shutters, and a rat scurried across her path. She stifled a yelp, jumping as it skittered into a pile of old rags crammed into the corner of a stairwell.

She'd arrived in the rookery.

A sign hung over one establishment halfway down the block, where light poured from every window. With such frigid temperatures gripping the city, no one lingered on the street. A man hurried from the opposite direction, head bent. He glanced up but wasted no time ducking into the tavern.

As Charlotte slowly approached, she could make out the sign swinging in the wind from two icy chains. Each swing squeaked, emphasizing the quiet everywhere else.

The Hog's Head.

The sign was in the shape of a barrel—a hogshead—but also bore the carved likeness of a pig's head.

Just the head. Severed and sitting atop the barrel.

She swallowed. A most uncouth advertisement for a public house.

Still, she'd come this far, and a public house open at this hour might be the best place to inquire as to the Cashel residence.

Girding herself with what remained of her courage, she put her hand on the door and pushed it open.

Inside, a room crowded with tables, chairs, men, and talk greeted her. Only a few heads looked up at her entrance, but one by one, conversations ceased and eyes fastened on her. Her heart thudded painfully, and her lungs felt tiny and crammed into the top of her rib cage.

The odor of stale beer and unwashed male hit her, and she winced. A fire roared in a massive fireplace, and to the side, a large, unkempt man came up a set of stairs from below with a barrel on his shoulder. At the sight of her, he lowered it to the floor with a *thunk*.

"Sharkey, me eyes is going wonky. I b'lieve I better be done for the night," a man to her left said, setting down his glass. "If I didn't know better, I'd say a girl had just walked in here."

"It is a girl, you buffoon," the large man with the barrel called out.

"Cor, get a look at her." The loud whisper came from the back of the room. "She ain't from around here, that's certain."

"Here, lovey, come sit wif us." A pockmarked man jumped up and grabbed an empty chair.

"No, come sit with me." A rotund man with a florid face scooted his chair back and patted his thigh. His eyebrows waggled, and his lips shone wetly in the light from the fireplace.

Charlotte's mouth went dry as she searched from one face to the next for any sign of . . . well, perhaps for someone who didn't look either disreputable or lascivious . . . or both.

Several chairs scooted back, and their occupants rose, fanning out and approaching her slowly.

Her knees felt quite mushy, and her heart threatened to batter its way out of her chest. Which made her angry. Why should she cower? These men had no right to frighten her so.

"Gentlemen, I will ask you to mind your manners. I'm in need of some information, not attention." She kept her chin up and tried to make her eyes fierce, but the crack in her voice didn't fool even her.

They continued to advance, crowding her back toward the door. She held the basket in front of her, and with one hand strove to find the door latch behind her without taking her eyes off the men.

"What information are ye lookin' for, me dove?" A hulking fellow with a beard that seemed desperate to hide his entire face grinned, showing off a few gaps where his teeth should reside.

For a moment, Charlotte couldn't remember why she was there. She blinked. "I need to find the home of Amelia Cashel and her daughter, Pippa."

The men stopped moving. The biggest man scratched his cheek, his fingers rasping in his beard. "Whatcha lookin' for Pippa Cashel round 'ere for? She ain't 'ere. She's too good for St. Giles by a long stretch. She's up in King's Place. Is that where you come from? If ya do, I'm going to have to save my pennies and visit you up there." His eyes flared, and he licked his lips.

Charlotte shook her head, unable to look away. This must be how a mouse felt when facing a snake. "No, I was told she lived in St. Giles. Her mother told me just today."

"Her mum lives 'ere, but not her."

Disappointment seeped in, and for a moment Charlotte forgot her precarious situation. She wasn't going to meet her sister tonight.

"What you want with her anyway? We'll keep you company tonight."

Her fingers found the latch behind her, but before she could open the door, the large man planted his palm on the wood over her head and leaned close. His hot, nasty breath puffed against her cheek, and she pressed away from him only to find that another man had come up on her left. His eyes were gimlet sharp.

"Been a while since we saw a fresh face around here. You do look like you could be a King's Place dolly-mop yourself, though yer dressed more like a nun. But still, there might be somethin' interesting under all that fabric." His hand, nails crusted and filthy, reached for her hood, yanking it back. The abrupt motion and Charlotte's endeavor to evade him tugged pins from her hair. Her yellow curls tumbled down about her shoulders, and several men sucked in quick breaths.

"Blimey," one man breathed. "Look how clean her hair is."

Charlotte tried to stuff her curls out of sight and tug her hood back up, but with only one hand, she made the situation worse, feeling pins slide and tangle in her hair.

"I'm sayin' it now. I get her first." The big man shoved the smaller man aside. As his giant hand reached for Charlotte's arm, she squirmed around, icy fingers scrabbling for the latch.

A whistling sound followed by a thud froze everyone in the room. Glancing up, Charlotte spied a bone-handled knife vibrating softly, embedded in the door. Was it possible for blood to truly run cold? Her vessels felt like the Thames ran through them.

She feared if her eyes widened more, they might come right out of her head. A knife? What had she been thinking, venturing alone into the rookery at night? She was an idiot. She should be committed to Bedlam.

"Stand down, gentlemen." A deep voice, all the more frightening because it was so calm and controlled, filtered around the bar patrons from the back of the room. "I'll be taking the lady."

Some of the men on the fringes resumed their seats, but the few right around Charlotte scowled and remained where they were.

A cloaked and hooded figure advanced, weaving between the tables. As he came, he tugged his muffler up to cover the lower part of his face. Digging into an inner pocket, he flicked a gold coin toward the bar. "Drown your disappointment, boys. I'll shout a round for the house."

This moved several more away, but the Big Beard stayed planted in front of Charlotte.

The hooded man reached around him and plucked the knife from the door. It disappeared under the cloak. "Barney, didn't the last time you crossed me teach you anything?" His voice dropped to a whisper that feathered across Charlotte's skin.

She looked from one to the other. Were they going to brawl right here and now? And could she escape while they were thus engaged?

But the giant's shoulders went slack, and he bobbed his head like an ox. "Sorry, Hawk."

With a small flick of his fingers, the cloaked man motioned Barney aside, took Charlotte's arm, and opened the door. Behind him, men crowded the bar, clamoring for their complimentary drink.

The man called Hawk—what kind of name was that?—steered her out into the cold darkness, his grip on her elbow firm.

"What on earth were you thinking? Are you lost, or have you merely misplaced your reason?" His voice remained muffled behind his scarf, but his breath puffed in clouds through the wool.

"Neither, sir. Unhand me." She jerked her arm in his grasp, but he held on. "Let me go, or I shall be forced to scream." Terror built in her throat.

"Then I should be forced to silence you." He leaned close, and his breath brushed her cheek. "I've no intention of harming you, but keep quiet. You've drawn enough attention to yourself—and me."

He sounded at least a bit educated, and . . . kind? Though impatient too. He set off the way Charlotte had come, his strides long and Charlotte trotting to keep up. The basket thumped against her leg with every step.

"Where do you live? From the look of you, it can't be St. Giles. No St. Giles girl would be so foolish as to beard a public house full of strange men at night." His tone said he thought she had pillow ticking for brains.

If he hadn't just rescued her from such a ridiculous situation, she would've had more of an argument for him.

Without waiting for an answer, he hurried toward the Tottenham Court Road. For a few minutes she trotted at his side, but finally, out of breath and out of temper, Charlotte jerked hard to free herself from his grasp and stopped. The cold air seared her lungs, and her breath hung in silvery mist as she gasped.

"Sir, I am not a barrow to be shoved along the street." She set the basket down and righted her cloak and hood, her hair still tumbling over her shoulders. "I thank you for your assistance back there, but I am quite capable of seeing myself home."

"I doubt that. Any woman who would stroll into the rookery at night, when she's clearly well out of her element, shouldn't be trusted to find her way home again." His voice came from deep within his hood, and his features, other than the glitter of his eyes, were obscured.

Charlotte bristled, a hundred hot words leaping to her tongue, but she remembered in time that he had rescued her and that her mouth had already gotten her in trouble once today. With an effort, she said, "Sir, I assure you, I am fine now." She stooped to pick up the basket, realizing she hadn't accomplished her mission at all. "Oh, slipslops and malaprops, I didn't find Amelia Cashel's house. Now I have to go back." She jerked the basket off the cobbles, but the man halted her with his hand on her wrist.

"You're not going back in there, not now, not ever. You have no idea how close you came to disappearing forever tonight. Now, come with me." He took the basket from her and laced his fingers through hers, tugging her along, but more gently this time. Her hand warmed, nestled in his, even through his gloves. When they reached the main road, as if by a conjuring trick, a carriage appeared.

"Where to, sir?" the cabbie asked.

The man looked at Charlotte. "Well?"

"Portman Square," she muttered.

She felt rather than saw the surprise in her rescuer's expression. Because of her plain cloak, he probably thought she looked more like a housemaid than the daughter of one of the owners of a house at that prestigious address. Let him assume. He handed her up into the carriage, and before she could tell him that she had no money for the fare, he swung up beside her.

"Really, sir, there's no need. I'm safe enough now."

"I might as well finish the job." He settled back against the hard wooden seat. No frills or plush squabs in this carriage. Tall as he was, he seemed to swallow up all the space inside.

When the carriage lurched into motion, he asked, "Why on earth were you looking for someone in the rookery at night?" He kept his face turned away from her, the muffler still covering the lower half, and the deep hood concealing the rest. He might be a common villain or the prime minister himself. Who could tell in the darkness like this?

She pressed her lips together. Disappointment and despair settled into her chest. She'd set out with such great hopes of meeting her sister. Of perhaps beginning a relationship . . . a friendship. She said nothing, knowing that it was foolish.

"Perhaps you're just now realizing what a dangerous stunt you attempted? Good." He tugged off his gloves, finger by finger, and bunched them in his hand, laying his fist along his thigh. The quality of his clothes was fine, the cloak thick, his gloves without a single hole that she could see.

Odd that his fingernails were so clean, not at all like the other men in the public house. And his diction was better.

And he smelled better.

"If you must know, I was hoping to deliver a few things. I met—" Charlotte stopped, wondering. She supposed that Amelia Cashel was a miss, since she'd never married, but she was old enough to be Charlotte's mother. "Madam Cashel this afternoon, and I could see she was in need. I only sought to help her." A blanket, some food, some candles, a shawl. Hopefully, none of the staff would notice these few items missing and report them to her parsimonious father.

The man actually grunted, as if barely comprehending her actions. "A noble thought, I suppose, though badly executed. If you leave the basket with me, I will see that it is properly delivered."

"You would do that?" Suspicion laced her words. "You aren't just trying to get your hands on the contents, are you?"

His silent offense was as cold as the February air. Finally, he asked, "What is your name?"

"Tell me who you are first." She didn't want to reveal her name, lest word get back to her father, so she stalled.

"Young woman, I have no need for such an exchange of information. If I put my mind to it, I will know your identity in less than twenty-four hours."

Indeed. Arrogant man. She pressed her lips together, determined to give him no clues.

"Let's see. Though you are plainly attired at the moment, you speak with an educated tone. Therefore you are probably genteelly born. Also, you haven't the sense God gave a chicken, though come to think of it, that doesn't narrow things down much. I've heard society ladies are a bit addlepated."

She stiffened, as if poked with a stick, but she bit hard on the inside of her cheek in order not to rise to his baiting.

"However, I do know you live on Portman Square. There cannot be that many beautiful young ladies who call that prestigious address home. An empty-headed society miss shouldn't be that difficult to identify. Though, you might be a governess, or a ladies' maid? Perhaps a paid companion? Still, the list of occupants in Portman Square isn't that large, so who you are won't be difficult to diagnose."

She fumed that he would think she had no sense, though she'd certainly behaved that way tonight. But she took satisfaction in the knowledge that he only thought he knew where she lived. She'd given a false address so he wouldn't be able to find her later and so she wouldn't bring any shame to her family.

No more shame than she'd discovered that her father had brought on them today.

The carriage rolled to a stop on the south side of Portman Square, and before he could stop her, she slipped out, leaving the basket behind, and hurried away.

As she ducked around the corner, she realized she hadn't given him proper thanks, though after his insult to her intelligence, he didn't deserve it.

Too bad she would never see him again. At least he'd been interesting to talk to. A rookery ruffian perhaps, but intelligent and capable of rescuing her from her own folly.

A unique man to be sure.

He also had one other uncommon opinion that predisposed her to favor him.

He had called her beautiful.